HEROIC AUTOGRAPHS

Danielle Ackley-McPhail

Gail Z. Martin

Larry N. Martin

Bryan J.L. Glass

John L. French

Walt Ciechanowski

Kathleen David

Robert Greenberger

James Chambers

PUBLISHED BY
eSpec Books LLC
Danielle McPhail, Publisher
PO Box 493,
Stratford, New Jersey 08084
www.especbooks.com

Copyright ©2015 eSpec Books LLC

Cover Art Copyright ©2015 Angela McKendrick
Interior Art Copyright ©2015 Jason Whitley

ISBN (trade paper): 978-1-942990-03-1
ISBN (ebook): 978-1-942990-15-4

Icons: Mike McPhail, McP Digital Graphics

Interior Design: Sidhe na Daire Multimedia
                  www.sidhenadaire.com

DEDICATION

To Christopher Reeve
The Man of Steel
1952 - 2004

Contents

INTRODUCTION

*The only thing necessary for the triumph of evil
is for good men to do nothing.* —Edmund Burke

Here I Come To Save the Day! —Mighty Mouse

ONCE UPON A TIME, IN A CENTURY NOT TOO LONG AGO, WE ALL RECOGNIZED what a hero looked like. What they did. Why they did it. Once upon a time, we were more concerned with discovering the secret of who they were, than what their weakness was or what mistakes they may have made.

People need heroes. They need to remember what it is to stand up for the little guy, the oppressed, those preyed upon by others. They need to remember that one person can make a difference and it needn't be about superpowers or expensive gadgets—though we happen to think those things are great—but about the willingness to step forward, put on that spandex suit, and say "not today, Evil, not today."

People need an example to live by. They need hope.

We would like to remind you of that bygone era of heroic figures doing what is right because it needs to be done, from the small things to the large, with no need for reward and knowing the cost may be sacrifice. But more important yet, let us remind you that one need not risk life and limb to be heroic, to make another's life better. Open these pages and watch these tales unfold, then take them with you into the day-to-day, and ask yourself: In what way can I be a hero today?

Danielle Ackley-McPhail
"The Hugger"

GHOST WOLF

Gail Z. Martin and Larry N. Martin

"GO BACK WHERE YOU CAME FROM." JUST FOR EMPHASIS, THE SPEAKER slapped a length of lead pipe against his palm. "We don't need your type. Damn Pollacks and Ruskies."

Six men blocked the sidewalk in a shadowed section between streetlights. They were young and out for trouble. The four men whose path they blocked were older and weary from working swing shift in the foundries and iron works along Carson Street. Their faces were streaked with soot, hair lank with sweat. Just another block and the steep tracks of the Monongahela Incline would take them up Coal Hill to their homes.

"Leave us," one of the workers said. "We have no quarrel with you. Be gone."

"Funny—that's what we'd like you to do. Be gone," the tough replied, and his friends laughed mirthlessly. They were strong, young men, not much over twenty years old, with muscles built from unloading shipping crates or working in the steel mills. The leader wore his blond hair shaved close to his head, and a scar through one eyebrow and a notch in an ear gave him the look of a junkyard dog.

"Go back the hell to where you came from." He advanced, holding his pipe like a weapon. The gang of men behind him produced chains, cut-down two-by-fours, and brass knuckles. "Or we'll send you there in a box."

The section of the city was deserted at this hour. To one side stretched the rail yards, empty and quiet. On the other side was the steep slope of Coal Hill, overgrown with gangly trees and scrub brush, littered with trash. The streetlight overhead was broken, creating a dark area between lights.

"We don't want trouble." The speaker was the oldest of the workers, and in his youth he had been as strong and brash as the bald young man with the pipe. Twenty-five years of hard, dangerous work and uncertain fortune had left their mark. His dark hair was graying and thin, and his features were as much a testimony to his heritage as his accent. The men behind him eyed the toughs warily, holding the lidded metal buckets they used to carry their lunches like weapons. The unmistakable click of switchblades opening upped the ante.

"Then you should have stayed where you belong." With that, the toughs surged forward. The workers swung their heavy buckets to keep the attackers at bay, and from the pockets of their jackets produced hammers, knives, and wrenches to defend themselves.

A wolf's howl echoed down the dark, empty street. There was a flash of gray, a *snick* like sharp teeth snapping together, and a blur of motion. One of the toughs went flying into the underbrush, hitting hard against the hillside. A gray figure interposed itself between the workers and the toughs. The figure's face was hidden beneath a wolf's head and a cape made from a wolf's pelt fell partway down the figure's back. The wolf's eyes glowed red.

"What the hell?" the gang leader muttered, and swung hard at the gray figure's head with his length of pipe. The fighter dodged away with inhuman speed and grace, landing a roundhouse punch with one furred fist that broke the gang leader's jaw with an audible *crack* and sent him sprawling.

Two of the ruffians dove for the gray fighter, pummeling him with their fists and brass knuckles, to no effect. He stayed a step ahead of them, turning on his attackers with a snarl. Sharp claws extended from the gray fighter's fists, and one swipe laid open one of the attackers from shoulder to hip, slicing easily through his jacket and shirt and raising four bloody slashes. One of the toughs tried to flank the gray creature, but it slapped him away with a powerful backhand that slashed across the man's face and sent him tumbling.

Emboldened by this unexpected champion, the older men whooped and dove into the fight, taking down three of the gang members with craftiness and experience more than brute force.

The last of the ruffians ran away, toward the Mon Incline. Five

of the troublemakers were down for the count in bloody heaps, while the four older workers appeared generally no worse for the wear than a few split lips and blackened eyes. The gray creature howled and set off after the fleeing tough like a streak, catching him easily and hoisting him with one clawed hand thrust through the collar of his jacket.

"Go to hell!" the tough shouted, kicking and swinging at the gray man-beast, who held him at arm's distance before hoisting the ruffian up and looping his jacket collar through one of the uprights of a tall iron fence.

The gray creature turned back to where the workers stared, still holding their makeshift weapons as if afraid their savior might turn on them. Sirens were already sounding, getting closer.

"Get out of here," the creature rasped. Then it turned and bounded away, running upright like a man but impossibly fast. The creature leapt up to the steel braces that supported the Mon Incline as one of the funicular cars began to clatter up the mountain, and in another jump landed easily on the top of the car. It paused just long enough for them to see its silhouette in the moonlight, part man and part beast, and to give another feral howl before it vanished into the shadows.

◄ G ►

In a quiet neighborhood atop Coal Hill, a figure slipped quietly through the shadows, finding its way to a ramshackle spring house that stood in disrepair in the stretch of woods behind a two-story stone home. The gray man glanced furtively from side to side and then, assured he had not been seen, let himself into the spring house and closed the door behind him. He knew his way in the dark from here. Off to the right, he heard the trickle of water in the cistern. To the left, halfway down the wall, a wooden panel covered with stones slipped out of place, and he crawled backward into a tunnel barely wider than his shoulders. He fit the panel back where it had been and shuffled on his hands and knees until the passage widened and he could crouch. The press of a button activated the red eyes in his helmet, enough light to make his way down the tunnel to where it became a room.

He lit a kerosene lantern from the table on one side of the room, and sat down heavily on a wooden chair. "I'm getting too old for this shit," he muttered in Polish.

Off came the furred reinforced gauntlets, and then the cloak and wolf skull helmet. He laid them carefully on the table, then eased out of the specially-built boots. He set aside the shaped buffalo horn that made the wolf-like howl. Finally, he unbuckled himself from the wood-and-metal exoskeleton. Then he set aside his cloak and shouldered out of the backpack of compressed gas cartridges the cloak and costume concealed. Some of the outfit Piotr had put together himself, but the ingenious pieces, the ones that gave him almost magical abilities, had been the covert gift of a local inventor who was one of the few to know Piotr's secret identity.

He looked up as a door opened on the far side of the room. Mrs. Szabo hustled in, bearing a pot of hot coffee and a chunk of ice wrapped in a dish cloth. "Busy night, Piotr?" she asked, taking in his disheveled appearance.

"Too many busy nights," he muttered. "Always the cops show up too late, when the fight is over, or they don't care who started it and they just come to rough people up." He swore under his breath, then blushed. "Sorry," he said.

Mrs. Szabo waved off the apology. "No harm done. You should have heard my Oskar cuss when he thought I wasn't around." She sighed, looking at the bruises that were beginning to purple. "Let me have a look at you. There's supper in the oven upstairs once we get you cleaned up."

"No matter how many nights I go out, there's more to do, and always a fight somewhere I didn't stop," Piotr said tiredly.

Mrs. Szabo clucked her tongue at him. "Enough of that. You're a hero, even if the Ghost Wolf gets all the credit. Every fight you break up is lives saved, and families that won't go hungry with their men out of work because they got busted up by ruffians." She winked conspiratorially. "The Ghost Wolf is becoming a legend. I've heard that just the name is enough to scare off some troublemakers."

"If the name alone scared off more people, I wouldn't get so banged up," Piotr replied.

Piotr winced as Mrs. Szabo daubed at the scrapes and bruises. The ice felt good. His special suit had blunted the killing blows and deflected the worst of the damage, but beneath the disguise he was still flesh and blood.

"What happened?" she asked, liberally applying the homemade salve she kept on hand for the aftermath of his nightly excursions. Piotr told her, sparing her any details that were unlikely to be in the newspaper, just in case the police ever came to call.

"God bless you," she said, and took a break from bandaging up his injuries to hand him a steaming cup of black coffee. "Those rough boys would have killed those men," she added. "Just like my Oskar."

We make an odd pair, Piotr thought, sipping the strong coffee. Mrs. Szabo was old enough to be his mother and determined enough to stand behind his cause. He was in his thirties, scarred from a life of hard work, first with traveling carnivals back in Poland, and then taking whatever work he could find in America: day labor, steel mill, longshoreman. As a younger man, he'd been a carnival magician and acrobat and then a bare-knuckles fighter, anything to make enough to keep body and soul together. Now, those skills helped him protect his fellow immigrants, so no one else had to lose a beloved husband to roving gangs.

"You're going to have some bad bruises," she fussed, being as gentle as possible though her touch made him catch his breath. "Bruised ribs," she added, shaking her head. "Oh—that's a deep cut. I'll have to stitch up you and your outfit." She kept up a running narrative as she cleaned and bandaged his wounds and wrapped his ribs in strips from torn bedsheets. Her poultice smelled of herbs and tea, and Piotr knew from experience it took out the soreness and kept cuts from going sour. He gritted his teeth as she took black sewing thread, waved her needle through the flame to cleanse it, and set to closing up the gash on his arm.

"When this is all over and you're back in your room, you should have a slug of that whiskey you keep under the bed," she said sagely, with a sly sideways glance that let him know she was onto his secrets. "Oskar always preferred vodka."

Mrs. Szabo was a thin woman old enough to be his mother. Her ropy muscles and long, skinny legs made him think of the scrawny chickens back home in the farm towns outside Warsaw. Like those chickens, Mrs. Szabo was a tough bird, capable of taking care of herself in a strange country when the gangs left her widowed and her children grew up and moved away from New Pittsburgh's smoky valleys.

She'd found him one night, after one of his more disastrous fights. That was before he had his new, improved equipment, when he was just an over-the-hill former prize-fighter with a doomed one-man war against the immigrant-hating gangs that roved the city's streets. When he awoke, he had discovered himself here, in a room once used to hide escaped slaves, beneath the old stone house. She told him that she had seen him fight off a gang so a group of boys from the neighborhood could get home safely. There had been no one to do that for Oskar. Since then, she had been part landlady, part fussy aunt, and part co-conspirator.

"I was careful," Piotr said. "No one followed me."

Mrs. Szabo nodded. "Good." She was nearly done, with a neat row of stiches to show for her work, a testimony to her skill as an expert seamstress. Tonight, he had fought the Irish to protect the Poles. But just as many times, the situations were reversed, and if it was Poles beating up Irish workers, he stepped in, too. That meant both sides equally hated and loved the Ghost Wolf, and he was just as likely to get killed by one side as the other. His goal was a corridor of safe passage through the Birmingham and Limerick neighborhoods and up to the top of Coal Hill. It was a never-ending battle.

"I heard them talking down at the market, about the Ghost Wolf," she added, refilling his coffee cup. "The tales get taller with the telling. Some think he's a real wolf, or a werewolf, come from the old country to protect us. A few think he's a demon, and they cross themselves when they speak his name, but in the next breath they say they're glad he protects their men. The rest seem to think he really is a ghost." She grinned. "I know exactly what the Ghost Wolf is," she added. "Hungry."

"*Dziękuję*," he said, when she gathered her things and turned back to the stairs.

"You're welcome." She gathered her skirts. "Hurry up. You don't want the stew to burn. Leave the outfit down here. I'll come back tonight and patch it."

◄ G ►

Early the next morning, Piotr Janacek was back at work, mop and bucket in hand. The pawn shop on Liberty Avenue was shabby, but the offices on the next two floors were in much better shape. He made a point of speaking broken English at work, knowing that most people would assume his understanding of the language would be just as limited. They would be wrong. While his English was heavily accented, he spoke, read, and understood it fluently. He had long ago realized the benefits of being under-estimated, especially when it came to eluding suspicion as a masked vigilante.

"*Dzien dobry.*" Piotr looked up as Agent Jacob Drangosavich greeted him. Tall and broad shouldered, with a long face and pale blue eyes, Dragosavich looked like most of the men down at the mill, except for his business suit. Drangosavich's Polish carried a hint of a Croatian accent, but Piotr appreciated the gesture.

"Good morning," Piotr replied in Polish. "Beautiful day today."

Drangosavich's gaze lingered for a few seconds on the bruise on Piotr's cheek. "It's nothing," Piotr said, ducking his head. "Walked into a door in the dark."

"Take care," Drangosavich said, though from his eyes Piotr was uncertain the agent had believed his excuse.

It had taken Piotr less than a week on his new job to realize that the pawn shop was not what it seemed, nor were most of the people who came and went through the store. *Spies,* he thought. Those had been common enough back in Poland. It was easy enough to listen as he mopped and swept, or to read the notes jotted on the blackboard in the conference room. *Government agents,* he realized. *Secret agents who look for ghosts.* That intrigued him, though he was careful not to appear to be interested for fear the agents might become suspicious.

"Is the coffee ready? Adam hasn't had a cup in at least an hour." Agent Mitch Storm strode toward Piotr with his usual confident swagger. Storm was shorter than Drangosavich, with dark hair and a five o'clock shadow despite being clean-shaven. He was handsome and cocky and probably had raised plenty of hell in his younger days.

"Coffee is making, sir," Piotr replied. Then he spotted the guest behind Storm and ducked his head, wishing he could become invisible.

Adam Farber, the young genius inventor from Tesla-Westing-house, was headed his way. Tall and lanky, with sandy brown hair and wire-rimmed glasses slightly askew, Farber looked as if he'd already had enough coffee to be twitchy. To Piotr's relief, Farber swept past him, joking with Storm, as if he had not noticed the janitor in the shadows. But for a split second, Piotr saw recognition in Farber's eyes. Only to be expected, since Farber had built Piotr's wolf-suit exoskeleton.

When the men were past, Piotr let out a breath he hadn't realized he had been holding and moved his bucket down the hallway. He had already learned that the heating ducts carried sound through the building in strange ways. If he timed his work right, he could find tasks that kept him in hearing range for most of the agents' meeting. And with Adam Farber involved, Piotr was very interested to find out what was going on.

After some chit-chat in the small kitchen, Storm, Farber, and Drangosavich made their way to the conference room. Piotr noticed that Farber had his cup in one hand and the entire pot of coffee in the other. They closed the conference room door behind them, and its pane of frosted glass kept Piotr from seeing what they were doing, but he suspected they would leave the half-erased chalkboard for him to clean, as usual.

No one else was in the office space at the moment, so Piotr could move about as he wished, so long as he kept up the appearance of doing his job. He pushed his broom down the hall and got out some brass polish to work on a light fixture near one of the best grates for eavesdropping.

"Since when does the Department of Supernatural Investigation get involved with hooligans?" Farber asked.

"It's not the hooligans we're interested in," Storm replied. "It's the ghost."

"Actually, it's both," Drangosavich put in. "The ghost—if there is one—on principle, since that's what we do. But HQ has every department on alert. The hooligan gangs are getting out of hand. HQ is worried there could be a turf war, maybe even a bombing, if this anti-immigrant talk goes much further."

"From what I read in the paper, the Ghost Wolf seemed to have the gangs on the run," Farber said off-handedly.

"Which is why we haven't investigated before this," Storm said. "But we've heard from our informants that the Rail Rats gang has been trying to hire a witch to take care of this 'ghost wolf'. So while the police and the guys from the Department of Justice are worried about a bomb that could take down a city block, we're more worried about a witch who could—oh, I don't know—open up a portal to Hell or put a curse on the whole south side of the city."

"Mitch exaggerates—as usual," Drangosavich replied with a sigh. "But the danger is real, and growing. People spoiling for a fight are taking it out on the city's newest residents. There've been a lot of ugly incidents, and the police aren't always as quick to step in as we'd like. Or they're just as bad as the troublemakers, and the immigrants end up deciding they have to form gangs of their own for protection, because they don't trust the police or the politicians to help them."

"And they would be right about that," Storm added. "The Oligarchy is making plenty of hay on the notion that foreigners should go home." He snorted. "Good for votes. So we can't expect any support from the Oligarchy, the cops they own or the politicians they pay for."

"And that drives your problem underground," Farber noted.

"Exactly," Drangosavich said. "So what do you have for us?"

Piotr clumped along the hall with his bucket, making sure he made enough noise so that they knew he was hard at work. He moved to another good listening post, and pulled out a wrench to fiddle with the radiator.

There was a thump like something had been placed on a table. "I've re-tooled the Maxwell box a bit, just for this," Farber said. "If your Ghost Wolf really is a ghost, and you decide you want him to keep his distance, the box will do it. But," he said, pausing for emphasis, "if you intend to call ghosts, I'd have a care about where I did it. The venom these gangs are spewing isn't new. It's been around since before the War, even though New Pittsburgh couldn't run its factories and mills without the immigrants the gangs are bashing. Choose the wrong location, and you might rouse ghosts that join the fight on the gang's side."

"Then maybe we pick our battlefield," Drangosavich mused. "If we want the ghosts on our side, then we force a showdown in Birmingham, near St. Adalbert's, instead of in Limerick near St. Malachy. Dead Poles will be friendlier to the cause, I warrant, than dead Irish."

"Most of the attacks have been down toward the Limerick neighborhood," Mitch mused. "Typical. The new kids off the boat get beat up by the last bunch to get off the boat, who got beat up by the previous bunch."

"There's been retaliation by the Poles, too," Drangosavich pointed out. "The Ghost Wolf seems to put an end to the fights, regardless of who starts them."

"What about the *Logonje*?" Farber asked. Piotr frowned. That was a phrase he had only heard whispered, a group of demon-fighting Polish priests he wasn't even sure were more than a myth.

"We've already alerted them. They're looking into the possibility of a real magical threat. If they think the stakes are high enough, they'll get involved. If not... we're on our own," Mitch replied.

Piotr had cleaned the glass on a nearby door until it shone, then got his mop and started to work on the floor. He would have to move out of earshot soon. It was dangerous to linger, but the information he gained made him loathe to leave.

Another sound, like metal sliding across wood. "Here's the new and improved EMF locator box," Farber said, sounding like a proud papa. "I've tweaked it a bit. Been following the work of a daring young man, William Duane, at the University of Pennsylvania and Harvard. I won't bore you with the details, but it has to do with whether we're made up of light or particles." Farber's voice was alive with curiosity.

"Anyhow... I started thinking about science and magic, like those waves and tiny particles. Maybe it's not either/or. Maybe it's both, and they're just on different frequencies. So I've been tinkering."

"Can it block magic?" Storm asked.

"No," Farber replied. "But it can... phase out a small space." He sighed. "It's hard to explain without doing the math. But imagine that you could put a bubble around someone in a rainstorm. They wouldn't get wet, although it was raining all around them. Now make that bubble a really fragile energy field and the rain is magic."

"So you can block magic," Drangosavich repeated.

"Not really," Farber said. "But whoever has this gadget can elude it for a very short period of time. Seconds, maybe. I haven't fully field tested it—"

"Have you tested it at all?" Storm pressed.

Farber cleared his throat. "Renate and I went a few rounds. It worked—mostly."

"You're overwhelming me with confidence," Storm said drily. "Anything else?"

"Not yet, but I'm always working on something new," Farber replied, seemingly immune to Storm's tone.

The sound of chairs pushing back from the table was Piotr's cue to move far down the hallway, where no one might suspect he had been listening. *At this rate, the floor will shine like a mirror,* he thought.

Storm, Farber, and Drangosavich joked with each other as they emerged from the conference room and headed for the door. To Piotr's surprise, Farber bumped him as he passed, and Piotr felt a bit of paper slip into his pocket. He steeled himself to keep his expression neutral.

"Sorry," Farber muttered, but he met Piotr's gaze intently, a signal to have a look at the paper when Piotr was in private. Then the two agents and the inventor were gone, leaving Piotr alone with his mop and bucket.

He reached into his pocket and withdrew a receipt for tailoring. He frowned, then read the address. The receipt was for a man's suit, and the seamstress was Mrs. O. Szabo. An additional note was hastily scrawled in a man's neat handwriting. *Pick up alterations. 8 pm tonight.*

Piotr put the note carefully into his shirt pocket, where it would not be dislodged. *That means Farber will be by the house. I wonder what he's got for me. This should be interesting.*

◄ G ►

Mrs. Szabo, like many widows, took in borders and sewed and washed other people's laundry in order to make ends meet. Piotr rented a room that had belonged to one of his landlady's sons. A river pilot paid rent on the second bedroom so it would be available when he came through town. Most of the time, it sat empty. Piotr's rent included breakfast and dinner plus a sandwich for lunch. He helped out whenever he could with chores and repairs. It was his opinion that Mrs. Szabo worked too hard, but he knew better than to say so out loud.

Meals were served in the kitchen, because the small dining room had been turned into a sewing room. The room got good light, and was suitable to host customers who came for a fitting or to drop off their mending. Wash tubs and a mangle for laundry were down in the basement, as well as the flat irons. Piotr finished washing dishes as Mrs. Szabo put the leftovers in the ice box, wrapping his sandwich for the next day in waxed paper.

The tapping at the back door made Piotr look up. Clients came through the front door, and hardly anyone came around back. Mrs. Szabo lifted the blind and then opened the door with a wide smile. "Miska! What an unexpected surprise!"

Miska Kovach seemed to fill the doorway. Tall and muscular, it wasn't hard to believe he was a former army rifleman, now a private security chief. "Brought you some of mama's *goulash*," he said with a grin. "She makes too much."

"Ohh," Mrs. Szabo said appreciatively. "It'll be dinner tomorrow!" She quickly wrapped up a dozen of the cookies she had just baked and pushed the package into Miska's hands. "Here. Tell her I said 'thank you'."

Miska chuckled. "She likes your cookies so much, I think this might be a plot." Then he glanced toward Piotr. "Big night?" he asked, raising an eyebrow.

Piotr nodded. "Yeah. For what it's worth." Miska had connected him with Adam Farber, though neither would say just how the unlikely pair knew each other.

"It's worth a lot," Miska replied. "Just keep yourself in one piece."

A knock at the front door came just as Piotr finished cleaning up. "I'd better go," Miska said. "Remember—stay safe. Leave the martyrs to the Church."

Mrs. Szabo went to greet the visitor as Piotr closed the back door behind Miska. Customers dropped off washing or mending throughout the day, nearly until bedtime. The frequent comings and goings were good cover for Piotr's exploits.

"Mr. Farber—so good to see you," Mrs. Szabo greeted the newcomer. "Will you share a cup of tea with us?" She did not wait for an answer before she bustled in to get the kettle and the tea tray, which Piotr had readied.

Piotr followed her in to the sewing room. Farber grinned. "Hadn't expected to run into you downtown," he said. "Don't worry—your secret is safe with me." At that, he lifted a large carpet bag onto Mrs. Szabo's worktable. He removed a tangle of shirts for mending and laundry, which he set to one side. "The usual," he said with a tired smile. Mrs. Szabo nodded.

"I'll have them back to you next week. Now, let me get you some of those cookies I just baked." Mrs. Szabo retreated to the kitchen. The clatter of dishes did not fool Piotr in the least. He was certain his landlady was listening.

Farber reached into the bottom of the bag and withdrew a few strange objects. "These are for you," Farber said, pushing the items toward Piotr. One was a metal box with a dial and two buttons. The second item was a man's vest. At first glance, it appeared to be made of many layers of silk. When Piotr looked more closely, he could see that the silk had a thin coating of metal.

"What are they?" he asked.

"Added protection," Farber replied. "I know I can't talk you out of what you're doing, so I thought I might keep you a little safer." Farber held the box up.

"This is completely experimental," Farber warned. "But it's worked well in trials. It might be of help if someone tries to jinx you, but it won't hold off a strong witch for more than a few seconds, if that, and it won't stop a big blast of power."

He handed the box to Piotr. "It works off a battery," Farber continued. "That means you've probably got one usage before the battery drains. I couldn't make it last longer without making it heavier and bigger."

"It's good," Piotr replied. "And the vest? Rather fancy." He chuckled.

Farber grinned. "It's not for show. Silk is woven very tightly. The strands are tight enough that on occasion, a silk pocket kerchief has stopped a small bullet." Piotr raised an eyebrow, impressed. "There are thirty layers of silk in that vest," Farber continued. "It's not armor, but it's a lot better than nothing, and you should be able to move easily with it, unlike metal plates."

"Why does it shine?" Piotr asked, holding up the vest and turning it in his hands to catch the light, which reflected more than could be accounted for by the silk's luster.

"Because each layer has a light coat of aluminum," Farber replied. "Something I'm playing around with. Ideally, I'd like to coat the silk before it's woven, but there wasn't time."

Piotr nodded. "Thank you."

Farber fixed him with a look. "Mitch and Jacob—the two agents I was with this morning—think the situation is going to get worse. Don't take foolish chances. One man can't stop an army."

Piotr lifted his head and squared his shoulders. "No. But in my country, a handful of men have stopped armies by being fast and clever."

Farber clapped him on the shoulder. "Then take care. And good luck."

Just then, Mrs. Szabo bustled back in with a package of cookies wrapped in cloth and tied with string. "Here," she said, thrusting the bundle into Farber's hands. "I baked these just this afternoon. Fatten you up," she said with a motherly smile. "And your mending. It's done. I checked all the buttons too; made sure they were on tightly. No extra charge."

Farber thanked Mrs. Szabo profusely as he slipped the payment into her hand, gave a nod to Piotr, and then left, carrying the carpet bag filled with freshly laundered and mended clothing. Piotr closed the door behind Farber, then moved to take the vest and box down to the hidden room.

"There's talk at the fishmonger's about the gangs," Mrs. Szabo said. "Problems are getting out of hand. Too many incidents in too many places for even the Ghost Wolf to take care of them all, they say."

Which is exactly what the government agents also said, Piotr thought. "And what else are people saying?"

Mrs. Szabo shrugged, but Piotr could tell she was worried. "Depends on who you talk to. Mrs. Baczkowski at the market says that the Irish might bring in more ruffians from Boston or New York to cause our boys problems. And at the butchers, I overheard the men saying that if the gangs get out of hand, the mill owners might call the Pinkertons on them." After the bloodshed of the Braddock riots and the Pullman strike a few years back, New Pittsburgh's steel workers feared having private security forces or even the army brought in to put down trouble.

Not good. Not good at all. The Pinkertons come in and split heads open. That's all they know how to do, Piotr thought. *Half the cops are Irish, and the other half belong to the fat-cat mill owners who pay them. They'll be no help.*

Piotr mustered a smile. "Maybe we can stop it before it gets that far," he said, more confidently than he felt. "Farber's friends, the government agents, they sounded like they might help."

Mrs. Szabo sighed, and looked suddenly older. "I wish I believed such things, but I don't anymore. Not after all I've seen." She shook her head. "It is the history of our people for others to try to take things from us. Only when we stand up to them ourselves does it stop. Counting on help from outsiders is a fool's errand." She paused. "Stay here. I have something for you."

Piotr waited as Mrs. Szabo went up to her room. When she came down a few minutes later, she had a piece of folded fabric in her hands. She stopped in the kitchen long enough to retrieve a salt shaker, and brought both items to him.

"I found this in the attic," she said, handing him the folded cloth. Piotr unwrapped it to find a faded belt embroidered with strange symbols and words. "It's a *ladanki.* Belonged to my grandfather. He said it had protective magic. I tried to get Oskar to wear it, but he didn't think such things were 'Christian'." It went without saying that Oskar had forfeited the belt's protection for piety, and had not survived.

"I want you to have it," Mrs. Szabo said. "Wear it in good health. And take this," she said, thrusting the salt shaker into his hand.

"Salt?"

She nodded. "The old women in the village where I grew up believed salt kept away evil spirits and bad magic. The *ladanki* and the salt together may help you, if there really are witches about."

Piotr accepted the gift with thanks, wrapping the belt around his waist beneath his shirt and dropping the salt shaker into a pocket of the jacket he pulled from a hook near the door. "I'm going out for a bit," he said as he headed toward the kitchen and the door to the secret room. "Not to fight. Just to clear my head." He glanced back over his shoulder. "Don't worry."

She made the sign of the cross. "Of course I worry." Then she muttered a phrase Piotr remembered his grandmother saying, a warding against evil.

Piotr headed out, pulling his jacket up against the evening chill. He headed down the block to Luczak's Bar, where most of the men in his neighborhood spent their evenings. The air was heavy with the aromas of roast pork, stuffed cabbage, and beets, mixed with cigarette smoke and the smell of dark Polish beer. He shouldered through the crowd to the bar. In the back corner, he heard the shouts of men playing darts and betting on dice.

"Gimme a beer," he said in Polish, no one else was speaking English.

Marek, the bartender, slid a lager his way, and collected the coins Piotr put down on the bar. "Haven't seen you in here in a while."

Piotr shrugged. "Working. You know."

Marek nodded. "Yeah. I know." He eyed the bruise on Piotr's face. "Trouble?"

"Nothing important. Took a shortcut; got slugged by someone looking for a fight." Technically true. His mask and outfit could not completely protect him from the hazards of his nightly excursions, and the frequent bruises, black eyes, and split lips were one reason he did not show up at Luczak's more often.

Piotr took a sip of his beer and looked around. Luczak's wasn't as crowded as usual. He said as much to Marek.

"It's the Irish," Marek replied, adding a curse. "Damn gangs. It's got so people don't like to go out at night." He laughed. "But not these guys. They're not going to let any damn Irishmen get between them and a good beer."

Piotr sat at the bar for over an hour nursing his beer. He listened to the conversations around him. Much of it was trivial. But even among the bets on sports teams and race horses, the vulgar jokes and the tall tales, it didn't take long to pick out comments that let Piotr know the ruffian gangs were never far from the bar patrons' thoughts.

"Dead rabbits." The phrase caught Piotr's attention, and he kept from turning around with effort. He had the feeling the man wasn't talking about game hunting, or picking up stew meat for dinner.

"...big in Boston. Even the cops can't shut them down," the voice was saying.

"Boston's a long way from here," another man replied.

The first speaker gave a bark of a laugh. "You know the Irish. Every one of them Micks is related to all the others. Mark my words, those Muckers'll come here if one of their Paddy friends calls for them. There's gonna be blood." The two men moved on, and the cheers from the dart game in the back drowned out the rest of their conversation. All he gleaned from the rest of the conversations was that feelings were mixed about the Ghost Wolf, since the mysterious vigilante had trounced Polish gangs as often as he attacked Irish ruffians.

"...he's a menace. Whatever he is, he needs to get out of the way and let us settle this with the Micks our way, once and for all."

"...takes balls to do that. My wife thinks he's a hero for making the streets a little safer. Me, I think he must be nuts..."

Piotr finished his beer, tuning out the idle gossip. His thoughts went back to the comments he heard earlier. *Plenty of Irish in Boston,* Piotr thought. *Big city, big gangs. Could 'Dead Rabbits' be a gang name?* Piotr didn't have a way to find out, but the Ghost Wolf did.

◄ G ►

The Ghost Wolf hunkered on the rooftops, just a shadow in the night. The part of town they called Limerick was dangerous for anyone who wasn't Irish. Small, dirty houses huddled not far enough from the soot-belching rail yards of the P&LE Railroad, a world away from the palatial concourse where swells caught trains to and from much fancier places.

Limerick and its Irishmen were at the bottom of Coal Hill, where the Polish settled. The Irish had come first, and claimed New Pittsburgh as their own. Now it was the Poles' turn to be strangers in a strange land, and the Irish weren't about to give up what they had gained with sweat and blood to a new crop of broad-backed men eager to work for whatever wages the mill owners and factory men would pay. *Play one group off against the other, and they never realize that the man in the middle is picking their pockets equally,* Piotr thought.

The exoskeleton Farber created enhanced his natural agility. He prowled like an alley cat, staying in the shadows, watching his prey. He'd had the men in his sights for a while. Not all of his nightly runs ended in fights. That was only when there was no helping it, when gangs of armed men stalked through the night, looking for victims. On the other nights, Piotr did reconnaissance, like his father who had been a sniper in the army before he joined the carnival.

His father had been part gypsy, *Polska Roma*, and hadn't been above picking a few pockets when necessary to keep food on the table. Piotr didn't hold with thieving, but he had his father's eye for a mark, his quick reflexes, and his ability to deflect attention until the strike was made. They served him well in his one-man war.

The Irish boys were drunk. Liquor made them mean. More than once, Piotr had smelled the stink of cheap whiskey as he fought ruffians still sober enough to go looking for easy prey to harass. But this night, the men staggered home without bothering anyone. Piotr sighed in relief. He had a more important quarry in mind.

It was hardly fair to call most of the ruffians on New Pittsburgh's streets 'gangs'. They were usually groups of friends, neighbors, or co-workers who went looking for trouble. The Ghost Wolf ensured they found more than they had expected. But the majority of the fights he broke up were spur-of-the-moment spitefulness.

So far, both the loosely organized Polish and Irish criminal gangs had stayed out of the fights, sticking to making money off making book and selling cheap whiskey. But if they got into a battle over who owned the sidewalks of the South Side, it was likely to end in disaster for both sides especially if the Pinkertons or the Army got called in to put down the unrest.

Not if I can stop it.

Tonight, the hunters were about to become the hunted.

Piotr stifled a cough. New Pittsburgh's skies were dark with coal smoke at all hours of the day. It was worst at night, when the air was still and the soot and fumes of the mills hung heavy, almost blotting out the moon. He glanced around, getting his bearings, and saw that he was near the Duquesne Incline, in a part of Limerick where only a fool would venture if he wasn't Irish.

Guess that makes me a fool, Piotr thought grimly, not the first time he had come to that conclusion.

Talk of bringing in Irish gang members from Boston worried Piotr. So he made his way to a building he had been watching for a while, a coal company's headquarters near the P& LE tracks that Sean Brennan, the Crime Boss of Limerick, had taken for his own.

Lights were on in the old building, dimmed by worn, stained

blinds. The streetlights near the building did not work, something Piotr doubted was an accident. Farber had made him special goggles that let him see better at night, and he spotted four guards despite the deep shadows. The trick would be to get close enough to hear what was going on. He hadn't made up his mind yet about fighting. That decision would come later, when he knew his enemy's plan and had a counter-strategy.

The coal company had left behind a mess. That worked in Piotr's favor. Even without his exoskeleton, he could have climbed the rusting equipment and piles of rubble easily, but with his equipment he could jump farther and move faster. He went over the heads of the guards, and made it to the building's roof. From there, he let himself down on a rope-and-pulley he had built for just these kinds of occasions. It allowed him to descend noiselessly and if necessary, ascend much faster than he could go hand-over-hand.

Darkness hid him, and his gray outfit blended with the shadows. The old windows were high off the ground, keeping him well above the guards' line of sight. If he gave them no reason to look up, they were unlikely to see him. Holding his breath, Piotr edged as close as he dared to the window.

Sean Brennan, the Crime Boss of Limerick, sat behind a mahogany desk that was in much better shape than the building he had chosen for his headquarters. With him were two other men Piotr recognized as Jamie MacCabe, Brennan's bodyguard, and Cian Maguaran, a slim, dark-haired man with the look of a Traveler whom many claimed was a warlock.

"Of course I don't want the damn Dead Rabbits in New Pittsburgh," Brennan said. "Just like the bloody live rabbits—first you've got two of them, and then they take over." He lit a cigar and shuffled through a folder on his desk. "But the idea of a proper gang from Boston coming here to bash some heads together is enough to put those Oligarchy bastards on pins and needles. All we've got to do is spread the word, provide a little provocation, and wham!" he said, slapping one hand against his desktop. "All the little vermin show up to fight, and the Pinkertons do our work for us."

"You want the Pinkertons?" MacCabe said incredulously.

Maguaran chuckled. "He wants them to pull the trigger for us.

Let the Oligarchy pay the 'exterminator'. Get rid of the rabble."

Except that the Pinkertons will take the Poles down too. And when everything's done burning and they mop up the blood, Brennan's political machine will own Birmingham as well as Limerick, and probably Coal Hill and all the South Side.

Piotr shimmied up the rope and squatted on the roof, taking in the lay of the land around Brennan's headquarters. He was watching the movements of the guards, planning his next steps. *Ginning up my nerve, because this is a lot bigger than scaring off some half-drunk hooligans.*

There was no way to alert Storm and Drangosavich without admitting to his—highly illegal—alter-ego as Ghost Wolf. If the government didn't put him in jail, he'd be dead in a day on the street from reprisals from both sides. It would take too long to warn Farber. And if he went home and did nothing, Brennan would provoke enough unrest—maybe even stage a riot—and the Pinkertons would end it with a bloodbath. Much as Piotr hated the ruffians, wholesale slaughter was worse.

And there was no one to stop it except him.

He drew a deep breath, muttered a curse, said a prayer, and made a decision. *First things first. Get rid of the guards.*

The Ghost Wolf was known for showing up out of nowhere, running off the hooligans, and disappearing into the night. Taking prisoners wasn't part of the plan. But he'd had an inkling that tonight might require different tactics, and so he had brought a small pack with him with handy objects, just in case. Rope, lock-picking tools, other useful items. Not for the first time, he questioned his decision to forego a knife or gun. *I may be a vigilante, but I'm not a murderer. At least, not yet.*

The first guard never knew what hit him. The Ghost Wolf bounded from the depths of the shadows, and a single swing of Piotr's blackjack laid the guard out before he could make a sound. Piotr dragged him behind a piece of rusted machinery, bound and gagged him for good measure, and resumed the hunt. The second guard fell just as easily, and Piotr trussed him up and hid him with his companion.

Something made the third guard wary. Piotr used the man's suspicions to his advantage, luring him into the shadows with the ping of a few pebbles thrown against old equipment.

"Who's out there?" the guard called.

"No one's there," the fourth guard mocked. "You're just daft."

"I swear, I heard something," the third man insisted. He moved a few steps toward the shadows, then paused to look over his shoulder.

The fourth guard had vanished.

Piotr wrestled the downed guard out of the way and circled the last of Brennan's protectors. He could see indecision in the man's face, fear that his colleagues might be playing a prank on him, or that calling for back-up might look like weakness, versus the reasonable impulse to yell for help.

In that moment of indecision, Piotr vaulted from the darkness, slamming the guard to the ground, following up the tackle with a smack of the blackjack. The guard went limp. "Still breathing," Piotr muttered. "Don't envy you the headache."

He finished tying up and gagging the last two guards, watching over his shoulder to assure that he had not been spotted. If the rumors about Brennan's man Maguaran were correct, then it would take more than speed and acrobatics to get past the thick-necked bodyguard and a warlock.

Piotr fingered the 'magic' belt for good luck. He listened beneath the window for a few seconds, making sure that Brennan and the others had not moved. Then he slipped around to the back of the building. It took only a moment to jimmy the basement door lock and find the electrical panel, then pull down the lever and plunge the building and grounds into darkness.

He froze, listening. Brennan and his allies were right overhead. MacCabe shouted to the guards, but no one answered. Silently, Piotr slipped out of the basement and circled the building, staying to the shadows. He was already in the hallway when MacCabe warily peered from the room. Piotr used the exoskeleton's added strength to grab MacCabe by the shoulders and pull him abruptly into the darkened corridor, simultaneously turning him so that the bodyguard's gun pointed away.

Before MacCabe fully realized what was going on, Piotr leaped, and the steel toe of his boot caught MacCabe under the jaw. The bodyguard went down like a sack of potatoes.

From inside Brennan's office, Piotr heard the sound of a revolver's hammer being cocked. Maguaran began to chant.

Too late to turn back now.

Piotr grabbed MacCabe's gun. He knew how to shoot; he just preferred not to, if there was another way. Then he leveraged his exoskeleton to haul MacCabe to his feet and push the big man's unconscious form into the doorway.

Six shots rang out as Brennan unloaded his bullets into the lumbering shadow. A flash of white light and a shout in a language Piotr guessed was Gaelic sent the smell of smoke and burning cloth into the air as a blast of power struck MacCabe square in the chest. As MacCabe's body slumped to the ground, Piotr hunched beside the doorway, shooting out one of the large windows with a crash of breaking glass and then the other.

In the instant when Brennan and Maguaran turned their weapons toward the windows, expecting a threat from outside, the Ghost Wolf lunged and dove. He came up shooting, intentionally taking a line of fire across the room to force the crime boss and the warlock to scramble for cover.

Maguaran was the first to make a move, lobbing what appeared to be a ball of green fire right at the spot where the Ghost Wolf had been seconds before.

Maguaran might have magic, but Piotr had technology. The special goggles Farber had made for him let him see although the room was almost pitch dark. He had discarded the empty gun, and the blackjack was in one hand and Farber's little box in the other.

Propelled by the gas cartridge that ran the exoskeleton, the Ghost Wolf sprang for the warlock in the darkness. Green fire flashed toward him. Piotr pressed the button on the box, felt a second's disorientation, and realized the fire had missed him. The *ladanki* belt pulsed once with a soft, golden light. Before Maguaran could recoup, Piotr slammed the warlock to the floor, pressing the magical belt against the small of the magic-user's back and giving the button on Farber's box another push, just for good measure. The air around him crackled with power both electrical and magical. Piotr cracked his blackjack against Maguaran's skull and dove out of the way in case Brennan had a second gun.

He rolled and came up right beside Brennan, swinging his weighted, metal-clawed gauntlets. One swipe slashed down across the crime boss's face, opening four deep, bloody slits and nearly blinding him in one eye. Brennan cursed and fell back a step. Light flashed, a force struck Piotr in the chest, and he staggered.

Brennan clutched a Derringer, his hold-out gun, its shot spent at close range. Piotr swung his blackjack. Brennan managed to block him, clamping down on Piotr's wrist with an iron grip.

"You should be dead," Brennan growled.

"And you should be in jail." Piotr bent his knees and pushed off. The exoskeleton vaulted him toward the ceiling, taking an unprepared Brennan with him. Piotr ducked, but he yanked on Brennan hard, slamming the crime boss's head against the plaster ceiling. The apparatus cushioned Piotr's landing, but he let Brennan fall hard, and as his enemy stumbled, Piotr brought the blackjack down with a satisfying crack.

Only then did Piotr take in what had happened. He clutched at his chest. The small caliber bullet had torn through the gray cloth of his costume, slowed by the silk of the vest beneath. But his ribs felt as if they had cracked with the impact, and warm blood trickled down his belly.

First things first. I'm going to get what I came for. Piotr had sized up his options and made preparations before he launched his attack. Now, speed was of the essence. It was only a matter of time before more of Brennan's men showed up. Piotr had no desire to leave Brennan and Maguaran for the local cops, who were likely to be on Brennan's pay. He gasped with pain as he dragged first Brennan then Maguaran to the back door, and went back to grab files from Brennan's desk to make sure the two men were fully incriminated.

He had hog-tied both men, gagging and blindfolding them for good measure. Swearing under his breath, he hauled them with the last of his strength to the large wooden crate that sat in a boxcar ready to leave the yard with the midnight train. Only his exoskeleton enabled Piotr to heft first Brennan and then Maguaran into the crate. He watched them both to make sure they were still unconscious, dropped the files from the desk in with them, then dumped salt over Maguaran, just in case.

Piotr gritted his teeth as he nailed the wooden crate shut. He had marked the shipping recipient when he prepared the crate. In the distance, he heard a train's whistle. In a few hours, the rail spur would bustle with the night shift. With luck, it would give him enough time to get home.

Piotr stuck to the darkest shadows, limping away from the coal company. After many a successful fight, the Ghost Wolf had triumphantly ridden atop one of Coal Hill's inclines, but tonight, Piotr was too injured to execute the necessary acrobatics. In his disguise, he dared not be seen by passers-by, so riding in the passenger compartment of the incline was out of the question. That left the long trek up the switchbacks of Indian Trail, a winding route that made its way up the steep slope of Coal Hill.

Piotr had always considered Indian Trail beyond the territory he patrolled as the Ghost Wolf. But he had heard rumors that forest spirits wrecked their own particular vengeance on anyone who tried to prey on the weary souls who climbed the dark, winding trails. As Piotr forced himself onward, he was certain eyes watched him from the shadows beneath the trees.

I've got to get shelter before daylight, he thought, pushing himself on. *I don't dare be caught dressed as the Ghost Wolf. And more to the point, I'm bleeding.* The silk vest was soaked with blood, and fire lanced his chest with every movement, every breath. The vest might have stopped Brennan's bullet from putting a big hole in him, but the slug had done damage, nonetheless.

Piotr's breath was labored, loud in the still night. He was injured and many blocks away from home, in enemy territory. And while he had put an end to Brennan's scheme, Piotr wondered if the price had been his own life.

There were no railings along Indian Trail, and no markers. Piotr stumbled, nearly falling. He was certain that he heard footsteps behind him, and equally sure he had no fight left in him. No streetlights marked the trail. It was an old path, and the factory workers and mill hunks who climbed this trail knew to carry a lantern for the trek home.

It was too early for the night shift to be getting off, too late for the swing shift. That meant no one else had good reason to be on Indian Trail, unless they were looking for trouble. Piotr gasped as he caught his boot on a root and nearly fell. The exoskeleton was keeping him upright, helping to bear some of his weight, giving him a spring in his step to counter his exhaustion. But the compressed air tanks were nearly empty, and when they were spent, Piotr knew he would not be able to go on.

If the cops don't get me, the Micks will.

He reached a place on the trail where the tree canopy opened up to the sky. Moonlight filtered down, and he saw three men not far behind him, gaining fast. Piotr tried to pick up his pace, but the world spun, and he pitched head-long onto the trail. The men were running now. Maybe they had recognized him and saw their chance to capture or kill the Ghost Wolf. Piotr had heard that there was a bounty, put on his head by ruffians with a grudge. He gritted his teeth and tried to rise, just as four new shadows emerged from the trees. A sound like thunder made his ears ring. His pursuers cried out in fear and their running footsteps receded. Piotr struggled to reach his knees, knowing he needed to defend himself from this new threat or at least escape into the woods, but even the exoskeleton could not keep him from collapse. *I'm a dead man.*

◄ G ►

Piotr woke slowly. First, he realized that he wasn't dead. Then he gingerly moved his wrists and ankles, fearing police shackles. When he realized that he was not chained, he panicked as it dawned on him that someone had removed both his Ghost Wolf outfit and the exoskeleton. He opened his eyes, and found himself in a small room that held a bed, a small desk and a chair. A crucifix hung over the door.

When he tried to sit up, his ribs protested. Piotr's chest was neatly taped, with fresh bandages that smelled of herbal poultice. A homespun nightshirt replaced his clothing, but as he took in his surroundings, he realized with relief that the exoskeleton leaned against the wall behind the door, and the rest of his outfit lay on the desk, next to a pitcher and a glass.

Just as Piotr was thinking about trying to get to the pitcher for a drink, the door opened. A woman in a nun's habit entered, and looked him up and down like a boys' school matron. She was in her middle years, plump and round-faced, with a solid build and broad hands that suggested a life of hard work.

"I see you're awake." Her voice had a strong Irish lilt, and Piotr's heart sank. Her lips quirked, as if she guessed his thoughts.

"Relax. You're safe here, Pole or Irish." She paused, and he thought he saw a glimpse of mischief in her eyes. "And for the famed Ghost Wolf, you have the best room our poor cloister has to offer."

"You were on the trail? The ones who saved me?"

The nun nodded. "Aye. Did you think the Ghost Wolf was the only one trying to make sure our young men stay in one piece on their way home from work? We watch over Indian Trail, since it comes out just below our cloister house. Sister Aideen had a vision in which the Holy Mother herself sent us to protect the trail, and so we have taken it as our calling."

"That noise... did you *shoot* those men who were following me?" Piotr knew it was probably impolite—not to mention unwise—to ask so many questions of his rescuer, but he had no idea what he had just gotten himself into.

The nun laughed. "Rock salt," she replied. "Stings like the devil, but won't put much of a hole in them." She sobered as she regarded him. "Unlike the bullet we dug out of you," she added, raising an eyebrow.

"It was a busy night," Piotr said. He had no desire to add to his sins by lying to a nun, but since he had acquired that bullet from two Irishmen, he thought it best to say as little as possible, here in an Irish convent. "Where am I?"

"You're in the cloister of the Sisters of Saint Athracht," she replied. "And I am Sister Muread."

"What do you intend to do with me?" Piotr asked, deciding it was better to get to the meat of the matter.

Sister Muread gave him a quizzical look as if he might still be addled from his injuries. "Heal you and send you on your way, with the blessings of the Saints and the Holy Mother," she replied.

"But I'm... not Irish."

This time, Sister Muread chuckled. "Sure'n your not, that's true. An' we know the stories of the Ghost Wolf, even up here, how he stops our boys fighting with your boys, which is as the Good Lord would have it. So you're welcome here, Sir Wolf, under our protection, 'til you can safely go home."

"Thank you," he said, managing a wan smile. "I'm grateful to you and the Sisters."

"We've found some fresh clothing for you," Sister Muread said. "Come nightfall, you can put your other items into a sack and throw a sheet over the larger pieces," she added with a nod toward the exoskeleton. "Our groundskeeper can take you in the wagon where you need to go."

"How long was I out?" Piotr asked.

"Just a day," Sister Muread replied. "Our healer dosed you with medicine to help you sleep, and cleaned your wound, bound up your ribs. With a good meal in you, you should be mostly mended."

I've missed a day of work, Piotr thought. *I might have saved the South Side, but I've probably lost my job.*

◄ G ►

With a heavy heart and aching ribs, Piotr went in to work the following day. He had spent the prior evening reassuring Mrs. Szabo that he was fine, and feeling very guilty since she had stayed up all of the previous night waiting for him, worried sick, and had gone out looking for him. Now, a different kind of worry gnawed at him, but he squared his shoulders and entered the pawn shop by the back door, as he always did.

"Piotr! Where have you been?" Agent Drangosavich was the first to spot him.

Piotr doffed his cap and looked down. "Apologies, sir. I fix things for my landlady and I fall from ladder. Knocked out." He tapped his knuckles against his temple. "But I have a hard head. Good as new."

He steeled himself, waiting to be fired. "Good to have you back," Drangosavich said. "Probably for the best you weren't around yesterday. Damndest thing. A box showed up at headquarters with two men inside. Troublemakers—from New Pittsburgh. Made for a busy day with the brass trying to figure out how they got to Washington, D.C. Lots of people in and out of here, and now there's dirt tracked all over the hallway." He gave Piotr a sidelong glance. "You'll take care of that right away?"

Piotr grinned. "Oh yes, sir. Don't you worry. I'll get it done." He went to fetch his mop and bucket, sensing that Drangosavich watched him walk away. But if the agent suspected anything, he chose to save it for another day.

Good to know the railroad runs on schedule, Piotr thought. *I'd have hated for that box to get lost.*

Furious in

Don't You Know Who I Am?

Bryan J.L. Glass

THERE WERE THREE GUNMEN ON THE ROOF OF THE HIGH-RISE HOTEL. They were most likely the reason police and news helicopters were staying well beyond firing range from the penthouse suite.

Furia was confident they couldn't see her, as the size of one relatively diminutive figure set against the wide expanse of sky would make observation difficult—and wearing a sky blue bodysuit definitely aided in her concealment.

As the only human being on Earth for whom unaided independent flight was a reality, embracing the gaudy hues derived from the realm of fictional super-powered heroes appeared to be Furia's only option. Unless the super-heroine otherwise wanted to embrace subservience to some random nation's military/industrial complex. Put on a costume. Hide one's identity beneath a blonde wig and biker goggles. Add actual super-strength, some form of invulnerability when it really mattered, and the bona fide ability to defy gravity at high velocity guaranteed Furia was the real deal. All she needed to complete the package was a genuine victim to rescue.

Circling the penthouse from a thousand feet above the twelve-story Regency Riverfront Hotel, the flying woman identified where each of the gunmen were stationed atop the triangular structure. Each had one compatriot in view at all times, eliminating the ability to drop in on one without immediately alerting the others to her presence. That might prove unfortunate for the hostages inside.

Furia lowered her binoculars. In the comics, movies, and on TV, every hero had their gadgets and a supporting cast that always included at least one tech genius. If she was the star of her own weekly television series, the tech boy or lab girl would have had her goggles outfitted with zoom lenses in the previous episode, just in time to save the day *this* week! Instead, she realized her spandex didn't even offer her anywhere to conveniently stash the binoculars once she'd committed herself to a course of action.

She could circle the hotel for the next several hours awaiting the cover of darkness, but her enemies offered no security in that scenario. One innocent woman was already in need of hospitalization, and Furia was sure the ticking of the clock was working against them both. By her own experience, she couldn't distinguish a true mercenary from any Hollywood stuntman, but this rooftop trio carried themselves just like every soldier of fortune she'd ever seen in front of a camera. And the high profile of their presumed target inside suggested they were the genuine article—lock and load, shoot first, let God sort out the details. Furia needed a strategy; and she needed one before anybody else was injured or worse.

Through her lens, she saw one gunman move, the barrel of his automatic weapon rising even before his own head looked up. In an instant, Furia realized the angle of the sun reflected one instant of sunlight off her goggles to the watchful eyes below. It wouldn't take a professional to be on the lookout for the one and only super-powered heroine this world had to offer; and if one was audacious enough to take a job in this town, then anyone worth their commission was going to keep at least one eye on the sky.

Furia watched the gunman's aim track with her as she allowed herself to drift with the upper air current. This wasn't a random motion. She'd been targeted. Without any plan of attack whatsoever, she knew she had to strike immediately. She could see the gunman's mouth moving, communicating her presence to his fellow flunkies on the roof, and most probably to those on the inside.

She'd blown her opportunity...and she still had no place to tuck away the binoculars. And to think this had all started with that blowhard Justin North actually believing the sun revolved around his star...

◄ **G** ►

"It's great to be here," Justin North spouted to the camera, eyes hidden behind his oversized trademark sunglasses. "Between LA, New York, and the rest of the world, I rarely get to experience middle-America from sea level."

He might be spouting gibberish, but Justin North was too much of an A-List commodity for any typical local journalist to ever call him on it. That simply wasn't how the entertainment game was played.

Far from typical, News 33 Reporter Jesus Martinez definitely had experience playing the players, and said, "You're such a global phenomenon, Justin—can I call you Justin?"

North smiled, cocking his head with a practiced ease, allowing the profile camera to catch a glimpse of the 24-karat caps he wore to compliment his brown skin and accent the gold around his neck.

Martinez continued, "Thank you, Justin. But we're just surprised you agreed to perform at our annual Charity Concert after the public spectacle you made last year in turning our local community down."

North splayed two fingers to indicate the wealth on his teeth and around his collar. "What you see here is just an outward expression of the true gold that springs from my heart."

"Of course. But what made you change your mind?" Martinez asked.

North adjusted his sunglasses. "It's such a worthy cause. What you got going here... touches so many lives." He coughed into his hand and quickly added, "What is it again?"

"Fem-Now," said Martinez with a sly grin, knowing it was quite acceptable to give the player as much rope as they asked for. "They're an umbrella organization specializing in women's issues, supporting a wide spectrum of smaller charities within, from equality to health to single parent families and the needs of their children."

"That's right," North chirped. "Good causes. I'm all about supporting the women and their [BLEEP]—can I say that on TV?"

Martinez smiled. "We're on a seven-second delay, so just speak from that heart."

"Yeah…" North nodded as if lost in thought for a moment. "Equality. I'm all for women and their rights…just so long as they know their place and don't get all up in my face about it—y'know what I'm saying?"

North conjured such apparent magic that he could spout the deepest offenses, break the Internet for a day, and yet the women of the world kept downloading his singles, and buying out his concert tours. He was the exception, and he knew it.

Yet Martinez was confident as well, knowing how Nielsen courted controversy, that he'd win the local ratings war yet again. He pressed his advantage. "I'm sure many in our audience would disagree. But now that your heart's on your sleeve, so to speak, I'm curious why you chose News 33 over the larger affiliates for an exclusive interview?"

North's grin never wavered, but the length of his pause spoke volumes. "Well…what can I say—I dig your suit. You're the station that introduced the entire wide world to that little blonde flying babe."

"And who might that be?" asked Martinez coyly.

"You know who I mean…*Furious!*"

"She calls herself 'Furia'," Martinez corrected.

The reporter had been the first to dub their super-heroine "Furious," only it hadn't taken long for the elusive flying woman to beat him at his own game. Martinez could respect that, and conceded it would be in his own best interests to release himself from any professional grudge against her.

"Y'see…it's that right there," North smiled as if he held all the cards, "That's why I picked you, Jesus. If anybody in this town knows how to get in touch with your little miss, Furious, it's gonna be you."

North had stepped into Martinez' arena, and the reporter knew just how gently to nudge the conversation. "Can you elaborate then, on how you feel someone of Furia's stature and power might be compelled to grant anyone as ordinary as you or me such an audience?"

North's head cocked backward ever so slightly. Behind his unwavering smile, he bristled with genuine offense. "Don't you know who I am?"

The absurdity hung in the air, invisibly like a personal cloud of passed gas.

"I'm sure she does...Justin. Only it appears to this reporter that you're simply trying to con the media into giving you a phone number you can't get on your own. Would I be correct in that assumption?"

North still smiled, only the edges curled giving him a sour expression. "Small fish, Martinez. And it's a big, big pond."

It was Martinez' turn to maintain his decorum. "That would be a yes?"

"We're done here," said Justin North as he stood, pulling his Lavalier microphone from his lapel. He scratched his chest with a middle finger as he walked from the set.

Jesus Martinez stifled his inner feelings as he verbally passed the segment back to the news desk anchor. Furia didn't need his protection, but that wouldn't stop the reporter from jealously guarding territory he still considered his own.

— G —

Furia had but a split second to take action. She was already grazing the gunman's bullet as it raced to meet her, singeing a few stray hairs of her blonde wig as they passed each other on her way down. She angled her trajectory just enough to mimic a cyclone approach. Harder to hit should the gunman rattle off a second shot, but an even better way to allow gravity to accelerate her descent.

With no place to put the binoculars, Furia opted to hold them in one hand right in front. It was the first thing the gunman felt as they shattered on impact. Her fist was the second. But Furia was already en route to the next before the first dropped to the penthouse patio's tiles.

Calculating reaction amidst a decade of outrageous acts had never been her strong suit, but since acquiring these equally outrageous new powers she was getting better at her estimates. If she'd worked her tailspin as intended, the same flight arc that landed her in the face of #1 should be sufficient to lead her straight into #2 without so much as a nick or tuck.

The second gunman had only just turned to face her approach when her forearm slammed into his knees. She heard a double crack of bone but felt no remorse. What had been done to that teenaged girl she saw on TV was enough to hold responsible every single one of these ass-hats brandishing an assault weapon.

Only gunman #3 remained.

The last of the outside rooftop trio was going to require a slight mid-course correction. Furia still sucked at mid-course corrections. She considered it Divine Intervention when she made any contact with the gunman at all. Unfortunately, she slammed into his assault rifle, spinning the man around like a top with enough centrifugal force that his body whirled to the rooftop rail and tipped over the side. The twelve-story drop welcomed him.

━◄ G ►━

Justin North stood on the platform before City Council, flashing his literal million-dollar smile. The gold on his teeth was real. The gold plating on the Key to the City was not. But Mayor Bloomquist still presented it as if the symbolic gesture truly opened the hearts and minds of every constituent that might reconsider their vote against him in the next election.

Following that debacle with Jesus Martinez on News 33, any other media outlet would have leapt at the chance to assist in damage control, only North never wanted to appear quite so needy as he actually was. And he'd learned that no one kissed your ass better than a public official.

"What can I say, but that it's great to be here," North spouted to the cameras, reporters, and politicians assembled in the Council Chamber. "And Fem-Now! What's up with that?"

It wasn't a statement. It was barely even a question. But that didn't thwart the applause. Only North knew his constituency was global, and salivated over every telecast word he uttered. That's what Martinez had claimed to understand yet failed to grasp. Just tell His Honor you wanted to shake his hand before the cameras, and he'd make it a catered, red carpet affair. This was the world according to super-stardom.

"But thanks for the key, your Honor," North continued. "And to all you ladies out there," he jangled the oversized tool in his hand, "this little baby opens the lock to what I just know you're all thinking about."

More than one reporter blushed.

"But I wanted to take this opportunity before all my adoring public, not only to thank your Mr. Mayor here for all his gracious hospitality, but to give each and every one of you a chance to join my payroll for a day, if you'll help me track down the whereabouts of one elusive fan…"

The Chamber may as well have been a concert hall, as Justin North did what he did best: preened before the cameras as if they were a million adoring fans.

"She flitters, she floats, she flies…you know who I'm talking about! She kissed that Martinez chump goodbye; told him where to stick it 'cause she's flying high. You all know her name…your one-of-a-kind female Super-Fly—FURIOUS!"

Reporters and politicians alike were stunned in silence. Bloomquist was mortified. North wasn't phased in the slightest by the lack of verbal support. "She can't be living that far in the future without her Internets a'buzzing? That those tight little blue panties are hot flashing for me just as I know I have that effect on all of you!"

Bloomquist shuffled uncomfortably, and tried to reign in the spectacle before he could be blamed for it. "Yes, yes. Thank you, Mr. North. As the kids say, my um, panties are hot flashing for you too—is that what they say?"

But there was no stopping the idol of millions once he'd started. "Your Honor, please…you're embarrassing yourself. Leave the public speaking to those professionals more qualified."

Bloomquist was not the first to suffer such public humiliation at North's charisma. Nor would he be the last, as that old North wind just kept on blowing. In moments, North had transformed the formal ceremony of the press conference into a full-blown Tent Revival for the Gospel of Justin!

"I know you can all hear what I'm saying, what I'm askin'. And what I want is whichever one of you has the hotline to her little blonde hotness…tell her to get on the horn to my press agent—I trust all you responsible networks are gonna put that contact info up on your little screens there—make sure she knows I'm in town…for CHARITY! As a good cause is served from the overflow of my heart."

He thumped his chest with a clenched fist. "This heart is gold, as all my fans will attest. So this is her only chance for Furious to meet the only man who can show her what being "super" is really all about!"

The news media reran highlights 24/7, as North had yet again broken the Internet.

— G —

They always made it look so damn easy in the movies.

In less than three seconds, Furia had taken out what she presumed to be three highly trained mercenary gunmen from the roof of the swanky Regency Hotel…only the third was plummeting to the ground while she was swooping upward in a looping arc.

The creeps deserved whatever they got, but Furia was determined to not play judge and jury. No one was going to die here if she could help it…and most especially not by her own actions!

Her flight arc was extreme as she circled back toward the falling gunman. She sensed her muscles were screaming in red alert mode, yet due to the mysteries of her power set she felt no pain. That would come later while she lay in bed, waves of nauseous ache oozing through her as if the agony were a tangible energy slowly dissipating from her system. Only that was happening with less frequency these days, so perhaps this time her good deed might go unpunished.

She'd had experience with this particular form of rescue before. Only this instance was from a much shorter height, less time to snag the victim, and most likely no clearance whatsoever to bank them both skyward and to safety. She was still suffering in public opinion polls after her last save had left a multi-million dollar swath of destruction across the city landscape. She could take comfort only in that no lives were lost as collateral…and no one knew who the mystery woman was beneath the oversized goggles, or where she lived!

Furia caught the gunman at about the third floor, startling one who was already staring death in the eye. "Don't fight, hang on," she shouted while spinning the much-larger man's back to her chest, and awaited the impact with her own shoulders. Less than two seconds remained. His legs and arms would probably shatter, and she'd feel a bit guilty about that, but at least he'd get to live with what he'd done.

As they struck the ground, the polished marble walkway cracked, and the concrete beneath vaporized into a plume of dust that instantly obscured them from the media cameras chronicling their fall. The gunman cried out only until his brain shut down from the shock. Furia felt the brunt of the impact smash into her upper back, and felt both shoulders dislocate.

Furia floated in the euphoria of pain-free stasis, as if her consciousness jumped ahead to another time zone before any injury might catch up with her...yet feeling no pain didn't prevent her decompressed lungs from coughing up a shot glass's ounce of blood.

◄ G ►

"Media: OFF!"

Cadence Lark commanded her large-screen monitor to shut down. She couldn't take the media assault any longer. Justin North seemed to be on every station, every hour of every day. She felt that damned charity concert couldn't arrive fast enough...and was fed up with the weeklong publicity show North had made of his own participation. It wasn't even about Fem-Now any longer, or any of the services its organizers represented, but had been transformed, co-opted into Justin North and his libido.

"He's a damn media whore—no, that's not right." Cadence muttered to no one but herself in her sprawling but mostly empty luxury apartment. She could afford the penthouse if she'd wanted, but her days of ostentatious display were over. Nothing remained of that desire to flaunt, that desperate need for approval and how it yearned for pity.

"A gigolo—that's it...he's a damned media-circus GIGOLO!"

But more than that, she considered the man a genuine monster—as such monsters came in both genders, all flavors, and were never limited by race, creed, or color. From personal experience, Cadence knew all too well how media culture was interested in only one thing: keeping the beast well fed.

Cadence wandered to her bathroom mirror for the seventeenth time that evening. With her pixie cut, black-dyed hair, and total abandonment of designer fashion...no one ever suspected who she had been. She had nowhere to go, and no one to talk to regarding what actually bothered her about all of this. North wanted Furious, so only one thing was certain: Furia would not fly until "Elvis" had left the building: *gonna bid my blues goodbye.*

That's the way it had to be. North lived off and for his own fame. The moment she let her own world be dominated by that similar need for attention again, there would be but one difference between the infamous Cadence Lark and notorious Justin North. Cadence would prove the scarier monster.

◄ G ►

SWAT and medical personnel swarmed in, hands holding M16s swatting at the clouds of dust left above the impact crater. They confirmed her voice before visual identification.

"I don't care how much it hurts him, but get this guy the hell off of me!" It was Furia laying six inches beneath the broken sidewalk squares bench-pressing the dead weight of a man she didn't appear to have the physical frame to lift.

"Are you okay?" asked one EMT.

Blood oozed from both ears, one eye, dripped from both nostrils, and bathed Furia's chin and chest in a wet, red bib. "Just get this guy taken care of before somebody up there gets killed!"

As Furia had expected, both the arms and legs of the gunman were shattered ruins, so a quartet of EMTs took his frame by both shoulders and either side of his trunk, and lifted his unconscious bulk onto the nearby gurney.

A SWAT officer extended his hand to Furia.

"Are you sure you want to do that?" she asked eying him with suspicion, knowing how many in law enforcement regarded her.

"It would be my pleasure, ma'am."

She took his hand and, with biceps over twice as large her own, he gently raised Furia to her feet. "I'm too young to be anybody's ma'am," she scowled as she popped her shoulder blades back into place.

The officer's eyes were filled with wonder and twinkled at her humor. "Are you sure there's nothing else we can d—"

Before he could finish, Furia had launched herself skyward.

◄ G ►

The evening before the Fem-Now Charity Concert was to be held, a Special Report cut into every local station and media service provider: armed terrorists had stormed the Regency Riverside Hotel and taken hostage famed entertainer Justin North and his entourage.

The majority of the guests and staff were permitted to leave the building until all that remained were a dozen black-armored gunmen and the party held captive on the penthouse floor. Within minutes, gunmen with assault rifles covered every entry into the hotel above and below. Only one message was conveyed by those allowed to escape: keep the cell towers on (as it was standard procedure in such situations to disable all communication). The Chief of Police consulted with Mayor Bloomquist, and the cellular lines went unblocked.

Cadence Lark's first reaction was to assume the out-of-control celebrity had staged the entire thing for publicity, and to lure Furia out of hiding.

"There is no way I'm giving that bastard what he wants," she quipped. Yet like most of America under the age of 30, Cadence remained fixated on her over-sized monitor, or pocket cellular device for social media updates throughout the night.

All proved silent and uneventful for the first several hours, with the exception of rooftop warning shots to scare back the news and police helicopters. Yet at midnight precisely, a text was dispatched to all local media with a list of demands: a trio of helicopters— pilots to be replaced upon landing—to fly the terrorists and their hostages to the airport, where Justin North's private jet was to be fully restocked and fueled, as well as a flight corridor cleared to the Middle East (Saudi Arabia boasted the largest male fan base the singer had).

That was it. No money. No political maneuvering. It was almost as if some foreign country didn't want to wait for North's next International concert tour, but had arranged to kidnap the popular rap vocalist months in advance; perhaps even a private performance for one royal family or another. But in today's climate, even that paranoid scheme was being debunked on websites, chat rooms, and podcasts that specialized in conspiracy.

Not surprisingly, those who appeared the most fixated on Furia making an appearance were the broadcast reporters, their trusty camera operators already on location, each one maintaining one eye on the drama behind the walls and the other on the skies, to see which studio would score the first sighting of their super-savior playing right into the "victim's" hands.

Every one of them could take a number in hell's waiting room as far as Cadence was concerned. Her couch was especially comfy this evening, and the fragrance from the kitchen commanded her presence.

As the night wore on, Cadence remained fascinated. Practically anything concerning North already possessed the power to compel one's attention, yet this event had taken even his disreputable showmanship to an entirely new level: that which was usually reserved for spectacular tragedies broadcast in cycles of slow-motion repetition. This time, she couldn't bring herself to close her screen down for even an instant.

Cadence must have nodded off at some point, as the dawn and a drastic turning point in the saga snapped her brain wide-awake. Another message sent directly to the media at 5:47 am, not quite the clockwork timing of the first, and this one in the form of a video: a teenaged girl assumed to be 18—but would probably be revealed as a minor—a member of North's entourage picked up locally just the other day to experience a once-in-a-lifetime opportunity to party with her favorite superstar...now appeared on screen, eyes blackened, cheeks pummeled, nose broken and bloody, a clump of hair ripped from her scalp. She appeared to be alone in the presence of her captor, isolated in one of the lower rooms where it could be assumed the atrocity had taken place. Her captor spoke off-screen, urging her to tell the camera exactly how she felt.

When she opened her mouth to speak, it was obvious several teeth were missing. She spit out blood and uttered but one word in answer to her tormentor's curious question: *How do you feel?*

"Fuh...f-furious."

—◄ G ►—

Furia cursed the window of opportunity she'd missed between taking out the rooftop gunmen and safeguarding the third before his death could have been attributed to her action.

In a moment's retrospective, she honestly wished she'd allowed the man to drop to his fate. She couldn't get the image out of her head of the teenaged girl from the news—confirmed as 16-year-old Jessica Reid. She was still inside—somewhere—and Furia vowed she'd be saved long before a finger was ever lifted on North's behalf.

Three down. And if news reports were reliable then that left nine more within, five below, and four most likely with the hostages; all of them much too aware that she was on her way.

Furia's entrance came boots first, straight through the center of the twin glass patio doors, blasting them from their hinges while shattering the glass to either side. She was finally learning how better to not endanger the very people she intended to save. Little by little she was becoming the hero she intended to be. Thus the sight that met her took her completely by surprise...

In the large common room of the luxurious penthouse suite sat Justin North's entire entourage sprawled on the couches, still drinking with the dawn, three young women in lingerie with two young men barely clothed, laughing hysterically at Furia's grand entrance, stoned out of their minds. North's private chef Papa Hopp was serving eggs onto plates from a still-steaming pan, as if he'd fully stocked the penthouse larder for the length of the siege. North's private physician Dr. Rahadyan Sastrowardoyo knelt, tending the wounds of Jessica Reid who giggled with the rest, through the bloody wrappings about her jaw.

Rahadyan looked up with apologetic eyes. "She doesn't feel any of this," he said, as if it might justify whatever was going on. "Mr. North will see she is well compensated. And she signed a waiver."

One of the gunmen stood nearby, gun danging from its shoulder strap, both arms raised abdomen-high as if to assure he posed no threat. "Hey," he said to draw Furia's attention. He gestured toward her bloodied face. "He wasn't supposed to take a shot at you. Sorry."

Smoke and mirrors. The truth behind entertainment: nothing was ever as it appeared. And Furia of all people should have clung to her initial instinct. She could feel her anger intensifying, and that wasn't going to be good for anybody, but in the moment she no longer cared. Signed "waiver" or not, the bloodied 16-year-old wasn't legally responsible for anything she'd consented to in securing her next emotional high. She didn't possess North's magic charm; once her medication wore off, she'd have to live with her choices.

"Which one of you did that to her?" Furia demanded, pointing at the giggling stoner.

The gunman pointed to his partner exiting the kitchen with a plate of eggs and potatoes, his own rifle slung over his shoulder. He appeared completely unperturbed by the sound of crashing doors and shattering glass from moments before, as if everything unfolded according to some previously concocted master plan.

"What?" was all he uttered from behind a strip of bacon held between his fingers and teeth.

Furia's speed surprised even her. She really was getting better at her reactionary timing, if not her reactionary decisions. She flew across the room faster than the turning heads of the others could track, and slammed shoulder-first into the unprepared gunman. Only his body armor saved him from an immediate expiration. That remained something Furia definitely needed to work on before her luck ran out.

The gunman dropped his plate and his gun, but the strip of bacon remained clenched in his teeth as Furia unloaded a rapid series of wild punches to his chest and abdomen. She still couldn't throw a proper punch, but her speed and strength more than compensated.

The previous gunman was on her in an instant, twice her size and locking her upper arms in a vice-like grip. "That's enough, little g—"

He too was unable to complete his sentence before Furia launched them both into the ceiling with enough force to buckle the roof at the gunman's expense. As they landed again, Furia let the gunman on her back collapse to the floor in a heap.

The gunman she'd pummeled was still hunched against the wall, gasping for breath from within the buckled-in body armor crushing his chest. Furia grabbed him by the hair and pulled him onto the floor. All 5'4" of her frame dragged the 6'5" tough guy across the carpet toward Jessica, whose giggles had faded. Her jaded eyes conveyed some understanding that something serious was occurring.

"Was it him?" Furia demanded an answer from her.

Chef Hopp let the remaining eggs fall to the floor for housekeeping to take care of, and raised his cast-iron skillet in both hands in a defensive posture. He backed up regardless.

Dr. Rahadyan raised his hand blocking the girl's view of Furia's handful of gunman. "Please! The girl is in no condition for any more of this!"

Furia glared through her goggles, baring her teeth through her own bloodied lips. "You volunteering to be next?"

"If need be," he answered. "Each of us makes our choices, even after we realize the mistakes we've made."

Furia tried to rein in her breathing. The doc was either spouting more gobbledygook in some lame effort to cover his own ass at the last instant...or offering some profundity she'd be wise to heed. She decided she preferred the second option.

A great bass voice shouted from behind her: "Furious! What the holy hell do you think you're doing?"

Furia turned to see Justin North, unharmed yet enraged, flanked between the two remaining penthouse gunmen, both targeting the heroine and clicking off their safeties as one.

Justin swatted both barrels toward the ceiling before any shots could be fired. "Nobody's getting' shot here," he shouted.

One of the underwear-clad entourage on the couch burst out laughing once more.

North whirled on his staff, commanding, "Jacko—shut the fuck up!"

Jacko shut up, as if he was more afraid of his boss's disapproval than anything else in the room.

North continued to control the situation through the sheer force of his personality. "There's nothing funny about this. We got people hurt here that should have never been hurt—and they wouldn't have if only everybody had done what they were supposed to do."

The room remained silent.

North turned his attention back to Furia. "You. Furious. Why couldn't you have come crashing in to save my ass last night like you were supposed to? Get yourself in the bathroom and wash yourself up. There's no way I'm kissing that face."

Furia just stared at him. She couldn't believe any human being could be so utterly self-absorbed; even in her own worst moments, she had never descended to such a depraved cluelessness.

North remained locked in his own world. He whipped off his trademark sunglasses to reveal furious eyes, as if he'd intended the facial pun. "I told you what to do, girl. You'd better do it."

Furia didn't move.

Jessica's voice broke the silence. "Whu... where's my mommy...?"

Furia glared at North. "Did you give the order?"

North glared right back. "For that?" he said, indicating Jessica. "I told somebody to make sure you got your ass over here. However they did it wasn't any of my concern. If there's a cost, I'll cover it. But whatever it was, it got you here—now don't you go gettin' all up in my face about it!"

Furia could have flown at him in the blink of an eye. Instead she walked, making sure every step was a conscious decisive choice. She walked so that North would see her coming.

The two gunmen stepped in to block any show of aggression as they'd been paid to do. Furia wasn't interested in their assignment. She threw one awkward punch. The burlier of the two caught it easily enough taking hold of the heroine's thin arm in one meaty grip. Only she gripped right back, clamping upon the mercenary's wrist. She casually tossed the man into his partner, using him like a bludgeon until he released his hold on her, and his partner stopped moving.

North finally seemed to realize he'd made a serious mistake.

Furia grabbed him by the chains around his neck and tossed him over the couch, sending his entourage scrambling for the floor. She followed him, catching a glimpse of Dr. Rahadyan on his cell phone placing a call that he probably should have made hours ago. Chef Hopp lowered his skillet with an equal personal conviction.

North struggled to stand when Furia grabbed him again, and tossed him through the broken doors. He tumbled thirty feet out onto the roof deck where the first of the helicopters was intended to land, bruising muscles and scraping large patches of exposed skin.

Furia continued her pursuit, truly not knowing how this confrontation could possibly end without crossing the line of her guilt. She hadn't wanted to become any part of this, only now she was committed to seeing it through.

Catching up to her target, she hefted him to his knees with both her fists clenched at his lapels. His head rocked back on a spine that had finally lost the will to keep it raised. Her contempt was palpable. "Whatever am I gonna do with you...little man?"

And that's when she saw the first spark of recognition dawn in North's eyes moments before he spoke. This was it, the real reason she'd wanted nothing to do with this entire escapade...

"Cady?" he said through a daze. "Cadence Lark? My god, it's you!"

━◄ G ►━

It was just after Cadence turned eighteen years old, at last becoming her own woman on the heels of a Hollywood youth. In one afternoon, she'd acquired the age of consent, dyed her innocent brown locks a provocative fiery red, hired new career management, and publicly fired her own father from the same position via an appearance on live TV. It would only take the next three years for Cadence to completely self-destruct.

But for the first night at least, she was still the reigning queen of her own media empire. Her new manager had scored tickets for Cady and her entourage to attend a concert at LA's leading Hip Hop club that same evening. She wasn't actually interested in the headline band, but it was important she be seen and photographed having the time of her life.

It was the warm-up act that caught her eye: a young rapper that had only just started making a local name for himself. He claimed to be 21, but looked on the younger side of 15 years old. That was his gimmick, accentuating the sexuality of his own youthful appearance.

The young flaming redhead in the audience drew his attention. He had no clue who she was, only that she was beautiful and seemingly entranced by his every move. As the performance progressed, it seemed that each was caught in the other's spotlight, the harsh glare blinding them to anything but each other.

The later evening found them in each other's arms. She'd had to dismiss her entourage, ditch her own bodyguard. But when the aspiring headliner had taken them to his shoddy apartment, she told the cab driver to wait—even the cockroaches were dangerous in that neighborhood. It took little prompting to get the young man back in the vehicle and off to a far ritzier destination where only her name would matter. By dawn, each had taken the other to new heights. But in the end their brief encounter proved about one thing...

"Justin...Justin North," she cooed gently from beneath the sweat-soaked sheets. "Someday you're going to be somebody."

His face was beautiful; eyes child-like yet a little sad. He said, "I'm never going to see you again, am I?"

Her heart sprung another leak as she silently mouthed her one word answer.

A lone tear rolled down his cheek. "Then one more," he said. "So I'll have something to remember you."

To be honest, she wanted the same. Only this wasn't about desire or need.

"Whatever am I gonna do with you...little man?" she said.

His eyes widened with confusion. Then Cadence pushed him off the bed with a knee to his groin.

She grabbed the sheet to cover herself and made a run for the open doorway. He struggled to his knees just in time to grab the last corner of the bedding, stopping her mad dash. He wept from more than just pain.

She glared at him with such utter contempt, and then bit her own lip until blood flowed. "You bastard," she screamed, spitting her blood over him. She punched him across the face. It wasn't a very skilled punch but it proved enough. The sheet came free and she ran from the room, out the door, into the hall, and then conjured her tears within the elevator to the lobby.

Security caught Justin North hobbling to don his second shoe. His shirt slung over his shoulder serving only to smear Cadence's blood across his chest. He was held until the police arrived, and a tear-wracked statement was drawn from his purported victim. His arrest only added to her publicity. The gracious decision to withdraw her charges against him one week later reminded America she was still their "sweetheart" after all, and kept her name prominently in the press and social media for another week. He was all but forgotten, left to struggle in his career until Cadence Lark crashed and burned three years later beneath the full gaze of the media lens...and every entertainment news agency in the world suddenly wanted the opinion of jilted lover Justin North.

Cadence hadn't made him the monster he became after that. She just taught him how to get away with it.

━ G ━

Furia stood on the rooftop deck holding the past in her bloody hands yet again. Some stains—some sins it seemed—would never wash away.

Shaken, bruised, and bloody, Justin North kneeled at her feet as she clutched him by the front of his shirt. Despite the momentary recognition, she still saw confusion in his eyes as he desperately tried to overcome his fear with a rapid calculation of whatever facts and details he knew. And then she sensed the abrupt change in his posture, as if he'd thrown a switch somewhere inside himself that restored his unflappable demeanor.

"Oh Cady," he cooed, "How could I ever forget you." North grinned his golden smile, and she felt her stomach twist in a knot.

Furia rocketed skyward, taking North with her. That brought the fear back into his eyes. Like reporter Jesus Martinez a week ago, she pressed her advantage hoping to leave a memorable impression that might threaten him into silence.

"I could drop you..." she hissed, "and you'd deserve it. So this is how it's going to—!"

North cut her off. "You're not gonna do a damn thing, Cady."

She wasn't the only one who'd spent her previous life perfecting an act. Suspended in mid-air, 10,000 feet above the world, Furia witnessed the professional survivor within Justin North reassert control.

"You've been a mess since your daddy died," he shouted at her. "And whatever this thing is you've got going now...I don't know how you do it, but I guess I'm the only homeboy that knows you're just desperate to ditch the Karma."

He might play the self-absorbed buffoon, but North was sharp. He was correct on all counts. She'd never do it. She'd already lived that media circus life of irresponsible horror, and she'd never go back.

It had taken the loss of everyone she'd ever cared for, but Cady finally saw the truth of her own monster. It was nothing to be embraced. She hit rock bottom and should have stayed there. Only a miraculous chemical formula—and perhaps the Grace of God—lifted her from that pit of her own making, purged her of her demons, and left her with these *powers and abilities far beyond those of mortal men*...or women.

To turn her back on that gift, this second chance at living, would betray the losses of all those who'd given their lives so that she could finally do the right thing. That was the burden she carried every day of her life, and most days, not all the super-strength in the world was enough to carry the weight.

But the martyrdom of her own pride in this moment would mean nothing to North. He'd gleefully ruin her last shot at redemption if only to stroke his own ego, and break the Internet yet again.

She couldn't take action on his vanity or her own. She had to remember the bloody face of Jessica Reid, broken to appease the whim of Justin North. Furia could fall on the sword of Cadence Lark's guilt, but North would just go on using and abusing.

It wasn't Furia's place to pass judgment. Where did the hero end and indestructible self-righteous goddess begin? The question proved the proverbial straw upon the camel's back. She opened her fingers and let North fall...

◄ G ►

Twelve thousand feet is standard skydiving height, enough to give the jumper one minute of glorious free fall before engaging their parachute.

Cadence gave Justin thirty seconds to realize his own past had finally caught up with him.

That's when Furia caught him and accelerated...ever downward, even faster, so that North never even realized the long banking curve she was taking him along.

Leveling out, they practically skimmed the surface of the river that flowed right past the Regency Riverview. Over the water, she granted North a moment to ponder his own reflection. His star power would prove enough to see him past even such a debacle as this latest, but it wouldn't be easy. He'd have his fair share of sleepless nights before him, and she wanted him to relive and ruminate over every second of this fiasco.

If there were second chances for Cadence Lark, then she could offer no less.

Furia mused that it was more than either of them deserved.

It was time to take him back up, and play her final card.

◄ G ►

A thousand feet above the hotel from which his scam had begun, Furia could smell the stink coming from Justin North's pants.

The super-heroine proved sufficient for the broad strokes, but it would take an Emmy-nominated actress to sell the last act—sure she'd lost, but in the entertainment business, even a nomination counted for something.

"Here's how it works, Justin," she said, pulling his face close enough to kiss. "If you ever tell another living soul what you learned today, whether you're drunk or under some drug-induced stupor—I'll know! And I'll find you...wherever you're hiding...and starting with your tongue...I will take you apart: piece by bloody piece. Do we have an understanding?"

The fear in his eyes betrayed the last hope in his blubbering voice. "Buh-but...you're a hero?"

"Oh you silly man..." she let her own eyes seal the performance. "Don't you remember who I am?"

She should have won an Oscar.

FIERY JUSTICE
A story of the Phoenix

John L. French

THE IMAGES FIRST APPEARED EARLY MONDAY MORNING. BY NOON they had circled the globe, with everyone who had a computer, tablet, AI-Phone, or imPLANT having viewed them more than once.

It was one of *those* moments, a "where were you when" question asked over and over—VE Day, the Kennedy Assassination, 9-11, the Cubs winning the seventh game of the World Series. It was something no one had wanted to see but that everyone had to view.

It was the death of the Cowboy.

He had come to the most dangerous city in the country, one whose name was synonymous with crime, corruption, and moral decay. Within a month he had shown the citizens of Harbor City that one brave man could make a difference. Street crime started to go down as the average thug never knew when or where the Cowboy would appear next. Then he went after the drug dealers, and their suppliers, and their wholesalers. Without a steady supply, addicts were forced to seek treatment and rehab.

The Cowboy became a national sensation. Brave and ruggedly handsome, he carried a gun but never shot to kill. Unlike most urban vigilantes, he did not go masked, depending on a turned-down hat, quick entrances and exits, and a remarkable knowledge of when a camera was pointing in his direction to hide his identity. He lived by a moral code and kept within both the letter and spirit of the law he supported.

He was, by every definition of the word, a hero. He was loved by the people, feared by the criminals and, grudgingly, accepted by law enforcement.

That's when he made his mistake. The same mistake all men and women like him make sooner or later. He was not content to be a hero. He decided to become a savior.

"You're a damn fool, Tex," Detective Theodore Cobb had said when the Cowboy told him of his plans.

"I keep telling you, Detective," the crime fighter said in a much-practiced drawl, "I'm not from Texas."

"You're Tex to me until you tell me your real name. And you're still a damn fool. Look, thanks to you and people you've inspired, street crime is down, drug use is down, gang activity is down. Call it a win and enjoy being a hero."

"Crime is down but not out. And we both know that much of what is left—the gangs, the drugs, the girls, and the rest—is all controlled by one man. Take that man down and the city's rackets fall apart. Easy picking for the HCPD."

"It's been tried before—the masks, Devlin—it worked for a time, then it didn't."

"Then we keep trying until it does."

◆ G ◆

"I was wondering when it would come to this."

Basil Haynes was not a name the average citizen knew. He wanted it that way. And what Basil Haynes wanted he generally got. Haynes did not run organized crime in Harbor City, Haynes *was* organized crime. He organized it, financed it, enforced it when need be. True, he allowed independent gangs to operate and even flourish if they could. "Cop bait" and, more recently, "Cowboy bait" he called them, making sure that his informants steered both police and heroes to these lawbreakers and not the ones under his control.

The police knew him, so did the prosecutors and the politicians. None could touch him. Arrest, indictment, trial, and conviction—they all required evidence. But the Cowboy's awareness of his existence was a different story. Vigilantes need not respect the niceties of the law. And someone who was willing to risk his life was likely to risk his freedom to put an end to the city's crime boss.

So word went out on the Undernet. A Crimefunder page was started, with Haynes contributing the first hundred and fifty thousand. Soon the bounty on the Cowboy was up to a quarter million. Traps were set. The Cowboy avoided them all, except for the last.

How he was taken no one knew. What was known was what was shown worldwide early that Monday morning. The Cowboy, his hat off, his once ruggedly handsome face now bruised and battered, his body tied to a chair, cut and bleeding. The slow rising and falling of his chest showing him to be still alive.

For five minutes that was all that was shown. But even as the police, private citizens, and government agencies tried to find his location, a man came into view. His clothes were black, as were the hat pulled down low over his eyes and the bandana tied around his face. What was not black was the shiny .45 revolver he drew from the holster around his waist—the Cowboy's holster, the Cowboy's gun—and put against the hero's head.

The man, who was quickly dubbed the Outlaw, did not speak. Instead he slowly pulled back the hammer of the .45 and just as slowly squeezed the trigger. There was a loud explosion, a spray of blood, and the Cowboy was dead.

During the funeral that followed the citizens of Harbor City mourned not only their fallen champion but their city as well. The Cowboy had given them life and promise and now there was nothing but death and despair. They had been lifted up and now had been dashed down.

The Cowboy was dead and, with him, so was all hope for Harbor City, and both were buried in the same grave.

Hope returned one cloudy night. It fell like a meteor from the sky. When it landed it took the form of a young woman, one whose hair was red, orange, and yellow—all the colors of the flame. The only witness to her arrival was one of the few remaining homeless, one who so far had avoided being forced into an educational shelter. He watched in amazement as clothing formed around the woman.

She saw him then, and decided that he was not a threat to anyone but himself. Too much cheap drink, too many nights in the open. When he shivered from the cold she gave him some of her warmth. Then she was gone.

She prowled the city in search of prey. Those who saw her, the ones she saved, described a flash of lightning, a swooping bird, or

just something bright and hot. Others, the ones she hunted, could only remember a hunter's eyes and a predator's smile, and considered themselves lucky to have escaped with only non-fatal burns.

Rumors began. Some said it was the Cowboy returned as an avenging angel. Others that it was a scheme by the city officials to make it seem so. Others swore that it was a crazy man with a flamethrower.

The stories and rumors were put to rest when a fire broke out in the Williams Street warehouse district. There had been several fires in that area recently. The district was slated for redevelopment and its buildings were far less valuable than the land they were on.

This fire, however, was less controlled than the others. It was possible that this was a rare blaze, one that was truly accidental in origin. Whatever its cause, it burst from the warehouse and began to spread, first to other buildings and then to the residential neighborhood to the north.

The firefighters, brave men and women all, but like most public agencies in Harbor City, understaffed and underfunded, were hard pressed to contain the blaze. Their chief had just decided to let the businesses burn and concentrate on saving what homes they could when *she* appeared in the night sky, a small flame above the larger one.

For a time she hovered above the inferno, enjoying its heat, losing herself in the patterns the flames created. Then, slowly, she drew the fire into herself. She let it feed her, strengthen her, fill her with a kind of ecstasy that humans only felt when two of them came together as one. And when the fire had been reduced, when it shrank to the point that it was no match for the firefighters, she flew out over the harbor that had given the city its name. There she discharged what she did not need into the night, creating a display the likes of which had not been seen since Independence Day.

Alone in the night sky, watched by all who were not fighting the fire, she waited until the blaze was extinguished before landing among those present. With her hair and clothing the colors of the flames that had just been defeated and still giving off some of their heat, she walked toward uniformed officers.

"Which of you," she asked, "is in charge?"

She allowed herself to be escorted to police headquarters. There, in a small interview room, she was met by a detective.

"I'm Theodore Cobb. And you are…"

"Yes, I am," the woman replied in a near lyrical voice. When it became clear to Cobb that that was the entirety of her answer he tried again.

"What shall we call you?"

"I am the Phoenix."

"Phoenix," the detective repeated. "A good name, it suits you."

"Not 'Phoenix,'" the woman corrected. "*The* Phoenix. There is no other."

"Do you have a civilian name you'd like to give us?"

"No."

"Would you mind telling me your purpose in coming to Harbor City?"

"No."

When again the Phoenix did not elaborate it occurred to Cobb that he was dealing with a very literal woman, or one that liked to mess with simple detectives just doing their job.

""What is your purpose in coming to Harbor City?"

"That, Detective Cobb, should be obvious." She went to the window, looked out. As she did so, it seemed to Cobb that the temperature in the room rose several degrees.

"Who are they, Detective? And why are they still out there?"

The music in her voice had changed. It was harsher, more direct—*Wagner instead of Mozart*, he thought.

He ignored her question, followed his orders. "Let me explain how it works, Phoenix. The reason you're meeting with me instead of the Mayor or Police Commissioner is that neither City Hall nor the HCPD can have any official contact with you. Anything you do, any actions you take will be as a private citizen. The city cannot support or condone your actions. Is that understood?"

She did not reply, but the look she gave him spoke eloquently of her contempt for the cowardice of government. Cobb felt the need to explain.

"Partly it's to protect the city from lawsuits. Mainly it's so that any arrests made as a result of your actions do not get tossed out of court. The rules of evidence do not apply to private citizens. Do you understand?"

"Yes, I believe I do." The room cooled by a few degrees.

"I should caution you, however, that as a private citizen you are subject to the laws of the city and the state. Break those laws and you could be arrested."

The Phoenix smiled at Cobb as if he had said something funny. "You could try. May I go now?"

"Eh, just one more thing. With your permission, I'd like to take your fingerprints."

Another smile, again she said, "Again, you could *try*," as she held up a hand to show flames dancing around her fingertips.

"We'll skip that then." Cobb gestured to a window. "Since you can fly you may want to leave that way. There's probably a crowd outside—the curious, the media, people who can't wait to be among the first to post your image."

"Then they should not be disappointed."

The Phoenix walked past the detective, down the hallway, out the front door, and into the night and the crowd.

Cobb followed, managing to get ahead of her at the last moment.

"Ladies and gentlemen," he announced. "May I present a visitor to Harbor City? She is called the Phoenix."

A dozen voices clashed.

"Where is she from? What does she want? Is she being charged? What is her real name? Are you holding her? Is that her real hair?"

Cobb shouted the crowd down.

"The Phoenix is not being charged. Helping to extinguish a fire is not a crime. She was simply giving a statement of her actions as a private citizen. As for holding her—I *am* a married man." After getting a bigger laugh then he deserved Cobb withdrew and left the Phoenix to the mercy of the crowd.

Maybe she'll melt a few reporters, he thought hopefully.

The Phoenix did not wait for questions. In a voice that rang out like a gospel singer's solo she said, "I am here because a month ago a brave man died. This man protected you, fought for you, and died for you. I am here to bring his killers to justice because the people of this city are too cowardly to do so."

"So you're here to avenge the death of the Cowboy?" one TV reporter asked needlessly.

The voice of the Phoenix lashed out like a whip. "I seek justice. Pray that I succeed. For if Vengeance falls upon this city, that dark lady will harshly judge all."

With that the temperature of the air rose suddenly. The Phoenix's clothing blazed. She rose up and was gone. Live feeds went dead as the heat and light of her departure overwhelmed all the recording devices.

━ G ━

For the next few weeks, a streak of fire fell upon those who would do evil. Robbers and thieves had their hands scorched. Drug dealers had their product burned. Those who lived by the knife and the gun had their weapons melted and too bad if they failed to drop them in time. As for rapists and other such offenders the flames were localized, painful, and designed so as to leave the would-be assailant incapable of committing similar crimes.

Some were spared their deserved fate, the few who could answer first the question "Who?" and, later, "Where?" Each one questioned had seen the Phoenix's appearance. Each one knew why she had come. Each one knew to whom she referred.

Most refused to talk, thinking that as a hero, the Phoenix would at the least spare their lives, something the one who truly ruled the city would not do. But some were more afraid of the fire in front of them than future consequences and so told what little they knew.

Each name led to another, and that to another, and so forth. It took a month before the Phoenix heard the name Basil Haynes.

— G —

"She is close," Basil Haynes said to his assembled lieutenants. "It is time to act."

"We're ready to go with the crime funding, Mr. Haynes," said one of his men. "Just give the word and we'll raise the money. They'll probably call this one 'The Extinguisher.'"

With a shake of his head Haynes vetoed that idea. "The last time was too theatrical. The sheep almost rose up. Let's do this one quietly and once we're successful, once her body is lying on the floor in front of me, we'll have our contact announce that the Phoenix has abandoned Harbor City as not worth saving. That should crush whatever spirit they have left. Now then, any ideas?'

Suggestions were offered, plans were made.

"If I may, Mr. Haynes and, er, ladies and gentlemen."

The voice had come from the back of the conference room. It belonged to Karl Darby, the IT guy whose job it was to make sure that the technical part of these meetings went smoothly. It was the first time he had ever spoken up.

"Yes, Mr. Darby?"

Surprised that Basil Haynes even knew his name, Darby sputtered a bit before saying,

"Those were all excellent ideas and I'm sure that at least one of them will work. But..."

"But they may not and you have a better one? Is that it?"

"Not necessarily a better one, sir. Rather, call it a 'what if they don't' contingency plan." He told them what it was.

Haynes nodded. "Not bad. Why not try this first?"

"There is some risk to yourself, sir. And it will take time to set up. In the meantime the other plans could be tried."

Haynes nodded his approval. "Start working on it. Get whatever you need. When this is over, see me and you'll get whatever, or whoever you want."

— G —

The fiery beacon of the Phoenix blazed across the sky. Once it appeared, a frightened voice cried out, "Help! Help me!"

A raptor diving after its prey, the Phoenix descended.

In a dark alley suddenly made bright two men were halted in their assault of a woman. She was bruised and her clothing was partially torn off. On seeing the Phoenix the men ran, but not far.

She drew the heat from one, leaving him to collapse when his body temperature fell to a barely survivable level. She gave the heat to the second. He too fell, shivering as a high fever ravaged his body.

As she turned to the woman, the Phoenix saw her draw a gun from behind her back, then aim and fire it at the no longer blazing hero. Instinctively she sent a wave of heat toward the rushing bullets, melting them as they flew toward her. So quickly had the Phoenix reacted she had not the time to directly target the oncoming missiles.

The wave struck the would-be killer with the power of a blast furnace, instantly reducing her to ash and charred bits of bone.

Feeling no regret at this taking of a life, the Phoenix turned toward the men still suffering on the ground. She took just enough heat from the fever victim to slightly warm the other then said to them both,

"Look at what's left of your friend then tell Haynes of the fate that awaits him." She then flew off.

When the men recovered they decided to simply report what had happened and not to pass her message on to Haynes. It was said that he did not take bad news well and might decide to involve them in future schemes to kill this flaming bird of prey.

A second attempt was made. An unused warehouse on the edge of town set ablaze. The HCFD was advised that their services would not be needed, although their equipment would.

As expected, the fire attracted the Phoenix. When she flew in to investigate its nature and to bathe in its flames, powerful hoses struck her from all sides, extinguishing her fire and causing her to fall into the inferno below. Thus renewed, she flew out again, hovering over the still-burning building.

Lyrical laughter was heard on the ground. Again hoses were trained on her. But this time their waters turned to steam. More laughter, this time mocking the foolishness of the mortals who dared assault her thus. When she tired of her steam bath, she swooped and flew low before flying off. Soon after the false firefighters tried to leave, only to learn that the tires of all their vehicles had been melted off their rims.

More attempts, more traps, more challenges. The Phoenix met them all. Haynes's men discovered that fire extinguishers, no matter with what they were charged, had little effect on her. The three men who took the phrase "Fight fire with fire" too literally were lucky that their attempt had amused the Phoenix more than angered her and so all she did was set their shoes and pants on fire.

The most imaginative attempt was made by two men and a woman who again used the "woman in peril" scenario to lure the Phoenix to street level. Once she had landed, two men wearing 10th generation Nomex© firefighting gear and whose bodies were coated in fire-resistant gel were able to grab hold of her.

Had this happened inside they might have had a chance of subduing her. As it was, with both men holding her tightly she flew into the open sky, continuing her upward flight until the men began to tire. When she spun, their grips loosened and they discovered that for all their precautions, they were not protected from the combined effects of height and gravity.

◄ G ►

"It will be soon," she told Detective Cobb as they walked along the waterfront during one of their rare meetings.

"I expect so," the detective replied, trying to keep his mind on business and not on the shapely woman beside him or the music in her voice. "All these failed attempts are making Haynes look weak and ineffective."

"No, these so-called attempts did not fail. They were never meant to succeed. They merely probed my strengths and weaknesses. Soon he will strike for real, and he will be there."

"You think so?'

"One hunter knows the other. We are each raptor and prey. He will not allow anyone else the pleasure of the kill."

"So you think he might kill you."

"He might, if he is clever enough. If he does he will regret doing so."

"As you regret the woman in the alley?"

"Which woman is that, Detective?'

"Ashes and bone, remember?'

"She killed herself. When one hunts a predator, one should expect to become prey."

"And the two men the other night?"

"I did not kill them either. It was their sudden stop."

Her clothing began to blaze as she prepared to fly off. Before she left she said, "Get word to Haynes if you can. Tell him that payment is due. Ask him the time and place."

Two days later a woman walked into the main branch of the Harbor City Public Library. She was, in most ways, nondescript, except that her hair was all the colors of fire. That wasn't unusual. Since the advent of the Phoenix salons all over town were coining money by offering their own version of the hero's hair style and coloring.

Like most people the woman was not there to read or borrow a book. In the digital age most people had never held a real book, doing their reading, watching their movies, and living their lives from a handheld screen. Those who could not afford one made do by using the public ones at the library.'

The woman in plain clothes and fiery 'do was taken for one of those. She waited her turned, logged on, then quickly checked her email account. There was just one new message— simple text with a place and time. She logged off and quickly exited the building. Sticking to alleys and side streets, she walked away with determination. As she did, her clothing subtly changed until it matched that of her hair. As soon as it did, the Phoenix flew off.

G

Our traps are set, thought the Phoenix as she arrived at the designated place. *His and mine. Tonight, one or both of us dies.* She did not fear death, never had. "A big adventure," the Pan had called it.

She smiled as she considered her ways into the old garage. Saw the invitation of an open window and decided it would be rude not to accept. She flew in, her thoughts of an old lover and what he might say at a time like this.

Time to play.

She landed in a small, open space. As she did, she heard the sound of windows and doors sealing themselves shut. Then came the whooshing, sucking sound of air being rapidly drawn from the room.

So it is I who am to die, she thought, disappointed in how simple the trap was and how easily she fell into it.

"As you have no doubt guessed," came a voice from several Wi-Fi speakers, "soon you will be in a total vacuum. Whatever your powers, you will not survive it long. Farewell, Phoeni..."

The speakers went silent. Just as she needed oxygen to support her flame, they needed air to transmit their sound. As their sound faded, so did she. Blackness fell over her. What little flame there was sputtered out and what heat she had cooled. Within minutes of entering the garage, the Phoenix was dead.

This time there were no recording devices, no posting of her demise. Harbor City did not need another martyr to be avenged. She would be buried unmourned in an unmarked grave far out of town, soon to be forgotten except by those who cursed her name for having abandoned them.

As fast as it went out, the air was pumped back into the room. When it was deemed safe, Basil Haynes emerged from the back room from where he had watched the brutally efficient murder of a hero.

"Why do they bother?" he asked those lieutenants that accompanied him. He pointed to the body. "Dispose of this...thing. And when you're done, do something about that Darby. He's much too smart for our good."

"Sir, Mr. Haynes, look."

Like Haynes had a few seconds before, the lieutenant was pointing to the body. It was moving, heat coming off it causing ripples in the air above. Smoke began to pour from its every orifice.

Fire appeared, flames all over the body. They began to grow. And spread.

"Sir, we should go, and go now."

But the doors were still locked. And the windows were still sealed tight. There was no time. There was no escape.

The body of the Phoenix renewed itself in a tremendous burst of light and heat. Metal parts, tools, workbenches, and auto lifts melted. Walls reinforced to withstand a hero's power buckled. Basil Haynes, crime boss and secret ruler of Harbor City, had just enough time to realize that "Phoenix" was less a name than a description before his quick and painful incineration.

The garage burned through the night, the HCFD, despite their best efforts, were unable to put it out. No Phoenix appeared to help them. Instead, she stood in the center of the inferno her rebirth had created, drawing strength from it and rejoicing in its caress.

━ G ━

A few days later, the Phoenix and Theodore Cobb again walked along the waterfront.

"You said Haynes would regret killing you. You were right. Now he's just ashes and bone."

"Like the woman, Detective."

"Yes, like the woman."

"How did you know about her, Detective Cobb? Only Haynes and his men knew. And how did you convey my challenge to Haynes so quickly?"

"Phoenix, what..."

"The Cowboy was smart, very smart. I knew a man like him once long ago. It is unlikely that he would have fallen into Haynes's trap. But the Cowboy trusted you. You led him there. Did you merely turn him over or were you the Outlaw?"

"What are you suggesting?"

"I am suggesting that slowly burning to death is a horrible way to die. Believe me, I have suffered it enough to know. A bullet is quicker. Or, here there is no one about, no one to see. In seconds you can be ashes and bone."

"Phoenix, I assure you…"

Her eyes blazed. "Look me in the eyes and assure me, Theodore Cobb, knowing full well the price of a lie."

He could not look her in the eyes. His head down, a nod was his confession. "Do it," he said. And that fast he was ashes and bone.

— G —

Fire burns, fire cleanses, fire purifies. Those were the thoughts of the Phoenix as she stood atop the Longfellow Hotel, the tallest building in Harbor City. From this aerie she looked down on the town and wondered why any place so corrupt had been allowed to continue. Sodom had burned. Troy was no more. Pompeii had been buried. Roanoke erased. More recently, the flames had almost claimed both Chicago and Baltimore, but like Nineveh long ago, they had been saved by divine intervention.

Perhaps this was the city's last chance and if they fell again, then would come the floods, or the ground would shake, or they would just tear the city and themselves apart.

That judgement was not for the Phoenix to make. Her self-appointed mission had been to seek justice for one brave man. That job was done. From the top of the Longfellow, she launched herself into the night.

Third Time's a Charm

Walt Ciechanowski

Something exploded in the Factory District.

Something was always exploding in the Factory District.

The Metropolitan took to the air from the Millennium Needle and wove between the skyscrapers of Midtown toward the flames. Mercurio burst through the doors of a downtown theatre and raced through traffic at what seemed to be the speed of light. Athena leapt from the roof of her laboratory as fast as the turbojets in her power armor could take her. The Lynx raced out of her hidden garage on her custom motorcycle while the Psion, perhaps a bit unceremoniously, took a cab. All of them were united in investigating and containing the latest threat to Vanguard City.

The one hero who wouldn't be there was Prince Charming.

Ironically, Prince Charming happened to be in costume this evening. Standing near the summit of a large hill on one side of the valley that cradled the city, he sported a white Renaissance shirt, brown faux-leather boots, and a wraparound black mask, all somewhat hidden by a red, hooded cloak. Once, not long ago, he would have called the Metropolitan or Athena to pick him up so he could join the battle. Unfortunately for him, his days as one of the Protectors were long over.

It's not that they would have expected his aid, of course. Prince Charming wasn't that type of hero. All he'd effectively been as a Protector was a source of comic relief, a hero with powers of dubious benefit when confronted with alien war machines, giant monsters, and armored villains. No, the other Protectors were the heroes of millions, gallantly saving the day, while Prince

Charming was the laughingstock of blogs, tabloids, and late-night monologues. In his quest to become a hero, all Prince Charming managed to become was a bad joke.

That would end tonight.

He watched the scene in the city unfold from the edge of the Overlook as he took a healthy swig out of the glass whiskey bottle he clutched with thick fingers. The whiskey helped ward off the bitter night cold that nipped at his exposed cheeks above his full, thick beard. The wind whipped his red cloak, once his trademark, about his now-obese frame, which was currently testing the limits of his already over-sized shirt. In spite of being in costume he'd had to leave his faux-leather pants at home—they hadn't fit for years—and the black sweatpants he wore instead did little to insulate him from the cold.

He pulled out a reusable canvas shopping bag from the back seat of his old, beaten, electric red '98 Dodge Neon and shut the door. He affectionately tapped the roof as if for the last time before walking away in the snow. He'd been lucky to make it this far in the car, given that he'd needed a few drinks to steel his nerves, but it was only a short walk to the bridge and, in his inebriated state, he didn't trust himself driving around the last couple of curves. If he was going to do this, then he was going to do it properly, in spite of his limp.

As he tenderly began his final walk toward the Valley View Bridge, Prince Charming caught sight of the flashing lights of the police and the spotlights emanating from their helicopters. He chuckled a bit, wondering how it must feel to be a Vanguard City police officer, spending all those months in the Academy just to be relegated to highlighting villains for the costumed heroes and keeping innocent bystanders out of the way. The Protectors even had a nickname for them, "The Containment Crew."

He laughed grimly at himself. Even the Containment Crew was more useful than Prince Charming.

As he carefully walked across the Overlook memories flooded back. This parking area offered a beautiful view of the City and was a popular place for love-struck couples to sit under the stars and enjoy each other's company. Tonight, however, the Overlook was eerily quiet, as the falling snow had kept even the most romantic souls away from the slippery hillside roads. He sighed as he gazed at the empty row of parking spaces.

This was a place that Prince Charming knew well.

He'd spent many a night here in his youth; each crunching, halting step he took along the snow-covered parking spots reminded him of a different girl, a different conquest that he enjoyed while sitting in his car parked along the railings' edge. Unfortunately, every pleasant memory he could conjure was laced with pain. Prince Charming let the tears fall—Jack Daniel's could only dull so many memories—and once again Prince Charming looked to a spot in the valley to remind himself of why he was there.

It wasn't the battle playing out before him. Even as the growing flames in the Factory District began to contort and form into a semblance of a face, Prince Charming tore his eyes from what he was certain was the origin of another megavillain, focusing past the police helicopters surrounding it and the skyscrapers of the Business District, to a relatively quiet suburb further down the valley. The name of the town was Springdale, and it was where Prince Charming had been born and raised.

He was fortunate—some would say "charmed"——to have been born into a comfortable upper middle-class family. He and his siblings never wanted for anything and in spite of busy lives his parents always found time for them. He'd spent much of the first decade or so of his life deciding whether he wanted to be an engineer like his mother or a surgeon like his father. He'd have the best education money could buy, start a career, buy his own house in Springdale, and start a family—and Veronica Sanchez was the girl he wanted to have that family with.

And then his budding teenage dreams came true and crashed in a single night—his Bar Mitzvah.

Prince Charming took another swig from the bottle. He couldn't remember when he first noticed that Veronica was "different" or when his feelings went from ignoring her, to finding her strange, to being infatuated with her—as time passed he refused to admit it was love—but in the months leading to the day he became a man he certainly remembered pining for her. Unfortunately, Veronica had her eyes on someone else: Hopper Lang.

Hopper Lang was one of Prince Charming's best friends in elementary school. His real name was Frederick, but everyone called him "Hopper" because of the unique way he ran. He always thought it was a budding superpower, but in the end it was nothing special, just strange, and Prince Charming teased him mercilessly for it. Still, the two of them were thick as thieves and it was a great blow to Prince Charming when Veronica agreed to go with Hopper to the first Junior High Dance. In spite of all Prince Charming's teasing, it was apparently Hopper who had the last laugh.

In spite of how he felt about Veronica, Prince Charming had played along as well as he could. He welcomed her into their circle of friends and soon counted her amongst them, even if it did bother him whenever he saw Hopper reading a text from her or the two of them holding hands when the teachers weren't watching. It was all so innocent back then, but in his twelve-year-old mind Veronica was Hopper's girl and Charming resented it.

Still, Veronica was enough of a friend that Prince Charming made sure she was invited to his Bar Mitzvah party. His parents had pulled out all the stops, renting the Grand Ballroom at the Downtown Station Hall and procuring the then-popular Letter Jacket Gang, a local swing band back when neo-swing was a thing. Even now in his drink-addled state Prince Charming could recall the cardigan-clad band playing old favorites and current songs. Fully half of his friends showed up in zoot suits and poodle skirts as they tried their best to swing dance.

Yet Prince Charming, on the night he was being celebrated for becoming a man, wasn't happy. He'd even left his own party, pretending to get some air as he stood out on the deck and gazed at the mountains —the elder Prince Charming imagined that he had been staring at himself and offered a toast—but really the sight of Veronica having a good time dancing with Hopper was just a bit too much for him. He figured a few moments alone would be all he needed to put his brave face back on and finish the party.

And then Veronica approached him.

The elder Prince Charming felt a tear roll down his cheek as he remembered her touch, lightly gripping his shoulder as she asked him what was wrong. It would have been so easy to brush her off, to send her back to the party and Hopper, as he thought that there was nothing she could say that could soothe him. Instead, as only an angry and hurt teenager could, he unloaded on her with his true feelings.

That was when his power first manifested.

Prince Charming, of course, didn't realize it at the time. He poured his heart out to her, confessing his love and desire to be with her even while screaming and cursing at her for refusing to acknowledge him. He also berated her for being with Hopper, calling her every insulting name that came to mind. He expected Veronica to scream back at him or flee in tears. Instead, Veronica simply stood there and took everything he gave her without a word. When he finished, she did something completely unexpected.

She kissed him.

However fleeting, it was to be the happiest moment of Prince Charming's life. He protested at first, suddenly feeling as if he'd betrayed his friend, but Veronica was adamant—she didn't want to be with Hopper, she loved him. She'd always loved him, and she wanted to be his girlfriend. In short, she said everything he told her he wanted to hear and when they went back inside, she told Hopper that too. Hopper then punched Prince Charming and left the party in tears. Prince Charming had lost a friend.

The next day, Hopper confronted him at the lockers and demanded to know what he'd done to Veronica. After the party he'd called her to demand an explanation and she claimed that she didn't love Prince Charming at all—she remembered kissing him, but she swore he must have done something to her. Prince Charming tried to protest, but all Hopper was spoiling for was a fight—that is, until Prince Charming asked him to stop—and he did, apologizing for his behavior.

Things got even more confusing when he spoke to Veronica. She claimed she thought she loved Hopper, but whenever she saw Prince Charming she fell in love with him all over again. She couldn't explain it except that whenever she was alone, she thought about Hopper and how badly she was betraying him. Worse, she said that Hopper was conflicted too; he claimed to hate Prince Charming, but couldn't remain angry in his presence. Prince Charming just seemed too nice a guy to hurt.

Prince Charming didn't quite understand what was happening at first, but he understood enough to realize that something was wrong—or maybe right—with him. Certainly there were costumed heroes and villains with ESP—Psion and Cerebral Killer sprang to mind—and it was possible that Prince Charming had a similar power. He spent the rest of junior high testing his theory. By the time he entered high school, Prince Charming knew he had something special.

Another smaller explosion down in the valley brought Prince Charming's mind back to the present. He watched a couple of fireballs ignite nearby buildings in the district before taking another swig of his bottle and continuing his walk past the Overlook. As he crossed each parking space, it conjured a memory, or several, of girls he dated in high school and, when he finally got his driver's license, brought up here to see the city lights and enjoy each other's company.

"What a jackass," Prince Charming spat, referring to the teenager he once was.

But it was true. Prince Charming could have any girl he wanted in high school. While Veronica was a memory—her mother took a new job that necessitated moving into a new district—there were plenty of other girls available. And that's when Prince Charming began learning the limits of his powers. He could "make" anyone like him and try to help him out, but he couldn't make them actually do anything they didn't want to do without concerted effort—and sometimes even that wasn't enough.

He kicked some of the snow at a parking space, pretending his then-brand new Neon was parked there. Most girls weren't so totally in love with their boyfriends that they wouldn't come with him to the Overlook, but once they were here the pangs of regret crept in. Nor did Prince Charming want to make them do anything they didn't want to do—that would make him a villain and a rapist. Thus he was reduced to begging and ultimately giving up before driving them home and, in spite of promises of friendship, never really saw them again beyond passing them in the halls.

Even when a girl did seem really interested in him, Prince Charming had trouble trusting her. He always wondered whether she truly meant it or was just saying it in his presence. Even the phone calls, cute texts, and romantic emails did little to assuage his fears. In the end, he always ended up breaking it off "just in case." By the time he graduated high school, he felt completely isolated and alone.

Worse, his grades had slipped. He'd banked on being able to talk his way to straight As, only to discover that his power usually only granted him second chances in terms of make-up work; Prince Charming rarely wanted to apply himself that much. His hygiene also slipped as well; why eat properly, exercise, and go to the gym when you can get people interested in you the way you are? As a kid Prince Charming was short and scrawny; by the time he'd graduated, he was still short, but he now sported a pot belly and pudgy face.

His average grades were enough to kill his chances of becoming an engineer or surgeon, but he did enroll in community college to try and "find himself." That only provided him with a new pool of young women and Prince Charming simply continued the trend of bringing them up here and getting turned down. Eventually, he had to do something to stop the self-loathing and grim hope that things would change. He needed help.

Finally passing the last parking space of the Overlook, he trudged up the slope as he continued to watch the scene below. The flames that flickered in the Factory District bent and morphed into a giant humanoid shape. Prince Charming realized that he was right; he was witnessing the birth of yet another villain. He sighed and took another swig of whiskey. The new flaming creature seemed to roar at Metropolitan as she flew straight into it and burst through the flames out the back of its head. Now there was a woman with real powers!

Real powers.

Prince Charming recalled the day he met Psion. It took quite some time to arrange a meeting. Sure, Psion was one of the Protectors, but unlike the comic books, they didn't sit around in the Protectors Headquarters waiting for the next crisis. They all had secret identities with jobs and normal personal lives; well, except for Mercurio. He'd been inadvertently outed when someone accidentally caught him running while not in costume on a Smartphone and slowed down the footage. Now he was the pitchman for several commercial products and even had his own Reality TV series.

No, Prince Charming had to do a bit of legwork to find Psion, scouring internet chat rooms, blogs, and even old newspapers and interviews for some hint on how to find him. He'd fallen victim to a couple of scams where a blogger had claimed to know Psion and could arrange a meeting for a fee. Prince Charming paid the fee but the blogger's promises went unfulfilled. Fortunately, one of the bloggers was eventually caught and, when he learned of the crime, Psion agreed to meet with the victims.

His brain was starting to swim but Prince Charming could clearly remember the day that he met Psion. The Protector was wearing his white jumpsuit with a blue eye emblazoned on the chest and a skintight mask that covered his eyes but left his nose and mouth free. Prince Charming recalled sitting at a table in one of the college study rooms and trying not to stare at that unsettling bright blue eye. Still, Psion immediately put his mind at ease when he told Prince Charming that he had ESP; his "encephalic aura" as he called it was quite visible to him.

It dawned on him that he could be a hero.

They'd spoken for the better part of two hours before Psion offered to take him to the Protectors; to this day Prince Charming couldn't remember if it was Psion's idea or whether he wanted to be a hero so badly he pushed Psion into it. Certainly Psion, "master of the mysteries of the mind," claimed that he could block Prince Charming's power, but his unsettling eyes betrayed him when he said it. In any event Prince Charming soon found himself standing in Athena's laboratory, which was as close to a "Protectors Headquarters" as they were ever likely to have.

The slope seemed steeper now as Prince Charming got closer to the bridge. He remembered that day well; all of the current Protectors were there. Metropolitan, Vanguard City's Mightiest Hero, looked absolutely stunning in her stars-and-stripes red, white, and blue jumpsuit that made her look like an Olympic athlete. She had the power to create force fields around her body that enabled her to, among other things, stop bullets, punch with the strength of ten people, and fly.

If Metropolitan was the leader, then Mercurio was the heart-throb, the one Prince Charming often saw posters of in women's bedrooms and dorm rooms. He never bothered with a costume beyond a pair of wrap-around sunglasses; he wore whatever was fashionable at the moment. Mercurio was perpetually tanned and spoke with a Latin accent that Prince Charming suspected was a bit put-on. If anything, Prince Charming felt that he was over-compensating for a CNN report that dubbed him "the Quickest Man in the World." It went viral, and Mercurio found himself the butt of many off-color jokes. Prince Charming was pretty certain that couldn't have gotten better after his unmasking.

Athena was the engineer and reminded Prince Charming quite a bit of his mother; that is if she were about a decade younger and confined to a wheelchair. Early in her career Athena was injured when the supervillain Cockroach attacked a project she was working on and her subsequent tinkering to regain some mobility resulted in a powered harness.

Finally—excepting Psion—there was Deadspot. She was young, sultry, and beautiful, with the power to dampen most biological superpowers by essentially shutting them off if they got too close to her. She was a recent recruit and quickly proved her worth by teaming with Athena. The armored Athena would simply drop Deadspot off near a supervillain, she'd shut down his superpowers, and then the rest of the team would clean up the mess.

Prince Charming paused and steadied himself against a tree to catch his breath before continuing up the slope and take the pressure off his bad leg. He remembered the belly laughs garnered from the other superheroes as Psion explained his power. "Attracting people with his animal magnetism" paled in comparison to force fields, super speed, and power dampening. Besides, Psion could already read minds—Prince Charming just seemed re-dundant. And, on a shallow note, he'd look terrible in a costume.

Still, Psion made a convincing argument that Prince Charming might be good for public relations—interacting with journalists and bystanders during and after slugfests; Deadspot surprisingly backed him up. Mercurio wasn't convinced, likely because he saw himself as the resident lothario, and asked for a demonstration. After Prince Charming made Metropolitan and Athena swoon, he was offered membership.

But he wasn't truly a hero.

No, he wasn't like any of the heroes he now watched battling the flaming creature. He could already anticipate their moves in his mind. Mercurio was likely using containment, racing around the creature to keep the flames in check. Athena was no doubt analyzing the chemical composition of the new villain before reshaping whatever was at hand into something that could snuff it out. Psion was trying to get into the villain's head while Lynx, a new superhero added to the team after Prince Charming left, was probably going through the nearby buildings and rescuing second-shift workers caught in the chaos.

He remembered dozens of similar fights: the Terrible Three, Mechaton, the Mighty Brain, and Tesseract, just to name a few. He was absolutely terrified during those first few battles; he'd never really fought anyone before, and he couldn't hide behind battle armor or force fields. Occasionally he could talk a villain into staying a likely death blow or retreating, but it was nothing the others couldn't do with enough firepower and threats at their disposal.

And the media! Oh, the media!

As befitting the name "Prince Charming," he needed a costume that reflected his image. Mercurio helped him pick it out, an outfit that looked seductive yet functional at the same time. The oversized shirt helped hide his pot belly, but Athena's idea of a ballistic armored cloak had to be abandoned because it proved too heavy for the out-of-shape Prince Charming to maneuver in. Unfortunately, that was only after the local news got footage of Mechaton beating the daylights out of him as he awkwardly and ineffectively tried to defend himself. And while Prince Charming's power made anyone nearby infatuated with him, it didn't translate over media. He looked ridiculous and the footage sparked a feeding frenzy for media commentators.

The only person who seemingly believed in him was fellow Protector Deadspot. He wanted to believe her so badly; for the first time, he'd met a woman whom he knew couldn't be swayed by his power. She flirted with him, laughed with him, and spent time with him. For the first time since Veronica, he was truly happy again, in spite of all the teasing he had to endure. It was she that convinced Athena that Prince Charming's skill set suited him for watching her laboratory while the team went out on missions.

Frankly, it didn't take much swaying; Athena was constantly upgrading her powered harness and other gadgets and having a fellow Protector watch over the lab while she wasn't there seemed like a good idea.

Once Prince Charming was trusted with the security codes, however, Deadspot used him to break into Athena's laboratory and steal the Mark V harness for her true master, Professor Havoc. He remembered how he pled with her once he realized what she was doing, how he reminded her of what they had together. Unfortunately, like so many journalists and talk show hosts, she simply laughed at him. Her feelings for him had all been a ruse and she had out-charmed Prince Charming. And then, to add insult to injury, she shattered his leg with one of Athena's experimental weapons before taking off.

Prince Charming took a final swig of his whiskey and threw the bottle into the snow.

That betrayal was simply too much to bear, especially since, armed with the latest Athena battle harness, Professor Havoc put Psion in the hospital and probably would have killed Athena had the hero not managed to exploit a weakness in the new design before the final blow. Deadspot, unfortunately, got away clean. No doubt she was now resting at one of Professor Havoc's offshore properties, waiting to be used against a vulnerable hero again. While Athena used her professional contacts to ensure that Prince Charming's leg was reconstructed as well as possible, he resigned from the Protectors. In spite of their platitudes, he was pretty sure that they were relieved to see him go.

It wasn't much further to the summit now where the road met the bridge. In the years since, Prince Charming had kept a low profile, wallowing in self-pity and getting even more out of shape. He had tried and failed to be a hero, and his power only made him a danger to everyone around him, including himself. He'd even gotten a telemarketing job just so he could sit at home and avoid people while hoping the "Latin Lover" shtick he'd borrowed from Mercurio would help him sell refinancing packages. It rarely did.

But now it was time to end it all.

He had made it to the top of the hill when his bad leg, combined with his own inebriation, finally gave out. Prince Charming unceremoniously fell to the ground, just as another major explosion rocked the Factory District amidst the light show caused by the fire creature's recurring gouts of flame. As he collapsed, he let go of the canvas bag he'd been holding. It spilled out its contents as it hit the ground—a 9mm semi-automatic pistol.

Prince Charming had planned to jump off the bridge with prejudice.

He reached for the pistol as he tried to ignore the sharp pains emanating from his bad leg. The gun was his insurance policy— if the bullet didn't kill him, then the fall from the bridge would, or vice versa. He laughed hysterically at himself as he dug through the snow looking for it; amidst everything else he couldn't even get this right. He finally felt the cool steel of the barrel and relaxed just a bit—his plan was safe after all. He dragged himself over to a sign that warned about icy conditions on the bridge and used it to pull himself back to his feet.

That's when he noticed he wasn't alone.

Someone had beaten him to the bridge. It looked like a man, but he was bundled up and it was difficult to see through the snowfall, even with the full moon shining down on them. Given the virgin snow that Prince Charming had limped through to get up here, it was likely that the man had come up from the other direction—that slope was even steeper, so he probably parked his car further down as well. What was more important was that the man was standing on the ice-covered planks beyond the railing.

He was going to jump.

Prince Charming followed the general incline of his head to the scene below. The man probably came up here intending to jump and got distracted by the impromptu battle taking place below. Judging by the creature's sudden evaporation, that battle was almost over and the would-be jumper was going to remember why he was here. Prince Charming had to do *something*.

He tossed the gun into the crevasse and lurched forward to grab the end of the railing near the bridge. All he needed to do was get close enough for his power to work, but his leg rebelled with searing pain. Prince Charming clenched his teeth and re- fused to scream. In spite of all of his pain, in spite of all of his failures, he couldn't watch this man jump or inadvertently prompt it, not while there was a chance to save him. He tightly wrapped his arm around the railing and called out to the man.

"Please don't," he said softly at first, his lips trembling as he tried not to sound intoxicated. He repeated himself, only more loudly. "Please don't!"

The man flinched a bit in surprise, but thankfully he recovered quickly.

"Why not?" asked the man without turning. It was a choked response; he was obviously crying. He picked up a foot and dangled it over the edge. "Don't try and stop me. I'm not worth it."

"What are you talking about?" Prince Charming answered, slowly clawing his way closer. The jumper was still out of range. If he could only keep him talking…"Of course you are. Everyone is."

"Not me," the man answered. He sounded young, probably in his twenties. "I've got no job, I'm being evicted from my apartment, and my fiancé left me for my best friend. You don't know what it's like."

"No," Prince Charming admitted, ignoring the pain as he inched closer. "I won't pretend to know exactly how you feel, but I do know what it feels like to be lonely and isolated, what it feels like to have the whole world laughing at you, and how it feels to be betrayed by the ones you love most. It hurts like hell."

"Then you do understand," he said as he leaned forward and looked down. There was nothing but sheer crevasse for hundreds of feet.

Yes, I do, Prince Charming thought to himself.

"What I understand is that you're at the bottom," Prince Charming said, "and if you take that final step there are no second chances. You have to believe in second chances, or third chances if need be. You have your whole life to learn from this, to become stronger because of it. Don't just throw it all away."

Almost. Prince Charming was almost close enough.

"You just don't want me to jump," the man shouted. "Who are you with, the police?"

"No," Prince Charming corrected as he steadied himself, trying his bad leg once more. "I'm…"

He didn't get to finish. The man turned to face him and Prince Charming saw the stunned recognition in his face. He knew exactly who he was facing.

"Oh my God, y-y-you're Prince Charming!" He stammered. "You don't care about me; you just want to get close enough to—to stop me!" He let go of the railing and turned on his heel.

"No!" Prince Charming screamed as he lunged forward, almost falling off the railing himself. He'd hoped he was close enough now as he concentrated, like Psion had taught him, to focus his power for maximum effect.

It seemed to work. The man's face softened as he shook his head. "No, I don't want to..."

But it was too late. He'd already started to jump and the slippery plank caused him to stumble. He toppled over, but thankfully he was still within range. He just couldn't bring himself to fall and upset Prince Charming, so he reached out and grabbed the end of the plank. At the same time, Prince Charming dove forward and grabbed his wrist.

"Don't worry, man. I've got you."

It had been a long time since Prince Charming had worked out in a gym or lifted anything heavier than a plate of spaghetti. Still, he summoned all of the strength he had to hold on until the man could find a support railing with his feet. Within a few minutes of coaxing and tugging, the man was once again atop the bridge, sitting next to the fallen and equally exhausted Prince Charming as they both caught their breaths.

"What's your name?" Prince Charming asked.

"Trey," the man replied. "Trey Hoffman."

"Well, Mr. Hoffman, if you wouldn't mind helping me up, we need to get you somewhere where you can be looked after for a bit. This gets better, I promise."

The young man gingerly stood and then helped Prince Charming up. "Call me Trey."

Prince Charming smiled. He knew exactly why Trey's demeanor had changed, but for once he was okay with that. It was his power keeping the man from making a second attempt. Fully embracing his power, perhaps for the first time, he wrapped his arm around the man's shoulder for support.

"We should probably take your car, Trey. I'm really in no condition to drive mine."

Trey obviously wasn't going to argue. He simply nodded and added, "Have you been drinking, Prince Charming?"

Prince Charming smiled. It was the first genuine warm smile he'd had in a long time. Maybe the doctors wouldn't be able to do anything for Trey. Maybe he was too far gone and would only try again. But, if so, that was for another day. For now, in this moment, here in the bitter cold atop a dangerously high crevasse, his power was enough to save someone, if only for a day. Perhaps the flames were now extinguished in the Factory District, but here, high up on the Valley View Bridge, something had finally sparked.

"Indeed I have, Trey," Prince Charming laughed as he playfully slapped the man's shoulder. *"L'Chaim!"*

Trey laughed with him as Prince Charming followed him toward his car, which was parked just a few yards down the steep slope on the other side. When he came up here, he was ready to end his life. Now, all of his problems seemed a bit foggy. And as Trey began to descend that slope to what was hopefully a brighter future a hero limped down the mountain with him.

THE HAND JOB

Kathleen David

FRED GREENLY WAS A DECENT PUPPETEER. IF YOU ASKED OTHER puppeteers about his form, they would say it was good and precise. But if you pressed the matter further they said that his performance was technically good but rather lifeless. He had auditioned for some of the big companies and gotten only so far before he was cut from the auditions. He had managed to carve out a career in puppetry but it was fighting for every inch. He watched as others who were not as good at basic technique sail past him and into his dream jobs.

He watched and grew resentful.

"You're good at building," he was told. So he started a puppet-building business and found himself making toys as well. He made a small name for himself as a toy maker. He even had large toy companies pay him to design toys for them. He watched as the toy companies made lots of money off the toys that he designed. His toys were very popular. He tried to change the terms from a flat fee to a percentage for his work and found himself out of the toy-making business for "being difficult".

Again, he watched and grew resentful.

He reinvented himself on the Internet and started to make toys that weren't for children but for collectors of the rare and strange. He had art gallery showings of his work. The last toy company that had kicked him out now sued him for supposed breach of contract because of his new work. He counter-sued and brought out the toy companies' dirty laundry. He lost. He found himself without his new designs, which were owned by the toy companies because of a very long and involved contract he had signed so many years ago.

He watched as his designs became even more popular and grew resentful.

Now any time he walked around the city, he saw young hip people wearing his designs on their shirts, bags, and sneakers. His designs were used to create very popular series for kids and adults. The kids loved it and the adults were crazy for his characters. There were conventions that he was not invited to. His original work was going for serious dollars on eBay but due to the contract he had signed so many years ago, anything new he created would also be owned by the toy companies. Then the cruelest cut of all: his creations were turned into puppets and became the most watched TV series among both children and adults.

He watched and grew resentful.

He sat in his workshop trying to figure out how to get out of the box he found himself in. He couldn't even use his puppets in his own shows because of that damn contract. He felt like he had sold his soul to Satan and made a really poor bargain. He tried to find other work but his lawsuit against the toy companies had been too visible in the press. No one wanted to take the chance that he would sue them.

The more he thought about what had happened the angrier he got. It should be him as a producer and performer on that show. It should be him raking in the cash for the things that he had designed. It should be him receiving accolades and signing autographs at conventions for the clever characters he had created. He was tired of being marginalized and made to feel worthless.

He'd lost everything and they just kept getting richer.

◄ G ►

He looked down at the paper and saw that Captain Quikk had apprehended the Notorious Naga for the third time that month only for the villain to slip out of police custody and slither back into the sewers. He had tried it their way. He had tried to follow the rules and be a good person but it had gotten him nowhere rather fast. Villains always seem to win in the end, or at least they got respect. Respect would fix everything for him.

"But how?" he thought, "How to do it?"

What kind of villain could he be? He went onto the Internet and started researching villains, trying to find some guidance on how he could start his new career. He found, strangely enough, various fan message boards for villains. He read up on what they did, what worked and didn't work. Should he be a Robin Hood type or a plain, nefarious ne'er-do-well?

And how would he accomplish his villainy? What could he do that other villains couldn't, wouldn't, or hadn't done already? He certainly didn't want to be accused of being a copycat.

His mind kept coming back to his puppets and toys. How he once had control over them and their fates but didn't anymore. He thought back to what he was told about his puppetry, technically good but lifeless...

Lifeless.

If there was only a way to bring his creations to life.

One of his favorite stories growing up was *The Adventures of Pinocchio* by Carlo Collodi. Not the watered-down Disney version but the original tale where the cricket didn't make it through the first half of the book. As a child he went around listening to blocks of wood hoping that one would talk to him so he could create his own friend. Magic is what made Pinocchio move and magic was the answer to his problems.

Fred Greenly started his quest to find real magic. He gained a reputation for debunking fakers. He exposed people and their powers to the world. And he searched the world to find the real thing. But he would find hints and rumors of magic tomes and real wizards and magic users. It was just enough to keep him on his quest. He would hear a tale and go to seek the origins of it. He became well versed in the religions and mythology of the world.

It wasn't until he came back home that he found what he was seeking in an old bookstore he had visited as a boy with his father. He had been all over the world and the answer to his problems was the shop just two blocks from his workshop and home. He went in to browse the shelves for more reading material on the cult of the Illuminati when he came across a very strange-looking book. At first it looked like a tome of standard stage magic tricks published sometime in the Victorian era. He had seen its like before and in fact had a number of them in his collection. But something about this one felt different. He could swear that he felt electricity running up his arm from just brushing the spine with his fingertips. He bought it from the old shopkeeper who still looked the same as he had long ago.

◄ G ►

That night Fred sat down and started reading. This was it! This was what he had been seeking. This was real magic written down in a concise form that he could follow. If only it would really work.

He cleared out the center of his workshop and with chalk recreated the diagram exactly as the book told him to. At the point he had to put the object to be animated, he looked around his shop.

Up on the shelf was a rather battered hand-and-rod puppet that he had created when he was a teenager. It was one of his earliest efforts. He had used a brown feather boa for the hair and blue doll eyes that caught the light. The skin was a light pink fabric his mother had bought him. He had never found the fabric again. The last costume he had made for the puppet was still on it. It was a white T-shirt and black leather jacket. There was no need for pants, because the body stopped at the bottom of the puppet's torso. The puppet rods were made from welding steel and were slightly bent and twisted from many years of use. He had called the puppet Bonzo and had used it in his first professional puppet show. He picked up Bonzo and put the puppet in the circle. He continued working his way through the ritual until he discovered he needed some things he could only find in either a new-age or pagan shop. He sighed and closed the book. The workshop had grown dark except for the candles he had lit outside the circle.

"So close, Bonzo," he said. "We were so close."

"So close to what?" came the voice from the center of the diagram.

The hairs on Fred's forearms stood up. He recognized that voice. He had created it for Bonzo. It was his voice and yet not his voice. He walked to the wall switch and turned on the lights. In the middle of the large chalk drawing Bonzo "sat" with his arms crossed, the rods dangling to the floor. Bonzo looked at him with a puzzled expression.

"Bonzo?"

"Yes?" answered the puppet.

Fred stared in disbelief at the puppet in the middle of the floor.

"Bonzo, can you come here?" asked Fred. Bonzo nodded yes and moved across the floor dragging his rods, which blurred the chalk lines. The movement was more of a hover as if Bonzo had legs that could not be seen.

Fred got down on one knee to meet his puppet. "Bonzo, do you know who I am?"

"You are the creator. You made me. We played together and made everyone laugh."

"You remember that?"

Bonzo shrugged. "Bits and pieces. I remember being on the high shelf for a long time. That was sad for me but you are the creator so you must have known what you were doing."

Fred patted Bonzo on his fluffy head. "I did indeed. Now, Bonzo, I need you to stay here until I call for you. If someone else comes, I want you to hide."

"I understand."

Fred left his workshop and walked up the steps to his apartment over the shop contemplating what his next move was going to be. Bonzo sat and waited for his creator to return.

The next morning after Fred woke up, he rushed down to the shop. He didn't see Bonzo through the window. He entered the shop and called out, "Bonzo?" There was no reply. Maybe the whole thing had just been a dream. But the chalk diagram was still there smudged by the marks that Bonzo's rods made. He heard the sound of metal on concrete and watched as Bonzo hovered his way toward Fred.

"You said to hide," said the puppet.

"That I did. You are a good puppet," said Fred. He picked Bonzo up and looked in his blue-glass eyes. Bonzo looked back at him. "I have big plans for you."

Fred learned that the magic had limits. He created new puppets and redid the diagram but they didn't work as well as Bonzo. They had movement but not the abilities that Bonzo did. He finally worked out that the older the object, the more animated it was. In a short time he had created his army so he could wreak havoc on those that he felt wronged him.

—◄ G ►—

Bonzo sat on top shelf that had been his home for so long and watched his creator bring to life his brothers, sisters, and what-nots. The creator had told him what was to come but Bonzo wasn't sure it was right. None of the other toys or puppets seem to have a problem with it, only Bonzo. So he kept his mouth shut and observed from his perch.

The first job was a simple bank job. Fred left a bag with his toys in the bank lobby. Since they were so small, they slipped under the radar. They managed to walk out with about a million in negotiable bearer bonds, which were to be taken from the bank the next day to the Treasury. They left a toy based on Fred's design with the words "The Toymaker" inscribed on its side.

In short order other banks found themselves relieved of cash and other negotiable commodities, always with an inscribed toy left behind. The next job didn't go as smoothly. The banks went to the heroes for help. The toys were seen and they lost two of their number that night. Bonzo had barely gotten out when the whole thing went down.

"Why?" he asked Fred.

"Because you were seen," said the Creator, "But that is alright. I am ready to start the next phase of my plan."

Bonzo hovered back up to his shelf and watched.

Bonzo found that he was spending a lot of time on that shelf. Whatever the creator was up to, it seemed to involve his computer. Bonzo watched the TV when Fred had it on. He enjoyed watching the news. He loved seeing the heroes help people. He remembered that when he had been performing with the Creator, he had been a hero. It felt good to make children laugh and applaud; oh, how he missed the applause. He knew what the Creator was doing was wrong but he couldn't go against his wishes.

Fred Greenly used the money that he had obtained to buy stocks. He carefully bought stock in the various toy companies that had ripped him off. He bought stock in the parent company of the network that aired the TV shows. He carefully accumulated bits and pieces of any company involved, covering his tracks as he went.

One night he gathered his toy troops and said, "It is time we start the next phase of the plan." The toys bowed to their creator. "We are going to convince a not-nice man that he needs to sell me his shares in his company or there will be consequences."

As he hopped into the black duffle bag, Bonzo noticed that Fred was dressed in his old puppeteer blacks with his hood flipped back.

Bonzo could hear everything through the bag. He had learned to sort the sounds out. Sometimes conversations were hard to make out but he did all right. This time he could hear conflict between his creator and another person.

"Greenly, what the hell are you doing in my house?"

"Ah Mr. Linstrom, haven't changed a bit have you? Still watching that blood pressure? Wouldn't want anything to happen to you..."

"I should call the police and have you arrested for trespassing."

"I don't think so."

"What the hell?"

Fred unzipped the bag and pulled out Bonzo. He put his hand up Bonzo's body and Bonzo could feel the creator's hand inside his head as he had so many times before. If only he could be the one in control. He saw that the other toys were holding Linstrom in place in a chair.

"You are truly mental, Greenly."

"Oh really? Maybe if you hadn't screwed me over, I could have had health insurance and it wouldn't have come to this."

"We paid you well for your designs. You signed the contract."

"Ah, the contract. I was desperate and you knew it. You took advantage of me and now I will return the favor. I want your shares in the company."

"No way in hell."

"Wrong answer." Fred picked up Bonzo's rods and had the puppet punch Linstrom in the gut. Fred had discovered by accident that the spell had given his creations super-human strength and the longer he had the puppet, the more the strength. Bonzo was his strongest puppet.

Linstrom gasped as he felt his guts get slammed into his spine. He tried to catch his breath but it was so hard. He felt as if his diaphragm was spasming.

"I trusted you," said Fred through gritted teeth, "You told me that you would take care of me. Instead, you hung me out to dry. You stole from me and now you are going to pay for that theft." He used Bonzo to hit Linstrom in a rather delicate place. Linstrom's eyes rolled up into his head and he passed out from the pain. Fred looked at the unconscious man and boiling rage filled him. He picked up Bonzo's rods and proceeded to pummel Linstrom from this world to the next. Bonzo felt as if his arms were getting longer and bigger as the beating continued.

Bonzo was horrified but he could do nothing. He couldn't close his eyes because he didn't have eyelids that worked. He couldn't control his actions because his creator had taken control of him. The battered and bruised body in front of him finally breathed its last.

Fred stepped back and looked at the carnage. It was almost cathartic to see Linstrom's broken body in front of him. He had taken back what was his. Fred removed Bonzo and called all the toys to the bag. He removed the papers from the safe and loaded the contents of Linstrom's company hard drive onto a memory stick. They left Linstrom cooling in his study.

Fred pulled Bonzo out of the bag and put him on the workbench. Bonzo looked at him. Fred checked Bonzo over for damage and any bloodstains. He found a slight rip in an arm seam. Stuffing was showing. He pulled out a needle and thread and started repairing the arm.

Bonzo watched as his arm was being repaired. He looked at his hands with disgust. He didn't want to hurt anyone. He was a hero, but his creator was making him a villain. But this was his creator. The conflict inside his head felt as heavy as when Fred's hand was there.

Bonzo sighed.

Fred finished the stitching and sat Bonzo up. "You did well tonight."

Bonzo stared at Fred.

"Stop staring at me! He deserved it. He screws all of us over without a second thought."

Bonzo continued to stare at Fred.

"I order you to stop staring at me! Go back to your shelf."

Bonzo hopped off the table and dragging his rods behind him made his way to the bookcase where he resided. He hovered his way back to the top of the shelves and settled down looking out into the workshop.

He contemplated what happened and tried to understand what he had done. He had, for just a second, total control over himself. He had disobeyed a direct order from the Creator! How had he done that? How could he do that? He sat on the shelf and pondered the implications of that small action. Could he do more? Could he take control?

The next day Fred seemed very agitated as he searched the television news channels and the Internet for any report of Linstrom's demise. Nothing came up. *I didn't leave anything behind,* he thought, *that might tie me to the crime.* He had accounted for all the toys that he had brought with him. He checked and cleaned them all up so there would be no evidence of what he had done. Once he was past the panic stage of the enormity of killing another human being, he started justifying it to himself. He had just paid Linstrom back the pain that he had felt all at once rather than dragging it out over many years. It wasn't until Monday that someone found Linstrom's body. Linstrom's maid had come to clean the house like she always did and found the broken and battered body sitting in an overstuffed chair in the study. The cops came into the crime scene to find out that the security hard drive had been wiped along with Linstrom's computer. The body had unusual contusions all over it. The coroner was going crazy trying to figure out what the weapon was and how it did so much damage. They compared it to all the other data they had collected from various crime scenes with known villains and came up empty. Eventually it went into the unsolved cases room to gather dust.

Fred breathed a sigh of relief as the case faded from the front page, to page 6, to a mere mention in a column ranting about how the superheroes and villains needed to go.

Bonzo watched and waited. His revelation that he could go against his creator had been a large one. He started trying things on his own. Small things at first and found that he could control himself with concentration when ordered to do something.

He discovered by accident that he could, given the right circumstances, actually take control of his creator if Fred was wearing him. Fred had to be distracted for it to work. If Fred was focused on Bonzo, then Bonzo was mostly in Fred's thrall. It was such a small thing. Fred had put Bonzo on and was playing with him. Having Bonzo punch and jab the way he had the night they killed Linstrom. Bonzo didn't like that at all. The phone rang and Bonzo pulled his right hand rod out of Fred's left hand by making Fred open his hand ever so slightly. He could feel his control of his creator's hand in his mind. He had done that, not Fred just dropping a rod.

Fred dropped the other rod and picked up the phone. As Fred was talking on the phone, Bonzo focused and turned his head toward Fred. As soon as Fred put the phone down he picked up both of Bonzo's rods and found himself looking into Bonzo's blue glass eyes. "Huh," said Fred out loud, "I don't remember turning your head."

"You must have done so," said Bonzo, "I am merely your puppet."

Fred put Bonzo back up on the shelf and went to his computer. Bonzo watched as Fred searched the Internet for information on the CEO of another toy company that Fred felt had wronged him. But Bonzo noticed that from time to time Fred would glance back at Bonzo with a very puzzled look. Bonzo stayed still and watched.

◄ G ►

The break in to the house went smoothly as always. The toys had that part of burglary down to a fine art. They knew how to cut the wires and screw up the electronics that guarded these types of houses.

Once into the house, things started to fall apart. They found someone else in the house with the CEO; someone that had already broken into the house.

Bonzo gazed up at a stunning woman. One of the most beautiful he had ever seen. She was sleek and graceful in a black cat suit. She had her hair under a black stocking cap and Bonzo thought the cap was moving slightly against her movement. She turned and looked at the toys through night-vision goggles she was sporting.

"*Toys?!?!*" she exclaimed.

Bonzo couldn't place the slight accent he heard but he loved the sound of her voice.

Fred came in the door that the other toys had opened for him and stopped short as he encountered the woman.

"Who is this?" he asked.

"Creator, we don't know," answered one of his dolls.

"Who are you?" asked Fred still sorting out that this was not the person he was looking for.

"No one you need to concern yourself about, my dear. I hope we aren't here for the same thing." She held up a flash drive, "Since I have already gotten what I came for."

Bonzo could see that the safe behind her head was open and empty.

She went to the window and jumped out onto the roof of the garage, vanishing into the dark.

Fred gathered up his toys and fled the house.

"She saw my face!" Fred ranted after they got back to the workshop, "What if she knows who I am? I have to find her."

"Creator," said Bonzo after he was tired of listening to Fred rant and rave, "She is a thief. If she reports you then she has to admit that she was in the house as well. You are safe."

Fred didn't seem convinced but calmed down a bit, "I'll just have to rethink how I am going to do this. I will have my revenge."

Bonzo remained quiet, not wanting to agitate Fred further. He thought back to the lovely woman he saw and wondered what color her eyes were.

Things were pretty quiet for a time after that. Fred spent a lot of time scouring the Internet to see if there was any mention of his presence at the CEO's house. He checked both the Hero boards and the Villain boards for anything. But nothing came up. The break in at the CEO's home had been connected to the death of Linstrom because the way the house was broken into but it was still not traced to Fred.

— G —

Late one night Bonzo watched as the lovely woman came sliding in through the door of the workshop. He watched as she went to Fred's computer and started to work a hack on it. All the toys were witnesses but they hadn't been ordered to do anything so they sat and watched.

Eventually Bonzo's curiosity got the best of him. He hopped off the shelf. The woman heard the sound and turned around quickly. She stared at Bonzo who hovered his way to her.

"Can I help you?" asked Bonzo. No reason not to be polite.

"You can talk?" came the response.

Bonzo watched her carefully. Again he noticed that her hat moved slightly around her head. "Well I am speaking to you," he replied.

"Am I speaking to Mr. Greenly?"

Bonzo cocked his head slightly to the right. "No, you are talking to me."

"And you are?"

"Bonzo."

"Bonzo, I thought I recognized you. I used to bring my daughter to Mr. Greenly's puppet shows when she was very young. You were usually the hero of the piece."

Bonzo was taken a bit aback. She knew who he was. She had seen him perform. He nodded slightly. "May I ask again: can I help you?"

She crouched down close to his level and he hovered slightly higher so he could look her in the eye.

"I am looking for something that I think Mr. Greenly might have acquired during his crime spree."

"I wouldn't call one dead company president a spree."

"What would you call it?"

"A start?"

The woman chuckled. It was like the music of bells to Bonzo's ears.

He said, "I have introduced myself and it would only be polite if you did the same."

"My, you are very old school aren't you?" said the woman, "You can call me Zola."

"Well Ms. Zola, care to explain what you are looking for?"

"Are you going to call the police?"

"Not yet."

"I am looking for some bank records that weren't on the flash drive I took from the CEO's house. I got the financials but I need the codes to transfer the money from his secret account to my account."

"Secret account?"

"Oh, you don't know. Well let's say there was a lot of skimming the cream off the top going on at that company.

"What do you need the money for?" asked Bonzo.

She hesitated and said, "I guess it wouldn't do any harm to tell you."

"I won't tell anyone," said Bonzo.

"Listen, this is not the best place to do this. Do you know the abandoned brownstone about four blocks from here?"

Bonzo thought about the neighborhood and remembered how it looked to him traveling on Fred's arm oh so many years ago, "Brown's pharmacy?"

"It hasn't been Brown's pharmacy in a very long time, but yes that's the building."

"I don't get out much these days or when I do it is usually in a duffle bag."

"I could see how that might be an impediment," she said with a slight smile. "How about we meet there tomorrow night?"

Bonzo thought through what Fred had been doing. He didn't remember seeing anything to indicate that they were going out to do anything for a while.

"I should be able to do that. If I am not there it is because my creator has other plans for me."

"Your creator?"

"Mr. Greenly."

"He would be that, wouldn't he," said Zola rather absentmind-edly. "Well I guess I should go, Bonzo. I hope to see you tomorrow." She slipped out as quietly as she slipped in but Bonzo swore he heard a slight hissing noise as she passed him. He went back to his shelf and continued his vigil.

Since Zola had not taken or touched anything, Bonzo didn't see the need to tell Fred what had happened the night before. Nothing was gone and nothing was damaged. The other toys seem to be totally in the creator's thrall. They never spoke unless spoken to and only answered questions when asked directly. So he wasn't worried about them spilling the beans of what had happened the night before.

Fred was latched to the computer for the day researching what Bonzo figured was going to be their next job. He seemed agitated about something but Bonzo knew better than to ask. So far the Creator hadn't figured out Bonzo's growing independence and he wanted to keep it that way. He thought about his encounter with Zola and plotted how he was going to get out and back to the workshop.

Finally Fred switched off the computer and left the workshop, locking the door behind him. Bonzo waited for a while to make sure Fred was gone. He hopped off his shelf and crossed to the other side of the room. He hopped up on the shelves next to a very small window. He quickly disabled the sensor to the window and cracked it open. Once he got his head through, the rest of the body was easy. He looked around cautiously. It seemed quiet. Bonzo slowly made his way over to the ex-pharmacy. He ducked in and out of shadows and tried to keep his arm rods off the ground. He saw a stray dog limp by him but the dog didn't bother him nor did he the dog. Finally after what seemed an eternity but was about twenty minutes, he arrived at the storefront. The door was closed but the window above the door was open. He hopped up and slid his head into the abandoned store. He looked around and saw the dust had been disturbed recently. There were footprints from the front door toward the back.

Bonzo pulled himself into the store and hopped to the floor. Cautiously he followed the footprints. The first feelings of dread tickled at the back of his mind but he went on, wanting to know more about this Zola and why she was at the CEO's house.

The trail led into a back office. There was a light on in the office. He thought he saw Zola's silhouette but her hair was out and moving around her head. He couldn't figure out how her hair could do something like that but put it down to Zola having a secret that she didn't want to share...yet.

He cleared his throat so as not to startle her.

"Just a moment, Bonzo" came the melodious voice that Bonzo found so fascinating. Her silhouette changed shape as Zola put on a large floppy hat.

"Come in." The invitation had been given and Bonzo glided his way into the office. Zola was seated behind a big antique wooden desk. She motioned to a stool that stood in front of the desk and Bonzo hopped up onto it. He appreciated being at eye level with Zola. It was a nice gesture he thought.

"So..." started Bonzo and then his voice trailed off.

"So," she repeated, "I believe yesterday I promised you an explanation."

"Yes, you did."

"Tell you what, let's play exchange information. You tell me what is going on with Greenly and I will tell you what I am up to. Just know I can detect lying. I have gotten very good at ferreting out lies over the years."

"How old are you?" asked Bonzo.

She smiled at him. "Oh Bonzo, you know it is impolite to ask a lady her age."

If Bonzo could have blushed he would have done so, instead he said, "I apologize. I am still learning about social customs. As for lying, I don't know how."

"You don't?"

"I'm a puppet and a hero puppet at that. I have always told the truth or kept silent."

"Well this should be a fascinating conversation, Mr. Bonzo."

"Just Bonzo, please."

"What is your....Creator trying to do?"

"I believe he is trying to get justice for the wrongs he has suffered in life. I am a little unclear as to what they all are but he does talk about them a lot."

"But he killed a man."

"Technically I killed him and my creator just controlled me. He has come to the conclusion that villainy gets you further than heroics. He tried to play by the rules and found himself almost destitute."

Zola made a derisive snort. "The rules. The rules change like the wind."

"Some do and some don't. Some are absolutes."

"Like do not kill?'

"Well, he has decided to be a villain," replied Bonzo.

Zola gestured toward Bonzo. "Your turn."

"Why do you need the funds from the CEO's accounts?"

"Because I have a dream and I need money to make my dream a reality."

"What sort..."

Zola raised her hand and cut him off, "Question for question, my dear. Those are the rules."

Bonzo nodded.

"Have you always been alive?" she asked.

Bonzo thought for a moment before responding, "Not an easy question to answer. In some ways, yes. Every time that I performed I believe I came to life. I remember performing in front of crowds at various places. I can remember my lines and what got the biggest laughs from the crowd. Even after he stopped performing, my creator would slip me on for old times' sake and talk to me and have me respond. But as I am now," he gestured with his arms, "This is pretty recent. My creator found a book of magic that was not just simple slight-of-hand tricks but actual spells that worked. He animated me first. I had been with him the longest so I think he has a soft spot for me."

"A book of spells? You have got to be kidding."

Bonzo shook his head, "I don't kid. Remember you said we would tell each other the truth. My turn, what is this dream you so want so much that you will steal to make a reality?"

"Well, that's rather harsh."

"Did you steal?"

"Yes, but that's not the point. And that's two questions."

"You didn't answer the first one, Ms. Zola."

"Just Zola please, Bonzo. I have a dream and I think it is a good dream. I want to turn this place into a bar, but not just any bar. A place for heroes and villains to not be heroes or villains but just to be themselves. Have a drink and some food. Neutral territory. A safe place away from prying eyes of those without powers."

"How?"

"How what?"

"How will you know?"

"I have my ways," she said with a sly smile on her lips, "and that was three questions in a row."

Bonzo shrugged, "I honestly don't think you are going to have too many more for me."

"You might be surprised," she said. "Do you eat or drink?"

"No. In fact I actively avoid such activities. Stains can be a pain to get rid of."

"Including blood stains?"

"Again, I was not in control that night and I think we are even again."

Zola nodded and gestured to Bonzo to ask his next question. He thought a bit and asked, "How are you going to keep the peace?"

"The peace?"

"You are trying to create neutral territory. There is going to be bad blood between these people from previous encounters."

"I have my ways, Bonzo. Don't worry about that."

Bonzo shrugged, "How much more do you need?"

Zola thought for a moment. "I am not far off. If I can get the account codes to access the money that was skimmed then I would have enough to buy this building and alter it to suit my needs. Will you help me?"

Bonzo thought for a moment, "How?"

"Do you know where the files Mr. Greenly took are?"

"The files that we took from the house are in the workshop. My creator was trying to get evidence to secure his hostile takeover of several companies that he feels have wronged him. I know right where they are."

"Will you give them to me?"

"That's two questions Zola and I think it is time for me to leave." He hopped off the stool.

She stood up, squatted to his level, and handed him a business card. "That's my number. If you want to help, call me. Be my hero."

Bonzo took the card, folded it in half and put it in the pocket of his shirt. He snuck back home, reset the alarm, and went back to his shelf thinking about everything that had been said.

Fred seemed more agitated than usual to Bonzo. Something was bothering him. "So close," he muttered. "So close. Oh, I am so close to everything I want and my revenge."

He picked Bonzo up off the shelf and Zola's business card fluttered out of Bonzo's pocket.

"Bonzo, what is this?"

"It looks like a card."

"Zola." Fred read. "Who is Zola and why do you have her card, Bonzo?"

Bonzo kept quiet.

"Bonzo, I made you and I can disassemble you just as easily. All it would take would be a pair of sharp scissors."

"No," said Bonzo very carefully.

"Did you just say No to me!?!"

"Yes, I said No to you. My creator, you are not yourself. The path you are traveling is not the one we first started down so many years ago."

"I was an idealistic fool then. I thought I could succeed at anything."

"And you have. You have had success in many fields."

"But no one knows that it was me. Others have taken the credit and accolades that I deserved. I can't walk the streets without seeing signs of my failure. Everyone is wearing it or carrying it or playing with it. I can't escape it. I am tired of being in the shadows and marginalized. But you are getting me off the subject: who is Zola? Answer me."

Bonzo debated whether to show his free will to his creator but decided to hold that card close to his vest.

"She was the woman we met at the CEO's house who had opened the safe."

"How did you get her card?"

Bonzo hesitated but decided in for a penny in for a pound. "She came to the workshop the other night looking for some papers that you took from the house."

"What kind of papers?"

"Codes to some off-shore accounts that the CEO had money hidden in. She took the flash drive that had all of the information on it except the codes."

"Why didn't you tell me that she had broken in here?"

"You didn't ask."

"Well why don't you invite her back here?" Before Bonzo could do anything Fred shoved his hand into Bonzo's head. "I'll dial, you talk but don't worry it will be like old times, I'll tell you exactly what to say." Bonzo didn't like the tone in his creator's voice. It was the same tone he heard the night that Fred had him pummel Linstrom to death.

Fred dialed the phone and put it on speaker.

"Yes, Bonzo? Did you think about my offer?" came the voice on the other end of the line.

Fred moved Bonzo's mouth, "Yes, why don't we meet at the workshop at midnight. It should be clear then."

"Is everything okay, Bonzo? You don't sound like yourself."

"Everything is fine. See you at midnight." Fred pushed the speaker button off.

Fred turned Bonzo toward him and looked into his glass eyes unflinchingly. "And we will have a little surprise for Ms. Zola, won't we, Bonzo?"

Bonzo let Fred bob his head up and down but inside he felt wrong. This was wrong! Zola had nothing to do with this except being in the wrong place at the wrong time. Bonzo focused his mind on Fred and Fred turned his head to the left and looked at the door. Bonzo relaxed his control over his creator and Fred's head came back to meet his gaze. He took Bonzo off and put him on the workbench.

"Bonzo, is there something you need to tell me?"

Bonzo shook his head no. He didn't feel like talking to Fred.

"Well then I shall get the place ready to greet our visitor. We must put on our best show."

Bonzo found himself conflicted. What could he do? He was a puppet in all senses of the word. Yet he had to do something to save Zola. He sat on the workbench and pondered his options, while Fred spoke quietly to the other toys.

Fred made a show of locking up the workshop and going upstairs. Bonzo turned his head toward the cable box, looking at the time. 11:45. Fifteen minutes to decide what he was going to do. Or rather what he was going to try to do.

Almost at the stroke of midnight, he heard lockpicks in the door. It opened and Zola entered carefully. She saw Bonzo on the table. As she crossed to the workbench she was attacked on all sides by Fred's army of dolls and toys. They quickly immobilized her and tied her to a chair.

Fred entered the room. "So, you must be Zola."

"And you are Mr. Greenly. I remember your puppet shows in the park quite fondly."

That gave Fred pause. "You know my work?"

"I have two of your original dolls before the toy company made you stop. The first set, not the second. They hold a place of honor in my home. You do quite lovely work."

Fred smiled. "You are trying to distract me."

"Is it working?"

"You were at the house."

"I am sure Bonzo has told you everything. I do have another appointment this evening so can we get on with whatever we are getting on with?"

"Rather flip for someone pinned to a chair."

"Mr. Greenly, I have been around the block more times than I care to count. I have a tendency toward bluntness these days. Why did you want me here?"

"You are the only one who knows who the Toymaker is. You are the only person who can tell the police what I did. For my plan to work, I must eliminate you."

Zola laughed a deep and throaty laugh. "Others have tried but I am still here".

"Others aren't me."

Bonzo sat and watched Zola. Again, he could swear that her hat was moving independent of any motion she made. From his view, her hair seemed agitated. It was almost like...he stopped that thought because it was absurd.

Bonzo found himself being picked up and put on. He felt his creator's hand inside his skull and he didn't like it much.

"Well, Miss Zola, it is time to turn you into a cold case file."

Bonzo found himself punching Zola in the gut. He heard her gasp in pain. The sound went right through him and something within him changed. He softened the next blow to her cheek but it still made an impact. With each blow he pulled his punches a little more.

Fred stepped back. "You're a superhero aren't you? What's your power? Invincibility?

Zola said, "Oh, my dear boy, nothing that crass. Why don't you ask Bonzo what is going on?"

"Bonzo?" Fred was very puzzled. And then Fred knew fear as Bonzo turned his head toward Fred. Fred tried to move Bonzo's face away from his own but he couldn't.

"You are not going to hurt this woman any more than you have," said Bonzo.

Fred's brain was trying to process his puppet talking to him while Fred was in control. However, Fred was quickly figuring out that he was not in control. In fact he was not certain he was even in control of his own body. He dropped the puppet's arm rods and tried to reach for the puppet to take him off.

"I don't think so," said Bonzo.

Fred felt a pressure build in his brain and found himself opening HIS mouth and saying, "Let her go." The toys did as they were ordered and let Zola go.

A scream of terror built in Fred's throat as Bonzo took over. It was if a fuzzy arm had reached inside his brain. Fred fought against it but that only made it worse.

Zola watched as the stare down between Bonzo and Fred went on. Then something strange happened. Bonzo seem to grow in size as Fred shrank. It looked as if Bonzo was absorbing Fred into himself. As Fred shrank, Zola heard a strangled scream coming from his throat. Zola looked down and saw that Bonzo and Fred were in the middle of a very strange looking diagram. Fred vanished leaving her eye to eye with Bonzo, now a human-sized puppet.

Zola said cautiously, "Bonzo?"

Bonzo replied, "Yes?"

"Bonzo, what happened to Mr. Greenly?"

Bonzo looked at her with a twinkle in his glass eyes and said, "Let's just say that he got caught up in his work."

Zola decided not to press the issue, still not entirely sure of what she had just seen.

"You needed some codes I believe?"

Zola nodded. Bonzo floated over to the desk and picked up a file folder. "I think what you need is in here."

Zola opened the folder and flipped through the papers. She removed a single sheet.

"Thank you, Bonzo. For everything." And she started to leave.

"Wait."

Zola stopped and turned toward Bonzo.

"I want you to promise me something. That this is it. After this you take the money and turn Brown's into a bar. No more thievery. You need to go on the straight and narrow. Someone should be able to fulfill their dreams."

Zola nodded slowly. "And what are you going to do?"

Bonzo shrugged, "I am not entirely sure."

"Where…?" Zola started to ask and then thought better.

Bonzo finished the question for her, "Did my creator go?" Bonzo tapped his head. "He's in here, where he can't do any more harm. I am no longer his puppet."

Zola watched as Bonzo glided toward her. She thought her eyes were playing tricks on her but she swore she saw the bottom of a forearm sticking just out from Bonzo.

"Zola, I want to be a hero. Let me help you."

Zola thought for a moment, "Okay, how about once the bar gets going, you help me keep the peace. I am pretty sure you are impervious to just about any power that might be thrown at you. And you do throw a mean punch."

"Sorry," said Bonzo, "I wasn't myself then."

"I know." She kissed him gently on the forehead. "I don't blame you at all. So how about it? Want to be Keeper of the Peace?"

"I think this is the beginning of a beautiful friendship, Zola."

Making a Difference

Robert Greenberger

Gravel and grit forced their way into his mouth as he felt his boots drag along the street, kicking up the debris as the car picked up speed. He held on tight to the front bumper, willing his hips and legs to swivel into action, letting him scale up to the hood. His mind fought to control multiple inputs, starting with the foul taste in his mouth, the ache in his calves, and the strain in his biceps.

Willing his body to behave, he once more moved into action and somehow wound up exactly where he wanted to be: riding a speeding car, weaving in and out of light Manhattan traffic at three in the morning, with police sirens beginning to fill the air. His gloved hands gripped the sides of the tapered hood and he stared through the windshield at the driver, a greasy-haired, pock-mocked kid of maybe twenty. Normally, he wouldn't have bothered with a simple car theft except for the other occupant in the vehicle—a screaming infant, safely buckled in the car seat in the rear.

The driver's eyes bulged and the hero saw his mouth work and finally form the name: "Crusader".

He hated the name but it had been pinned on him on the very first night he sought to make a difference. When he decided to don the black-and-gold outfit, he had been mulling over names but after stopping a riot in the wake of an unfavorable legal decision, a reporter quipped, "Hey, caped crusader, where's your cape?" And, that was all it took, suddenly he was the Crusader.

There were worse names, he supposed, and he'd grown accustomed to it, but he'd much rather have had a say in his alter ego's name.

A sharp swerve to the right shook him from his reverie and he nearly lost his grip on the polished metal surface. With a severe gesture, he made it clear he wanted the panicky driver to pull over and surrender.

Rather than obeying the command, the driver braked hard and came to a sudden stop, the momentum dislodging the hero. Crusader rolled to the street, taking the brunt of the impact on his right shoulder, but the sound of the door opening, sneakers hitting the pavement, and the wail of the frightened infant shocked him into action. With an effort he regained his footing, checked to make certain the infant was still in the car, and took off after the thief, certain the impending arrival of the police would mean the kid would be looked after. The scumbag who stole the car, though, needed some justice. And the way the Crusader felt right then, it would be rough justice.

◄ G ►

Harmony looked up in alarm when the Crusader appeared in the doorway to her bedroom. He tended to call ahead or at least knock to alert her of his arrival. Instead, given the late hour, the costumed figure slipped a key from a belt compartment and let himself in, the sound waking her.

"Its 4:30 in the mor…" her complaint trailed off when she saw him somewhat stagger to the edge of the bed where he heavily let himself down. "My god, you look terrible."

"Feel worse," he said in a hoarse voice. She turned on the night-table lamp and in the illumination saw the black streaks from his most recent activity. His mouth was bruised and swollen and even the skin was raw, trickling blood, adding a new color to the gold piping on his outfit. She noted that spots were worn through the costume and his boots were scuffed. The stylish outfit was one of the first things she focused on when they initially met. It was thick leather, providing him with some protection, creased and crinkled here and there but being mostly black you needed a strong light to notice. The helmet and faceplate cowl had a gold design that led to piping down both sleeves, disappearing under tight gloves. It was far less garish than some of the outfits other heroes appeared in, especially the women who clearly were using their cleavage to distract criminals from their fists.

"What happened?" She rose and kneeled beside him, totally unconscious that she was wearing her oversized Crusader night shirt, his grinning, cowled face looming large from shoulders to hips.

He began to speak of the evening's activity but she placed two fingers on his lips, silencing him as she headed into the bathroom and came back with all the usual first-aid supplies. By then, he had peeled out of the leather and Kevlar-fitted jacket, exposing the various older yellow and fresh black bruises that created a pop art image on his body. She deftly applied antiseptic cream and bandages. His breathing slowed and resumed a regular rhythm.

"Was it worth it?"

"I saved a baby, so yeah," he told her, which caught her attention. *Children always do that to heroes and civilians alike, it must be hardwired into humanity,* Mike Kinnard thought. Finally loosening his cowl and peeling it away, his brown eyes met hers and they silently communed for a minute.

"You're a mess," she said, breaking the silence which had been growing uncomfortable. "You never used to finish the night like this. You must be getting sloppy or..."

"...or old," he finished for her. This had recently become the centerpiece of their conversations when it came to his colorful alter ego.

She nodded, closing up the first aid kit. "How much longer do you think you can keep this up?" she asked, the anger clear in her tone.

This was far from the first time she raised the question but tonight, this morning, was the first time he actually considered a real response. He ached. Seriously ached and not for the first time this year, he realized. He was not healing as quickly as he used to.

"There's still work to be done," he began before she could cut him off. "As long as I can make a difference."

"That's a pat, bullshit answer. You're closing in on forty and are still trying to act like someone half your age. It's no longer safe. You go out, beat the shit out of the bad guys, and come back here to be patched up. You make time for me as *convenient,* but even then you'd have to be inside me before you'd consider staying, rather than answer a cry for help."

"Harm, that's not true or really fair."

She pulled a stray lock of hair away from her eyes, tucking it behind her ear. "Fair? Fair is us being together, making a life for ourselves, actually planning more than a few hours out. I fell for *you*, Mike, not the Crusader."

"I *am* the Crusader," Mike Kinnard told her, some heat of his own in the words. "You knew that from the moment I yanked the rapist off you." That had been four years ago, when he could still patrol the streets for hours, bust some heads, and go to work without getting tired. He felt strong and vital then; in love, real love, for the first time in his life. Mike could not now imagine his life without Harmony St. James, but she was challenging that idyllic vision and he was not in the mood to consider it. Letting a deep breath out slowly through his nose, Kinnard kept his mouth shut, not daring to let this escalate into something ugly. He was weary and sore and did not need a fight with his lover to finish off a tough night.

"Yeah, I knew you as the Crusader first," Harmony went on, clearly not reading his mind or his body language. "But I came to love Mike Kinnard and you're making that very hard right now. Before you, I wasn't sure I'd ever find someone I could imagine growing old with, but then you swooped in and became my personal hero. But for *us* to grow old together, you need to stay alive and, you know, healthy."

He winced at that, much as he winced at the aching muscles that screamed for Ben Gay or a whirlpool. His local gym was a 24-hour place and he wanted to go there before he had to make an appearance at Count on Kinnard, his private accounting company.

"I can't do this without you," he began. When she shot him a look, he let the sentence die mercifully.

"Do you want us to stay together? Get married, settle down, skip the picket fence and kids, but experience things as a couple? Answer yes and that will tell you what you need to do. Answer no then you've set the timer on our relationship starting tonight."

He didn't answer her and he didn't believe she truly expected an answer at this late hour. She deserved one and he wanted to say the former but knew full well he was not done fighting for his city. The Blockade, Doctor Bizarre, Lightspeed, and the other heroes were still going strong and together, they were keeping

Manhattan from becoming more dangerous. It felt like he'd be betraying them but then again, they had their powers to protect them. He was just an extraordinarily gifted athlete with an above-average intellect. Right now, though, he was not feeling particularly smart.

"Mike…you have to slow down. Take some nights off. Make some time for us. I don't want to make an ultimatum, but we're getting really close to having that 'me or the mask' conversation. The one you told me you never wanted us to get to."

That conversation started about a year back, after he fought to stem a gang war while still wearing a splint, a trophy from battling the Gentleman. It was then he began to notice the wear and tear on his body and the impending onset of serious middle age. He always joked forty was when the warranty would end and his body would fall apart. What he didn't realize at the time was that he wasn't being sardonic but prophetic.

He soaked and slept and trained and felt somewhat better the next day. During that time, even while meeting with his clients, his mind was turning over the conversation with Harmony. She meant everything to him, and yes, he wanted to be with her until death do they part, but he hadn't created his heroic alter ego lightly. The city was mired in petty crime that the other heroes ignored and politicians gave lip service to. He created his identity to wade into the streets and tame the criminals, cow them into towing the line or staying in the shadows.

The Crusader burst onto the scene fifteen years ago and quickly became a fixture in the city. With the advent of social media, his whereabouts were tweeted and Instagram images were posted nightly. The criminals, though, didn't seem to fear his growing fame. They continued to buy and sell drugs, weapons, and people. From the Battery to the docks, he would find activity that cried for his attention. He let the powerful ones handle the bigger threats while he handled the muggers, robbers, and thieves. Lowlifes of every kind knew they risked getting up-close and personal with his fists if they tried to ply their trade. Not that it mattered, because there were more of them than the one of him and they liked to gamble.

On more than one occasion, some media pundit would question whether he was making a difference compared with the Silver Centurion or the others. Kinnard would sometimes wallow in self-doubt after one of these pieces ran, but Harmony was there to bolster his spirits, pat him on the ass, and send him back out to fight the good fight.

So, imagining her hand on his butt, he suited up for another night.

As he checked over his outfit, he noted that he needed to order new boots, the toes rubbed ragged thanks to the previous night. He polished his helmet and used a microfiber cloth to polish his faceplate and saw a new scratch that stubbornly resisted his efforts.

Crimefighting was not an occupation for the poor. It wasn't until he received an unanticipated inheritance that he could make his imaginary hero a reality. It was a pain to find a variety of suppliers for his gear at the outset but after debuting and then meeting other protectors, he learned of the network of fabricators and manufacturers who serviced the heroes, their prices buying their services and their silence.

Since Harmony had an evening event at the Museum of Modern Art, where she worked in its acquisitions department, he felt safe to go back into the night and continue to make a difference. From a rented space, he eased out his powerful motorcycle, nondescript enough to blend in when he was not astride it, normally cruising (albeit with license plates he regularly stole from the police impound yards to avoid being traced) in search of danger.

Doubts still popped up now and then, but most nights, he prowled the streets and rooftops certain he was making Manhattan safer for its millions of inhabitants. Sometimes he imagined his very presence on the streets, as his image was flashed across the Internet, put the criminal element on notice. Some were savvy about it and tracked him while others, too many he considered, ignored it and went about their business. Of course, their business was *his* business so they'd invariably butt heads.

For example, he saw a cruising police car two blocks up ahead near Union Square suddenly switch on its lights. He revved the motorcycle to catch up and see if he could lend a hand. It took him a block before he caught up with the vehicle near 15th Street, heading west. The Crusader hung back a bit, prepared to lend unofficial support but then he spotted the figures. Four men, all in leather biker jackets, scattering. Two veered off, going toward 16th so he followed them, confident he could bring them down easily while the police chased after the other pair.

The cycle narrowed the gap with ease although it was clear they were running flat out. He was still faster and took a moment to observe them: both Caucasian; one muscular, one with a beer belly; neither with an obvious weapon. He timed his move and withdrew a cord from a compartment on the cycle. The ready-made lasso was twirled overhead, gaining speed as he eyed his targets, carefully taking aim. With a sure hand, he let loose and the flexible cord sailed from motorcycle to thug and ensnared Beer Belly. The man's momentum was broken and he stumbled, nearly tugging Crusader from his mount. The hero recovered and wrapped his end of the lasso around the handlebars. The other man was gaining distance so Crusader gunned the engine, pulling the captured man off his feet and forward, legs scrambling to try and keep up.

The man turned right, heading onto Park Avenue South and heading uptown. The Crusader measured the distance between them and risked a leap from the motorcycle. He sailed through the air, tackling the running figure. The landing felt rougher than usual, likely because he was still sore from last night's carjacker. Behind him, Beer Belly practically ran over the discarded motor-cycle, which fell to its side, engine still running. The idiot tugged at the lasso, trying to disengage himself but the knot was tight and he couldn't reach it.

The Crusader crawled atop the more muscular figure and landed two quick jabs to the man's face to stun him. The second blow hurt his knuckles, but also landed with a satisfying crack. Kneeling to hold one arm in place, the Crusader reached to his belt and neatly withdrew a zip tie and bundled the perp's wrists together. The other man wrestled with his hands, snarling in frustration and rammed his head into the Crusader's chest. The blow carried enough impact to send him backward and off the figure, who wasted no time scrambling to his feet and resuming his sprint up Park.

Bypassers squawked as they were shoved out of his way, but the suspect continued to move like a linebacker, moving up field. The Crusader sprung to his feet, glanced over his shoulder to note Beer Belly was still tied to the motorcycle and struggling, so felt free to pursue his quarry. He still had the endurance that years of Ironman training left him, and he immediately began closing ground. Being just after 10 p.m. on a Thursday night, Crusader had to contend with fairly busy sidewalks, which his target used to his advantage, sending men and women tumbling, turning his path into an obstacle course.

The Crusader jumped over some, weaved around others, and never lost sight of his quarry. He spotted a bench and mentally calculated speed and angle, concluding he could use the bench as a way to close the gap. Quickening his pace, he ran a few more steps, then crouched and leapt. Sailing over a ducking pedestrian, the Crusader bent his knees and landed on the bench, using it to propel himself forward, narrowing the gap and putting the suspect in his grasp.

He sailed through the air, pleased this would not only work but look pretty cool.

The perp unexpectedly surged ahead and rather than land on the fleeing figure, the Crusader crumpled to the concrete sidewalk, rolling to the side, nearly bowling over a strolling couple, oblivious to his miscue. This had never failed before. In fact, this was something he had practiced at the gym numerous times, forcing his muscles to memorize the movements so it would come off smoothly. Still, he came up short.

The escaping man saw the hero on the ground, let out a loud bark of a laugh, and continued to weave through the crowd, putting a lot of distance between them.

Letting out more than a few curses, the Crusader sprinted back to the motorcycle, pleased to see a police officer already snapping cuffs on the captured man. The cop nodded at the Crusader, who hurriedly coiled the rope and righted his bike. Gunning the engine like an animal bellowing a challenge, he roared down the street. There was no way he would let his blunder result in a single criminal escaping. There'd be some harsh payback even though there was really no one to blame except for himself.

G

The following week was a rough one. He was black and blue from head to toe, or so it felt. He ached beyond the reach of non-prescription pain relievers and had sworn a long time ago never to resort to stronger stuff for fear of addiction. As a result, each morning was a challenge to get out of bed and get dressed for work. His time with Harmony was strained. Their intimate acts caused more than a few winces and for the first time, she wasn't trying to be gentle with him, as if making his choices now painful punishments.

She wisely left the topic remain unspoken. Instead, they both seemed to silently invest themselves in keeping the relationship together. Their actions spoke louder than the words they had already spoken. Mike loved her, he did. Still, his sense of duty and obligation forced him to go back to the streets every night.

There was unfinished business. Three of the four men were apprehended, but a fourth remained free. It turned out they had been spotted beating a gay man and a good Samaritan had called it in. The Crusader was in the right place at the right time when the responding patrol car passed by. Thankfully, the imprisoned men turned on their colleague and provided details on where he could be found and a friendly cop shared the intel. Of all the crimes the Crusader dealt with, hate crimes were the ones that emotionally hurt him the most. Thankfully, the final criminal was tracked down and caught. And his knuckles were still raw from the beating he administered that night. His growing anger with criminals seemed in proportion with how long it took him to recover. He was still going out and patrolling but was being more careful with each action, thinking things through, resisting impulsive action. The results were good but he disliked the need to slow down. It felt...old.

He and Harmony continued to avoid the issue of retirement. She began to ignore his wounds, her way of protesting his indecision. He avoided the issue, feeling that as long as he could be *needed,* he *should* be out on the streets.

So that's exactly where he was. On the streets of Manhattan at two in the morning, a light rain beginning to fall, as he traded blows with the Gentleman once more. Each fist landed against the reinforced fabric that made up the Saville Row suit that never seemed to wrinkle. The Gentleman was always well-dressed, always sporting expensive suits, ties, and shoes, rarely repeating an outfit. Experience taught the Crusader that everything from the collar stays to pocket square were all weapons and over the years, he had tasted them all, living to learn not to try them again. His longtime foe was always after high-end valuables, usually sculpture, jewelry, and the like, easy to access and carry off.

Tonight, the criminal accidentally tripped a secondary silent alarm he missed disarming while robbing the mansion of a tech mogul. The Crusader rushed across town, attempting to beat the police and arrive in time to stop the criminal. They'd fought often enough through the years that they had grown comfortable with one another. Crusader, unlike the police, knew all about the Gentleman's weaponry and his penchant for causing excessive property damage to aid in his escapes.

Of course, all the Crusader needed to do was seek out the most expensive foreign car in the vicinity to know how his arch enemy intended to escape. Sure enough, the Gentleman emerged from the service entrance of a nearby condominium tower, removing the night goggles that somehow tastefully matched his dark charcoal gray suit. The tie was a pleasing red-and-gold weave but the Crusader recognized, from painful experience, the clasp; a small explosive.

"Good evening," he said to catch the man's attention.

The Gentleman, who real name was Ali Kokmen, paused for the briefest of moments and bowed deeply toward his opponent. "You're looking the worse for wear," he said.

The Crusader cocked his head.

"Your boots are terrible," the Gentlemen explained.

"Yeah, they need a good brushing. You looking to make some quick cash and give them a polish?"

"You couldn't afford me," the thief said, his left hand slowly moving up toward his tie.

"Ah, ah," the Crusader said, wagging a finger at the other man. "Hands away from the tie, Ali." He knew using his given name irked the criminal and it always gave him a little thrill of delight to watch his face contort in disgust.

"Oh very well," the Gentleman said. As usual, his voice barely rose, maintaining a civil tone and cadence. It was after the man's fourth, or was it the fifth, arrest that Mike learned he had been sent to the finest schools in Europe, trained to be the perfect gentleman's gentleman but he rejected a dead-end career in favor of robbing those he was trained to serve and live as they did. When things grew complicated in France, he immigrated to New York and had a very successful first year until the Crusader finally managed to track him down.

"I'd say your entire ensemble could use replacing," the criminal said, lowering the hand.

"It'll do for now. Maybe when the new fall collections go on sale," Crusader said, taking a step toward the other man.

"Really, my dear fellow, can you not get a new bespoke outfit?"

"Unlike you, I have to earn my spending cash," Crusader said, stepping to his left. They continued to circle one another and he took in all of their surroundings, weighing and measuring options as they bantered. No doubt his adversary was doing the same thing.

"Hopefully you do something cerebral since you're not much of a strongman," the man said with a smirk.

"I'll happily take your surrender and save us both some bumps and bruises," the Crusader replied, refusing to address the jibe.

The Gentleman took a step toward the colorful figure. "But then I will have to face arrest, trial, and possibly incarceration and that just won't do. I have a busy dance card this year."

"Which reminds me," Crusader said, closing the distance between them by another step. "Where is your booty?"

"Booty?"

"Ill-gotten gain?"

"Ah," the man in the suit said, taking yet another step. "Thankfully, it's something small and easily transported. Never you fear, it's safe for now."

The Crusader decided they were close enough. "Last chance," he said.

"Oh tosh," the Gentleman said, his right thumb rubbing the underside of the gold ring on his hand. Something clear poured out of the ring that glistened in the street light. Crusader suspected he best not come into contact with the liquid, hoping the drizzle would help to dilute it.

With surprising speed, the Gentleman's left hand, fingers extended, came darting toward him. He leaned back but didn't bend far enough. The jab caught him just under the rib cage, forcing him to violently exhale. As he bent over, the Gentleman unleashed a vicious leg sweep that upended the hero. He fell on his right shoulder and saw that the coated right hand now swung toward his face. The Crusader curled into a ball, tucking his head low so the blow hit his left shoulder. Once the punch landed, he extended both feet forward, into the Gentleman's shins, forcing him backward, his arms windmilling to help maintain balance.

The Crusader got to his feet and rushed the still-moving criminal. "I have to warn you," he said. "I've had a crappy few weeks and am more than happy to show you how I feel about it." He used an uppercut to emphasize his point. The punch struck the side of the villain's face and the Gentleman was knocked to the ground.

"You know I can keep this up all night," the Crusader said, his voice deep and grim.

"And you know I can take it all night," the Gentleman said as he rubbed his jaw. He looked thoughtful for a moment. "That sounds naughty does it not?"

"Sure does, and I'm ready to keep pounding you until you surrender. Give it up now and we can move things along."

The Gentleman staggered to his feet and the Crusader backed out of arm's reach, to be safe. He eyed the dapper figure noting the fabric seemed a touch tighter on the normally thin figure. "Are you actually putting on a few pounds?"

"Aren't we all?"

"Sure, but I've added more time in the gym," the Crusader said, flexing his muscles and subtly sucking in his gut.

"And a macrobiotic diet or some such rubbish, no doubt. You've probably added Spanx or their heroic equivalent to remain a dashing figure."

"You can leave my figure out of this," Crusader said. "Come and get it or give up. Your call."

"I would rather not set a new record for the shortest battle," the Gentleman said. "It speaks to weakness."

"Or age."

"That too. You have to admit, we're both getting a little long in the tooth to be doing this every few months."

The Gentleman nodded at that and began to move with almost balletic preciseness. He cut a semicircle to the hero's left and the Crusader matched him, practically a mirror image.

"I don't know about you, dear boy, but the recent financial crisis has cut deeply into my retirement account. Trust me, I do not always do this for the thrill of the crime. There are bills to pay, mouths to feed, you understand."

"All too well," the Crusader agreed without trying to think about how the economic calamity had definitely hurt his accounting business, nearly a quarter of his clients wanted to declare bankruptcy. As long as the economy yo-yoed, people would resort to crime and that meant job security for the Crusader. Mike Kinnard's business, on the other hand, might need to downsize a bit until things improved.

The Gentleman tugged his vest neatly and then lunged forward with surprising speed. He wrapped his arms around the Crusader and forced him into the brick wall. He yanked the costumed champion back a few steps then rammed him again.

"My future was never the brightest but now it's a sad mockery of what might have been," the criminal said as he rammed his opponent a third time. He then released the slumping figure and punched with piston-like regularity into the solar plexus. "I need to work. I'd rather be on a beach somewhere but we can't always have what we want."

The hero raised his arms between the still-moving arms of the villain, throwing them to the sides. He then lowered his head and butted the Gentleman, hearing the satisfying crunch of his nose breaking.

"Damn you," the Gentleman cried out.

"As long as you keep doing this, you force me to come out here and stop you. I'd consider retirement if I thought you and your ilk would stay in jail." The Crusader realized he meant it.

"Did you actually use 'ilk' properly in a sentence? You've come a long way since our first encounter when your monosyllables were less interesting." He stepped back and grabbed for the pocket square, using it to staunch the trickle of blood from one nostril.

The Crusader paused and stepped back, wary of whatever deadly trick might also be contained within the square.

"You knew the risks when you committed the crime, a little blood is par," the Crusader snapped.

"Do you know how hard it is to get blood out of this fabric?"

"Don't know," the Crusader said, lunging forward and swinging a roundhouse kick that connected with the man's arm, knocking him off-balance. This was an overly familiar dance and one that now felt old. He flashed on an image of the two of them chasing each other with walkers, flailing canes at one another. It wasn't humorous in the slightest. He ached. He was tired. He hated feeling like this.

"Don't care." An uppercut, perfectly placed on the Gentleman's chin, sent the bleeding man to the concrete.

He stated at the sprawled figure. "Got a Tide stick for that?"

He was already peeling off the costume as he entered Harmony's apartment. She was curled up in her favorite easy chair, having fallen asleep in place, dressed for bed but clearly waiting up for him. Just seeing her made him feel better.

She stirred and opened one eye, aiming it right at him. "Mugger? Grand theft auto? Cat in a tree?"

"The Gentleman," Mike said, tossing the bits of his costume to the carpet, standing there in sweaty undergarments.

"Again?"

"Again." The boots came off. The belt followed. Looking down, he realized Spanx were not that bad an idea.

"Poofta," she murmured and then stretched and he liked watching the curves shift under the filmy fabric.

"I'm calling it, Harm," he said.

"Okay, heads or tails," she said, still waking up.

"No, I'm hanging up the costume. I'm retiring."

The words seemed to energize her and suddenly she was in his arms, gripping tightly. They remained in place for a few minutes until finally she sniffed and asked, "For real?"

"For real."

"All right then," she said. "First thing a retired superhero does is take a shower. You stink. Come on, I'll wash your back."

In the shower, she gently lathered his hair and he stood there, steadying himself with his arms against the stall walls.

"What changed?" she asked gently.

"Him. I want to make a difference and guys like him keep coming back. Rather than playing whack-a-mole with him and the others, I realize it's not working."

She let him rinse his hair, not saying a word, letting him get it all out.

"Harm, I can't keep doing this and I refuse to keep fighting you and them. I know you want me to choose and I'm choosing you. *You*, not the bruises. *You*, not the criminals."

She was now soaping his back and letting her fingers gently work from shoulder to hip.

"The kind of difference I'm making today, it's not the same. I am only one finger in the dike and it's just not enough."

Her hand slipped around, soaping his belly and working lower. He stopped talking.

—◄ G ►—

He was elated all the next day, despite the dismal state of his business. There might be a layoff or two in his future but he'd manage. Kinnard had faced far worse crises. Besides, he felt free for the first time in ages. Even the bruises from the previous night didn't spoil his mood. His first resolution when he awoke that morning was not to give up on his exercise regimen. After all, now that middle age was fast approaching, he needed to keep working out or the muscle would morph into fat and that would never do.

After calling it a day, he stopped at the local market and picked up everything on the list he found tucked into his uniform belt that morning. He added a fresh loaf of bread and then stopped for a bottle of expensive wine to celebrate this new chapter. When he arrived at Harmony's apartment, they fell into an easy rhythm. Together they sliced, diced, sautéed, and mixed the ingredients into a casserole dish. He opened the wine to let it breathe and they sat side by side on the couch, her feet tucked beneath her, his stretched out. They didn't need to say much, luxuriating in one another's company.

As they prepared to put the completed meal on the dining table, a squawk caught his attention. It was the police scanner band on his communications gear, activated when certain key words were detected. He rose and went closer to listen; Harmony most definitely did not accompany him.

"Sounds like someone new," he muttered. "Golden armor, some sort of energy mace, definitely not someone I recognize."

There was suddenly silence in the apartment. The radio had gone silent, the oven was cycling off. The silence stretched like chasm between the two. Neither moved.

Then he began to reach for the belt and remainder of his outfit, which had remained in a heap on the floor all day like unwanted laundry.

Harmony turned her back to him, not wanting to see him break his word.

The radio squawked again, breaking the tension.

"Got a new cape," a female voice said. "On the scene. Young, can fly, seems strong. The mace isn't having an impact."

"Wonder who he could be," Mike muttered as he dropped the costume and walked into the living room and switched on the television. Sure enough, CNN cut to a live feed of the fight and the woman was right, this was someone new. He studied the fleet image and readjusted his expectations. *She* was powerful.

Kinnard was so caught up in watching, he didn't notice Harmony had come in to join him on the couch. The mace definitely didn't harm her but she was also strong and broke the criminal's arm as she grabbed it, snatching the mace and tossing it to a nearby cop. She was smiling from ear to ear, a hero making her debut in spectacular fashion.

"Smooth," Kinnard said, more to himself than Harmony.

"I'd kill for those abs or that ass," Harmony commented.

"Well, I could train you," he offered, sliding an arm around her waist, pulling her close. She broke free and got up from the couch, clearly not interested in joining that side of his life.

As an EMT worked with two other cops to treat and subdue the bad guy, a series of microphones were thrust in the new hero's face.

"What do you call yourself?"

"What can you do?"

"Where'd you come from?"

"Have you registered with the Mayor's office?"

"Do you have a boyfriend?"

"Do you have a girlfriend?"

Mike chuckled at first, remember what his first night felt like. He leaned forward, oblivious to Harmony returning to the room, settling herself beside him, silently handing him a glass of wine.

The young hero seemed more surprised by the microphones than when she was confronting the unnamed perp. She stammered a bit and then shot into the sky, gaining speed and altitude until the television camera lost her in the night sky.

"She was terrible, blew her moment," Harmony said. "It's like she needs a press agent."

They clinked glasses as an idea began to form in Mike's mind.

— G —

The Crusader entered the meeting room of the Champions, the government-sanctioned headquarters for the good guys. He was in a new, slightly modified uniform that had a little more give to it. He was pleased to see everyone was already there since he liked making an entrance. They were young, puppies to his eyes, even the powerful young lady front and center, the one who inspired this moment. All eyes were on him and he took in the moment.

"Good afternoon," he said. "I'm glad you accepted our invitation. This is the beginning of a seminar on good conduct. Today we begin with how to work with the local and federal law-enforcement agencies. We'll cover jurisdictional issues as well as crime-scene etiquette. Next week will be press relations…"

And the week after, he thought, *I offer them tips on where to get equipment made and their taxes done. Maybe I'll even suggest some investments from endorsement deals.*

There was still some good the Crusader could do, even if it meant training a new generation of crimefighters as opposed to busting his knuckles on the same old rogues.

Mike Kinnard, the Crusader, was a man in full.

EIGHT MILLION STRONG

James Chambers

@TheAlbatross
7:43 A.M. Two drug deals, three burglaries—stopped. A kitten rescued from a dumpster. Solid night's work! You're welcome, Boyelle City. #NightPatrol

@TheAlbatross
7:46 A.M. Tonight's Citizen-Protectors: Allie Park, Little Korea. Dabney Simms, Kirby Gardens. The city thanks YOU! #Citizen-Protectors #8MillionStrong

@TheAlbatross
7:51 A.M. Beautiful sunrise over St. John's River! Only we can protect Boyette! Don't let me down. #StJohnsSunrise #8Million-Strong

Lacie Ross lowered her phone and dropped her Giella designer handbag as she flopped into her chair. She stared at the small, gray box on her desk, worried if she opened it, she'd find something mundane inside rather than the fulfillment of a hope she'd cherished since sixth grade. A glance around the cubicle farm revealed her sleepy-eyed coworkers trickling into the office, coffees in hand, starting another uneventful day. They emanated invisible waves of tedium that failed to diminish Lacie's excitement.

Her fingertips slid across the smooth cardboard.

Once she opened it she would have to choose.

Biting her lip, she flipped back the lid.

A pin of etched, gray steel in the shape of a stylized seabird nested on a silk cloth inside. The logo of the Albatross. Its eye—a red LED—blinked, inviting Lacie to become one of Boyette's Citizen-Protectors, unlikely heroes who sacrificed their time and effort to protect the city. Some provided expertise or access to specialized information. Others used their jobs or social positions to monitor criminals or draw them out with misleading information. A few performed special assignments never made public. All earned the city's gratitude.

Lacie knew by heart the Albatross' slogans from his public service ads on the Internet, TV, and posters on the streets and subways, all branded with his signature avian silhouette.

Boyette City—Eight Million Protectors Strong.
If You See Something, Say Something—I'm Listening.
Your Streets. Your Duty.
Hang the Albatross Around the Neck of Crime.

Boyette's anonymous defender flew watch drones around-the-clock in every part of the city and monitored it through thousands of mobile devices whose owners downloaded his "Eyes Everywhere" app—yet Lacie had never thought he'd ever really see *her*, let alone choose her for a Citizen-Protector.

She balanced the pin on her fingertips. The eye winked on, off, on, off.

Those who accepted wore their pins every day, marked for life as Citizen-Protectors. Those who declined only waited until the blinking ceased and an acid reservoir dissolved the pin from the inside out. Growing up, Lacie's circle of friends had asked each other a thousand times how they would choose.

"Morning, Lacie. I swear the subway gets more crowded every day. If I didn't—" Sarah Lagos shuffled into their shared cubicle and plopped her tote bag by her chair before the sight of the pin startled her. "You've been called! What does he want?"

"I have to wear it to find out."

"Are you going to?"

Pulse racing, Lacie smiled then pinned the gray bird to her blouse.

It perched above her heart, a badge of honor not yet earned.

She downloaded the Albatross's app, which she'd never expected to need, and a gray bird, identical to her pin, appeared on her phone screen. "Connecting" flashed across its wingspan. The pin's eye blinked from red to green. Lacie's phone buzzed. The steel bird vibrated in reply, syncing, and its eye dimmed to a steady, cool blue.

A grid of four options resolved onscreen. Lacie tapped the globe icon and opened a map of the city's downtown waterfront. The social media icon led to a swarm of links to follow the Albatross. A gear icon brought up a menu of app settings. The last icon, the Albatross' logo, revealed her mission. She tapped it, and the word "Accepted" appeared at the top of the screen beside a running count: "22 of 30." Then Lacie's phone buzzed and the count rose to "23."

Sarah looked over her shoulder. "What does he want you to do?"

Lacie skimmed the text. "Go to a warehouse on Morcey Avenue by 10 a.m. and wait for more instructions."

"Do you think when he watches us he sees us…you know, in the shower and *stuff*? Rick and I were *bad* last night."

Lacie laughed. "You're awful. Pathetic and awful."

"Yet *very* satisfied," Sarah said, smirking. "Mr. Harris is going to be pissed. We have an audit this morning."

"Tough, the law's the law, and I accepted the call."

@TheAlbatross
8:22 A.M. Boyette, this safe, peaceful morning is brought to you by YOU! Never lose your streets again. #8MillionStrong #YourStreetsYourDuty

@TheAlbatross
8:24 A.M. Never forget the mean streets and the bad old days. Download "EyesEverywhere" in all app stores. #8MillionStrong #EyesEverywhere

"No friggin' way," Smitty said.

Marc Thorner groaned and stared at the blinking red light. The pin sat in its open box beside his huddled camera bag and a palisade of lenses and partly disassembled cameras. He tried to decide what agitated him more—the call or Smitty's overheated reaction.

"What are you going to do? You've been called, and the clock's ticking, man. You have to choose."

Thorner flashed Smitty a warning look. "I *know*. For Pete's sake, the thing's blinking right in front of me."

"Let it burn itself out. We've got work to do."

"If I accept, maybe I can help someone."

"If you ignore it, you can help *me* with the shoots we've got scheduled today."

"I mean I could help someone in need, not someone who double books his gigs."

"Well, fine, and all you'll give in return for the opportunity to help an anonymous psycho is your tacit approval of the Albatross' monstrous invasion of our privacy, your efforts, time, and expertise, or whatever he needs—uncompensated, I might add—and oh, yeah, maybe risk your life. All to play sidekick to Big Brother with a messiah complex."

"We've been safe for years, haven't we? Remember the Little Korea shoot and $35,000 in gear? Nothing like that's happened since the Albatross. He took Boyette back. We have to keep it. Don't we?"

Smitty rubbed his eyes. "Sure. *Eight million protectors strong.* Or as I think of us: eight million rats in a maze with a narcissistic, voyeuristic, tech-freak owner."

"It's not like he watches us all 24/7. How could he? Algorithms tell him who can help."

"He still records it all. No one asked him to do what he does. You owe him nothing."

"I wouldn't be doing this for the Albatross," said Thorner.

"He's the only one asking."

"Uh-uh. How many hundreds of people have stepped up as Citizen-Protectors since he pulled the city from the brink of disaster? How can I enjoy the safety they sacrificed to provide and then refuse to do my part?"

"You're allowed to decline."

Thorner frowned. "Boyette's our home. When Nass Corp tried to move the Peacemakers to a stadium across the river you blew your stack, but this you have a problem with? You want fifteen murders a week again and the old mean streets back?"

Smitty frowned. "Nass Corp messed with *our* city."

"And we stopped them."

"The Albatross messes with it even *worse*."

"Ah, forget it, man. I have to do this."

Shaking his head, Thorner pinned the gray bird on his shirt and synced it to his phone. He found a map directing him to 10 Morcey Avenue then opened the mission instructions. The count at the top of his screen rose to "24 of 30."

@TheAlbatross
8:58 A.M. Ready to open the gray box? Stay fit & train to be a Citizen-Protector at any accredited CP school. #8MillionStrong #YourStreetsYourDuty

@TheAlbatross
9:04 A.M. Hello, hello? This thing on? Are the sheep listening? I hope so. I have stories to tell. #TheAlbatrossLies

Robbie Nunez chewed on his fingernail and stared at the gray box atop the hood of his beaten-up Honda Acura in the alley behind his mother's row house. He flicked the top open, and the steel bird pin inside blinked at him. It made no sense for the Albatross to recruit a punk he'd almost nabbed on half a dozen night patrols. Robbie counted himself lucky for his freedom. His old high-school crew sat rotting away up in Morrow Penitentiary, while he hustled counterfeit designer handbags and stolen cigarettes for Gary the Skeeve. Not exactly Citizen-Protector material.

Let it dissolve.

Forget you ever saw it.

Except Robbie had never forgotten how it felt to wonder. A glimmer of memory inspired him to snatch up the pin, and for a moment he fell back into his six-year-old self with swimming goggles on, brandishing a water pistol, playing the Albatross with all the kids on the block. None of them understood the hero's name except that it had come from some old poem about a sailor who kills a lucky bird that brought good weather then hangs the carcass from his neck for punishment. They took turns as the hero, back in the days before they learned how the streets worked, when Robbie still believed he could grow up better than his brother and his father, become a fireman or an EMT or maybe a teacher. Anything but the punk he'd grown into.

He put on the pin and synced it with his phone.

The count rose to "25 of 30."

@TheAlbatross
9:06 A.M. Bright sun, safe streets, rotten odor. Enjoy your last morning as prisoners! It all changes today. #YourStreets YourCage #TheAlbatrossLies

@TheAlbatross
9:10 A.M. Rainbows swirl in a toxic film on the St. John's. Let's sink this false savior where it belongs. #FoolPatrol #YourStreetssYourGarbage

@TheAlbatross
9:12 A.M. Carrie Jones. Ned Lopez. Kami Takahashi. Citizen-Protectors who never came home. An indifferent city shrugs. #CannonFodder #FoolPatrol

Keysha Warner nearly crushed the gray box on her stoop as she stepped out for morning coffee....

Chetan Majumdar found his with his morning mail at the convenience store he owned by the 18th Street subway station....

Lester Goldberg's awaited him by his favorite seat at the diner counter where he ate a knish every morning....

Nancy Chernenko picked up her gray box from the back seat of the limousine that drove her to work in the financial district....

Sam Carter tossed a wet paint brush into a shadowed corner and pinned the steel bird to his jacket...

...and the count reached "30 of 30."

@TheAlbatross
9:21 A.M. Traffic Tip: Three-car accident blocking Giordano Drive, north of Biro Ave. Try the 47th St. bypass. #MorningPatrol #EyesInTheSky

@TheAlbatross
9:23 A.M. Traffic Tip: Stay home. Draw the blinds. Think for yourselves. Own your lives. #EyesOpen #TheAlbatrossLies

@TheAlbatross
9:24 A.M. If You See Something, Say Something—He's Listening. To everything you say. All the time. And recording it. #8MillionWrong #TheAlbatrossSpies

Dust painted a furry skin on Kara Rawlins' fingertips as she unwrapped a pottery shard from the Egyptian Third Dynasty. The artifact bored her, but she cataloged it with the rest of the articles delivered from the Cairo Museum for a six-month-long exchange with the Boyette World Culture Museum. She hoped to finish before the Albatross brought the Gray Bird into the hangar two floors below for refueling. Her computer beeped an alert, and the monitor lit up, indicating a Citizen-Protector pin going live. Raising an eyebrow, Kara set down the shard, moved to her keyboard, and launched her tracking software. A map of Boyette appeared with avatars to show the location of the pins—twenty-five of them converging on Morcey Avenue. Two more came online while she watched.

Kara, who'd never seen so many pins live at once, shot back in her chair, and dialed the phone.

A gruff, weary voice answered. "Morning, Kara."

"Morning, boss. You in trouble?"

"No. City's quiet. Drone 73SJ is posting sunrise shots of the Gray Bird over the St. John's to InstaSnap. Why?"

"A pin lit up on the grid."

"I haven't called anyone since Park and Simms. We deactivated them hours ago."

"Right, so you probably also didn't put out twenty-seven calls."

"Hell, no." All weariness left the Albatross' voice. "I'm launching the tracker. What the—? Run the pin numbers, make sure they're not old ones coming back online somehow."

"Did it while we were talking. They're fresh but out of sequence from your last round." Kara sighed and rubbed her eyes. "Maybe someone stole a bunch of pins?"

"Like winning the lottery. It's *possible* but damn unlikely. And why the delay on the alert? The first one came online at 6:20, but they started pinging only a minute ago. Someone's in our system."

Kara gasped. "Three more just came online."

"I'm cutting to the west side waterfront now. The first ones will reach Morcey before me. Dig deep with your diagnostics. Keep me in the loop."

"Roger that, boss."

@TheAlbatross
9:33 A.M. You help more than you know. No one is called to do more than they can. Do your part for Boyette. #CitizenProtectors #YourStreetsYourDuty

@TheAlbatross
9:38 A.M. Help the Albatross! Play sidekick! Get maimed! Tracy Martin lost an arm. Eleanor Kozloski lost a leg. Yay! #CannonFodder #8MillionWrong

@TheAlbatross
9:40 A.M. I helped the Albatross and all I got was a lousy pin, a total loss of privacy, and traumatic stress disorder. #GuiltShamed #8MillionWrong

The Gray Bird cut downtown over Guardineer Heights, running on autopilot. The Albatross drew a cup of coffee from the cockpit carafe then ripped open a protein bar and bit into it. A collage of scenes from the phones and drones monitoring the west-side waterfront flared to life on his video feeds. People wearing the pins lit up red. Their likenesses auto-sorted into rows, where biometric recognition programs tagged them with personal data.

The Albatross recognized none of them.

His database listed the Morcey Avenue warehouse abandoned after a bankruptcy. It came as no surprise to find, beneath layers of corporate camouflage, that a Nass Corp bank now held the title. No matter how often he exposed their corruption, Nass Corp crept deeper and deeper into life in Boyette, an ultra-rich cabal intent on taking the city.

On the tracking display, thirty avatars rushed toward the unknown.

Someone had wanted the Albatross to see them all responding only after it was too late to stop whatever had been set in motion.

The Gray Bird's engines revved as the aircraft shifted into hover mode. On the video link, the warehouse doors hung open as would-be Citizen-Protectors trickled into the building.

He dialed Kara. "Status?"

"I'm on it, dammit, don't rush me!"

"Clock's ticking, Kara."

"You think I don't know that? We've been hacked hard. Did you see the Twitter feed?"

"No, the AI is running it."

"It was. That's hacked too. They're posting the names of dead CPs."

"Shut it down."

"Trying! I'm mostly locked out. The malignant code is covered up better than a redhead on the beach at noon, but there's something familiar—oh, no!"

"What'd you find?"

"A tease embedded in the code. We were meant to find this. It's Sebastian Volchenko. He's freelancing for Nass Corp. Says they're going to pull the ground out from under you so Boyette falls."

"Are you sure? Volchenko hasn't been active for two years."

"I don't know anyone else this good. It's going to be hard to purge."

"Do what you can."

The Albatross cut the connection and then lifted his gray-and-white hooded mask from where it hung bunched at the base of his neck. He drew it over his head, leaving only his chin, mouth, and nose exposed. The mask's lenses switched on his heads-up display, continuing the video feed. Parking the Gray Bird in hover, he dropped into the cargo compartment, left empty while his custom SUV that usually occupied it remained at the hangar for repairs.

The lower hatch opened onto empty sky.

@TheAlbatross
9:49 A.M. Citizen-Protector program suspended! Report gray boxes to albatross@albatross.com or BCPD. Do not open! #CitizensAlert #8MillionStrong

@TheAlbatross
9:52 A.M. Due to ethical difficulties, the Albatross will soon be suspended. Open your eyes, not gray boxes! #Citizens Alert #TheAlbatrossLies

"Hello? Anyone here?"

"Back here."

Lacie followed the deep voice into a cavernous, empty storeroom, walking through shafts of gauzy sunlight that leaked in via high, grimy windows. The air smelled of overheated dust and damp wood. A man in a fedora, an Albatross pin on his jacket, and a camera case slung from one shoulder, stood with a group, all wearing identical pins. They gathered around a sloppy rendering of the Albatross' logo on the floor.

"I'm Marc Thorner," the man said.

"Lacie Ross. What's this?"

"An answer without a question. The paint's still tacky."

More people entered the room, and Thorner waved them over.

A young man in frayed jeans and a black muscle shirt stood aloof, chewing his fingernail.

Thorner frowned at the man. "You all right, buddy?"

"Something's wrong here," he said.

"What do you mean?" asked Lacie.

"This many CPs? It ain't right."

"What's your name?" Thorner offered his hand, and the man shook it.

"Robbie. You ever see the Albatross thank this many CPs after a patrol? Uh-uh, no way. Two, three at most. This is bogus. Maybe it isn't him. Maybe these pins are fakes."

Lacie shook her head. "No way. The pin's as real as it gets."

"Yeah? Think you would know?" Robbie pointed to Lacie's Giella handbag. "You buy that in Macy's or Aparo Square?"

"Aparo Square."

"Then the closest Giella came to that bag is if he flew over Boyette City while I drove it in from Swanderson in the trunk of my car. One-hundred percent made in Malaysia, and you can't tell the difference. Show's what you know."

Lacie blushed.

"Alright, easy, now. If you're right then who gave them to us?" asked Thorner.

A rumble and a crash rolled from the depths of the warehouse. Dust drizzled down from the ceiling. The hum of hidden motors filled the lull.

Backing away from the group, Robbie shook his head. "Don't know. Don't want to find out." He heeled around and ran as another rattling crash vibrated the building.

A gray-blue blur flashed by one of the high windows like a giant, gliding bird before hidden gears clanked and steel barriers dropped over every opening. Only three steps from freedom, Robbie stumbled trying to stop and slammed against a steel plate that lowered over the exit.

"Damn, no!" He smacked his hand against the blockade.

Murky shadows descended, and cries of panic rose from the crowd. Rectangles of light shone in the gloom as people tried to use phones without a signal. The eyes on everyone's pins changed from cool blue to fiery orange. Then every phone in the room rang or buzzed. Their screens brightened with a video of the group in the warehouse gathered around the Albatross' logo on the floor, which segued to a clip from a different angle, then to a view of three Citizen-Protectors crossing Morcey Avenue. More clips cycled in a slideshow documenting the CPs from when they found their gray box that morning to now.

A fervent voice came over the speakers.

@TheAlbatross
10:02 A.M. All citizens are advised to avoid the lower waterfront by Morcey Ave. Use alternate routes. #CitizensAlert #EyesEv-
erywhere

@TheAlbatross
10:03 A.M.: All citizens are advised to avoid the Albatross. Don't be owned, Boyette! Fight the real enemy! #TheAlbatrossLies #EverythingChangesToday

On the warehouse's shaking rooftop, the Albatross glimpsed the slideshow in his heads-up display. The videos revealed a warehouse of sagging boards, peeling paint, cracked plaster and a group of anxious CPs. He dialed up the volume: "...montage compiled from the Albatross' own video surveillance to show Boyette City how naïve they are to trust their so-called protector. The Albatross' drones watch every inch of your city. His messages play on all your devices. They bombard you in your homes and bedrooms and offices so he can drag you into a fight he started for his own glory but sells to you as your own. Why do you trip over yourselves to leap into danger for his benefit when he calls? Do you simply swallow his lie that if you don't comply the bad old days will come roaring back?"

Voice recognition software produced no matches, suggesting disguised audio.

The Albatross sized up the steel barriers visible in the warehouse backgrounds then he leapt off the building and snapped open his jacket to unfurl his gliders, riding them until he lit beside a window. His fist, protected by a thick glove, shattered a glass pane, exposing the steel plate behind it.

"You trade freedom for plush cages and clean streets. You prostrate yourselves before the all-knowing, all-seeing eye of an aerial, would-be god, mistaking his presence for a good omen rather than a sign of peril. Let me be your Ancient Mariner, Boyette. Let me take this Albatross from 'round your neck. At 10:30 this morning, thirty of the faithful shall die for their trust in the Albatross and his ludicrous campaign against imagined threats. The Albatross cannot save them. No one can. You can save yourselves only by breaking free of the cage you've built around your city."

A liquid stream ate into the steel plate, melting it as the Albatross used an acid spray from his equipment belt. A sequence of eye blinks launched aural filters in his cowl, dampening ambient noises, such as the wind and the Gray Bird's engines, while amplifying sounds from within the warehouse. Crying. Shouting. Footsteps.

The acid dissolved the upper corner of the plate. He angled it to a lower corner, which soon gave way, and two minutes later the other corners disintegrated too. Voice commands summoned the Gray Bird, which dropped a rescue line from its cargo hatch. The Albatross grabbed the line and swung away from the warehouse to build momentum. As he threw his weight against the steel plate, a series of growling booms quaked the building from within. Breathing deeply, the Albatross slammed feet first into the steel barrier.

It plunged into an inferno. Fire licked out chased by threads of smoke rising on rippling heat. The Albatross pulled a breathing mask over his mouth and nose and then hurled himself through the opening.

@TheAlbatross
10:24 A.M. Morcey Ave. and the lower waterfront are closed. Keep streets clear for first responders en route. #CitizensAlert #EyesEverywhere

@TheAlbatross
10:25 A.M. Freedom frightens, fire does too, Albatross is a psycho, who wants to use you—and toss you away lIke garbage. #KillTheBird #BreakTheCage

Flames covered the warehouse walls where incendiary tape ignited. Black and gray smoke filled the room. The Citizen-Protectors dropped to crawls.

"Only ways out of here are through the roof or underground," Robbie said.

Thorner pushed back his fedora and wiped sweat from his brow. "If you know how to reach either one, lead the way."

Coughing on smoke, Lacie pointed at a high window. "Wait! What's that?"

The steel plate jolted inward, toppling to a floor-shaking impact. A gray-and-white figure leapt in through the opening. Acrid smoke wrung tears from Lacie's eyes, blurring everything, and she lost sight of him.

The heat rose, and the smoke grew thicker. The other Citizen-Protectors bustled past Lacie on hands and knees, desperate for a way out. A rooftop explosion shook everything and sent a massive rain of wood, steel, and plaster into an empty corner. The fire surged as it gulped fresh oxygen. Lacie's eyes burned. Her throat ached for moisture, her lungs for cool air. She wanted to run and pound on the steel barrier, but she watched someone try and only burn their hands. A shadow appeared in the haze above the hole in the ceiling.

Rising smoke corkscrewed, caught in the Gray Bird's hover-jet stream.

The ship spit streams of white foam that fought back the fire, generating massive clouds of steamy white smoke. Soupy fire-repellant poured down, dousing the area below the hole, and then three lines unfurled into the room.

Lacie glimpsed the Albatross, powerful, assured, his gray-and-white uniform a beacon in the chaos. The Citizen-Protectors rushed to him, and he sent them up the lines one at a time, the Gray Bird's winches hauling them into the cargo compartment, dropping fresh lines for each one that rose. Lacie, Thorner, and Robbie helped those disoriented or overcome by heat and smoke then waited to ascend with the Albatross. As they finally breached the roof and cool air washed over them, the Albatross slipped off his breathing mask. He smiled, and gave Lacie a thumbs up. The gesture made her feel vulnerable yet strong for weathering the fire and helping the others, for being a Citizen-Protector. Adrenaline electrified her. She wondered how anyone could do this every day. Then hands from above pulled her into the Gray Bird's crowded cargo compartment as the aircraft rose away from the burning warehouse.

> @TheAlbatross
> 10:37 A.M. BCPD asks all citizens to avoid Morcey Ave. below 19th St. until a warehouse fire is under control. #CitizensAlert #EyesEverywhere

> @TheAlbatross
> 10:42 A.M. All citizens are asked to understand there is more than one way to kill a bird and his ugly ducklings. #CannonFodder #KillTheBird

"Kara, alert Sutton Memorial. I'm bringing thirty patients to the E.R. Smoke inhalation, maybe worse. ETA, four minutes."

"Roger that, boss."

The Albatross locked in the course then moved to the cargo compartment. The stares of the rescued drilled into him. In their faces he read a conflict between their trust of him and the way of life he'd brought to Boyette and the reality of the near-fatal encounter to which it had led them. Biometrics scanners in his heads-up display showed a roster of racing pulses and elevated body temperatures. Soot streaked their faces, inky smudges cut through by tears. Many of them coughed into their sleeves or wiped ashy mucus from their noses.

The Albatross took a deep breath. "I'm sorry you all had to go through that."

"Why'd you send us in there?" Nancy Chernenko asked.

"I didn't. You're wearing counterfeit pins. Whoever sent the video hacked my system and set us up."

"To die, to make you look bad," said Robbie.

The Albatross nodded.

"We trusted you," Chetan Majumdar said.

"I'm grateful for that, and I saved you," the Albatross said.

"We never should've been in danger in the first place," Lester Goldberg said.

"Aren't your systems secure?" Keysha Warner said.

"We're not expendable," Chernenko said.

"No, you're not. But did you think we could achieve what we have in Boyette without risk? You could've refused the call. Be proud you stood up for your city."

Majumdar dismissed him with a wave. "Maybe this Mariner guy's right. Nothing bad happens except where you're around."

An argument erupted, and angry voices filled the tight quarters. The Albatross tried to calm them No one listened. Only the few who'd helped others in the warehouse defended him. About half a dozen people.

He turned to hoist himself to the cockpit when a partially melted phone thrown from the crowd struck the side of his head. He dropped back to the cargo room. A fist sent waves of pain through his jaw, jarring him against the bulkhead. A sweeping kick knocked his attacker to the floor, but others came. Their eyes burned with fear and anger. They kicked and scratched him. He deflected the blows, straining not to injure them. Voices screaming for reason submerged beneath the rabble. Others, too hurt or shocked to act, cowered against the bulkhead. The Gray Bird banked, signaling arrival at the hospital, but it needed the

Albatross to land. He surged against the crowd, forcing a path to the cockpit.

An angry voice cut through the din, amplified and distorted like the one from the video.

"Stay, Albatross. Do as I say, maybe I'll let a few live to tell what happened today."

The crowd parted to reveal a thin man, with white hair and dark circles under his eyes. A gray bird pin hung from his lapel. He inched toward the Albatross, opening his threadbare jacket to expose two canisters strapped to his torso and wired to a trigger on his belt.

"I've been with you all morning, recording everything, like you, so no one will ever forget the horror you brought us."

"You brought this to us, not me," the Albatross said. "What's in the tanks?"

"Enough Saladino gas no one will be able to open the Gray Bird for a day after I release it. But I've brought four doses of antidote. Cooperate and I'll let you choose who survives—except you, of course."

"Maybe no one should if you think we're all so bad," the Albatross said.

"See? To you, we're nothing but resources to be wasted. Like my daughter was."

Seizing on the clue, the Albatross ordered a facial-recognition search of likely familial relations for the man in front of him. His computers matched him to a CP from five years ago, one of the few who'd died because she helped him: Joanie Carter, age 27.

"You're Sam Carter," the Albatross said. "I remember Joanie. I grieved for her, but the evidence she provided stopped crimes that would've killed dozens or more. She died a hero."

"She died heartbroken and alone because, like these fools, she idolized you."

"She chose to help," the Albatross said.

"That choice cost her everything. Did it never occur to you how intruding into people's lives might affect them? You left Joanie's pin for her inside her girlfriend's apartment. It scared Miranda so much that you'd broken in, she dumped Joanie. The trauma of working for you and lying to get you the information you needed was hard enough, but then losing Miranda—it was more than

Joanie could cope with. She broke down, lost her job, wound up in treatment for post-traumatic stress disorder. She fell into a depression, and six months after doing your dirty work, she took her own life because you made a ruin of it. You used her like you use all of us."

"He doesn't use us. We have a choice," Thorner said.

"Do you think we're all brainwashed sheep?" Lacie said.

"None of you said no when you found the pins," Carter said.

"We accepted the risk," Lacie said.

Thorner pulled a camera from his case, focused on Carter, and then snapped the shutter. "You're recording us? Fine. I want everyone to see the face of the murderer who killed us so they know we haven't pushed all the scum back into the gutters."

"Put down the camera," Carter said.

"No." Thorner snapped more shots, the images auto-uploading to the cloud.

"Stop taking my picture! That's what *he* does. This isn't about me."

Carter swiped at Thorner, who sidestepped the blow.

Robbie intercepted him, staggering Carter with a punch to his chin. As he recovered, Carter drew a handgun and aimed at Thorner. Robbie charged, knocking him askew as he fired. The report reverberated like a bomb in the small space, but the shot missed its mark, instead striking the Albatross in the chest. The impact knocked him to the floor, gasping for breath.

Lacie knelt by his side, trembling as she pushed his jacket open and looked for a wound she couldn't find. Kevlar mesh had stopped the slug from penetrating.

Robbie grabbed Carter's gun hand and pried the weapon away. Two other men seized Carter's arms and wrestled him to the floor. He slammed the back of his head into one's face, yanked his arm free, and grabbed the trigger on his belt.

"Fine, you all get to die like Joanie!" he screamed.

Lights on the canisters brightened as he pushed the trigger.

Gas hissed from their valves.

Aching and cold with sweat, the Albatross pushed Lacie toward the cockpit and urged her upward. He tugged his face mask back on, finding it harder to breathe through it, then staggered to the cargo bay control board, jerked it open, and tapped in a preset sequence.

Carter died first. His eyes rolled back in his head, and his lips drew to a thin, frozen line before he hit the floor. Then the men holding him fell, their faces twisted in the same hideous way. Then Robbie crumpled like a scarecrow without a stake. Slow to react, Nancy Chernenko and Lester Goldberg collapsed next.

Lacie screamed from the cockpit hatch. Thorner stood below her, holding his breath and still snapping photos. The others pressed themselves to the walls as far from Carter as possible, covered their noses, and stared hopefully at the Albatross.

He hit the final key of the code, and the cargo hatch opened two feet. Daylight streamed in from below. An opalescent mist sprayed out from roof vents, filling the cargo bay with a haze that neutralized the gas and forced it out in a glittering, inert cloud that dispersed behind the Gray Bird. The Albatross pulled his mask away to show the others it was safe to breathe. He gazed at them, Citizen-Protectors, hurt and scared, angry, brave and defiant, and those who lay still beside the body of a man whose pain could've belonged to any one of them.

The Albatross wondered if he'd failed them or if they had failed him, or if they simply walked in the shadows of good and evil, caught up in something larger than them all.

He ascended to the cockpit and landed the Gray Bird at Sutton Memorial.

@TheAlbatross
12:47 P.M. This morning a madman tested our resolve. Stand strong Boyette. Your city needs you. #8MillionStrong #YourStreetsYourDuty

@TheAlbatross
12:53 A.M. Today's Citizen-Protectors: Robbie Nunez, Novick Heights. A grateful city mourns. (1/30) #Citizen-Protectors #8MillionStrong #HonorTheFallen

@TheAlbatross
12:54 A.M. Today's Citizen-Protectors: Lester Goldberg, Lee Park. A grateful city mourns. (2/30) #Citizen-Protectors #8MillionStrong #HonorTheFallen

Lacie eyed the pins on the handful of Citizen-Protectors gathered around Robbie Nunez's grave. Hundreds had attended the funeral and memorial service to honor Robbie, and when the crowd left, only a few like Lacie and Thorner and Robbie's grieving mother remained. Mrs. Nunez wrapped her rosary beads around her son's Albatross pin and clutched it in her hand. Her daughters stood on either side of her, holding her up. Lacie saw pride in the woman's mournful expression, as if Robbie's last acts had proven something she'd known all along about her son—that he was a good boy who did the right thing when it counted.

Across the cemetery, a separate crowd loitered behind barricades and mounted police. They carried posters reading: *The Mariner Was Right, Take Back Boyette*, and *No More Prying Eyes*. The city hadn't seen as much turmoil in ten years as it had in the week since the Mariner and Volchenko hijacked the Citizen-Protector system. The Albatross had gone public about the event, live-streamed a speech from Palmer Park, answered questions, and laid out the evidence of how people involved with Nass Corp had hired Volchenko, goaded Carter to act, and funded his death trap. The Mariner's videos and Thorner's photos of those awful moments in the Gray Bird brought the truth forward but provided no answers, and people could make anything they wanted of the truth. Lacie fiddled with her gray bird pin, worn on her lapel and wondered if the damage could ever be undone.

BIOGRAPHIES

Award-winning author and editor **Danielle Ackley-McPhail** has worked both sides of the publishing industry for longer than she cares to admit. Currently, she is a project editor and promotions manager for Dark Quest Books. In 2014 she joined forces with husband Mike McPhail and friend Greg Schauer to form her own publishing house, eSpec Books ().

Her published works include five urban fantasy novels, *Yesterday's Dreams, Tomorrow's Memories, Today's Promise, The Halfling's Court:* and *The Redcaps' Queen: A Bad-Ass Faerie Tale*, and a young adult Steampunk novel, *Baba Ali and the Clockwork Djinn*, written with Day Al-Mohamed. She is also the senior editor of the *Bad-Ass Faeries* anthology series, *Dragon's Lure*, and *In an Iron Cage*. Her short stories are included in numerous other anthologies and collections.

She is a member of Broad Universe, a writer's organization focusing on promoting the works of women authors in the speculative genres.

Danielle lives in New Jersey with husband and fellow writer, Mike McPhail and two extremely spoiled cats. To learn more about her work, visit www.sidhenadaire.com, www.especbooks.com, www.badassfaeries.com, or look her up on social media.

Gail Z. Martin is the author of the new epic fantasy novel *Shadow and Flame* (Orbit Books) which is Book Three in the *Ascendant Kingdoms Saga*; *Iron and Blood: The Jake Desmet Adventures* a new Steampunk series (Solaris Books) co-authored with Larry N. Martin and *Vendetta: A Deadly Curiosities Novel* in her urban fantasy series set in Charleston, SC (Solaris Books); and. She is also author of *Ice Forged, Reign of Ash* and *War of Shadows* in *The*

Ascendant Kingdoms Saga, The Chronicles of The Necromancer series (*The Summoner, The Blood King, Dark Haven, Dark Lady's Chosen*) from Solaris Books and *The Fallen Kings Cycle* (*The Sworn, The Dread*) from Orbit Books. Gail writes two series of ebook short stories: *The Jonmarc Vahanian Adventures* and the *Deadly Curiosities Adventures* and her work has appeared in over 20 US/UK anthologies.

Follow her at www.AscendantKingdoms.com, on Twitter @GailZMartin, on Facebook.com/WinterKingdoms, at DisquietingVisions.com blog andGhostInTheMachinePodcast.com, on Goodreads https://www.goodreads.com/GailZMartin and free excerpts on Wattpad http://wattpad.com/GailZMartin.

Larry N. Martin fell in love with fantasy and science fiction when he was a teenager. After a twenty-five year career in Corporate America, Larry started working full-time with his wife, author Gail Z. Martin and discovered that his writing and editing skills transitioned well to fiction and that he had a knack for storytelling, plotting and character development as well. While *Iron and Blood* is their first official collaboration, readers have benefited from Larry's contributions on several earlier works. On the rare occasions when Larry isn't working on book-related things, he enjoys pottery, cooking, and reading.

Bryan J.L. Glass is the multiple Harvey Award winning co-creator/writer of *The Mice Templar* from Image Comics, and of *Furious* from Dark Horse Comics.

A contributor to DC Comics' *Adventures of Superman*, his Marvel Comics credentials include *Thor: Crown of Fools, First Thunder* and *Valkyrie*, as well as adapting *Magician, the Riftwar Saga* and Cirque du Soleil's *KÀ*.

Bryan's first work in the comic industry was in the role of photographer, providing photo covers and interiors to such 80s series as *The Elementals, Mage,* and *Punisher Armory*. His earliest writing projects in the '90s were *Spandex Tights* and *Ship of Fools*. After a brief hiatus from the industry, Bryan returned in 2003 with his first *Mice Templar* short stories, followed by *Quixote: A Novel* and *86 Voltz: The Dead Girl*. www.bryanjlglass.com.

John L. French has worked for over thirty years as a crime scene investigator and has seen more than his share of murders, shootings and serious assaults. As a break from the realities of his job, he writes science fiction, pulp, horror, fantasy, and, of course, crime fiction. Since 1992 John has been writing stories partly based on his experiences on the streets of what some have called one of the most dangerous cities in the country. His books include *The Devil of Harbor City, Past Sins, Souls on Fire, Here There Be Monsters* and *Paradise Denied.* He's also written several books with co-conspirator Patrick Thomas, the latest of which is *The Assassins' Ball.* John is the editor of *Bad Cop, No Donut, Mermaids 13: Tales of the Sea,* and *With Great Power....* One of these days John will get a website and a Facebook page but in the meantime he can be contacted at jfrenchfam@aol.com.

Walt Ciechanowski is an award-winning author and developer who primarily writes for the roleplaying games industry, contributing to such lines as *DC Adventures, Doctor Who, Dungeons & Dragons, Mutants & Masterminds, Rotted Capes,* and *Victoriana.* He is also a founding contributor to *Gnome Stew* and has co-written several books offering roleplaying advice. Outside of the roleplaying game industry, Walt has also contributed a short story to the anthology *The Stories in Between.* Walt lives in Springfield, Pennsylvania with his wife Helena and his three children, Leianna, Stephen, and Zoeanna.

Kathleen O'Shea David started working with puppets when she was 2, and over 40 years later she is still "wiggling dolls" for fun and profit. Along the way she picked up a few more skills and careers. She has done just about everything from cancer research to rock and roll. Some of her favorite jobs have been in puppetry, theater and publishing. With her husband Peter David, she adapted the first four issues of the Japanese Manga *Negima.* She is the author of the short story "On a Pedestal" in the Big Finish anthology *Doctor Who: Quality of Leadership.* She is currently an associate editor for *Time and Space* magazine. Her costumes have won numerous awards for both presentation and workmanship.

She is a book editor, the owner of No String Attached (Custom Puppets, Masks, and Dolls). Her puppets are in collections all over the world.

Robert Greenberger met his first superhero when he was six years old, never imagining that he would work alongside them at DC Comics and Marvel Comics for much of his adult life. Additionally, he created *Comics Scene*, the first nationally distributed newsstand magazine to cover the world of heroes and villains. His written works include nonfiction (*The Essential Batman Encyclopedia*) and fiction (*Iron Man: Femme Fatales*), celebrating the brave deeds of these characters. A co-founder of Crazy 8 Press, he is creating his own protagonists in new worlds. His alter ego is that of a high school English teacher and makes his home in Maryland.

You can learn more at www.bobgreenberger.com.

James Chambers writes tales of horror, crime, fantasy, and science fiction. He is the author of *The Engines of Sacrifice*, a collection of four Lovecraftian-inspired novellas published by Dark Regions Press which *Publisher's Weekly* described in a starred-review as "...chillingly evocative...." He is also the author of the short fiction collections *Resurrection House* (Dark Regions Press) and *The Midnight Hour: Saint Lawn Hill and Other Tales*, in collaboration with illustrator Jason Whitley as well as the dark, urban fantasy novella, *Three Chords of Chaos* and *The Dead Bear Witness* and *Tears of Blood*, volume one and two in his Corpse Fauna novella series.

His short stories have been published in the anthologies *The Avenger: Roaring Heart of the Crucible*, *Chiral Mad 2*, *Dark Furies*, *The Dead Walk*, *Deep Cuts*, *The Domino Lady: Sex as a Weapon*, *Dragon's Lure*, *Fantastic Futures 13*, *The Green Hornet Chronicles*, *Hardboiled Cthulhu*, *In An Iron Cage*, *No Longer Dreams*, *Shadows Over Main Street*, *The Spider: Extreme Prejudice*, *Qualia Nous*, *Reel Dark*, *Truth or Dare*, *TV Gods*, *Walrus Tales*, *Warfear*, and the *Bad-Ass Faeries* and *Defending the Future* series as well as the magazines *Bare Bone*, *Cthulhu Sex*, and *Allen K's Inhuman*.

He has also edited and written numerous comic books including *Leonard Nimoy's Primortals*, the critically acclaimed "The Revenant" in *Shadow House*, the Midnight Hour for *Negative Burn*, and the original graphic novel *Kolchak, The Night Stalker: The Poe Crimes*.

The Ranks of the Heroic

Ali T. Kokmen
Kelly Farmer
Evaristo Ramos, Jr.
Patrick McPhail
Sara Hefner
Susan Carlson
Robby Thrasher
Sam Tomaino
Missy Gunnels Katano
Larry "Lordlnyc" Nelson
Raphael Sutton
Meredith Peruzzi
Andrew Hatchell
Yes
Donald J. Bingle, Writer on Demand
Peter Young
Doug "Valhalar" Triplett
Chris Volcheck
Wrinkles Lord of the Lawn Chair
Phaminator
Andy Pavlik
Tom Bither
Tom B
Matt P
Anna Zahn
Tina Randleman
William Wiebking
Christa Brolley
Dion Smallwood
Sharon VanBlarcom

Evan Sturtevant
Lark Cunningham
Lee
Neil A Ottenstein
Cathy Franchett
Pat Hayes
Leave Blank
Andy Holman
That Blair Guy
Lorraine J. Anderson
Brendan Lonehawk
Eric Gasior
Lady Ozma
Bill Simoni
Josh Pritchett
Christopher J. Burke
Elaine Tindill-Rohr
Mike Thurlow
Launi Purcell
Jessica Reid
Ruth Fletcher Gage
M Burton Hopkins Jr
Mary Catelynn Cunningham
John Idlor
Pepita Hogg-Sonnenberg
Erik T Johnson
Yes
Katherine Hempel
Jenn Whitworth
Maurice Hopkins
Lora McQueen
Michael Abbott
Jerry Alexandratos
Heather Selbe
okay
"Raging" Randall Lemon
Lois Johnson
John L. French
Tom Berrisford

thatraja
Edward Greaves
Alan Danziger
Nicholas Ahlhelm
John Green
Chris Imershein
Danielle Ackley-McPhail
The Schneider Boys
Jeff Metzner
Guy McLimore
Ashley Stryker
Rich Gonzalez
Jay Zastrow
Maricus
Margaret S. McGraw
Jeffrey Jenkins
Svend Andersen
Umbroso Dragonsworn
Steve Lord
Anonymous
The Archive
Andrew Kaplan
Michael Kahan
Michael A. Burstein
Katherine Malloy
sam m
Janito Vaqueiro Ferreira Filho
JW
D-Rock
Amanda Johnson
Andrew J Clark IV
Samantha Bryant, Author of *Going Through the Change*
Stephen Ballentine
Lisa Panzer
Brian Lintz
Cindy Allen
Sean McGarry
ed z
Mark Lukens

Linda Silverman
Tomas Burgos-Caez
Shiny
Alyce Wilson

and...
YOU

THE SIDE OF EVIL

Edited by

GREG SCHAUER
DANIELLE ACKLEY-McPHAIL

eSPEC BOOKS

Stratford, NJ

PUBLISHED BY
eSpec Books LLC
Danielle McPhail, Publisher
PO Box 493,
Stratford, New Jersey 08084
www.especbooks.com

ISBN (trade paper): 978-1-942990-03-1
ISBN (ebook): 978-1-942990-16-1

Icons: Mike McPhail, McP Digital Graphics

Interior Design: Sidhe na Daire Multimedia
                  www.sidhenadaire.com

Dedication

To Heath Ledger
The Joker is Wild
1979 - 2008

Villainous Autographs

Greg Schauer

James M. Ward

Drew Bittner

Janine K. Spendlove

Aaron Rosenberg

Peter David

Keith R.A. DeCandido

James Chambers

Contents

Introduction

We should be sincere enough to admit
that we love evil too well to give it up.
—Mahatma Gandhi

On its own, humanity is a destructive force.
It needs a master." —Ra's Al Ghul

SOME VILLAINS BECOME EVIL IN THE NAME OF A GREATER GOOD. Characters like Magneto and Ra's Al Ghul understand that humanity, or a subset of humanity, must be protected from itself. They are willing to do whatever it takes to create what they perceive to be a better world.

More often their brethren are motivated by greed, driven by ego to nefarious schemes that only benefit themselves. They may be collecting items that are thematically dear to them or merely acquiring great wealth. In either case, they are all seeking the spotlight to gain what they covet.

Others are driven by revenge seeking to redress some real or imagined slight by a hero that has now become their archenemy. Creating newer and grander plots with better equipment to foil, embarrass, or preferably kill their enemy.

Then we have villains like the Joker, sociopaths who don't care what happens during their reign of terror, obsessively trying to fulfill some inner need for destruction and possibly greed.

But whatever inspires them, villains are nothing if not goal-oriented. Whether it is personal, global, or galactic, there is always a goal.

Ya kinda have to admire that.

Think about what it takes to craft such schemes and carry them out. A vision is needed first, robbing a bank or ruling the world, a villain needs a master plan. Then there is acquiring the elements to put the plan into action: Technology or magic or brute force. Whatever it takes to make it happen. Then, and only then, can the vision be carried out. And let none stand in their way or suffer the consequences.

Sure, sometimes there is collateral damage. People die, buildings fall, economies crumble, cities and planets disappear but what are such small sacrifices once one's hearts desire has been achieved?

Isn't that what we all want: our hearts desire?

You know you do.

BWAHAHAHAHA!!

Greg Schauer
"Pusher Man"

Doth Protest Too Much

James M. Ward

"By the work, one knows the workman."

Jean de La Fontaine

HER MOTHER AND FATHER WERE WAITING FOR HER DOWNSTAIRS at the family breakfast table. They were villainous lawyers, the most successful the world had ever known. Today, she would be allowed to start down her own path of true villainy.

"By the work, one knows the workman," the birthday girl of eighteen said over and over again. The quote had a world of meaning for her. She found herself repeating it before every difficult task she took up in her young life.

She skipped down the stairs, happy with her recent choices. Entering the breakfast nook she greeted her parents. "Good morning, Mommy; morning, Daddy."

Her dad closed his laptop. "Crimson, you are glowing today. Happy birthday to you, my darling daughter. By the way, I love the new uniform. That cape and those gloves set off the outfit perfectly."

Crimson Doom spun around in place, showing off her white outfit with the apple red cape. Seeing the smiles of delight from her parents topped off her high feeling of luck.

She sat down and reached for both the orange juice and tomato juice. It was definitely going to be a two-juice day. "Nice of you to say, Daddy."

"I trust it is bullet proof, fire proof, and can't be detected by infra-red or television cameras," her father said worried about his daughter.

"Oh, Daddy, you're so silly." Crimson laughed as she dumped a huge pile of eggs and watermelon on her plate. "We learned the cloak and dagger stuff in sixth grade villainy class. My suit is amazing, just like me. It is stuffed with all the nano-bots my superpowers let me make. It can also change my appearance from a busty female to an old man. The costume is perfect, just like your birthday daughter." She gave her dad a big smile; her mouth bulging with eggs.

Her mother sat down at the table and looked disparagingly at her hair. "Happy birthday, daughter. I still worry about a foe pulling your war braid," her mom admonished for the hundredth time.

"Mom, just stop right there. We've talked and talked about my hair. I am not you. War braids are the style this year for all female villains. Let's talk about something else," Crimson said as she gulped down her breakfast.

"Capital idea, daughter," her dad said smiling at the way she was packing in the food. He remembered his first day in court, thirty-two years ago. "Tell me what you have decided to do for your first act of despicable villainousness."

"I'm going to rob the Industrial and Commercial Bank of China in Macau," she said, bursting with pride. "It's the largest bank in the world. I'm only going to take ten million or so, but it's all going to be in paper currency."

She held up her hand, quieting her mother who was about to speak. "Mom, I have done my homework. The bank was acquired by Sociedade de Turismo e Diversoes de Macau in 1989, and is a wholly owned subsidiary. It was said to be the first bank in Greater China to offer a pre-paid debit card. There are 110 security guards on duty during the day and 47 at night. I've reviewed all the blueprints of the place. I know just where to cut communications with the outside world. I have two escape routes *and* I planned a little distraction for the police of the city."

"That's my birthday girl!" her dad said filled with pride.

"Honey, maybe we should send a few of our best lawyers over, just in case." Her mother had that worried protective tone in her voice.

Her father was having nothing to do with that idea. "Faith, dear, she doesn't want or need our help. We have done everything we can to make her successful in her chosen career as a villain."

"Thanks, Dad," Crimson said, deciding not to take a third helping of eggs and fruit.

As she got up her dad said, "Maybe we shouldn't show the world our true nature just yet." He pointed at her cape.

"Oh right," she said irritated at making a rookie mistake. She swirled and used her nano-bot powers to change her appearance to a pleasant Chinese school girl dressed in a white blouse and black skirt. It was one of many appearances she could change into in an instant using her nano-bot super power and the features of her costume.

She kissed both of her parents on their cheeks and left the house whistling a happy tune.

Crimson Doom's mother glared at her father.

"All right, all right, it doesn't hurt to be a little careful. I'll send a brace of lawyers and a squad of our best assassins. We'll have the bank and Macau's police departments covered like white on rice. However, if she finds out about them, you were the one that sent them." He reached back to his laptop and sent an email to the office and the head of security.

The flight from San Francisco to Macau was fast and fun. Crimson decided to fly first class because she had never been on a normal passenger plane before. A cab took her to the deluxe Hilton hotel. She looked at herself in the full-length mirror in her room. She saw a young woman with a red braid in a frilly sundress. Raising her hand, a million nanobots changed her to her archvillain costume. "I am the Crimson Doom. I'm the scourge of the world and don't you forget it."

The Crimson Doom would take a nap now, once she ordered a four a.m. wake-up call.

Hours and hours later the phone rang. The blurry-eyed young woman picked up the ancient hotel phone and heard the wake-up call recording.

"Don't they realize I'm the Crimson Doom? I'm tired," she hissed as she slammed the phone down on its base. Briefly, she thought about sleeping an hour more. Then her eyes blazed open. She was going to become infamous today. She would be the only

person to ever rob the biggest bank in the world. Interpol, the CIA, *and* the Chinese Military would all be after her. "What a great day!" she said jumping up and getting ready.

Using the nano-abilities built into her special costume, she morphed into her Chinese school girl persona. The Crimson Doom began generating highly specialized nanobot batches in the hundreds of thousands. She placed these about her person. They became invisible patches on her uniform, but she knew where every one of them was located and what their programed abilities were. Skipping, she traveled down the busy sidewalk to the front of the bank. The nanobots she'd activated were even now setting off alarms on the other side of town. Fifty stores were signaling robberies all across the north end of the city.

She casually tossed off more nanobots into the air by the outdoor alarm of *her* bank, to disable the system. More bots would shut off the bank's video cameras. A batch unlocked the front door and she walked in bold as brass; tossing nanobot patches to make the guards fall unconscious.

"Wait a minute," she said surprised. "Something is very wrong!"

The alarms and cameras were already turned off. Her nanobots told her there were 48 guards, but they were all using neural paralyzer pistols instead of guns. Bank security guards couldn't afford that type of weapon.

Suddenly, she was enraged. Screaming, she transformed. "Someone else is trying to rob my bank!" From the lovely, full-figured young school girl, her rage transformed her. Outrageous muscles bulged from her body. Odd black nano-bot cones, like thorns, grew from her uniform in the hundreds. She broke three off and threw them at the nearest guards closing in on her. Flying at many times the speed of sound, the cones burst through the bodies of the guards, killing them instantly.

Her nanobots told her she was dealing with reptile men. Ignoring the paralyzer fire, she killed batches of the fake guards. "Mark Forest, where are you?" she screamed. The world knew that Mark Forest was the supreme leader of the reptile men. Her nanobots told her he was in the vault. The vault *she* was supposed to open.

The other forty-seven fake guards were dead. In the vault, Mark Forest was pushing a very heavy, wheeled cart filled with cash and gold into a large, black dimensional portal.

So it's to be the old portal dodge, Crimson thought to herself. Not only was she crazy angry, she now added green jealousy to the mix. She couldn't make portals yet. She'd been working on the effect, but so far had no luck. She threw nanobots at all four wheels to seize the platform before it entered the portal.

Then she attacked Mark Forest.

Her jet-propelled nano-bot rockets bounced off her adversary.

"Miss Crimson, would you begrudge me a few million in stolen currency? What about honor among thieves?" Mark Forest said in a chiding tone.

"Never call me Miss Crimson. I am the Crimson Doom and you have invaded my territory. You aren't getting away with a single dollar of that money." She used three different highly specialized nano-bot attacks on her adversary. His mutations rebuffed them all.

"Well, I can see you are going to be snippy about this," Mark Forest said in a snide tone. "We will meet again under different circumstances, dear lady." Taking a single bill as proof that Crimson couldn't stop his theft, he calmly walked through the portal and it vanished after him.

"Dear lady!" she mocked. "Miss Crimson, I hate being called that!"

Crimson Doom stormed around the bank. She noted all the millions and millions of dollars lying around. She didn't care about them now. *What's the point if I'm not going to be the first one to rob this bank?*

Her nanobots avoided their mistress, knowing how angry she was just then. They started dumping reptilian security guards in a massive pile in the middle of the bank lobby.

An hour later the morning shift came in and found the Crimson Doom crying her eyes out over her lost chance. Several hours later she called her mother, not caring about the time difference.

Crying and hiccupping at the same time, Crimson Doom told her sad tale. Her mother tried to comfort her, explaining that sometimes luck isn't on the side of the mighty. Her daughter didn't want to feel better. She ended her woeful tale with, "And then that evil bank president presented me with a check for twenty million dollars as a reward for saving 300 million from being stolen. I was only going to steal *ten* million in the first place!" Her sobs filled the phone. "Mother, I'm sorry to have to ask this, but could you please sign me up with a bank account at your and Daddy's bank. I'll be home in two days with this stupid, fat check."

"Of course I can do that dear," her mother said. "You come home and you and I will go out to the family firing range and blow up some Abrams tanks. You have always liked doing that."

"Thanks, Mom, you are the best. See you soon," she said hanging up, tears of frustration still falling from her eyes.

It had been a week since the ruined bank job. The world was welcoming a new hero. However, no one understood why this hero would want a name like the Crimson Doom. Every time she saw herself on a newscast she went up to her room in tears.

"I'm a *villain,* doggone it. Why can't they see that?" She dried her eyes and stiffened her resolve. She would show the world or die trying and she was way too young to die. She went to the villain Facebook page and asked for ideas. After a day she had a hundred comments. Lots of them were wonderful. There was one that really struck her fancy. She started doing research. "By the work, one knows the workman," she muttered over and over.

Her reading gave her the following information:

It's a United States Army post in Kentucky south of Louisville and north of Elizabethtown. The 109,000 acre base covers parts of Bullitt, Hardin, and Meade counties. It currently holds the Army Human Resources Center of Excellence to include the Army Human Resources Command, United States Army Cadet Command, and the United States Army Accessions Command.

For 60 years, it was the home of the U.S. Army Armor Center and the U.S. Army Armor School.

Below the fortress-like structure lie the gold vaults lined with granite walls protected by a blast-proof door weighing 22 tons. Each member of the depository staff must dial a separate combination known only to them. Both the vault door and the emergency door are 21-inches thick and made of the latest torch-and-drill-resistant material.

The facility is ringed with fences and is guarded by the United States Mint Police. The Depository premises are within the site of Fort Knox, a US Army post, allowing the Army to provide additional protection. The Depository is protected by layers of physical security, alarms, video cameras, microphones, mine fields, barbed razor wire, electric fences, heavily armed guards, and the Army units based at Fort Knox, including unmarked Apache helicopter gunships. There is an escape tunnel from the lower level of the vault in case someone has been locked in accidentally.

For security reasons, no visitors are allowed inside the depository grounds.

Crimson Doom had every GPS map available. She had gone to visit the museum at the fort. She chose to dress in a frilly pink outfit with poodles on the skirt. She flirted outrageously with the troops while her nanobots flowed through the facility gathering security codes, door codes, and the layout of security cameras and microphones. Crimson Doom loved the fact that there were land mines in the area. The first part of her plan included exploding all of those mines at the same time and really messing up the front lawn.

After days of preparation, she stood in front of her bedroom mirror. "By the work, one knows the workman," she said over and over to herself. Her uniform was still awesome. The war-braid was tied perfectly and flowed from her head down her front. Once more she went down to breakfast.

"Honey," her dad said, clearly pleased to see her. "I'm so glad to see you are done pouting and have come out of your room."

"Thank you, Daddy," Crimson Doom said with a vague air about her. She was deep in thought.

"Is today the day you're trying again?" asked her mother.

"Yes, I'm traveling to Kentucky today," she told her parents. "I'll pull the job tomorrow and announce it to the world the next day. I think I have everything figured out. I only want to take 100 gold bars."

"Gold bars, darling? Where in the world does one get gold bars in Kentucky?" her father asked.

"I'm robbing Fort Knox, Father," she said with doubt in her voice.

"Well done, dear," her mother said patting her daughter on the back. "Getting back in the saddle is just what you need. Fort Knox, now that should put you on the villain map."

"Well that's the hope, Mother," she said, leaving the table with her food uneaten. She gave her parents each a hug and walked out the front door.

⟶ E ⟵

"What are we going to do? She looks terrible," said her mother.

"She has a plan. She has a goal. She's our daughter. I think she will do fine," said her father. He noticed his wife's look. "There are a few supervillains that owe me favors. I also have that four-star general in my pocket. I'll get right on it."

Kentucky was a lonely place for the Crimson Doom. She was in a nice enough hotel, but the people talked so funny. The next day started out bright and clear. Looking at herself in the hotel mirror she appeared to be dressed in a typical student uniform from a classy private school. Her nanobots had generated a white blouse and a long navy blue skirt. Knee socks and saddle shoes finished off the look. She couldn't help but wonder if girls really wore saddle shoes any more.

She drove into Fort Knox in a huge SUV. The shocks and suspension system had been radically transformed to easily carry the weight of 200 gold bars. *I know, I know,* she thought to herself. *I don't need all that carrying capacity, but a girl can't be too careful.* She remembered when her Aunt, the Purple Fate, had that problem with the cruise ship she tried to portal to Egypt. A horrific mistake like that wasn't going to happen to her.

Getting out of the van, she blew the outdoor security camera a kiss. Millions of nanobots flew from her lips and into the security system. She twirled with her hands and arms extended, in what looked like a fun expression of joy. Several million nanobots flew from her hands, finding new homes in the mine field. Other nanobots played themselves out as she entered the nearest door to the Mint.

A simple twist of her mind caused all of the mines surrounding the fort to explode in a hail of dirt and noise. She allowed alarms to ring while people ran around like crazed chickens. She had to laugh at that, as she changed back into her Doom uniform. Then the strangest thing happened. A marching band started playing. Music was part of her training; every villain needed a theme song. She recognized this music as a John Philip Sousa's piece called *The Rifle Regiment.* The music came closer and closer until the oddness of it all transfixed the Crimson Doom. From around the corner came a military marching band. It was led by a four-star general, two people with jackets sporting the presidential seal, and four guards pulling a pallet of gold bars. Her eyes grew wider and wider and wider. What was happening to her?

The general signaled for the music to stop. "May I call you Miss Crimson?" asked the general.

"No," she said quite rudely. "I am known as the Crimson Doom and I will thank you to always address me that way."

"Of course, dear lady, as you wish. We have several things for you that I know you will like." The general was clearly trying and failing to be gracious. "One of our scientists discovered your use of nanobots in our security systems when you first came to scope out our defenses. Your clever actions threw up alarm bells all over the facility. In fact, it was noted in the halls of the Pentagon as we realized we didn't have the proper defenses to stop such attacks. Our science jonnies developed several new defenses against your special powers. However, we weren't sure any of them would work against you. I'm pleased to say that all of them worked and your nanobots were completely neutralized as they invaded this facility. Ahem, I'm sorry to say that we didn't think to cover the land mines, but that's all right, we've been thinking of getting rid of them for years."

Crimson Doom got more and more angry. Nano-bot cones started appearing. Just as suddenly, she was surrounded by troopers wearing black hazmat suits. The general stood back a step.

"Yes, we have heard about what you can do with those nano-cones. I think you will find that these suits are proof against your thrown weapons. But feel free to give it a try."

The general politely waited a minute and then continued. "No? All right, then. Well the President has awarded you the Presidential Medal of Freedom." The two men in jackets walked up to her, one put a huge medal around her neck while the other read from a scroll thing.

"Crimson Doom has been awarded the Presidential Medal of Freedom for revealing an important failing in the defenses of the United States. Her action with nanobots has saved literally billions in defense spending. It is a grateful country that awards her this medal today."

"No, *no*, I came here to rob the place. I was after the gold," a bewildered Crimson Doom said.

"Oh we know," replied the general. "We didn't want you to go home unhappy or empty handed. Here are 120 gold bars. Please tell us where you want them sent, postage free of course."

In a distracted voice, she gave them her mother and father's address.

"Is there anything else a grateful country can do for one of its youngest heroes?" the general asked.

"Nothing at all," our distracted medal-wearing, unintentional superhero said. She rose into the air, using a nano-repelling ability and flew the 600 miles back to her parent's house.

Her father was reading the afternoon news at the kitchen table. He looked up from the paper. "Daughter, you're home early. Did everything go all right?"

"Not quite, Daddy. I did get the gold I wanted, but they *gave* it to me. I got the fame I wanted but only because they gave me the Presidential Medal of Freedom."

"Isn't that like the Medal of Honor for the military?"

"Yes, Daddy, it is." She bit her lower lip before continuing. "How bad would it be if the world regarded me as a hero and not a villain?"

He put the paper down and seriously considered the question. "I'm not sure. None of your Aunts would ever speak to us again. There are about 30 or so villains that would try to kill our entire family. I imagine your mother would be heartbroken. She had her heart set on you becoming the greatest villain of all time."

Walking up to her room she distractedly said to her father, "You might consider putting on some extra security. Our family is going to get some very bad press in the weeks to come." She rushed into her room with tears in her eyes.

He pressed his panic button.

Months after the Fort Knox incident, she visited New York City for the first time. The Crimson Doom found it to be a huge place. She had memorized several maps of the city and the surrounding ports. After getting a great hotel room along Central Park, she started exploring the various port districts of the Big Apple. She wanted to shock the world with her next effort. There would be no way her newest 'crime of the century' could be construed as something helpful.

The nanobots she planned on using for this ultimate villainous act were the most ambitious she had ever designed. Her plan was simple. Billions of nanobots would replicate themselves in the various New York harbors. Using the minerals and other materials found in the water, strong chains of nanobots would wrap themselves around the propellers of every ship, creating powerful nanotubes connected together in long chains of nano-webs across all five harbors. It would take several days to cover all of the vessels coming into port. Her nanobots would have to be exceptionally tough. She stared into the murky depths of the harbor, proud of her latest creations as they communicated with her.

Spending several days near the five ports of New York her nanobots invisibly filled the sea and started replicating themselves. A side effect of the growing population of nanobots was that the water became much clearer and free of pollutants. The nanobots were using those elements in the water as building materials to make more nanobots.

Days later, she snapped her fingers at dawn and her nanobots froze every single propeller in all of the harbors of New York City.

The Staten Island Ferry was the world's busiest ferry. It carried approximately 20 million people on the 5.2 mile route between Staten Island and Lower Manhattan 24 hours a day. With the snap of those feminine fingers the ferry stopped in place in the middle of its run. So did the dozens of other ferries serving the city.

Cargo and cruise ships all around New York lost propulsion. No matter what their captains ordered or their engineers tried, nothing could make ship propellers turn in any of the five harbors. The nanotubes resisted the tides pushing into the harbors and then hours later, pushing out again. Only a very strong tugboat could move any single ship in any direction and they all had their propellers fouled as well. Her plan was fool proof and deliciously villainous.

With a wicked laugh the Crimson Doom went back to her hotel to rest and relax for the day. Maybe she would take in a Broadway play. She had always wanted to see one of those.

⊏

Some very clever, union man saw an advantage to be had. Suddenly, a call went out for all dock workers to report to work, triple time was being awarded for any union man who could make it to the docks. If a certain villainous super heroine knew what the union leaders planned she wouldn't be very happy.

The next day, in the disguise of a stock broker, the Crimson Doom walked the streets of New York. She was filled with so much glee at the chaos she was causing that she waited an extra day before announcing her demands. On the afternoon of the third day the broadcasts on every channel in New York were interrupted by the face of the Crimson Doom in her uniform.

"I am the Crimson Doom. I have halted all shipping in the harbors of New York City. I hold thousands of vessels in the palm of my hand!" She closed her red-gloved fist for emphasis. "Tomorrow at noon, I will come to City Hall and expect to receive a check for one billion dollars. If I'm not given that ransom, I will sink every ship in all five harbors. Ignore me at your peril."

With a snap of her fingers, normal programming resumed on every channel. Filled with glee she walked down to Smith & Wolinski's for lunch. She loved that restaurant for its breads and perfect service.

Unknown to a certain villain, with her announcement, the Dock Workers Union redoubled their efforts. Working 24/7 they called in workers from other unions. News teams trying to film the activity on the docks were shut down by tough characters with unusually thick necks. No word would leak out about what was happening there.

The next day dawned bright and clear. The Crimson Doom got up and had a hearty breakfast. Dressed openly in her natty uniform, she flew using special lifting nano-bots to City Hall. What she saw there instantly depressed her.

Bright banners and a speaking platform had been set up on the steps in front of the building. When she appeared in the skies above the square, a band struck up the same blasted Sousa song she heard at Fort Knox. The mayor of New York stood there holding a huge, stupid gold key. A massive crowd formed in front of the building. There were dozens of news trucks on side streets. All of them were turned toward the speaking platform.

Crimson Doom couldn't help herself. She burst out in muscles and deadly nano-cones formed all over her body.

"There she is!" the loud speakers boomed over the crowd. "Ladies and gentleman, as the mayor of New York I would like to welcome our latest hero to the steps of City Hall. Let's give her a rousing New York welcome."

In a blind rage she flew down and threw three nano-cones at the mayor. Instantly, a figure in one of those military hazmat suits stepped in front of him. The deadly cones turned to dust as they touched the special surface of the military green suit. It was then that she noticed the twenty suited-up troopers in the mix of people on the speaking platform. Her best attack would be thwarted.

She landed in front of the mayor. "What are you doing? I held this city for ransom," she whispered.

The now-sweating Mayor realized how close he had come to being ripped apart. He had seen the images of the 47 reptile men from the bank job. He didn't want to experience one of those cones tearing through *his* body. Smiling as only a politician could, he talked into the microphones. "And now, Crimson Doom, the Dock Workers Union of New York has a special presentation to give you." The mayor stood back as two burly men came to the platform with a ten foot-long check made out for a billion dollars.

"I am Chris Clark, president of the Dock Workers Union of New York," the first burly man said.

"And I'm Tim Kask, vice president of the Dock Workers Union of New York," the second man spoke up.

"We are here to present this billion-dollar check to the Crimson Doom for her service in helping the dock workers of New York do their job. Let's hear it for the little lady!"

The crowd went wild.

In reaction to her despair, the hundreds of nano-cones withered and fell from her body. "How can this be happening to me?" she said in a trembling voice. "This is not the way to treat a world-class villain. I am to be *feared*, not *cheered*."

The check was put on a stand, while the president of the union approached the microphones.

"Because of the brave and valiant actions of this little hero, for the first time in twenty years of New York dock history; we are caught up! While all the ships were frozen in the harbors we were able to use the larger sailing ships to move cargo vessels in and out of the docks for loading and unloading. There was a backlog of six months for unloading important cargos for the city. Food that would have rotted was unloaded fresh and ready to use. Important medical devices were unloaded and sent to hospitals months ahead of schedule and are now saving lives. Never before has one single hero done so much for the prosperity and people of New York. That's why we have this check, whose monies were taken from a small part of the profits from loading and unloading so many ships. The second we got those full ships out of the harbors their propellers were free to resume shipping. What a great plan this was for the advancement of the union and New York City. People of New York, I present the Crimson Doom with one billion dollars!"

To say the crowd went even wilder was an understatement. As she stood there, taking in the cheering crowd she wondered what went wrong. Then the stupid mayor came up to the podium again. "And that's not all, folks. I now present the president of the New York Ecological Council."

"Hello, New York!" Frank Mentzer said waving to the crowd. "Some of you might not realize just how heroic this little lady is."

He tried to put his arm around the Crimson Doom. Aghast at the very thought, her nanobots levitated her ten feet in the air. The crowd loved it and cheered her action.

"Well, err, yes. Anyway, her nanobots used the impurities in the harbors of the city and made our waters as clean as they were in the 1600s. Those waters were a deadly mess before her actions. We were looking at spending billions on refreshing the waterways. Now we don't have to. I have a second Presidential Medal of Freedom to present to the Crimson Doom. Let's give her a round of New York applause."

Frank held the big medal up for everyone to see. He turned to try to talk the floating hero down to put it around her neck.

The Crimson Doom was heartbroken. What did she have to do to show the world she was truly evil? Briefly, she thought about just killing the thousands of people packed to see her get her rewards, but she restrained the impulse. There was really no artistry in that act.

"Oh...goodie...another President's Medal," she mumbled to herself. How can one refuse such a thing? She flew away from the crowd, doing just that.

It was a dejected Crimson Doom that tried to enter her house a day later. The news hounds were at every door, trying to get a picture of the nation's latest heroine. Her nanos made the lenses of all the cameras scratch and fog up. The young girl walked past the microphones not wanting to even say 'no comment.'

Her parents met her at the door. She flew into their arms.

"Mother, Father, I tried to be so bad. Nothing worked," she sobbed. "Who knew it would be so hard to be evil. Now I have a billion plus dollars in the bank and a pallet full of gold bars for my troubles and all our relatives hate us!" She wailed this last as her parents tried to comfort her.

"Honey, your mother and I have been right where you are in our youth," her father comforted. "For my first villainous defense case the obvious mass murderer got life imprisonment. I still write him every month."

Seeing the amazed look on her daughter's face, the mother jumped in as well. "My first case I was trying to keep two Mafia bosses from getting the electric chair. They were both judged guilty and executed, despite all the months and months of appeals. I know we have had this talk before, but what about trying Harvard for a year or two? Your dad and I can donate a couple of million dollars for a new law building and you could start in the fall. Just think of the challenge where your marvelous nano-power won't help you at all."

Crimson Doom went to Harvard and in her second year met a villain named Rail Gun. Soon after the world changed as this dynamic duo worked their special skills across the globe.

Henchmonster

Drew Bittner

See, here's the thing. I love being a monster. There's nothing like it. It's a rush, and that's coming from a guy who played pro football. Well, for all of five games, but that's not the point. Being a monster—you read the comic books and monsters are all sad basket cases, moping around or angry. We rip stuff up, we smash things, we hurt innocent people (especially our loved ones).

I've never met a monster who was like that, and believe me, once you join the club, you meet a lot of monsters.

The mouthy guy at the bar? He shuts up when ten shaggy feet of muscle sits down next to him. I don't even have to give him a look.

Jehovah's Witnesses? Not a problem, trust me.

Even telemarketers hang up when they hear my growly basso profundo. (I had to look that one up, because it sounds better than "really deep voice.")

So why am I a monster? Mostly, I needed a job...

Long story short, in my darkest hour, I found what I was looking for: a guy who hooked me up with MutaJen, a lady who makes monsters. That is, she turns people into monsters. That's her power. She took all the cash I had left in the world and touched me with her right hand—which wouldn't stop changing, from a monkey's paw to a chicken foot to a webbed and scaly mitt to...okay, you get the idea—and in a blaze of agony I was reborn as Woolly Bully.

I chose the name myself.

And I made that name mean something, though it took years to work my way up to the big time. Years spent working for a crime boss here, a wannabe villain there, little by little building up my reputation with the people who mattered.

You probably saw pictures of me on the news when I helped my boss, the Atomic Brain, fight the Northern Front. They had some rare earth stuff he wanted to use in making robots or something, so we went to grab it from them. I hadn't heard much about the NF before we slugged it out, but they're based in the upper Midwest for some reason and heck, all five of 'em were ready to fight. Seeing as I was now ten feet tall, covered in rust-colored fur, and about as strong as a team of elephants, I wasn't all that shy about mixing it up either. The Northern Front was good training for what was coming.

If you don't know me, you almost have to know my boss. The Atomic Brain is short, scrawny and has a head about four sizes too big for him, around which orbit what he calls his "danger-drones"—each one's a combination of sensor, video camera, and energy blaster. He wears a lab coat and sometimes likes to be called Doctor, even though he doesn't have so much as a bachelor's degree. He's one of those old-school bad guys, a supergenius inventor who's one bright idea away from taking over the world. He fought Dr. Phenomenal and his Tomorrow, Inc. crew a few times before I started working for him.

Man, you should hear him rant about those guys. He's worse than my old man going on about the Packers during an off season.

"Woolly, I'm ten times smarter than that glory hound," he'd mutter. "My tech is better, my insights more revolutionary. Hell, even my logo is better! Seems like every time we crossed paths, though, some lucky break let him win."

In hindsight, seeing how my boss could overlook small but important details, "some lucky break" was probably something obvious he'd forgotten to take into account. He could build an intercontinental teleporter or a death ray, no problem, but ask him to plan out a bank robbery and it'd be a Rube Goldberg mishmash nightmare, collapsing under its own weight. And not a dollar earned.

Where he got the money to pay me, I'm not sure. I think he had a few patents earning him bucks on the side. Like any self-respecting villain, though, he wanted to make his money the old-fashioned way: he wanted to steal it.

Except the Atomic Brain wasn't in it for money. What my boss really wanted to do was capture a powerful superhero—maybe even one of the Originals (you know, the first ones to undergo the Process)—so he could figure out how to get their strength and invulnerability. He had this idea he could make himself into a god or something instead of a hunched-over macrocephalic with male-pattern baldness, surrounded by a flying swarm of killer cameras.

And sure enough, one day...

"Woolly, I've chosen my target at last," he said, the chitinous armature around his oversized noggin working extra-hard to lift his eyes to meet mine. "There's only one being on the planet who has the boundless strength, stamina, and invulnerability to suit me. I must acquire those qualities for myself, so that my amazing mind continues in perpetuity!"

"Oh crap," I mumbled, looking around.

Had I mentioned that I was the Atomic Brain's only hench-monster at that time?

Reading back, I see I didn't and that's kind of important, so my apologies.

"We" was him and me. And I didn't trust him all that much, even though he was paying me okay money. For one thing, it was under the table and for another I didn't have insurance any more. I healed up pretty fast but we had to be talking A-listers here. He wasn't going to settle for taking what the Sharkmaster could give him.

"Um, who's your target, boss?" I asked, afraid to hear the answer.

Which is how we ended up facing the Ogre.

— ∈ —

Everybody knows the Ogre. He's one of the Originals, powerful enough to go toe to toe with Heroic and a bona-fide hero of the Jabberwock War, before he started running a motorcycle gang in the Southwest and dealing in every sort of contraband known. I had a couple of feet on him, height wise, not to mention a much longer reach, but he was probably twice as strong as me.

You can probably tell I wasn't eager to try myself against him. Some monsters are smarter than others. I might not be all that smart but I do have survival instincts.

Unfortunately, what I didn't have was a choice. My boss knew where he was, which meant I was going to go, unless I ran for it then and there. Considering Stella and I had bills to pay, running wasn't on my list of choices. Besides, he could just find me and teleport me there anyway.

It wasn't hard for a guy as smart as the Atomic Brain to find the Ogre. That's not a really big compliment; I could have found the guy in two minutes online. It's not like the Ogre makes it hard, even though the stories tell you he's always running and hiding. I don't think this guy hid one day in his entire life. I mean, for heaven's sake, he's eight feet tall and half as wide and has fists like engine blocks, and that's not even mentioning his metallic bronze skin. He can knock over a building with one punch or pick up a jet plane. He causes seismic shocks when he jumps up and down. People ten miles away could have told you where he was.

Does that sound like a hider to you?

"Go and have a chat with him, won't you?" the Atomic Brain told me.

"Boss, I'm gonna have to ask for hazard pay," I said. If one argument was likely to work, it would be hitting him in the wallet.

He scowled at me but it was hard to argue. The Ogre had beaten entire teams of heroes sent to "chat" with him. Sending me alone was a pretty rough assignment.

We haggled. He didn't try to talk me down all that much, which told me how eager he was to get his prize into his lab.

All I had to do was bring him in.

The Atomic Brain sent me via teleporter. He didn't own any kind of vehicle, claiming he got motion sick very easily, and thus he built a teleporter out of necessity. Even so, I was the one who went out for groceries and Redbox, so go figure. At least I didn't have to commute to work. He calculated the exact spot on which to dump me and zap, I was there a minute later. The teleporter made me a little queasy, but it never lasted long.

What did last was the damned dry heat. As Woolly Bully, I was made for cooler climates. The Pacific Northwest was my new vision of paradise. Ask yourself if a gorilla-bear-Muppet hybrid with overlong arms and short legs belongs in a freaking desert.

This was not going to go well.

"You lost?"

I turned around and, sure enough, there was the guy I'd come to meet, sitting on his motorcycle—a Harley about the size of a minivan—with a surprised look on his face.

"Not really. Came to see you," I said, already sweating buckets under my fur.

"That so. Not a lot of people come to see me...uninvited," he said, his expression darkening. "Not shaggy-assed tourists, anyway."

"My boss wanted you to come for a visit."

"And who's your boss?" He climbed off the motorcycle and took off his gloves. Seemed to me like he was getting ready to fight.

"The Atomic Brain. He wants to meet you."

He stopped and stared at me, his lambent yellow eyes wide. "You're kidding, aren't you?"

I shook my head. "He sent me out here thinking we'd beat the hell out of each other but I'd somehow make you come with me. How about I just invite you? We could have a beer."

"And why would I go? What's your name, anyway?"

"Woolly Bully. And curiosity."

"Now you *have* to be kidding me," he laughed. "Woolly Bully? Who else has he got working for him, the Leader of the Pack?"

"Just me."

"You got guts, buddy. Point to you. But why is curiosity going to take me to meet your boss?"

I shrugged. "I don't know, man, but it's my job and that's the only card I've got to play, short of trading punches. And who knows how that'd turn out? I don't think I want to find out bad enough to start up."

He chuckled. "This has to be the most screwed up brawl I've ever been in," he said. "Tell you what, I'll go along and if I want to leave, I'll beat the crap out of you on the way out for wasting my time."

"Fair enough."

So I used my communicator to signal the boss we were ready to come back, and zap, there we were in the secret lair. (It was a huge old place deep beneath a national forest. It might have been a military installation once.)

The Atomic Brain gaped at us. He seemed baffled and maybe a tiny bit scared out of his mind.

"You...you were supposed to defeat him!" he shouted.

"You said to bring him back," I said. "Here he is."

"I was going to load his unconscious body into my demolecularizer! It's part of the process!"

The Ogre shot me a look.

"Maybe we can talk this out..."

The Atomic Brain screamed, "I didn't hire you to be a diplomat! A brainless pile of muscles like you only has one use: fighting! You can't even do that right?"

The Ogre cleared his throat. "Seems to me your employee did what you asked. He's okay...but I'm not sure about you. Now, you can explain *why* you wanted me here or I can just destroy this place, put you in traction for a decade, and make my way home."

"I have the means to deal with you, even if my 'employee' proved ineffective," the Atomic Brain snarled. He fired up his wrist controls.

"Oh no," I muttered.

A twenty-foot-tall robot lumbered out of the shadows, its car-sized hands grasping for the Ogre. It was Crushbot, the Atomic Brain's hobby project. I'd wrestled it a few times, testing it out, and we learned it was stronger, slower, and lots dumber than me. Sending it to fight the Ogre was a bad idea.

"Boss, stop!" I yelled.

The Ogre got a really unpleasant smile on his face. "I do believe I'll get some exercise," he growled, leaping at his mechanical foe. His huge fist hammered Crushbot's faceplate and for a wonder didn't even crack it; the boss must have been upgrading again. The Ogre tried to smash in Crushbot's head again but Crushbot...

Well, you don't need the blow-by-blow to know that the Ogre made it out of the Atomic Brain's lair with his clothes shredded. The boss was seriously peeved, and I was both "on probation" and generally unhurt from the ruckus. He sent me home, or rather yelled at me to get out from where he crouched over the smoking ruin of Crushbot. Later he texted me that he needed time to "consider his options" regarding my employment.

—◄€►—

"Sounds like he wanted you to get beat up," Stella said, passing me a gallon jug full of cold beer.

"Yup," I said. "Maybe I should look for another job."

"There are other supervillains," she said. "You still get the *Black Market Bulletin*? They run help wanted ads all the time."

On my hands and knees, I rummaged through a stack of old papers piled up by the back door. I couldn't stand up in most of our house, but my wife Stella really loved the place and it was remote enough that a ten-foot furry goon wouldn't draw too much attention. Took a minute to find a *Bulletin* more recent than a month ago. Flipping it open, and taking some care that my claws wouldn't shred it, I looked over the small classified section.

"Hm. 'New villain looking to start a team.' Nah. 'Join a criminal brotherhood with a legacy of evil.' Eh, sounds like the Dreadfuls are recruiting again. Diabolicus runs through henchmen the way men run through singles at a strip club. Man, if only somebody like Nox was hiring. You know what that would mean for me? Working for the Darkmother would put me in the big leagues for sure."

"Mm-hmm," she said, eyes still scanning the paper. "There's one. Fimbulwinter—have you heard of him?"

"Yeah, he's a cold-weather, snow-and-ice kind of guy. He's been working Chicago, I hear."

"What do the Twin Cities have for him? He sounds like he might be a player."

I shrugged. "Probably the tech startups north of town," I said. "UltraTech, Tyndall Enterprises...a lot of big R&D firms moved in over the years."

"His contact info is here. Want me to send an email?"

"Sure. Thanks, baby."

She snuggled close, hands burrowing into my fur. "Anything for my monster."

Fimbulwinter was hiring. I got an invitation to come to an audition the next day, at an address well outside of the city. Stella drove our cargo van (and damn, I missed driving) and the GPS took us to an abandoned warehouse way outside of the city. There were a few other vans parked in the lot.

Here's a pro tip: when you see an unusual number of cargo vans in one spot, you're probably way too close to monsters.

"Looks like the right place," I said.

"Want me to stay?" She looked calm but I could smell the fear on her, and if I could, so could other monsters. Stella's a great girl but she's as nervous around monsters as most sane people.

"Nah. I'll be okay. Call you when I'm done." I slid out of the van and shut the door, then gave her a peck on the cheek. "Go find a place to get breakfast and wait for me. Love you."

"Love you. Get your game face on and don't take any shit from the others," she told me, before backing up and driving off.

Any wonder why I love her?

"...an age when the heroes are busy fighting each other, when they aren't becoming villains themselves," someone with an aristocratic voice ranted, as I stepped into the warehouse.

Oh great, he was monologuing.

You see it in the movies or read it in comics and think "Aw c'mon, nobody is going to waste time raving about their genius plan and give the good guy time to recover, escape, think up a way to fight back, or let the cavalry arrive."

And you would be wrong.

It must be in villain DNA. Every single one of them loves to chew your ear off about how smart/powerful/dangerous they are and why their plan cannot possibly fail, until of course it does.

A smart villain would just kill the hero, right?

Never seen it happen.

I guess they feel like they have to give their defeated enemy a sporting chance to survive.

"What's he saying?" I asked another henchmonster.

"He's talking about how old timers like him have a code of honor," said a dude who looked like an upright tiger. "They'll put a hero into a death trap but not take a gun and blow his head off. It's like they're playing a damn game."

"I'm Woolly Bully," I said, offering my hand.

"Bengal Bill," he said, shaking it with his oversized paw. "Didn't I see you...? Northern Front?"

"Yeah. I work for the Atomic Brain but I'm, uh, exploring my options."

Bengal Bill nodded. "Smart. I hear that mad scientists are hard to work for. They can turn on you."

And that's when it struck me why the Atomic Brain wanted me and the Ogre to fight. If we were *both* beaten up, he could run experiments on both of us.

Dang.

"Are we fighting for real or sparring?" I asked, trying to shake off the near-miss I'd so suddenly comprehended.

"Sparring. Fimbulwinter doesn't want us killing each other," Bengal Bill said.

"Good. My wife's kind of tired of seeing me slashed up," I said. "Seems like I fight a lot of heroes with claws."

"Well, well, if it isn't Fuzzy Wussy," a gravelly voice snorted behind me.

Suddenly my day was not getting better.

"Oh hey, it's Rip-bore," I said, turning around.

Riproar and I had history, going back to my early days in the business. We had MutaJen in common and had started out around the same time. I'd beaten him out for a couple of gigs and he hadn't forgiven me, even though he lost out because not a lot of people want to work with a homicidal psychopath. I knew we'd throw down one day but hopefully it wasn't today; I needed a job, not a blood feud.

"You two know each other?" Bengal Bill said, backing away.

Riproar gave him a withering look and bumped his chest into my abs. He might be short but his claws are as big as mine and he's a maniac when he gets going. "What are you here for, Wussy? Fim wants *monsters*, not losers."

"Fim? You on a first syllable basis with the guy, Harvey?" I sneered.

He growled low and angry; he does not like people throwing around his real name.

"You better stay outta my way," he rumbled, shoving past me toward another corner of the warehouse.

Yeah, it was gonna happen.

"He's one angry monster," Bengal Bill said.

"You'd be angry too if you'd been hybridized with a neutered alley cat," I said.

"Oh man, is that true?"

"Nah. He's just a jerk." I shook it off, getting my head back in the game. This was an audition, not a villain dance club or underground gladiatorial combat arena. (They exist.) I had to show Fimbulwinter what I could do.

"...distracted by fighting among themselves, giving us unprecedented opportunities!"

He was still going.

But he wasn't wrong. I don't know what had gotten into the heroes but they'd been fighting each other more than any of us lately. Northern Front had mixed it up with the Golden Eagles, the government's very own superteam, and the Garden State Guardians had brawled with the Broadway Knights in Times Square, of all places. Tomorrow Inc. had duked it out with Team Warlock (another government team, this one an enhanced spec ops platoon). It was *crazy.*

Mostly the villains sat back, grabbed some popcorn, and enjoyed the show. And pulled off a whole bunch of capers while keeping a low profile. The last thing anyone wanted was to be a problem the heroes had to handle.

The Atomic Brain had muttered about now being the time to take advantage of their disarray, but...villains don't get along and they weren't about to team up, no matter how great an idea it might be. Every villain sees every other villain as a rival, an enemy, or a useful dupe. It might help explain some things later on to keep that in mind.

"...show me what you can do!"

And that was the end of the welcoming speech. I signed in with a rather terrified temp, who gave me a number and asked me very nicely if I minded waiting over there, please? Some monsters get their kicks by terrorizing the help, but not me. Poor kid is just making a buck. I growled something agreeable and went to wait.

Maybe an hour later, it was my turn to show my stuff. There were huge weights everywhere, ranging up to ten tons, and I was able to lift them easily. I put a fist through a sheet of steel, jumped twenty feet straight up from a standing start, ripped an engine block in two, and...

SON OF A BITCH!!

"Hey! What the hell was *that?*"

The machine gun's barrel was still smoking. I wasn't hurt but .50 caliber slugs still sting; if you've ever been shot by a BB gun, you know how I felt. It was followed by something that fired green energy blasts at me, which I mostly dodged, and then a gas bomb full of a powerful sedative. It gave me a headache but didn't put me down.

"Impressive," Fimbulwinter said, gazing down at me from his elevated platform. "You are quite durable…Woolly Bully, is it? Correct me if I'm wrong but aren't you with the Atomic Brain?"

One thing I'd learned from lots of failed interviews, always stay positive and don't badmouth a former boss.

"I'm always alert for new opportunities, sir," I said.

"Quite so," he said, looking thoughtful. He waved me back to the waiting area and so that's what I did.

There were about a dozen monsters in the mix at the start. Some of them I knew a little bit, others were strangers—probably a mix of rookies and out-of-towners—but the field was winnowed down to four candidates by noon. One of them was a buddy, Snowball, who's a white beachball with stubby arms and legs and great big eyes, but no mouth. Even I can't shake his hand, because he gives off extreme cold by touch, which I guess fit Fimbulwinter's motif. There was also Glacier, who was a made man from Alaska, easily my height and probably three times my mass, trailing a wide wedge of ice behind him with every ponderous step.

And the fourth was Riproar.

Motherfu…

"What is going on here?"

A big insectile shape was among us and how had the damn thing gotten inside? But it was uncomfortably familiar.

It was a giant-sized dangerdrone.

The Atomic Brain had found me. Found me applying for a job with another villain.

"I knew it! Did I tell you? I *knew* he'd run off from his old boss," Riproar bellowed.

"Nevertheless, he has what I'm looking for in a henchmonster," Fimbulwinter said, running a hand over his albino-pale chin, his silver hair swirling around as he looked from me to the dangerdrone. He pulled his ermine-trimmed coat close around his narrow shoulders. "We've never met, Atomic Brain. I'm Fimbulwinter."

"You're poaching! You are stealing my employee!" the Atomic Brain shrieked.

"I've done nothing of the kind!"

"When you knew he was an employee of another villain, the rules say you must disqualify him from consideration," the Atomic Brain said.

"Those rules apply to unenhanced hirelings and you know it," Fimbulwinter said. "Any applicant who has superhuman capabilities must be considered a free agent until such time as a contractual dispute arises. Does Woolly Bully have a contract with you?"

"We...never got around to signing one," the Atomic Brain admitted.

"There you go, then. He's free to enter my employ," Fimbulwinter said, a bit triumphantly.

"This will not stand! If we do not enforce the rules of the Covenant to which we are all signatories..."

Covenant? What the hell was that?

"I know the terms as well as you," Fimbulwinter said.

"Then I claim right of retribution against a faithless employee," the Atomic Brain insisted, and the dangerdrone turned toward me, its energy weapons beginning to glow.

"I refuse! I make him an offer of employment here and now, and as such, he is under my protection," Fimbulwinter said.

"I accept!" I yelped, in case there was any doubt.

The dangerdrone was silent for a long and uncomfortable moment. "This is not over," the Atomic Brain said through his flying weapon. Which then wheeled around and flew out of the room through a hole it must have burned through the wall while we were otherwise occupied.

"Welcome to the Frozen Fiends, Woolly Bully," Fimbulwinter said, nodding in my direction.

I nodded back. Already I was wondering what the Atomic Brain was going to do to get back at me.

You're probably thinking I hurried to call Stella and got her out of town.

And you'd be wrong. Supervillains have a reputation for going after the family and friends of people who betray or otherwise cross them, but it's undeserved; they really don't want to wreak death when it's unprofitable. Besides which, most of them have families and friends too, so they're off-limits. Sure, there are some psychos who enjoy breaking the rules, but the Atomic Brain wasn't one of them.

No, he would come after me directly. It wouldn't be pretty either.

For now, though, I had a new boss.

None of us knew that the Villain War had begun.

I don't know who called it the Villain War. Probably some TV reporter or blogger of the weird, like that "Strange Trails" group, but it wasn't us villains.

It sure as heck was a war, though.

I hadn't been part of the Frozen Fiends more than an hour before not one, not two, but three Crushbots showed up to re-decorate the old warehouse. I have the feeling they were there to inflict more than property damage because two of them came straight for me as the third ripped apart the cinderblock walls.

"Fiends, defend me!" Fimbulwinter cried, even though he wasn't their target. No, that honor was mostly reserved for me.

"Dammit!" Then it occurred to me. Remember how I said the Atomic Brain sometimes overlooked simple but obvious things? I had been the guy field-testing these things; if anyone knew their weaknesses, it was me. "Okay, guys, here's what you do. Listen to me, I know these machines."

Riproar, right on schedule, came back with "I don't need a lecture from Fuzzy Wussy to rip up robots." He jumped at the closest one and I don't feel too bad that he was knocked through a wall by a kinetic cannon.

"Anyone else have a snappy comeback?" Hearing none, I said, "Go for the knees. The weapons cycle through every six seconds and have a limited field of fire above and below. Stay down or go real high and they'll have a hard time hitting you. Armor is weakest on the opposite side of the faceplate in front. Go!"

It took some doing but the three of us who were left managed to bring down the Crushbots. I tossed one hulk out of the warehouse in time to see a dangerdrone zooming away, discretion being the better part of valor and all that.

It was the opening salvo but hardly the only battle we were going to fight.

Fimbulwinter put out the word and someone gave up a teleportation node belonging to the Atomic Brain. I didn't know anything about it but apparently my boss needed devices like this to zero in his teleporter…and we could use it to find him. My new boss guided us to what looked like a former coal mine, which we used to get down way underground—and then break into the Atomic Brain's lair.

"Knock knock!" Riproar yelled, happy for the chance to commit some first-class mayhem. He found the lair held a half-completed Crushbot and a swarm of dangerdrones of various sizes , but the Atomic Brain was gone.

"Woolly, does he have a backup lair?" Fimbulwinter asked.

"Never saw one," I said. "But…oh hell, we gotta go." I pointed to a digital timer that was counting down way too fast. "Spoilsport bomb. Run!"

Nobody chose to argue.

The explosion chased us through much too much of the mine. Fimbulwinter had slowed the blast wave with walls of ice, but the shock still ruptured the decaying supports all around, bringing the mine shafts down behind us a split second after we got clear. It was a close call.

"This is war," Fimbulwinter said through clenched teeth. "And in war, you need allies."

The Atomic Brain wasn't all that popular with lots of his fellow supervillains and some were plenty eager to take a swing at the guy.

Of course, my old boss had come to the same conclusion, which gave us an unpleasant surprise soon enough.

It was a long couple of weeks. While Fimbulwinter worked the villains' network, I showed my new comrades where the Atomic Brain had constructed factories, stored materials (including some trophies), and even a couple of vaults I suspected held his cash. We weren't disappointed. The cash also helped us hire some foot soldiers.

At the same time, soldierbots had struck at Fimbulwinter's properties. An ice rink, an ice distribution company, a traveling circus...quite a few seemingly unrelated businesses were quickly, completely, and mercilessly destroyed. Fimbulwinter growled a whole lot of threats when the bad news came in.

Our forces clashed directly a few times. Improved Crushbots were a lot harder to beat, but as we took out Atomic Brain's factories, we faced fewer of those. We fought cybernetically enhanced beasts but only a few minor supervillains—people like the Princess, an old woman artificially de-aged to childhood and now surrounded with a techno-menagerie from hell. She looked and acted like a kid playing princess, hence the nickname. I almost felt bad about wrecking her army of killer stuffed animals. I got into a punching match with Dustup, a super-thug whose suit turns him into dust, and beat him by busting a fire hydrant and soaking him down. Riproar and I took out Updraft, who has antigravity tech, while Snowball and I were almost beaten into the ground by the Technomorph; this nanotech/polyalloy thing was playing bulldozer and we were ambushed good. Managed to fry him by pulling down a power line and getting creative.

Meanwhile, we had a few minor leaguers on our side too. Destroy Inc. worked on a couple of the Atomic Brain's holdings, reducing them to rubble in a few minutes apiece, while Homewrecker used her super-wiles on guys like Blastastic (those flying armored guys all think bullets or blasts, not wink-wink) and Titanic Tom, the guy with the size-changing gizmo. She put both of them out of commission by herself.

Things went back and forth, with neither side seeming to gain an advantage.

But it did attract attention, getting on the national news after the first couple of days.

Where were the heroes in all this? Busy licking their own wounds, mostly, which didn't do wonders for the public's confidence in them. The Golden Eagles and Team Warlock were the government response teams but we didn't see them; the others all begged off, saying they had local crises to manage or bigger fish to fry.

Har de har har. Let's be honest, they were waiting for us to kill each other off and then swoop in to administer the *coup de grace*.

It didn't make any difference to the higher ups. We even started to gain allies.

It happened like this. After those first couple of weeks, a weird sorting process worked itself out. The villains who were technology-driven, the inventors and armored guys and weapon-slingers and so on, sided with the Atomic Brain, while those with innate powers sided with Fimbulwinter. Without meaning to, we'd more or less turned this fight into a 'which is better, tech or powers?' argument.

It was crazy.

So naturally my boss wanted to have a villain summit meeting to speak to all of his new buddies. Mostly I think he wanted to preen a bit.

◄—€—►

"We have been doing well," Fimbulwinter told his guests. I hung back against the back wall; it didn't seem like a good idea to advertise that I was the reason we were fighting each other like the heroes were. Somebody might get the smart idea that killing me would end the hostilities and while that might be swell for them, it'd be bad for me.

Fimbulwinter's gaze swept the room. He had put out the word through the villains' grapevine. MutaJen, Diabolicus and his Dreadfuls, and a handful of other minor leaguers like Monsterboy and Thermal had answered the call.

"I intend to teach the Atomic Brain a lesson he will never forget," Fimbulwinter said, for perhaps the fiftieth time since hostilities had begun. "He will beg for mercy but my cold heart will grant none!"

I tried not to roll my eyes, honest.

Lucky for me, the other villains were eating it up.

"I have heard rumors that the Atomic Brain is also recruiting," Diabolicus said, his soft voice like a razor blade running over bare skin. Just being in the same room with him gave me the heebie-jeebies, and that's pretty darned hard to do to a monster like me. "We will not find him an easy or unprepared target."

"We just need to find him," Fimbulwinter said. "And we have an expert on him in our midst." He turned to include me in the conversation. "With our advantages, our victory is assured and we will carve up his holdings among ourselves."

I suspected it would not be that easy, and my fellow monsters seemed similarly dubious. Monsters can be pragmatic like that.

The temp chose that moment to slink into the room. "Um, boss, there's something on TV," he stage-whispered into Fimbulwinter's ear. Then he ran out of the room about as fast as he could; Diabolicus had looked his way. Can't say I blamed him.

Fimbulwinter shot Diabolicus a glance ripe with annoyance, then switched on the super-huge plasma screen TV we'd installed while setting up the new HQ. (Stella and I inherited his old TV, which took up a whole wall of our living room.)

What we saw was about the last thing any of us expected.

The Atomic Brain was monologuing at the now-ruined front gates of UltraTech, playing to an audience of reporters, soldiers, and UltraTech employees who couldn't quite bring themselves to abandon their workplace. He was flanked by the Technologist and...oh my God, that was Cyberoic.

The Technologist is world famous. He's the guy who's actually beaten more heroes than have beaten him; a winning record like that among villains is almost unheard-of. Like the Ogre, he had fought entire teams of heroes, holding his own with technology that was decades ahead of anything we had now. He was a supergenius inventor like the Atomic Brain, but was generally far more successful...and dangerous. Plus he was just damned cool in his armored suit.

Cyberoic was in the same league as the Technologist. He claimed to be the real Heroic, mutilated and left for dead on an alien world until he was rebuilt with alien technology and somehow returned to Earth. Considering we already had a Heroic, his claim was met with skepticism, to put it mildly, and he hadn't taken that well. He was a global-level threat...and he had sided with our enemy.

This was really not good.

"Well," Fimbulwinter said.

"Shh! Listen," MutaJen said. "Turn it up!"

"...challenge the foolish Fimbulwinter to face me here, at UltraTech, one hour from now. If you refuse..."

The camera panned around and...oh my God, that was Stella in the crowd. She was standing next to Ruth Fletcher Gage, the billionaire tech queen who owned UltraTech.

"...everyone here will die."

"That's my wife," I said.

"Did you get a chance to say goodbye?" Riproar asked with poisonous sweetness.

"We seem to have our next engagement chosen for us," Fimbulwinter said.

"He wants me," I said.

"I know. And he can't have you," Fimbulwinter told me. "We're not out of options yet. Let us see what happens."

And with that, the council of war was over and we were on our way. Looked like we were heading into a winner-takes-all fight and our enemy had chosen the battlefield.

Less than an hour later, we had arrived at the UltraTech compound. Lucky for us, the employees inside had secured the facility before the Atomic Brain could make use of what was inside, or it could have been even worse for us. As it was, though, I didn't like our chances. Fighting two tech geniuses and one Heroic-level cyborg was going to be ugly.

Stella caught my eye. She was scared, under the gun of some giant robot the Atomic Brain had cobbled together, but was holding up well. I gave her a nod.

I was going to pull his head off for this.

"Fimbulwinter, even you should see that true supervillainy rests with those who use their brains instead of relying on freakish powers," the Atomic Brain taunted from the depths of his armored exo-suit. Considering it looked like a hydrocephalic gorilla, it could have been more intimidating but it was probably the best he could do.

"You are simply jealous that you must build weapons instead of being one," Fimbulwinter said, the air around him swirling with frost.

"Enough of this," the Technologist said. "I came because my ally promised me your bodies to dissect. Discovering and perhaps replicating your powers could be invaluable to me. I see no need to delay in claiming what was promised." And he unleashed a barrage of violet-blue energy bolts that pretty much went through everything they touched. Luckily I was not one of those things.

There was a blast of air and it turns out Cyberoic nearly took my head off, except that Snowball shoved me out of the way. He had slapped Riproar aside even so. Guess if Snowball was going to save one ally, it was going to be me. I felt the subzero cold on my back even through the fur. Little guy saved my life. Cyberoic swooped back around, apparently annoyed that he'd missed me the first time.

Snowball decided to stand his ground.

Imagine a frosty beachball standing in the way of an elephant stampede. That was Snowy. Cyberoic crossed about half a mile in the blink of an eye. Snowball stuck out his stubby little hands and...I'm not sure I believe what happened, but Cyberoic hit a wave of cold probably a few degrees north of absolute zero. His metal prosthetics shattered and even his inhumanly durable skin turned blue-white with frostbite. He fell out of the sky and, being frozen harder than glacial ice, plowed into the ground and came to a stop more or less at the same time. More or less. The chunks of him did, anyway.

The Atomic Brain had noticed our encounter, because about a second later there were half a dozen napalm grenades unleashed on poor little Snowy. I batted them away as fast as I could, when I saw them coming, but he got tagged with a few. His hypercold metabolism couldn't handle so much heat and he burned alive, even as he struggled to counter the flames with his dwindling cold. I... well, I'm not proud to say that I was paralyzed for a moment, trying to think of something, anything, I could do to save him. But there was no snuffing those fires and he died there in the dirt, even as I tried to smother the flames with my hands.

Fimbulwinter saw what had happened and used his own ice powers to shatter the remaining napalm launchers on the Atomic Brain's side of the field. He wasn't going to fall for the same trick, especially when it had cost him such a surprisingly useful henchmonster as Snowball. Who could have imagined the little guy could take out Cyberoic? I mean, the cyborg has backup bodies—we all know that—but he wouldn't be jumping back into this fight any time soon. Still, killing Cyberoic even once was monumental. Snowball had earned a place in the Villains' Hall of Fame.

Glacier was holding his own against the Technologist, whose armor was keeping the cold at bay but just barely. His energy bolts ripped through Glacier's ice walls but they only sealed up again with fresh ice. Those two were occupied for the moment so...

I felt like having a word with my old boss.

Took me a couple of bounds to cross the field, coming in at an angle so hopefully he wouldn't notice me until too late. I was about one good jump from his exo-suit when I heard, "What in the name of all that is evil is going on here?"

Oh boy, we'd done it. It was the Darkmother.

I guess she'd had enough.

If heroes look up to Heroic, we sort of do the same with Nox the Darkmother. She's a nyktokinetic, wielding night and cold, as well as an energy vampire; she's held her own against *every* hero on the planet. Word was she had held downtown Manhattan *by herself* against a company of Jabberwocks. Nox was the one who'd come down on villains who were going too far. She was like the scary stepmother we were all afraid of. If there really was such a thing as a Covenant between villains, it was her doing.

She floated out of the sky, a swirling pool of inky blackness with a face floating near the top, so coldly beautiful that it might have been an ivory mask. Nox looked at the Atomic Brain, then at Fimbulwinter, and then at the rest of us.

"I have seen the heroes consumed with this madness, fighting each other like rabid animals, but I hadn't yet seen it in our ranks," she said, her voice carrying like an icy wind to the far reaches of the impromptu battlefield. "Why are you fighting? What cause has convinced you to destroy each other at such cost to yourselves?"

Nobody had much of an answer. I guess nobody thought that what had driven the heroes crazy could affect us too.

"You are the proximate cause," Nox said and...oh my God, she was looking at me. "And yet I do not consider you guilty of anything but looking for a new job. You're entitled to do that."

"Um, thanks," I said.

"I will call together a gathering of villains from around the world," Nox proclaimed. "There shall be a new Covenant, and a new understanding among us. We have let petty divisions drive us to bloodshed."

There were lots of villains who didn't mind bloodshed but nobody spoke up to correct Nox. Riproar in particular found the ground amazingly interesting just then.

"These two sides shall part in peace. In token of my services in ending this misbegotten war, I shall require tribute from all concerned. You will hear from me…or shall I say, you'll get my bill."

And then her darkness imploded and she was gone.

The Atomic Brain and Fimbulwinter looked at each other, not daring to do more than exchange baleful glares, and then they mustered their troops and retreated. I collected Snowball's remains and followed after Fimbulwinter, wondering what the heck just happened. When we'd all stepped back, I looked and Stella was gone. She knew the drill; don't hang around and don't make like you know anyone there. If the Atomic Brain had brought her, he'd let her go.

Okay then. Time to see what came next.

What came next was a letter. The handwriting was oversized and crude, but I had no trouble making it out. I was surprised it came to my home address, but rumor was the Ogre was a lot smarter than he let on. It read:

Hey WB,

I like guys with guts. That's why I gave you a hand and called in an old friend to break up that fight you had going on. Nox owed me a favor and now you owe me. I'll think of something I want and let you know.

You ever want to run with a gang of real monsters, look me up.

Ogre

PS, Nox says if you need a new job, give her a call.

Wow. I guess you never know.

Fimbulwinter didn't exactly fire me but he felt like he'd lost face, backing down to Nox. Supervillains get weird about stuff like that. I got called less and less, found out about meetings after they happened, and missed getting paid once or twice. I took the hint.

I called up Nox and it turned out she was hiring after all. I'm her one and only henchmonster.

So now I'm working for the scary godmother of the villain world. It's a pretty good gig.

I love being a monster.

Marvelous Man: Birth of Anarchy

Janine K. Spendlove

"You know, Lauren, now that you're eighteen the arrest will stay on your record." Jess gripped the steering wheel of her Prius, pulled back into traffic, and focused on the road before them, taking them away from Oakland and back to The City.

The sound of gum popping made Jess grip the wheel tighter. Lauren knew Jess hated when she did that.

"Oh come on, Jess, it's not like it was a felony. Just a widdle bitty miss-dee-mee-ner." Lauren stretched her pink gum out before her and wrapped it around her finger before popping it back in her mouth. Jess forced herself not to shudder.

Times like this she wondered if they really were sisters. Aside from not looking a thing alike—Jess was blonde and petite like their father, while Lauren had inherited their mother's dark Greek features and hefty build—they couldn't be more different in their personalities and interests either.

"So what was it this time?" Jess signaled left, looked over her shoulder, and eased into the next lane. Lauren would have just glanced at the mirrors and swerved over without so much as a "by your leave." Safely in the new lane, Jess couldn't help the bit of sarcasm that crept into her voice. "Another boot manufacturer killing baby seals? Rabbits being tortured by a cosmetics company?"

"No, it was NovoTech." At Jess's raised eyebrows Lauren clarified. "They're a pharmaceutical company that likes to experiment on primates." She placed her booted feet on the dash, though she knew Jess hated when she did that, and ran a black painted thumbnail along the side seam of her battered jeans. "And it's not like I started it. We were picketing peacefully—"

Jess snorted.

"*Peacefully*, and one of the NovoTech goons shoved me—"

"Probably more like pushed past you so he could get to work since I'm sure you were blocking the door."

"—So I shoved back, and one thing led to another…"

"Where's your sign?" They crossed the Golden Gate Bridge, and the low-lying fog still obscured a lot of the view of San Francisco.

"What sign?" Lauren popped her gum again as she stared out the passenger window.

"Oh come on, you *always* have a sign."

"Maybe I broke it." Lauren faced Jess, a large grin splitting her round face. "Maybe I broke it on that tool's head."

"Lauren!" Jess forced herself to keep her eyes on the road.

"What? It's not like I blew up the building or anything." Lauren was back to stretching out her gum and wrapping it around her thick index finger. "I probably should have, though. Would definitely have been more effective," she muttered before sticking the gum back in her mouth

"Look, I know you're just joking—you *are* joking, right?—but you can't go around blowing up buildings just because you don't like something. That would lead to anarchy. If you don't like the law, work to change it—you've got to allow the legal process a chance to work."

"But that would take years, and in the meantime more innocents will be killed." Lauren leaned her head against the passenger window, a look of dejection on her face so pitiful that Jess wanted to hug her and tell her everything would be alright. "Maybe we need a little bit of anarchy to effect some real change."

"Come on, Lauren, you don't mean that."

But Lauren didn't answer.

Jess opened the door to Ground Up and immediately felt herself relax. The smell of roasting coffee beans always put her at ease, as did the sight of her sister waving at her from their customary table in the back corner, with a perfect view of Nob Hill and the cable cars traversing it. No matter how things got between her and Lauren, the two of them always met for their Saturday morning chai date at Ground Up to touch base. After kissing their hellos, they both sat down just in time for Richie, the coffee shop's owner, to deliver their chai tea lattes.

"How are my two favorite rival sisters?" His dark hands contrasted sharply with the ceramic white mugs he placed before them. Jess had to force herself not to stare. She always thought he had the loveliest hands—big and strong, yet gentle at the same time.

Lauren snorted. "We're hardly rivals, Richie."

"But I thought you went to Berkley and Jess was an engineering wiz at Stanford." He swiped his hand over top of his bald head and Jess smiled into her mug.

"I'm far from a wiz, nor am I an undergrad. These days I spend most of my time dealing with recalcitrant students." She took a sip of her drink. "Why did I ever agree to be a TA?"

"Because Professor Anraku asked you to, and she's the best mechanical engineer ever and you wish you were half as cool as she is or something along those lines." Lauren barely dodged the kick Jess sent her way under the table and stuck her tongue out at her sister.

Richie raised two hands in surrender. "Okay, I'm out. Jess, call me when you need a refill." He gave her a wink as he left, and Jess felt her cheeks heat up in a brilliant blush.

Lauren smirked as she looked over at her sister. "You know, he never gives me free refills."

"Lauren…"

"He's pretty good looking for a thirty-something guy."

"Shut-up." Jess was already quite aware of how attractive Richie was.

"And he has his own business."

Jess readied her leg to launch another kick at her sister, when the sound of many people screaming assaulted her ears. She and Lauren both surged to their feet and another shop patron pointed up the hill at what appeared to be a cable car descending at breakneck speed.

"Oh my gosh!" Jess pressed herself against the window and heard Lauren quickly fill in Richie on what was going on while she dialed 911. "Why isn't the conductor using the rear wheel break?" Unable to sit and just watch the horror unfold Jess looked around for something, anything, that they could use to slow down the cable car before it passed them. Maybe if they slowed it enough, the passengers could leap to safety...

A blur of yellow and red landed in the street before them so forcefully, Jess felt her teeth clatter against each other.

Marvelous Man!

He held out his hands before him and just let the runaway cable car slam into him. It pushed him back about twenty feet, and he managed to tear furrows into the street with his feet. Jess inwardly cringed at the thought of how much energy had to have been transferred to both Marvelous Man and the cable car's passengers. She hoped none of them were injured too badly.

When Marvelous Man stepped out from the front of the cable car, Jess felt herself release a breath she hadn't even realized she was holding. He was okay. The crowd burst into applause and before they could surround him, begging for photos or autographs, the benevolent man from another world flashed them all a brilliant smile and zoomed back off into the sky.

"Jess!"

She jerked her head back from following Marvelous Man's trail across the clouds and looked over at a frantically waving Richie. He and Lauren were already helping the passengers out of the cable car, and Jess hurried over to join them.

"Wasn't that amazing?" she asked, as Lauren helped an elderly woman stand up.

"Amazing?" Lauren's eyes burned furiously as her mouth turned down. "While all those lookie-loos out there are taking pictures and cheering that alien asshole on, not a single one of them are worried about helping out anyone themselves." Lauren indicated everyone outside the cable car lining the streets and pointing up at the sky, and Jess felt her cheeks once again heat up, but this time from shame. Aside from her, Richie, and one or two other people, no one else seemed to even care about the injured people in the cable car.

They were too busy looking for Marvelous Man.

The following week blew by in a flurry of classes, grading papers, and explaining to Chand Svare Ghei, a student in her Structures 101 class, that hacking into FBI archives and telling her who really killed Kennedy would not garner him a passing grade. But overshadowing all that was the realization that her sister had been right—people were changing. They were becoming... lazier? Was that the right word? She couldn't quite explain what it is she had been noticing. She thought perhaps she just had a particularly bad crop of students this semester, or that people in The City were just more clueless or unobservant than usual.

During lunch that Wednesday, she munched on her cheddar avocado sandwich from her usual perch on the park bench. The spring breeze ruffled her blonde hair in its pony tail as she watched a group of college kids playing around with a Frisbee. It all seemed harmless enough until someone threw the Frisbee so hard it flew into oncoming traffic.

Jess jumped up shouting at the young man to be careful, as he dove for the Frisbee, seemingly heedless of the garbage truck barreling down at him. Time seemed to stand still as she closed her eyes, wincing in anticipation, and then... nothing.

The garbage truck rumbled on by, leaving a greasy stench of banana in its wake. Jess opened her eyes and saw a bright yellow chest emblazoned with a crimson "M" directly before her.

She slowly brought her gaze up to meet crystal blue eyes on a perfectly chiseled, beautiful face, and felt her mouth go dry.

"I believe you dropped this, Ma'am." His kind voice immediately put her at ease, and she felt him slip her forgotten sandwich into her hands. He gave her a brilliant grin—she could have sworn his teeth dang near sparkled—and with a toss of his black hair, was gone, leaving nothing but a swirl of fresh-smelling air in his wake.

Jess felt her legs go weak as she sank back down onto the bench. People were pointing up at where Marvelous Man had flown off, and a few were pointing at her—some even pulled out cameras and took her picture. The reckless Frisbee player was busy high-fiving his friends, and Jess watched in shock as they threw the Frisbee toward the street again. Thankfully this time there were no cars coming.

She needed to talk to Lauren.

The following Saturday when Jess bustled into the coffee shop for their chai date, she was a bit disappointed that Lauren wasn't already waiting for her. All her attempts at meeting up early were for naught, and she was desperate to get Lauren's thoughts on Marvelous Man.

"You're early." Richie waved at her from behind the counter, and Jess smiled back with a shrug before moving to her usual corner of the shop. Jess would wait for Lauren to arrive before she ordered their drinks. No point letting their chai get cold.

She pulled out her phone and texted Lauren "here," to which her sister responded "got a late start. tell u when I get there. almost 2 the muni station. c u in a bit."

Satisfied, Jess looked out the window and noticed they'd already paved over the furrows Marvelous Man had gouged in the asphalt. That didn't stop the tourists from gawking though.

"They've been coming here all week, like they're on a sacred pilgrimage or something." Richie set a mug of chai and a spoon in front of Jess. He then took the seat opposite her, cradling a cup of steaming coffee so dark and rich, it was almost a perfect match for his skin tone.

"Thanks for the chai." She stirred it with the spoon more out of habit than because it needed anything added to it. Richie always made it just to her taste. "You know you can't keep giving me free drinks."

"Sure I can." He took a sip of his coffee and smiled, his brilliant white teeth gleaming against his square jaw and strong cheekbones. Jess was momentarily reminded of another set of brilliant teeth and square jaw, and found she much preferred her current company. Marvelous Man, for all his attractiveness and allure felt... alien.

"It's my shop, after all."

Blushing once again, Jess looked down at her drink. "You know what I mean."

"I do. But I don't think you know what I mean." He reached out and engulfed her hand with his. "You're one of my favorite people, Jess. It makes me happy to see you smile, and you don't do it nearly enough. So, as long as you keep coming here, I'll keep doing what I can to make sure you keep smiling."

She peeked up at him through her blonde lashes, not understanding why her heart was racing and she was fighting another blush. "But I don't want to take advantage of you."

He removed his hand from hers and laughed. "Oh, Jess, you are not the only person I give free drinks to. Charlie, who lives in the box around the corner, gets a morning shot of Joe on the house every day. Diane, who works security for Wells Fargo gets a peppermint tea with honey every so often, and, well, I could go on."

Jess felt both worse and better. At least she wasn't a solitary mooch, but at the same time she no longer felt as special as she had before.

Taking another sip of his coffee, he smiled at her again, but then frowned as he noticed his watch. "Where's Lauren? Shouldn't she be here by now?"

Jess blinked, stopping herself from staring at his caramel-colored eyes, and checked her phone. Yes, Lauren definitely should have been here by now.

Not again, she thought.

Jess texted Lauren once more, but never received anything back. Eventually Richie had to go back to work—the line was getting long, overwhelming the other employees, and not even chatting with one of his "favorite people" could justify neglecting it. Another hour passed, and finally Jess left feeling well and truly stood up.

It wasn't until she got home and saw the police car that she stopped being angry with Lauren.

Jess sat numbly on the wooden chair at her dining table trying to process everything that had happened.

Lauren was dead.

Jess had identified the body and told their parents.

Her sister had been mugged on her way to the train station, and instead of just giving the guy her purse, she'd fought back. The mugger had stabbed her and left her for dead.

How did Jess know all this?

Because there were witnesses. Three people had seen the entire attack from start to finish, and not a single one of them had lifted a finger to help save her sister. Not one.

Why why why why why why why why why?

A stray thought broke through her chorus of "why" as she remembered the Kennedy assassination.

She picked up her phone with trembling hands and it took her several times to punch in the number correctly.

"Hello?"

"Chand?" She felt a tear leak from the corner of her eye. Her voice remained strong.

"Yeah, who is this?"

"It's Jess." The tear trailed down her cheek.

"Who?"

"Your Structures TA." Her tear hung for a moment on the edge of her chin before dropping down and splashing onto the surface of her clean, wooden table.

"Oh."

"I have a way you can pass the class if your hacking skills are as good as you claim they are."

⟤ ∈ ⟥

The following Saturday Jess sat at the same corner table at Ground Up where she'd first seen Marvelous Man.

"More like Monstrous Man," she muttered while gripping her now cold cup of chai.

"What was that?" Richie sat down across from her before gently prying her fingers off the cup and replacing it with a hot one. She knew that she should thank him for the attentiveness. She knew that somewhere in the back of her mind she was exulting over the tingly touch of his calloused fingertips across her knuckles. But all she could think of was the fact that her sister was dead, and it was all Marvelous Man's fault.

"He's a cancer to The City, and soon he will be to the entire world."

"Jess, I know you're upset that he didn't save her—"

"No!" She slammed her cup down, the hot chai sloshing over and scalding her skin. She reveled in the pain because it was at least a ghost of the agony in her heart. "You have no idea what I'm thinking or feeling right now. No idea whatsoever."

He held up his hands in a pacifying gesture. "You're right. I'm sorry. Your feelings are exactly that: your feelings." He pulled a dishtowel from the pocket of his apron and reached over to mop up the spill on the table. His kind, understanding gaze met hers, and she felt herself soften slightly.

"Richie, I…" She finally sipped her drink, cinnamon and cardamom exploding on her tongue, reminding her that Christmas was coming, and with it, her first holiday without her baby sister. "…I got a copy of the police report."

"How in the world did you get your hands on that? I thought they weren't done with the investigation." She just raised one blonde eyebrow and he once again held up his hands. "Please continue."

"Here's the thing, I'm not angry that Marvelous Man didn't show up. I'm angry with the witnesses who did nothing. They watched my sister get attacked and *murdered* right in front of them and did *nothing* to help her. Nothing at all." She took another sip of her chai. Her hand was shaking so badly that the mug clattered against her teeth.

"That's awful. Jess, I'm so sorry—"

She held up one trembling hand. "No, that's not the awful part. The truly awful part is that when questioned as to why they did nothing every last one of them, complete strangers to each other, said it was because they were waiting for Marvelous Man to show up and save her."

Richie covered her shaking hand with his and she felt herself still beneath his calming touch.

"I'm here for you, Jess. You know that, right? If you ever need a friend—"

She jerked her hand away, suddenly angry. "What good is a friend in this world? A world where people won't even stop a man from murdering someone right in front of them." She had to bite her lip to keep from devolving into tears.

"We can't just close ourselves off from relationships. They're part of what makes us human. If we stop caring about each other, that would lead to anarchy."

At Richie's words, Jess felt a hint of a smile tug at her lips. Lauren would like that. "Maybe a little anarchy is what we need."

◄■ Є ►

Jess felt the heat from flames as the force of the blast propelled her forward a few feet and knocked her to the ground. She groaned as she rolled over onto her back and beheld the glorious sight before her.

NovoTech was almost completely consumed in flames, and the view was almost enough to wash away the wave of pain along her back. She'd definitely been burned.

"Next time I need to be farther away or build a protective suit or something." She rolled to her hands and knees and went to pull herself up against the brick wall before her when a heavy hand descended on her shoulder.

"How about next time you don't blow up a building?"

Panicking, Jess flailed out her hands, kicking back against her attacker, before recognizing Richie's soothing voice. She stopped struggling and he loosened his hold on her, but didn't let her go. She could feel his deft fingers as he inspected her back.

"Did you follow me?"

"I'm worried about you."

"So you followed me here. That's kinda creepy." She winced as one of his fingers skimmed a burn.

"Says the woman who just blew up a building."

"Not just any building. This one was a worthy cause." Her face blossomed into a smile as she looked back at the building. One wall remained intact, with the word ANARCHY burning along its surface. That had taken some doing, but nothing a bit of engineering couldn't handle. Lauren would have been so happy.

"I agree with you on that point at least. NovoTech has done horrible things to this neighborhood. And the police here aren't much better." Richie dropped his hands and walked around her to face her. "You'll be fine. I've got some prescription burn cream at the coffee shop, so I think we can avoid a trip to the ER, but we need to get going before you get caught." He gave her arm a gentle tug, but stopped when she held up a staying hand.

"Not just yet."

He followed her skyward gaze, and Jess was grateful for the alien invader's obscenely bright yellow suit. It stuck out brightly in the night sky.

She watched as he used some sort of freezing breath to put out the flames, and also noticed that he was very careful not to go near the flames themselves. She didn't know if that was because fire could hurt him or if he was trying to preserve his suit.

"Are you studying him?"

Jess nodded. "Yes."

"Do you intend to fight him?"

"Eventually."

The alien picked up a heavy metal girder and tossed it aside like it was a feather pillow.

Jess flexed her free arm and looked back at the monster before her. "I'll need something to augment my strength. Just going to the gym isn't going to cut it. Maybe some sort of armored mech sleeve?" She started thinking of design potentials when she heard Richie snort.

"What? You don't think I could build a mechanical arm?" She didn't know why, but the idea that Richie didn't think she could do something bothered her more than it should have.

"You're one of the smartest people I know. I think you could build and entire armored suit and make it fly if you wanted to." He gave her arm a slightly forceful tug and led her down the alley, and away from the building. The distant sound of sirens blossomed in the chilly night air. "But super strength isn't going to win any fights with Monstrous Man if you don't know how to throw a punch."

Jess allowed him to help her up into the high cab of his delivery van, hidden away several streets over from NovoTech. She watched as he deposited a box full of day old pastries from Ground Up on the stoop of the homeless shelter they were parked across from. Either he was incredibly kind and generous, which perfectly suited him, or he'd known what she'd been planning and had an alibi ready for them both.

Probably both.

As he climbed into the driver's seat and started the van, Jess cocked her head to the side, remembering how easily he'd blocked her punches and kicks.

"You know how to fight, don't you?"

He shrugged. "Mostly wrestle, but yeah, I got in a few tussles growing up around here." He looked at the dilapidated buildings surrounding them, and Jess felt a chill crawl up her back, as if she was being watched with malicious intent by someone in the shadows.

"Impossible not to, really," he continued. "There's a reason Oakland is the most dangerous city in California."

Their eyes met and she held his steady gaze, feeling completely understood for the first time since Lauren's murder. Or perhaps he'd always understood her.

A streak of yellow zoomed up into the sky, breaking the spell, and Jess felt herself suck in a breath.

"Could you teach me how?"

"To fight?" Richie threw the van's gearshift into drive and stepped on the gas, narrowly avoiding a hooded figure stepping toward them. Jess could have sworn she saw a flash of metal in the stranger's hand.

"Yeah." Richie ran the next two red lights, and didn't ease off on the gas until they were well clear of the area. "I can teach you how to fight."

THE SHTICK

Aaron Rosenberg

"THOSE STUPID DO-GOODERS WILL NEVER—AW, COME ON!" WALTER C. Shticklemeyer whined as the costumed duo burst into the heart of his lair. "How'd you even find me?"

"Seriously, Eraserhead?" Twilight the Shade Prince asked, sharing a surprised but amused glance with his mentor and partner, Midnight King. "You stole the second-most valuable gem in the world—Number Two—from the Ticonderoga Museum. And now you're holed up in an abandoned pencil factory?"

"Let's face it, chum," Midnight King added in that distinctive growl of his as he strode across the room toward where Walter cowered behind his desk, "you're predictable. But then, evil always is."

"Oh, yeah?" Walter straightened as the dark-clad hero approached. "Well, predict this!" he raised his voice. "Pencil-necks, get them!"

Twlight giggled, arms crossed over his chest. "We already took care of your henchmen," he reported. "So you can go ahead and write them off." He laughed at his own joke, and Midnight King joined in with his raspy chuckle.

"Curse you, Midnight King!" Walter cried. The hero reached for him, but Walter managed to pull free, wailing—and punched Midnight King full in the face.

"Owwww!" The skinny little villain cradled his injured hand as the hero dragged him from the room. "That hurt!"

"Crime always does," Midnight King rasped down at him. "Crime always does."

"You're who, now?" The big bruiser who'd just cut in front of Walter asked, peering down at him with beady little eyes. "Erasermate?" Several of the other inmates in the prison cafeteria laughed.

"Eraserhead!" Walter replied indignantly, hands tightening on his lunch tray. "Eraserhead!" he pointed at his hair, which stood up several inches and was still cut in a perfectly circular flat top, thanks to First City's policy of letting inmates retain their distinctive looks as much as possible. Looking around him, he could see plenty of others with unique hairstyles, face paint, eyewear, and even a certain degree of jewelry. The big guy in front of him, however, had none of those—he was completely nondescript in his orange prison jumpsuit, just another giant slab of muscle as he slowly shook his head.

"Never heard of you," the bruiser declared, turning toward the cafeteria workers and holding out his tray to receive large scoops of equally nondescript prison food.

But Walter wasn't ready to let it go. "Never heard of me!" he practically screeched. "I fought Midnight King! Repeatedly!"

Now the bruiser laughed. "You? Fought Midnight King?" Again the dismissive once-over. "What'd you do, threaten to bleed on him?" That got more laughs. "Listen, pal," the big guy added, "most of us went up against that cowled clown, or worked for guys who did. That's how we wound up in here. That don't make you special." The conversation over, he took his now-loaded tray and headed toward the row upon row of tables for someplace to eat in peace. Plenty of others moved aside to let him pass.

"I am special," Walter insisted, but in a much quieter voice, nearly a whisper, as he surrendered his tray to the cafeteria workers. "I'm Eraserhead."

But even he wasn't sure he believed it anymore.

"I'm not special," Walter declared, slumping on the stool in front of a threefold standing mirror. "Hardly anybody's even heard of Eraserhead, and those who have think I'm a joke."

"So change," the woman at the long sewing table against the far wall replied. She glanced over at him and frowned. "You need a new—"

"Don't say it," Walter warned. Growing up, all anyone ever called him was "Shtick," and he hated that nickname, and the word in general. But she was right. Look at how easily Midnight King had found him last time. An old pencil factory? Could he have been more obvious? "I really am a joke," he decided, slumping even more. "I'm pathetic."

"Stop putting yourself down," his companion and hostess snapped. "Every time you do, you owe me twenty push-ups."

"What?" That made his head jerk up, at least, as he stared across the room at her. "But, Launi—"

Her glare stopped him cold.

"Right, sorry—Seamstrix." It was amazing how cowed he was by someone who was only five feet tall, but for all her short stature Launi Rombach, seamstress to the supervillains, was no one to mess with. And despite her height, with that long, straight silvery-white hair and her stern expression, not to mention her own costume—a leather dominatrix outfit, all buckles and straps, but covered in pockets filled with scissors and tape measures and needle and thread and lots and lots of pins—she was actually really imposing.

Which made sense. Why would you commission a supervillain costume from someone who couldn't even make a convincing one for herself?

The Seamstrix was the go-to choice for every supervillain in First City. And Walter had been going to her for years. They'd even developed a sort of friendship. In fact, in a lot of ways she was his closest friend. Which was why, as soon as he'd gotten out—which had only been after a few months, since even with First City's rather lax view toward costumed vigilantes it had still wound up being one costumed nut's word against another, because like most supervillains who'd managed to survive, Walter was at least professional enough to blank out all security cameras first, and to wear gloves the whole time—Walter had gone straight to her.

But his days of wearing a striped yellow turtleneck and matching leggings were over. Eraserhead was dead.

That hated word aside, Launi was absolutely right, Walter realized as he wearily climbed down off the stool, stretched out on his stomach on the floor, and began slowly, wretchedly doing push-ups.

He needed something new.

"This is ridiculous," Walter declared a few days later. He was standing once again, pivoting back and forth before the mirrors, studying his reflection. Which looked just as confused and horrified as he felt. "I look like an idiot."

"You look like a supervillain," Launi corrected, the words only slightly garbled by the pins in her mouth. "Stand still!"

He froze, letting her adjust the last elements of his new costume. Which was altogether preposterous. He was wearing an elegant dinner jacket that looked like it belonged in a Victorian drama, a silk waistcoat with an intricate paw-print pattern, and pinstriped pants. But instead of lace, fur protruded from his jacket cuffs, the pants were golden-brown to match the waistcoat, the jacket was tawny, and he wearing an elaborate silk ruff like you'd see in an old Shakespearean play. And a tufted tail stuck out from the jacket as well, waving slightly as Launi moved around him, hemming the pants over the cats-paw boots she'd stuck on his feet.

"Here," she said finally, straightening and handing him a silk top hat—also tawny brown, and with cat ears affixed to the brim.

Walter obediently placed the hat on his head, stared at himself a second, then pulled it off again. "No," he decided. "I can't. It's just too silly."

That earned him a glare, and a head-jerk toward the floor. And one word:

"Push-ups."

Sighing, he set the hat aside and dropped to the ground. This was already the twelfth time she'd made him do push-ups, and he'd only been out for a week!

"I'm going to be a laughing-stock," he muttered as he forced his stringy arms to lift him off the floor. "Again."

" 'Sincerely, the Dandy-lion,'" Twilight read off the handsomely engraved card. He looked up at his mentor. "Who the heck is the Dandy-lion?"

"I don't know," Midnight King admitted in his usual gravely voice. "But whoever he is, he's smart. Hit the Victorian Flowers exhibit and made off with the Cat's Eye, the centerpiece of Queen

Victoria's famous Jeweled Bouquet." The caped detective clenched a fist and pounded it against the now-empty display case. "We'll catch him, though."

"Sure," his partner agreed, though his expression behind the mask said otherwise. "Just as soon as we figure out who in tarnation he is!"

⟞€⟝

"It worked!" Walter did a little jig around the crowded sewing room, even going so far as to twirl Launi at one point. She barely cracked a smile, but that didn't stop him. "It totally worked!" He held up the fist-sized gem for her to see. "Look at it! It's gorgeous! And priceless! And that dundering fool doesn't have a clue who did it, or where to find me!" He laughed and spun Launi around again. "You're a genius!"

This time she did smile—just a little. "Glad you're satisfied," she said with her usual acerbity. "Bye."

But Walter had stopped dancing. "No no," he told her, shaking his head as he shucked the fancy coat with its tails—and tail. "That was fun, and I'm thrilled it worked, but this—this just isn't me. I'm sorry." He sighed. "I'm going to need something else."

Launi glared at him, but then her gaze shifted to the enormous jewel in his hand. "Well," she muttered, "at least I know you can pay me. Not like some people." She nodded. "Right. Strip."

She turned away to gather her tools, while Walter began to divest himself of the costume. He hoped the next one would be a little more...dignified.

⟞€⟝

"Okay, and I thought the last one looked silly," he announced as he examined himself in the mirrors the following week, after she'd finished putting together the new outfit. "This one is even worse."

He was wearing more stripes—what was it with her and stripes lately?—but now he was in a more traditional supervillain one-piece unitard, at least. And the stripes weren't so much solid lines as closely spaced dots, running all up and down his arms, legs, and torso.

As he stared at the form-fitting costume, Walter had to admit something: he really needed to work out more. And to cut back on those jelly donuts.

Launi was already glaring at him, and he knew exactly what she was going to say before she even opened her mouth:

"Push-ups."

"Yes, fine," he groused, though he didn't hesitate to comply. "At least I'll be nice and fit when they catch me and send me back to prison."

—◄E►—

" 'If you agree to these terms, sign…the Dotted Line,' " Twilight read aloud, holding up what looked like a contract but was actually a ransom demand. "Who?"

"Some new villain, obviously," his partner growled. "And he's taken Deputy Mayor Costanza—who's known as the Head of the Hard-line." Midnight King shook his head. "First that Dandy-lion, and now this. Who are these people?"

"What're we gonna do?" Twilight asked as Police Commissioner Ian McClellan approached. "We don't know this guy, so how're we gonna find him?"

That produced another growl from his partner, this one even more frustrated than the last. "We can't," he admitted softly, grinding the words out through clenched teeth. "Not in time. Which means the city—and Costanza's family, who're loaded—will pay the ransom. And we'll hope we can intercept it in time."

But judging by his tone, Twilight could tell his partner didn't really expect that to happen. This new criminal was too careful. Too clever.

And, because they'd never encountered him before, too unpredictable.

—◄E►—

"I can't believe that worked!" Walter shouted, throwing handfuls of money up in the air and letting the bills rain down around him. "It actually worked!"

Launi didn't say anything, though her quick hands did snatch several bills before they could hit the ground, depositing the money into her many pockets quick as a wink. But Walter didn't mind. He was too busy celebrating. And besides, he owed her the rest of the money for the outfit.

"First the Cat's Eye"—which he had already sold to a collector for a ridiculous amount of money— "and now this! It's amazing!"

"Glad you're satisfied," the costumed seamstress drawled, her gaze drifting very deliberately toward the door leading out of her concealed shop.

But Walter's joy had faded once again, his mood dropping as quickly as the ransom money now drifting to the floor all around him. "Happy with the job, yes," he agreed. "But with the costume? Not so much." He plucked at the fabric clinging to his thin arms. "It's too close. And it chafes."

The woman beside him sighed. "So you want something different?" she interpreted.

"Yes! Please!" He beamed down at her. "As you can see, money isn't a problem. I just need something a little more...classy. Less circus-acrobat and more...I don't know, business mogul?"

"Business mogul?" Launi had produced a grease pencil from one of her many pockets, and now tapped it idly against her chin. Finally she nodded. "Got just the thing."

Walter waited, fidgeting slightly, as she turned away to collect materials so she could start measuring and cutting. He hoped this new costume—and the identity to go with it—would be a little more to his liking.

◄═ E ═►

"Stripes? Again?" Walter exclaimed, looking at himself in his latest costume, which she had finally finished after several days and multiple fittings—and a whole lot of push-ups in be-tween. "Really? And what is it with you and fur?" He adjusted the fur-rimmed metal cap on his head. "Come on!"

His exasperation was met with the usual glare, and he lowered his head. "Yeah, I know," he said before she even spoke. "Push-ups." He grimaced. "At least those are getting easier!"

"Make it fifty, then," came the reply as he lowered himself to the ground. Walter knew better than to say no.

"Happy?" he asked twenty minutes later, as he levered himself back up with noodle-like arms. "But seriously, how does this make any sense?" He held out his arms. He was wearing a nice, classy three-piece suit, pinstripe gray—only it had studded leather pieces over the shoulders, a matching armored chestplate instead of a vest, fur-lined leather boots, and of course the helmet, which was like someone had wrapped a medieval knight's half-helm—or an old Army helmet—in fur, and added a spike on top.

"You wanted mogul," Launi reminded him sharply. She gestured at his new get-up. "I give you..."

"The Business Mongol?" Twilight asked, staring at the note the latest villain had left behind. "Where are these guys even coming from?"

"I wish I knew," Midnight King admitted, pacing the empty executive office, which was most notable for its fine furnishings—and its missing computer. "But with a name like that, it makes sense he'd strike here, stealing valuable trade secrets from this particular company." His fingers traced the company logo emblazoned on a bronze plaque on the wall. The words read "Temujin Industries."

Twilight was, as always, quick to catch on. "And Temujin," he said, "was the birth name of Genghis Khan—"

"The founder of the Mongol Empire," his partner finished. He slammed his gauntleted fists together, a sure sign of his mounting frustration. "If we'd known, we could have beaten him here. And next time, we will. But this time?" He shook his cowled head. "Without any prior warning, we had no way of even knowing this one existed, let alone where he'd hit."

"Don't worry, MK," Twilight assured his mentor, playfully punching the older man in the arm. "We'll get him next time."

"There won't be a next time," Walter insisted, tossing the fur-lined cap onto Launi's sewing table and narrowly missing the computer hard drive already resting there. "Oh, sure, it was a success and all—I've already got a buyer lined up for the secrets on this drive. But this?" He patted the heavy shoulder pieces atop his suit jacket. "I almost got stuck climbing in the window with these! And this"—he indicated the suit itself—"isn't exactly suited—ha ha—to an active life of crime."

He favored the diminutive seamstress with a smile. "Sorry, Launi—I mean, Seamstrix. I know you worked hard on this one. But I need something else. Something I can move in. Something"—he paused, staring off into space as he reached for inspiration—"something with a little more grace. More poetry."

"Poetry, huh?" She cocked an eyebrow at him. "I know just the thing."

Walter already knew the routine. While she bustled about the room, pulling out fabric and other elements to start work on the new costume, he began pulling off the old one.

And he dropped and did a few quick push-ups, too, just in case.

He made a mental note, though, to ask her if he could keep the suit. Minus the fur and leather bits, of course—but without those, it'd look nice for formal occasions.

Or for his next court date.

"I'm wearing a blouse!" Walter shouted when the latest ensemble was ready, waving his arms so the long, wide-mouthed sleeves swirled around him. "A freaking silk blouse! How am I supposed to intimidate anybody like this? What am I, the Hostage Hostess?"

Conversation paused then, as he did yet more push-ups. He was half-convinced the Seamstrix had been an Army drill sergeant in a previous life. Or maybe just earlier in this one, it was hard to tell.

"Not a dress," Launi corrected after he'd finished and was on his feet again, adjusting the sash tied about his waist and stepping back to take in the full effect. "A kimono. And hakama." She tapped the wide, flared pants that, honestly, Walter had thought was a skirt until he tried putting it on. Launi turned away for a second, and when she twisted back around she had a loose jacket or overshirt in her hands, with sleeves just as wide as the kimono's. "And haori," she explained, holding it out for him to slip into. "Traditional Samurai garb."

The mention of the ancient Japanese warrior clan calmed him down somewhat. "Samurai, huh?" Walter muttered, letting her tug the jacket about so that it hung properly, its sides loose, its wide lapels open to expose the kimono beneath. "Yeah, okay. Does that mean I get a—ah!" The exclamation slipped from his lips as the short seamstress presented him with a katana, a Japanese longsword, and then showed him how to slide it through the sash, the curve angled downward. "Well, all right, then!"

This time, when he struck a pose, Walter admired himself in the mirror. This really did look pretty good, he had to admit. With the full garb on, and the sword especially, he looked fierce. Capable.

Dangerous.

"So, who am I now?" he wondered, speaking to his reflection. "The Sinister Samurai? The Evil Swordsman? The Ronin Raider?"

But, standing just a little behind him, he saw in the mirror that Launi was shaking her head. "You know how to use that?" she demanded, tapping the sword's cloth-wrapped handle with a forefinger.

"Well, no," Walter acknowledged. "So?"

"So, you're no swordsman," she snapped. "Focus on what you're good at."

"And what's that?" he asked, half-afraid of the answer.

His incredulity and instant denial when she told him only earned him more push-ups.

At least I'll be in better shape when I go back inside, he told himself as he shoved off the floor fifty more times. *Too bad they won't let me keep the sword!*

◄ Ǝ ►

" 'Lovely as the sun/rare as a star fell to earth/beauty in my hand,'" Twilight recited. He held the small scroll out for his partner's perusal. "And there's this weird mark up in the corner."

Midnight King studied the small red box encapsulating several red lines, placed well above the black ink of the note itself. "It's a chop," he explained in his usual grating tones. "Like a cross between a signature and a seal. This one says"—he frowned as he studied the marks—" 'haiku,' which this is, and 'ou sama,' which means 'king.' The Haiku King." The masked superhero rubbed at his forehead through his cowl. "I hate haiku," he muttered in a low rasp. "It's the metaphors, they always mess with me."

"Well, this one seems pretty clear," Twilight offered, trying to hide his dismay at his partner's discomfort. Midnight King was a seasoned pro—he never let this stuff get to him. "I mean, he's talking about the rock he took, right?"

"He is," Midnight King agreed. "Moraeite. A new, super-rare element, said to be a close cousin to Lutetium, which until now was the most expensive natural element in existence. This was the single largest moraeite sample ever discovered, and unlike lutetium it's completely pure. Lutetium is worth thousands per gram—this was a rock the size of my fist, so close to three hundred grams, and its estimated value was over a million bucks." He shook his head. "That's not the only reason he went after this, though."

Twilight grinned. If his mentor was back in lecture mode, he must be feeling a little better. "What else is there?" he asked obediently.

"Its name, for one thing," Midnight King replied. He tapped the plaque on the empty case. "Moraeite. Morae are the Japanese equivalent to syllables, more or less. Haiku are composed of morae." He held up a finger. "There's more, though. This is the Shiki Institute," he explained, gesturing at the high-tech lab around them. "Masaoka Shiki was the writer who popularized the term 'haiku,' back in the nineteenth century."

"So this Haiku King really knows his stuff," Twilight summarized. He rubbed a gloved hand across his crew-cut. "How do we catch him?"

His partner sighed uncharacteristically, and his reply was so low Twilight had to strain to hear it. "I wish I knew."

—◄ E ►—

"I just don't get it," Midnight King exclaimed a few nights later, banging his fist down on the round table before him. "Everything was business as usual in First City, the standard costumed baddies would pop up and Twilight and me would put them down, there'd be robberies and kidnappings and the occasional bomb, it was all good." He pushed back his chair and crossed his arms, scowling at nothing and everything. "Now, all of a sudden, I've got this whole new slew of villains showing up out of nowhere!" Holding up one gauntleted hand, he began ticking them off on his fingers. "Dandy-lion. Dotted Line. Business Mongol. Haiku King. Who the hell are these guys? Where'd they all come from?" He shook his head. "And so far none of them have hit twice, so I haven't had a chance to predict their moves. It's making me crazy!"

Captain Solar nodded his sympathy. As usual, the alien super hero had declined a seat and was instead hovering in mid-air, his feet just a few inches off the ground, arms crossed over his powerful chest. "I wish I knew how to help, old friend," he intoned, his words echoing with power even though he kept them soft and his tone as conversational as he knew how. He frowned, the expression pulling at his sternly handsome face, his flared-sun eyes glowing. "I would be happy to scan your city for any trace of these villains, if you'd like. But unless they are currently in costume or committing felonies, I would not be able to detect them. Not without more to go on."

"There isn't any more," Twilight interjected, leaning forward to perch on the edge of his own seat. "These guys are careful, every one of them. They all wear gloves. They cut the security feeds. We don't have a single smidge of trace evidence on any of them!"

"I could zip through the city and look for them," the Streak offered, "but like the captain said, if they're not doing something right then and there I wouldn't have any way to know I'd even found them." He shrugged. "Plus, a lot of people get angry when I phase through their homes."

"That's because you insist on running around butt-naked," Lightshade told him. "Nobody wants to see that, dude."

"I'm in constant motion," their resident speedster insisted with what looked the start of a pout. "Everything's blurred out!"

"Yeah, we still know it's there." Lightshade shuddered. "Why'd you think we made sure each of us had our own special seat with our name on it? Nobody wants to sit in the same place as you and your boys."

"Perhaps we could discuss something else," Junoesque Justice suggested with just a hint of steel in her voice, though her lovely features had already darkened a few shades. Born on a small tropical island of only women, she still wasn't terribly comfortable with men in general, and naked ones in particular. "I would also be happy to assist in the search for these new foes of yours," the statuesque heroine told Midnight King, flexing her impressive arms, "if I only knew a way that I could help." Beside her, their other female teammate, Eagless, nodded in agreement.

"I could talk to the fish, ask if they've seen anything," Herr Meere said in his customary whisper, which was so soft only Captain Solar could usually make out what he was saying. "But unless they've been pulling crimes by the river or near the harbor, I doubt that will yield much. Sorry." He sank back into his chair, looking embarrassed. For someone who was essentially the ruler of the seven seas, he always seemed so uncomfortable speaking up, even here when it was just them.

Lightshade, on the other hand, propped his feet up on the table, casual as ever. "Sorry, guys," the Lightstone-wielding superhero said, nodding toward Captain Solar. "The big guy's right. We'd love to help, you know we would—that's what the Hero Bunch is all about, right? And if you've got a runaway satellite, a mad godling, a demon infestation, a crazed warlord, an army of murderous robots—we're there. But this?" He spread his hands, the flickering colors of the gem in his forehead casting strange shadows across the table and around the room. "This just sounds like a bunch of costumed baddies running loose in your city. That's really more your thing than ours." He shrugged.

"I know it's my problem," Midnight King grated, pushing back his chair and rising to his feet with his usual grace despite the heavy body armor he wore. "And I'll deal with it, me and Twilight. I just came here to—well, to vent, I suppose." He spun on his heel, cloak flaring behind him, as Twilight hurried to his side. "By next meeting I'll have this taken care of and First City back to normal."

"Great," Lightshade called out behind him as the duo headed for the door. "Your turn to bring the snacks!"

Midnight King grumbled something in reply, but too softly to make out. Then they were gone.

"Look at this!" Walter threw the newspaper down onto Launi's sewing table. In big, bold letters the front page declared "Wave of New Costumed Baddies Has Heroes Stumped!"

"Nice," the short seamstress acknowledged with a curt nod after glancing at it quickly.

"No, not nice," Walter argued, grabbing the paper up only to hurl it down again. "Not nice at all! 'Wave of New Costumed Baddies'? They have no idea it's me! They have no idea *any* of them are me, much less all of them!"

His companion studied him, her face stoic as always. "So?" she queried. "Isn't that a good thing? If they don't know it's you, they can't catch you. Isn't that what you wanted?"

"What? No! Yes! I don't know!" Walter slumped down onto the ever-present stool, head cradled in his long, thin hands. "I thought so! I mean, yes, it's nice not getting carted off to jail every time I pull a job. It's nice actually completing the jobs and raking in the dough and even being able to squirrel it all away. That's good. And it's nice to know I've got Midnight King and his obnoxious little sidekick completely bamboozled." He peered up at her through his fingers, his eyes wide and imploring. "But he doesn't know it's me! Nobody does! I'm finally beating Midnight King, and you're the only person who has any idea!"

She shrugged. "Still not seeing how that's a bad thing."

"Because," Walter whined, leaping up from the stool to pace the room. "Don't you get it? It's not about the money. I mean, sure, the money's great and all. But it's about the fame! The glory! The rep! And if they don't know it's me pulling all these jobs, making those caped clowns look like fools, well, then as far as anybody knows, I'm still a nobody." He sighed. "And that's not who I want to be."

"So?" Launi fixed him with her usual stony glare. "What're you gonna do about it?"

Faced with her irritation, Walter automatically dropped to the floor and started doing push-ups. She'd recently upgraded him to a hundred, and he was gasping for air when he straightened back up a few minutes later. But at least the exercise had helped him clear his head. "I'm going to need a new costume," he told her. "Sort of."

Then he told her what he wanted.

It only took the Seamstrix a few days to pull it together. "This may be the ugliest thing I've ever had to make," she told Walter critically as she watched him try it on. "And I once had to sew spandex diapers for Big Baby."

Walter disagreed, however. "It's perfect," he assured her. "It's exactly what I needed." Then he gave her a quick hug and a peck on the cheek and headed for the door. "I may not be back for a little while," he warned as he departed.

"Good, it'll give my fingers a chance to rest!" she shouted after him. But if Walter had turned around, he would have seen the worry in Launi's eyes as he left.

His own eyes, however, were firmly fixed on the future. His future. The one he wanted, and was finally going to reach out and grab.

⊰ Ε ⊱

"Midnight King!" Walter shouted as he strode into the ball-room. It was First City's annual Mayoral Fundraiser, and all the city's bigwigs were there. Which meant that the costumed hero had to be lurking nearby, too, in case the mayor and his friends needed protecting. "I know you're here," Walter continued, reaching over and yanking a diamond pendant off a stunned partygoer's neck, then snatching pearls from another. "Show yourself!"

Sure enough, a dark-clad figure stepped from the shadows in the room's far corner. "Who exactly are you supposed to be?" The hero grated as he stalked toward Walter with his trademark blend of fluidity and rage. Twilight pranced along half a step behind him.

"Me?" Walter spread his arms wide, knowing that the entire room was taking in his admittedly garish ensemble. He had on the Dandy-lion's waistcoat over the Dotted Line's unitard and above the Haiku King's hakama pants, with the Business Mongol's fur-lined boots and helmet. "I am—the Shtick!"

And finally, after all these years, the old nickname felt like it fit.

"It was you the whole time?" Twilight asked as the duo closed in on Walter. "You pulled all those capers?"

"That's right, Boy Shadow," Walter replied, grinning back at them. "It's been me the whole time. Walter C. Shticklemeyer. The Shtick. And you couldn't catch me, not one single time."

"We caught you now," Midnight King growled, stepping up to get in Walter's face, leaning in so close their noses almost touched.

"You couldn't catch a cold," Walter taunted. "I'm giving myself up." He laughed, and took a quick step back. "But first—" He cocked back his fist.

Smirking, Midnight King stood there and let Walter take his best shot.

Kapow! Walter landed a solid blow right on the cowled hero's lantern jaw—

—and was as stunned as everyone else when the Shadowy Sherlock toppled to the ground, out cold.

"Wow," Walter whispered, holding his fist up to study it, and the muscled arm it sprouted from. "All those push-ups really paid off!"

A second later, Twilight's knockout pellets landed at Walter's feet, and he felt his own consciousness fading.

But even as Walter keeled over, he was smiling.

━◀ ∈ ▶━

"Check it out!" Walter heard someone whisper as he entered the prison cafeteria. "You know who that is?"

"That's the Shtick," somebody else took up. "He ran circles around Midnight King!"

"Yeah, and then laid him out with one punch!" another inmate added.

The room was abuzz with the story, and with a general susurrus of awe—and respect. Walter could feel it like the warm glow of a sunbeam all around him, as the hardened criminals in line in front of him nodded and backed away, giving him a clear path to the food.

Walter sighed happily, the motion stretching the orange jumpsuit that was, without the Seamstrix's expert adjustments, a tad bit too snug across his newly muscular chest and arms. This was what he'd been looking for. Respect. Admiration. Fame.

And, when he got back out in a few months—since the only charges they'd been able to make stick this time were those two snatch-and-grabs at the ball, and a charge of brawling for knocking out Midnight King—he knew he'd go right back to what he'd been doing. He already had a whole list of new identities for Launi to craft for him.

Only this time, he'd make sure to sign each caper with his real name, as well.

Yes, Walter thought as he stepped slowly, proudly, up to the food line and held up his battered tray, he'd finally found his shtick.

THE FAN JOB

Peter David

"WAIT'LL THEY GET A LOAD OF THIS!"

Melissa Ronco stared at the array she had created on her wall for seemingly ever. She could not believe its quality. She remembered a few years earlier, when she had been competing in her school's science fair and had spent months working on a model of a volcano. It had seemingly taken forever and when she had done her demonstration for it, fake lava had exploded out of the top. She'd been so proud and actually won a ribbon for the first time ever.

But now she was in sixth grade, which meant that she had to turn her attention to something of greater import. And that something had presented itself just weeks earlier.

There was a knock at her bedroom door. "Come in!" she called.

The door swung open and her mother was standing there with a small tray. Balanced on it were a peanut butter sandwich (with the crust trimmed off), a glass of Coca Cola, and a small bag of chips. Her mother was smiling widely. "You didn't seem interested in coming downstairs, so I figured I'd..." Her voice trailed off. "What the hell—?" she asked when she finally got her voice back.

Melissa smiled broadly and gestured toward her product. "What do you think?"

"I'm not sure. What is it?"

She had covered an entire wall with pictures of superheroes. Any and all pictures of superheroes. Some of them were 8 x 10 head shots of the heroes smiling with their gleaming white teeth. Others were clipped from newspapers and were shots taken by photographers lucky enough to be on the scene when the superheroes went into action.

Melissa grinned in excitement. "And it's not just pictures! There's all kinds of captions about when and how they were taken! I've actually managed to start charting stuff about them!"

"Charting stuff? What kind of stuff?"

"They have territories!"

"What?"

"Territories. Although they probably called them something else. Zones. Whatever. The point is, I'm positive that they've somehow divided up the city into these territories, and they all stick to specific crimes or wrongdoings in those particular parts of the city! Except for Captain Quikk. He seems to go wherever he feels like at any time. I have no idea if he pisses people off when he does it. But who cares? He's probably the greatest superhero of them all!"

Her mother stared at the assemblage on her wall. At the dozens of pictures and the lengthy written notations that included projected height, weight, and known personal habits. "Well…I have to admit you've been very thorough. This is most impressive."

"Do you think the club will like it?"

Her mother stared at her. "Club? What club?"

"Oh! I forgot to tell you! I'm starting a superhero club with my friends!" She hesitated, her voice dropping a few notes. "Is that okay?"

Her mother hesitated, but then recovered quickly. Her smile returned as she said, "Why wouldn't it be? Why would I have a problem with that? It's not like I have a problem with superheroes."

"Good!"

"I mean," and she coughed for a moment, "sure, they've come out of nowhere. Ever since that speedster first showed up, there's been a bunch of them. More and more of them, in fact. Setting themselves up as…I don't know…extensions of the police. Without permission, I assume."

"Oh no," said Melissa firmly. "They have some sort of set up with the police or the mayor or somebody. They have to. They're superheroes. Superheroes would never act on their own and defy the authorities. That's totally against what being a superhero is."

"Yes, of course. I suppose you're right."

"I know I am," Melissa said with a confident grin.

Anthony Ronco sat in the living room, trying to ignore the giggling and high pitched squeals that were coming from his daughter's room. She wasn't alone; there were at least four girls with her, and all of them were talking about something that brought them great excitement.

"Martha!" he shouted. "Martha!"

His wife walked in from the kitchen, wiping her hands on her apron. She was in the midst of preparing dinner. "Yes, honey?"

"You want to tell me what the hell is going on up there?" He pointed upstairs.

"Oh. Melissa's just having some friends over." She turned and started to head back into the kitchen.

"Whoa. Whoa." He put up his hands in protest and she turned back to see what he had to say. "She's having some friends over for what?" When his wife did not respond immediately, he repeated with greater insistence, "For. What?"

She wasn't especially anxious to respond, but she really didn't see any point in lying about it. "She started a club. Those are friends who are in it with her."

"A club? A club for what?" When she didn't respond immediately, he pressed the point. "What is she having a club for?"

His wife hesitated and then, bracing herself for what she knew was going to come, said, "Superheroes."

"Are you kidding me?"

"Afraid not."

"*Are you kidding me*?!"

Martha tried her best to keep everything calm. "Come on, Anthony. Take it easy."

"That's simple for you to say." He tossed aside his newspaper and got to his feet. "They're up there celebrating superheroes and I'm supposed to what? Just deal with it?"

"Yes." Her voice was sharp and harsh. "Yes, that's exactly what you are going to do. You're just going to deal with it, Anthony. I don't care how you do it. But just deal. And do it in a way that won't infringe on your daughter's having fun. Is that clear?" When he did not respond immediately, she repeated the question.

"All right, fine." He rolled his eyes. "I won't say or do anything."

"Thank you." She sounded genuinely grateful.

"Don't thank me. I'm not doing it for you. I'm doing it for her. She deserves to worship whomever, even if it's not me. It doesn't mean that I have to approve. In fact, I don't."

"I know you don't. But it's still nice of you to let your daughter have her fun."

He looked sourly upstairs in the direction of the girls' laughter as he picked his newspaper up again. "Oh yeah. I'm a real sweetheart."

Several years passed.

Melissa developed into a lovely teenager. For years she had worn her hair in long braids; for her 13th birthday she got her hair trimmed to shoulder-length and darkened to solid black. She looked vaguely goth although she tended not to think of herself in that way. Her taste in lipstick tended toward bright red and, despite her mother's best efforts to provide correction, she wore far too much eye shadow. None of that, however, led to a change in her fundamental personality. She was still relentlessly upbeat and, even more importantly, had not lost her interest in superheroes.

In fact, that interest was amplified when she learned of the establishment of the DMZ. The notion that there was a superhero watering hole in town—a place where both superheroes and supervillains set aside their differences, drank and ate and just hung out with each other—was nothing but a massive dose of catnip to her. By the time she was 14, the DMZ was a regular stop for her after school. And it wasn't as if it was actually on the way home; it was in fact considerably out of her way. Yet not a day went by where she did not wind up outside the DMZ, trying to catch a glimpse of heroes and villains coming and going from the establishment.

A number of friends regularly accompanied her. The girls would stand outside the DMZ and call out and wave to anyone they saw going in or out. On several occasions they even screwed up their nerve and tried to enter. They never got very far, though. The bartender, an attractive blonde who apparently went by the name of Dutch, never hesitated to throw them out every time they set foot in the place. She would always say more or less the same thing: that the DMZ was exclusively for superheroes and villains, and not powerless teen worshipers. The fact that Melissa headed up an official superhero fan club never seemed to make the slightest bit of difference. They were still considered to be nothing but annoying outsiders. That was fine with Melissa. As much as she wanted to hobnob with her heroes, she was fully aware that she was simply a teenager while the heroes were their own thing.

Eventually, her superhero club became organized to the point where she was actually holding meetings in school. By this point the organization had acquired two dozen members, and they voted unanimously to put Melissa in charge. They started having biweekly meetings in the science class where they pretty much did what they had been doing in Melissa's room: talking about superheroes animatedly. There were a few people who seemed more interested in the supervillains than the heroes, but Melissa didn't worry about that. If people were going to freak out about villains, let them. It wasn't any skin off her nose. She knew which side she came down on.

The superhero club also engaged in occasional fundraising activities, and on this particular Wednesday their activity had been a bake sale. It had gone better than Melissa could possibly hope, probably due to the specially made superhero cupcakes that she had produced. It had been an impressive assortment, various superhero logos decorating the frosted tops. That, and the kids who bought them simply had no sense of what was proper to eat. So they had scarfed up the cupcakes continuously during the day and the club had benefited to the tune of over $200. Melissa was overjoyed with the results.

"What should we do with it?" she asked her best friend and club vice president, Whitney.

Whitney did not hesitate in her response: "We bring it to the bank, is what. We don't stick it in a cardboard box where someone could steal it. We put it in the club's account first thing."

"You sure?" Melissa herself was hardly certain. They had opened up the bank account at the strong suggestion of other club members and the teacher in charge. But Melissa was not sure she trusted the bank all that much. Banks, as far as she was concerned, served mainly to be major targets for supervillains. It seemed she was always reading about some new bank robbery that some supervillain was pulling off.

"Yes, of course I'm sure! Why aren't you?"

Melissa laughed. "Don't be like that. I'll be fine. The money will be fine. Everything will be fine." She glanced up at a clock on the wall. "It's 2:15 now. I can get over to the bank before 3 o'clock. Will that do?"

"Of course it will! Geez!"

Melissa carefully took the money and counted it out one more time before placing it carefully into her purse. She snapped it shut and tucked it under her arm. "No problem," she said as she patted her purse.

While her friend headed home, Melissa went straight for the First National Bank where they had the money deposited. She knew there was not a ton in the bank; indeed, the $200 she was going to deposit was probably going to double the checking account. But it had never been her intention to start the club for the purpose of making big money. The superhero fan club's role remained exactly the same as when she'd first started it, namely to worship superheroes.

As she headed for the bank, she once again gave thought to a recurring fantasy, namely that somehow she would become a teenage sidekick to a superhero. There were certainly plenty in fiction. Robin, Kid Flash, Wonder Girl, Bucky—all these and more were examples of teen sidekicks. Yet in her incessant following of real-life superheroes, she had yet to encounter a single adult superhero who had a teen sidekick. This was endlessly frustrating to her. She wasn't old enough to take on the superhero career by herself. If nothing else, she had a complete lack of any actual superpowers. On the other hand, if some superhero was willing to take her on—take her under their wing or cape or whatever—why then, anything was possible. For a long moment, she once again gave much thought to the prospect of battling alongside a superhero in the name of justice. She envisioned herself in some sort of flamboyant costume, punching out bad guys with reckless abandon and determination. And why not? Why should she not acquire a career all her own? There were some superheroes, such as Leatherwing, who did not seem to have any superpowers at all. Yet no one hesitated to describe them as superheroes. So, indeed, why not her? What was there to stop her from throwing her hat into the ring and becoming a super heroine in her own right? Nothing. Nothing except for the fact that, as near as she could tell, no adult superheroes wanted to have anything to do with teen sidekicks.

Maybe it had to do with child endangerment issues, which were certainly not a factor in the pages of comic books, but could pose serious legal problems in the real world. Nor could she think of any way to approach a superhero about the prospect of taking her on that would ameliorate such concerns. Even if one went on the assumption (which she did) that the superheroes were indeed operating with the tacit approval of City Hall and law enforcement, no one was going to be willing to stick their neck out over child endangerment.

For that matter, she really couldn't blame them. If she were in the superhero game, she'd be as reluctant as any other superhero about bringing a teen into life-threatening situations.

So what to do?

Nothing. That was all. Nothing. Superheroes would just go on doing their crime-fighting thing and she would go on admiring them from afar. That was simply the way it was going to have to remain.

Before she knew it, she was at the door to the bank. She checked her watch and was pleased to see that it was only 2:35. Plenty of time to make a deposit.

She strode in and was pleased to see that the line was very short. There was only one person standing on it, a businessman in his mid-50s. She stepped in line behind him. There was no need to fill out a deposit slip. This particular bank had done away with them. While she stood there, she counted one more time to make sure of how much was there.

Suddenly the front door banged open. A costumed man strode in, accompanied by two men dressed in plainclothes with black masks on their faces. As for the man who was leading them, he was outfitted entirely in purple. A cape fluttered off his shoulders and he wore a mask that concealed the entirety of his face. He raised his arm and Melissa was terrified to see that there was a gun mounted on it. To be specific, she could see a large, specially created gun barrel on his fist instead of a hand, presumably covering it. It rotated and clicked loudly into place.

"Attention. May I have your attention, please." His voice was staticy, and even robotic. Apparently he had some manner of voice changer under his mask. "My name is the Malevolence. As you may have been able to intuit, I am here to rob your bank. If no one attempts to get in my way—"

Abruptly he swung his right arm to one side and fired. When the gun on his fist discharged, it was like a blast of thunder in the bank's cramped quarters. Melissa put her hands over her ears but her head was already ringing.

The blast from the gun struck a bank guard squarely in the chest. Melissa had not even seen the guard; he had been off to the side, standing behind a pillar when the robbers walked in. He must've thought that they had not seen him and that he had a chance to surprise them. He had discovered that he was wrong.

What was astounding was that he was not dead from the impact of the shot. Nor was it a normal gun firing bullets. Instead a mass of electrical energy had burst out of the gun barrel, streaking across the room before striking the guard squarely in his upper body. The man had screamed and dropped his gun almost immediately as his body shook violently from the impact of the electrical blast. It lasted only three, maybe four seconds, but that was more than enough. The guard crumpled to the floor.

Immediately Melissa ran toward him. She only stopped when the Malevolence shouted angrily at her to do so. She stopped for a moment, then gathered herself and turned and started snapping back. "I'm just going to help him. Who knows what your electricity did to him!"

The Malevolence, much to her surprise, did not seem to know quite how to answer her. "He'll be fine," he said, but he spoke with a sort of hesitation.

"You don't know that. I'm going to go check. And if you don't like it, you can shoot me too!"

Then, without another word, she headed straight for the guard. The entire time, she mentally braced herself for what she was certain was the inevitable crackling of electricity that would certainly envelop her. To her surprise, nothing was forthcoming.

Instead, as if ignoring her was suddenly the greatest priority in the world, the Malevolence snapped at the men with him, "Get the money. All the tellers. Move like we have a purpose, gentlemen."

Immediately the other two men did as they were instructed. They quickly and systematically went to each teller, who each obediently cleaned out their money drawer and shoved it through to them. The empty bags that they had been carrying quickly filled up with currency.

In the meantime, Melissa checked over the guard to see what his status was. He was breathing, shallowly. His face was distinctly pale and she took his pulse. It seemed steady and relatively normal. At least she was guessing that it was. Fortunately enough the electricity hadn't had a major affect on him.

But what was even more important was that his gun was lying next to him.

Another girl might well have hesitated to try anything offensive. Melissa, however, was anything but another girl. A girl like her had spent years imagining herself being in a situation such as this. Presented with this opportunity, she was not about to let it go by. Not without taking some manner of action.

Slowly she reached for the gun. Her plan was incredibly simple: she was going to pick it up and start shooting.

But just as her fingers touched the cold metal of the firearm, she heard a click and a soft whining of energy building up mere inches from her head. Her gaze darted over and she saw that the Malevolence had his huge electrical gun pointed straight at her face. It would take no more than a split instant for him to discharge it at her.

"I wouldn't be doing that if I were you," he growled at her. "Pull your hand away from that. Now, please."

Slowly and deliberately she withdrew her hand from the gun.

"Stand up, please. You spent enough time with this gentleman."

She did as instructed. Her legs were shaking, her hand twitching in frustration. For his part, the Malevolence did not seem the least bit bothered. "Kick the gun over to me, if you would be so kind." Once more she did as she was told, giving the gun a push with her foot, causing it to slide across the floor to him. He crouched, picked up the gun with his left hand and shoved it into his belt. "Gentlemen, are you about done?"

The other two masked robbers shouted affirmation. They headed toward him, giggling, and one of them glanced at Melissa. "We should take her along as a hostage," one of them suggested.

Melissa's blood froze. The prospect of being dragged along with these criminals was absolutely terrifying to her. It was one thing when she thought that she could at least get her hands on a weapon. The prospect of being an unarmed hostage was horrifying.

Fortunately enough, it didn't seem like it was going to become an issue. The Malevolence glanced at her for a moment and then said, "Forget it. We don't need her. Let's go."

"But—"

"You heard me. I said let's go."

The other two bank robbers seem to forget about her and headed toward the front door. It seemed like that was going to be it. They had come in, grabbed their money, and now they were getting gone.

Suddenly, they stopped at the front door. One of them let out a loud profanity and ran back into the bank. The one who had cursed was hardly done. "What the hell are they doing here? How did they get here so fast?"

"I don't know," said the Malevolence. He was clearly annoyed. "It usually takes at least 10 minutes for the police to respond to a call. I assume one of you did this," he said with a snarl to the tellers. "One of you tripped a silent alarm? Anyone care to own up to it?" None of the tellers seemed especially inclined to admit to it. "Yes, that's what I thought."

"What are we going to do?" asked one of his men. "There's at least half a dozen cop cars out there!"

"I don't understand what they're doing here." It was as if the Malevolence hadn't yet processed that the bank robbery was effectively over. "It should take them at least another five minutes..."

"*Who cares*?!" The taller of the two bank robbers seemed fit to be tied. "The fact is that they are here, and if we don't do something, we won't be!" Then his gaze shifted toward Melissa and he started toward her.

"What are you doing?" The Malevolence seemed confused.

"She's going to be our ticket out of here," said the robber as he approached her.

"Leave her alone. We'll find another way."

"*There is no other way*!" He turned and shouted at the Malevolence. "Don't you get it? The cops are out there! They're going to be looking for reasons to shoot! I say we don't give them one. And the best way to do that is to put her between us and them."

The Malevolence did not seem convinced. "You are not going to use this girl as a shield. Do you understand? I said no."

"Screw you. You know, I could be working for Original Sin right now. Or somebody like that. But you talked a good game and you seemed like you had your act together. And we pulled some great jobs until now. Well this time it's gone off the rails. And now we have to do something about it. Now I don't know what your problem is with this girl," and he pointed at Melissa with a trembling finger. "But she is the ideal hostage and she's going to play that role. And if you don't like that, then you can lump it!"

The Malevolence took that in for a moment, and then shrugged his caped shoulders. "All right. As you wish."

The taller robber turned back toward Melissa and started to reach for her.

That was when a burst of electrical energy ripped out of the massive gun mounted on the end of the Malevolence's right arm. It enveloped the bank robber just before he could grab Melissa's arm. Melissa jumped back in surprise as she watched the bank robber tremble and shake in the electricity's grip. Then, without another word, he sank to the ground unconscious.

"Idiot," said the Malevolence. Then he turned and pointed at a female bank executive who was standing behind her desk. "You. Come here. Now. Or I will do to you what I just did to my own man. I strongly suggest you do not attempt to call my bluff ."

The bank executive nodded her head like a bobble-headed statue as she approached, with both her arms up in the air. The other bank robber grabbed her then and put a gun to the side of her head.

Melissa watched the entire thing as if she was seeing it through a fog. She had no idea why on earth the Malevolence had chosen to spare her. She wasn't knocking it; she simply didn't understand. And the Malevolence did not seem particularly interested in explaining it.

A voice sounded from a megaphone outside. *"This is the police. This message is for the bank robbers. Come out with your hands over your head and you will not be harmed."*

"How generous of them," said the Malevolence. He raised his voice and shouted back, "Listen to me carefully. I am the Malevolence. Perhaps you've heard of me."

"Can't say it rings a bell."

"How kind of you to say. Be that as it may, I am in charge of this situation, not you. And the situation is this: you are going to holster all your weapons and leash up your SWAT team. There will be no surprises and no impressive marksmanship. We have a hostage and are not the least bit concerned about blowing her brains out. You will stay right where you are as I go to my vehicle and we depart this place. If you attempt in any way to interfere, the hostage will die. Is that clear? A simple yes or no will suffice."

"None of this is necessary. I—"

"Apparently I did not make myself sufficiently clear." He pulled out the guard's gun and pointed it straight at the bank executive's head. "If you speak one more sentence that does not simply consist of the word yes, she dies. Quickly. Bloody. Have I made myself clear?"

There was a pause and then a grunted, frustrated response: "Yes."

"Good. At least we have that squared away."

They began to move forward and then all of a sudden a massive breeze blasted through the bank. It grabbed brochures and small papers up and sent them flying through the air. Melissa automatically grabbed at her skirt to prevent it from blowing upward even as her heart raced with excitement. She knew what was about to happen. Only one thing could be causing this type of abrupt wind.

The Malevolence let out an alarmed shriek and brought his gun up. He blasted out an electrical arc in a sweeping circuit, covering the entire entranceway to the bank. Even though there was nothing there; he appeared to be firing in advance of whatever was coming, as if he were anticipating it. But his timing was off. He had just finished discharging' his blaster weapon, when a red streak hurtled into the bank. It was moving so quickly that no one could make it out. The Malevolence tried to bring his gun up again to fire once more, but apparently it was too soon. The gun needed moments to recharge—moments that he did not have.

The red streak blew past them and the bank executive was no longer in the arms of the robber. Instead she was on the far side of the room as the red streak hurtled back the way it had come. Before the Malevolence or his sidekick could move, the streak had surrounded them and was moving at high speed in a gradually tightening circle. Moments later it broke off and the Malevolence and other crook were seated on the floor, tied together with rope. The gun had been detached from the Malevolence's hand and was lying on the floor next to him. The Malevolence and his companion struggled against the rope, but they were helpless to do anything to break it. They were trapped.

Melissa let out a screech of joy as the red streak skidded to a halt. Standing there right in front of her was none other than Captain Quikk. An impromptu cheer rose from the people in the bank and the captain tossed off a wave. He turned and noticed Melissa and smiled at her.

She tried to think of something to say. It was as if her entire life had led up to this moment.

She had nothing. Her mouth opened and closed several times but no words emerged.

And then, just like that, the captain was gone. He bolted out of the doors and, presumably, sped down the street and away. Mentally Melissa kicked herself. There was so much that she could've said, but she had uttered none of it. She had never been more frustrated with herself than she was at that moment.

Police came pouring in through the door. They were shouting useless instructions such as "Nobody move!" They were acting as if their actions were making some difference to the situation—a situation that had already been thoroughly handled by the captain.

They went quickly to the Malevolence and yanked both him and his partner to his feet. The other bank robber was still unconscious on the floor and they slapped handcuffs on. As for the Malevolence and his crony, they were still tied together and it was going to take a few minutes for the police to get to their hands. As it was, it appeared that they were simply going to escort them out of the bank at gunpoint.

Before they did so, however, they yanked the masks off of the Malevolence and his partner.

Melissa had never seen the partner before. He was just some guy with a lantern jaw and a receding hairline.

The Malevolence, however, she recognized immediately.

She couldn't believe it. For a moment she waited for someone to step forward and yell "Surprise!" And everyone would laugh that she had been so thoroughly punked. But that didn't happen. There was no punking. There was no laughter. There was no hint of any joke at all as she stood there and watch the police hauling her father, Anthony, out of the bank. Anthony looked toward her briefly just before they got him to the door and mouthed the words "*I'm sorry*" to her before they shoved him out the door.

Policemen and medical technicians came up to her then, asked if she was okay, asking if she needed anything. She did. What she needed was a world that would make sense again. Not a world where her father was a supervillain.

But that was the world that she was in. And she had absolutely no idea how to livc in it.

——◄ E ►——

Martha Ronco turned white as a ghost when Melissa told her what she'd witnessed. Slowly she sank into an easy chair in the living room as Melissa paced back and forth, completely distraught. "What are we going to do? My God, what are we going to do?"

"Well," said Martha, "I suppose we should get in touch with our lawyer. Get him on top of this as quickly as possible."

"Our lawyer? You mean Morrie?" When Martha nodded, Melissa said, "What's he going to do about it?"

"Oh, Morrie has quite a bit of experience at criminal law. I'm sure he can get all over this."

Melissa was practically trembling with agitation. "But isn't he going to be stunned that dad is a supervillain? Wouldn't anyone be stunned? I don't understand how..." Then her voice trailed off as a new realization settled on her. She almost fell backward and stopped herself at the last moment, reaching for a chair that she flopped into. "You knew." Her voice was barely above a whisper. "Oh my God. You knew. Did you know? You couldn't have known. Dad...Dad's a realtor. He's always been a realtor."

"Well...as a day job..."

"*Oh my God! You did know.*"

"Okay, you really need to get a hold of yourself..."

Melissa would have leapt to her feet and run out the front door if she had had any energy in her legs. But she found that she was stuck there. "How could you not tell me?"

"Tell you?" To her horror, her mother actually laughed. "When? When in all your superhero worshiping life were you ready to hear the truth about your father?"

"He *is* my father. You should've told me, you know, whenever."

"Whenever you had your friends over? Whenever you were staying late at school for your club? You have no idea what it's like raising a daughter who worships the other side."

"*How the hell was I supposed to know superheroes were the other side*?!"

It was as if her mother hadn't even heard the question. "You have no idea what you put your father through. How often he wanted to go up to your room and tell you the truth. But he never did because he knew how important the superheroes were to you. He didn't want to tell you that he was building your whole college fund on his illegal earnings. That's the reason we could afford to live the way we do was because of his illegal activities."

"The way we do? We live in this simple house! What's the big deal?"

"Here, yes. And we have houses in Los Angeles. And New York. And the Cayman Islands."

Melissa's jaw dropped. "Are you serious?"

"Yes, of course I'm serious," said Martha impatiently. "We were going to wait until you are 18 and then tell you about it. But that's blown, obviously."

"I...don't believe it. Is there anything else I should know about?"

"Various businesses your father owns, I suppose. They're all legal but some of them aren't especially profitable. His extra funds that he picks up from bank robberies and such is how he keeps it all going."

Melissa rubbed her temples, feeling a massive headache coming on. "So what happens now? I mean, once we pull in a lawyer and everything?"

"Well, I suspect your father is going to be doing some jail time. And it's quite possible that we will have the IRS going over all our bank accounts and seeing where the money came from. Things are going to get extremely problematic around here. So I strongly suggest you get used to that idea."

Melissa had no idea what to say. Finally she just nodded. "All right. Whatever happens, I guess we'll just deal with it."

"I guess we will."

Slowly Melissa rose from the chair. Mother said nothing further to her as she trotted up the stairs. She entered her room and closed the door behind her. Then she stared at the walls of her bedroom.

A huge poster of Captain Quikk was staring back at her. In the picture, he was giving a big thumbs up and grinning widely.

Other heroes likewise stared out at her from different posters. But it was the one of the captain that she kept staring at. The one from which she could not look away.

With a high-pitched, angry shriek, she grabbed the poster and tore it down from the wall. It ripped clean in half and it took her long moments to rip the rest of the pieces down from the wall. Eventually she managed to get all of it down and then she crumbled it all up into one big wad of trash. Then she shoved it in the nearest garbage can. For a long moment she stood there out of breath, and then she began taking down the rest of the posters as well. She didn't tear the others; simply removed the thumb-tacks and rolled them up. The end result, however, was the same. At the end of half an hour, she had denuded all the walls of any superhero posters. Instead the bare white walls stared back at her.

She collapsed to her carpet and began sobbing.

Anthony Ronco was astounded to see his daughter waiting for him on the other side of the visitors' window. He had been told that someone had come to see him, but had simply assumed it was his wife or attorney.

Other convicts were already seated along the row, phones to their ears, as they conversed with their visitors. Anthony, however, remained standing for a long moment as Melissa simply sat there and stared at him. Finally he sat down on the other side of the window and picked up the phone. Melissa did likewise on her side.

"Hi," he said.

She stared at him for a long moment, as if she had no idea what to say. It was an unusual situation for him. He was so accustomed to her knowing what to say about damn near everything. So this long, atypical silence from her was a little bit difficult for him to deal with.

Finally she spoke. "Thank you for not making me a hostage," she said.

He nodded. "Well, that was a no-brainer. You could have knocked me over with a feather when we burst into that bank and I saw you standing there. And the whole time I was saying to myself, Please don't let me get caught. Not today. Not with her here." He shrugged. "So much for that. I suppose God isn't one for answering prayers when you're..."

"A supervillain?"

"I guess."

"You guess? Dad... *Malevolence*? When you run around in the hood in a cape and have a big weapon on your hand, and you call yourself the Malevolence, there's no guessing involved. You're a supervillain."

"I suppose you're right. Except now all I am is a convict." He plucked at the orange jumpsuit he was wearing. "How do I look?"

"Orange isn't your color."

"If you say so."

"Dad..." She gestured helplessly. "What are we going to do? How could you do this? To yourself? To us?"

"Melissa, you're going to find as you go through life that all the excuses for everything all boil down to the exact same explanation: it seemed like a good idea at the time."

"Dad, come on..."

"I'm serious. Why did I become a supervillain? Seemed like a good idea at the time. Why were you doing 95 on the highway? Seemed like a good idea at the time. Why did you marry whomever you marry? Seemed like a good idea at the time. Anything I tell you will wind up boiling down to that. Everything else is incidental."

"What about mom and me? Are we incidental? What's going to happen to us?"

"Well, I have some thoughts on that."

"You do?"

"I do," he nodded. "I think it's about time that you got yourself a job. I know that you're only a teenager, but still, it wouldn't be a bad idea."

"What?" She gaped at him. "A job? Dad, that's ridiculous. Who would hire me?"

"Actually, I pretty much have that arranged. How would you like to work in a comic book shop?"

Her stunned expression became even more shocked. "A comic book store? What comic book store?"

"The one I bought about a year ago. Cosmic Comics over on Pico. Because you were so interested in superheroes. So I bought it and figured that it might be something you would become intrigued by. I was figuring to run it a few more years before bringing you into it, but now I figure, why not? Why not bring you in? Put you in charge of the place."

"Dad, this is insane!" She gripped the phone tightly to her ear. "I'm still trying to adjust to the idea that my father is a criminal, and you're talking about setting me up at a damned comic book store."

"Why not?"

"Why not! There's like a dozen reasons!"

"Not if we take away all the reasons that have anything to do with your personal shock. Once we get all those out of the way, we are left with the simple prospect of you taking on a job. A totally legit job at a place that actually turns a profit without my having to shovel illegal money into it. So you should consider yourself lucky."

"Lucky? How am I lucky?"

He smiled at her gently. "Because," he said, "you have a father and mother who loves you. You have a father who has set you up with the way of earning some cash at a time when money may wind up being tight. And eventually I will get out of jail. That's a fact. And we will be together again. One big happy family. By the way," and he glanced around suspiciously as if concerned that someone was listening in, "don't get yourself a new mattress anytime soon. Okay?"

"What?"

"I said don't get yourself a mattress…"

"Anytime soon, yes, I heard you. But I don't understand."

He stared at her. And he grinned.

And then she understood.

⇥E⇤

When she got home, the first thing that Melissa did was cut open her mattress in her bedroom. She tried not to squeal in demented joy as stacks of money fell out. She couldn't believe it. She had no idea when her father had shoved all the stolen money (she was assuming of course, but she was correct) into her mattress for safekeeping, but she knew she wasn't going to worry about it. Let the IRS climb all over their bank accounts; it didn't matter. Her father had made sure to provide for her and her mother.

Then, even though she didn't have to, she headed over to the comic book store. The moment she introduced herself, the store owner knew exactly who she was and what she was there for. By that afternoon she was safely ensconced behind the cash register. From that point on it would be where she could regularly be found on any weekday after school. And sometimes even when she should have been in school.

And as she sat there, she had her drawing pad flipped open and was busily sketching costume concepts on it. She was busily designing the most forbidding costume that she could possibly conceive of. She also had a name already etched across the top:

Dementia.

She had thought long and hard about it.

It wasn't remotely superhero like. Instead it was unquestionably the name that a supervillain would undertake.

A supervillain who was the total opposite of superheroes.

A supervillain would not go around trying to help people, but instead would be out solely to get whatever she could get her hands on to help her family.

A supervillain who would be just like her father.

Seemed like a good idea.

She smiled.

"Wait'll they get a load of this."

Send in the Clones
A tale of the Super City Police Department

Keith R.A. DeCandido

"*Who's* in the interrogation room?"

Detective Kristin Milewski, who simply had *not* had enough coffee yet, stared intently at Officer M.C. Cunningham as she asked the question.

For her part, Cunningham looked very reluctant to answer. "I *think* it's the Clone Master."

"You *think*?"

"Well, he looks just like him, but he's dressed up in that silly white outfit that all his henchmen wear."

"And he just showed up?"

Cunningham nodded. "Came in, went straight to Sarge's desk, wearing the whole outfit, saying he had to talk to a detective about the Clone Master. Then he took off the mask, and it *was* the Clone Master. Sarge had me take him up to Interrogation 2, and—well, you two are the only ones here."

Milewski turned to face her partner, Detective Jorge Alvarado, who held up both hands. "Whatcha lookin' at *me* for? I don't even remember which one the Clone Master is." Alvarado recently moved to Super City from Baltimore, and he still hadn't gotten all the superheroes and supervillains straight in his head.

Though he should have recalled this one, as he was the scourge of the homicide squad. "Clone Master's the one who keeps dying and then coming back. He's probably the most reckless of the costumes out there, and he's always getting himself knocked off. Every time that happens, one of us has to perform a death investigation, because the annotated code says that every time a body falls in Super City, the SCPD must perform an investigation.

Which, for the Clone Master, is a *huge* waste of time, because somehow he always comes back." She turned back to Cunningham. "And he's in there now?"

"Disguised as one of his henchmen, yeah. I don't get it, either, but he said he wanted a detective, so..." The uniformed officer shrugged.

Milewski stared at Alvarado, then stared at Cunningham, then declared, "I need more coffee."

Once she'd poured more of the squadroom sludge into the mug her mother gave her when she made detective, she led Alvarado into the video room. The interrogation rooms all had cameras that fed to monitors here.

In her years on the job, Milewski had never actually encountered the Clone Master in person. The last two times he died and there was the usual abortive investigation, Fischer and Billinghurst had handled it. Both instances were right after she got promoted to homicide from vice. She had seen his face a few times, though, in news reports, and once in the morgue when the M.E. was working on one of his clones.

The person she saw on the monitor for Interrogation 2 matched her memory of that face: large nose, weak chin, beady eyes, and tiny ears. He was drumming his fingers on the battered metal table in the center of the room, and rocking back and forth in the metal chair. That seat was uneven and squeaky and uncomfortable, all of which was quite deliberate, since the people who sat there were intended to be made as uncomfortable as possible.

The one difference was that this one didn't have a right eyebrow.

"That's the guy?" Alvarado asked.

Milewski nodded. "And he's wearing the same outfit his thugs wear. All the guys who help him on his jobs wear that froofy all-white thing that makes them look like low-rent Jedi, plus hoods to hide their faces."

"That's gotta fuck up their peripheral vision."

"Prob'ly, yeah." Milewski gulped down the rest of her coffee, which burned her throat a bit. "Let's dig out the casefiles on the last couple Clone Master deaths, and then we'll see what he's got to say."

They went to the file cabinets and retrieved the files in question, and then went into the interrogation room. The Clone Master stopped drumming his fingers and sat up straight. "Finally!"

"I'm Detective Milewski, this is Detective Alvarado. You must be the Clone Master."

"I'm Markos Balidemaj, yes. Or, rather, I'm Clone Number 78. I mean, I'm both. I'm a clone of the Clone Master."

Milewski sat down across from him, placing the two folders in front of her, while Alvarado chose instead to lean against the far wall. "So what do we call you. 'Mr. 78'? Or can we be casual and call you 'Clone'?"

"I wish I could answer, but I'm having trouble keeping track of who I am."

"Okay. Well, you came to us, so why don't you tell Detective Alvarado and I what it is you want to say?"

He took a very deep breath. "I want to enumerate all the crimes committed by all the various versions of Markos Balidemaj since 2007."

Alvarado asked, "Is that when the Clone Master first showed up?"

"Of course," the clone said as if it was the stupidest question ever.

"He's new," Milewski said quickly. "I remember when he—or you, whatever—first showed up. You took on Old Glory and got your ass kicked, but you got away. Two weeks later, the Bruiser fought you and you were killed. Everyone figured that was the end of it, and nobody understood why you were called the Clone Master."

"And then another Clone Master arrived to do battle with the Superior Six."

"When you also died."

Balidemaj smiled. "Well, I—or, rather, the Clone Master—can afford to be reckless."

Alvarado came off the wall and moved toward the table. "All right, hold it a second, I'm gettin' a fuckin' migraine. Are you the Clone Master or not?"

"I am—and I'm not."

Looking down at the seated Milewski, Alvarado said, "I don't know about you, but that just made my migraine worse."

Milewski, however, looked right at Balidemaj's beady eyes. "How can you be both?"

"Because Markos Balidemaj was a genius when he was alive. I know, because his personality lives on in me."

"All right, this is some bullshit." Alvarado moved toward the door. "I don't gotta listen to this."

Looking straight at Milewski with those damned eyes, Balidemaj said, "You believe me, don't you, Detective Milewski?"

"No—but I don't disbelieve you, either. First homicide I caught was the Claw case. My ex-partner and I broke that case on the basis of a place that, I swear to Christ, is called Dimension X and it turns people into evil versions of themselves. For that matter, Alvarado's first case involved dimensional travel. So I'm not defaulting to bullshit *just* yet."

"But you want to hear more."

"Like I said, you came to us."

Balidemaj nodded. "Okay. Here's the story. I'm Clone Number 78. About thirty-five years ago, a brilliant scientist named Markos Balidemaj made an amazing discovery."

Alvarado, who was now leaning by the door as if ready to bolt at a moment's notice, rolled his eyes. "We know, he discovered cloning."

"Oh no, Detective." Balidemaj shook a finger back and forth. "No, my—rather, his father discovered cloning back in the 1950s. No, it was in 1986 that I—I mean, that he made the much more important breakthrough. You see, cloning's easy, if you have the right equipment. No, the problem is that a clone looks just like you, has all your genetic characteristics, writes with the same hand—but it doesn't have the same experiences. It isn't you, it's your twin. And twins aren't the same person."

"Okay," Milewski said with a glance at a very confused looking Alvarado, "what did Balidemaj figure out in '86?"

"How to transfer someone's mental pattern into another person."

Alvarado was shaking his head. "What, so he can move his mind into someone else's body?"

"Yes, Detective."

"Y'know," he said, "I've seen a lot of crazy-ass shit in this job, especially since I moved here to Super City, but mind-switching? C'mon, that's a bad *Star Trek* episode."

"What I want to know," Milewski said, "is why you—or he, or who-the-fuck-ever—didn't just patent this thing and sell it?"

"Because there are side effects," Balidemaj said. "Mental instability being the biggie. He couldn't get any funding to continue the research, mostly because he used a bunch of alien tech his dad salvaged back in the '50s during that big invasion. Nobody legit trusted that stuff."

Milewski nodded. "So he worked on his own?"

"He inherited a lot of money from his family, and he had some patents. And then he had the breakthrough in '86. So he created two hundred and fifty clones."

At that, Milewski dropped her pencil. Alvarado reach down to pick it up. "Thanks," she said. "Did you say two hundred—"

"—and fifty, yes, Detective."

"And you're 78?"

He nodded. "There were a few that didn't work out, but yes, the original Markos Balidemaj died when he went up against Old Glory back in '07."

"Wait, I don't get it," Alvarado said, "why'd he wait so long?"

"Clones age at the same rate as everyone else, Detective," Balidemaj—or, rather, his clone—said. "They don't pop out fully grown. They had to age to maturity, which is why he waited as long as he did. In fact, he might have waited longer, but he was running out of money. You might recall that his first battle against Old Glory was a bank robbery."

"So when he died, what happened?"

Balidemaj hesitated. "Before I explain that, I should explain what our lives were like growing up. We were—well, indoctrinated. We were taught that the Clone Master was our god, basically. Our only mandate was to serve him. Everything we did, we did in service of the Clone Master, who would take over the world, and we would be his chosen ones."

"And you believed this shit?" Alvarado asked.

"For a long time, Detective, it was all I knew. Are you religious?"

"Raised Catholic," Alvarado muttered.

"And when you were a boy, did you believe?"

"Yeah. Then I became a cop."

Milewski chuckled, then said to Balidemaj, "So you got no other experiences?"

He shook his head. "We weren't allowed outside the compound."

"What compound?"

"Sorry, the estate that Balidemaj's family owns over in Willingham Gardens outside of town."

Milewski shot Alvarado a look. He gave a quick nod, then said, "I'm sick'a this shit. You wanna listen to this asshole, Milewski, knock yourself out." He stormed out.

Balidemaj looked at the door as he slammed it shut. "Your partner doesn't believe me?" He sounded crestfallen.

In fact, he was storming out under the pretense of digging up information on the estate mentioned. But good-cop/bad-cop was a cliché for a reason—it still worked as a tactic.

"Like I said, he's new." Milewski leaned forward. "So you were indoctrinated by the Clone Master for all your lives."

"And also trained. We learned various martial arts and got weapons training. We had excellent medical care, and only the healthiest food."

"No wonder he ran out of money."

Smiling, Balidemaj said, "Actually, he ran out of money before that, but he had loans and credit and such. Those have all been paid back, thanks to my—to our successful criminal enterprises."

"So the Clone Master has two hundred and fifty people who look just like him who worship the ground he walks on. Handy as henchmen."

"And as repositories." He took a deep breath. "The breakthrough in '86 was a way to wipe someone's mind and replace those engrams with someone else's. When the first Clone Master died, his mind was transferred to the supercomputer we have in the basement of the compound. The engrams only last an hour or two in the computer before they break down into component memories without a personality. Not sure why, but all the tests I did—he did—you know what I mean—they showed that the engrams didn't hold together as a personality in the computer for long."

Milewski frowned. "Okay. This leads me to ask how those tests were performed."

Balidemaj looked away. "On homeless people and other indigents. I told you I'd provide a list of crimes? Those tests are among them."

"Wonderful." She leaned back in her chair. "Go on. First Clone Master died, then what?"

"His engrams were automatically transferred to the computer. Clone Number 4 then got into the chair and Clone Number 10 operated the transfer."

"Dare I ask what happened to one through three and five through nine?"

That got a wince. "It, ah, wasn't pretty."

Holding up a hand, Milewski said, "I don't need to know anymore, then. So Number 4 got to be the new Clone Master?"

Balidemaj nodded. "The machine wiped his own memories and imprinted mine—or, rather, Balidemaj's—onto his mind. He was now the Clone Master, and the rest of us followed *him.*"

"And this kept happening?"

"Yes." Balidemaj blew out a breath. "Until me. Do you recall the last time Clone Master died?"

Milewski pointed at one of the folders on the desk and then opened it. "I didn't catch the case, but I remember Fischer and Billinghurst bitching about it. I don't remember the specifics, though—that was right after the Claw case finished up, so I was busy with that." She glanced at the case file. "And that was the night of that alien invasion during a rainstorm."

"Right. Well, that storm was pretty nasty. So nasty, in fact, that lightning struck the estate when the transfer was happening. See, Clone Master died when he jumped off that roof."

"Why did he jump off the roof, anyhow? According to Detective Billinghurst's notes, he just seemed to jump, but the rain washed away all the physical evidence, so they weren't sure what happened."

"I misjudged the distance." He shook his head. "I mean, *he* did. The Cowboy was chasing me—him—and I jumped, trying to make it to the next roof over."

Milewski rolled her eyes. "Of course, the Cowboy just left the scene. Asshole." The Cowboy was more of a showoff than a superhero. Unlike the Bruiser, who actually cooperated with the police, the Cowboy was an irritant who mostly just got in the way. People loved him, though, so he always got a free pass.

"Anyhow," Balidemaj said, "I was next up in the chair. I got in, thinking it was a great honor to become the vessel for the new Clone Master. And then lightning struck during the transfer. It was horrible, sent a nasty shock through my system, and I got a few electrical burns." He pointed to his right eye. "That's how I lost the eyebrow, not to mention half the hair on my right arm. And worse, something went wrong with the transfer. I got all the Clone Master's memories, obviously, but Clone Number 78 *wasn't* wiped."

Milewski nodded in understanding. "So you remember being Clone Number 78 *and* being the Clone Master?"

He nodded right back. "It's been a nightmare. My whole life was a lie! I was raised to believe that the Clone Master loved us and we'd be rewarded when he finally took over the world, but it was all a lie!"

"He was just using you guys as warm bodies."

"Oh, it's worse than that, Detective. He didn't even want to take over the world! The whole point of all of it was that we'd be by his side when he ruled everything, but he didn't *want* to rule everything! He just wanted more money."

Shaking her head, Milewski said, "That's all *anybody* wants." She shuddered, remembering her time in narcotics, where everything that ever occurred was motivated entirely by money— whether the dealers trying to make money off addicts or the addicts trying to get money so they could buy the drugs—and moving to homicide didn't really change much. On those occasions when the motive wasn't related to money, it was generally related to sex.

"So, here are the crimes that—"

Milewski held up a hand. "Hold on—at this point, I really need to read you your rights."

⊷ Є ⊶

After spending half an hour or so having Balidemaj read and initial all the paragraphs, and then finally sign the forms indicating that he waived his right to remain silent and his right to counsel, Milewski then took his statement enumerating all the crimes committed by Markos Balidemaj over the past four decades or so.

While that was going on, Alvarado had called the chief prosecutor's office and they'd sent a deputy prosecutor over. Michael Spila and his rather unfortunate comb-over were sitting in the guest seat at Alvarado's desk.

"Hey Kristin," Spila said. "Jorge here's been filling me in."

She tossed a yellow legal pad onto the desk, which landed with a resounding *thwap*. "Well, here's his statement. I'll have Zelda type it up all nice and formal into the computer."

A buzzing came from Spila's jacket pocket. He pulled it out and looked at the display. "My master calls. Gimme a sec." He got up, put the phone to his ear, and said, "Yeah, boss?"

Alvarado stared after him. "He calls the CP 'boss'?"

"Why not?" Milewski shrugged. "What'd you get on the 'compound'?"

Indicating the monitor of his computer with his head, Alvarado said, "The property's owned by a trust that was started back in 1951 by Emil Balidemaj."

"That's Markos's father?"

Alvarado nodded. "Apparently, Emil was a hotshot scientist at Cal Tech, and then he worked for the Army. They had him on Project: Flying Saucer back in the day, until he got fired for cause, and nobody ever heard from him again."

Milewski nodded. "That tracks with the statement."

Spila was wandering back toward the desk. "Understood. Talk to you later." He hit END on his phone and shoved it back in his pocket.

"So, Mike," Milewski said, "we got enough for a warrant on the Clone Master's compound?"

"Nope. In fact, we don't have enough to prosecute. File the statement if you want, but as far as the CP's concerned, there's no case here. Kick him."

Milewski stared blankly at Spila. "Excuse me?"

He held up both hands. "Not my decision, Kristin. Look, that guy in there?" He pointed at the interrogation room. "He didn't actually commit any of the crimes he just confessed to. They were all committed by other people who are now dead."

"Bullshit. If you run the prints and DNA that we found on all the open cases connected to him, they'll all match the guy we got in Interrogation 2."

"And his lawyer will then subpoena the DNA of the eighty gajillion corpses that have dropped since 2007." Spila let out a long, deep breath. "Look, this case is the textbook definition of reasonable doubt. This Balidemaj guy figured out a way to commit the perfect crime. Besides, the only case we have on him is for a bunch of robberies, B&E's, and assaults. He's never killed anyone—he's low-priority by costumed bad guy standards. Trust me, the CP won't touch this case with a ten-foot pole. You gotta kick him."

Alvarado was shaking his head. "You gotta be fuckin' kiddin' me."

"Like I said, not my decision. Believe me, I'd love to prosecute this jackass, but I just go where the boss tells me."

"Yeah." Milewski sighed. "I'm still having Zelda type up the statement. I want it on file."

"Knock yourself out. Maybe someday he'll kill someone and the CP will give more of a shit. Or maybe he'll run out of clones." Spila shrugged and headed toward one of the other interrogation rooms. "I gotta go see a man about a dog."

"Who talks like that?" Alvarado asked.

"Actually, he really does," Milewski said. "The Bruiser brought Canis in last night, and he's trying to work out a plea deal." At Alvarado's blank look, Milewski added, "Canis is part human, part dog."

"This town is seriously fucked up."

Milewski stared at the door to Interrogation 2. "Yeah."

Three days later, Milewski and Alvarado got called to a double homicide in an alley behind the Sinnott Building.

The reporting officers, who had parked their blue-and-white at the mouth of the alley, looked slightly weirded out. "According to the witnesses," one of them said, "the Clone Master was going at it on the roof with one of his thugs."

The other added, "I ain't never seen a bad guy beat the shit out of his henchman before. Crazy stuff."

Milewski and Alvarado exchanged glances. He asked her, "You thinkin' what I'm thinkin'?"

Instead of actually responding, Milewski went into the alley, where someone from the medical examiner's office was kneeling over the body of the Clone Master.

Putting latex gloves on, Milewski went to the other body, that of the white-robed henchman. She pulled off the hood to reveal a face that looked exactly like that of the Clone Master.

With one exception: he didn't have a right eyebrow.

The M.E. stood up. "Best I can tell, they both fell from the top of the building. I've got multiple broken bones, contusions, and the like. I won't know the specific CODs until I get them on the table, but I'm guessing they both died from the trauma of colliding with the ground at high speeds."

"Thanks, Doc." Milewski sighed and got to her feet.

"Whaddaya think happened?" Alvarado asked.

"My guess is the other clones realized that their new Clone Master wasn't right in the head, so they downloaded another one into that guy." She pointed at the guy in the Clone Master's costume. "Meanwhile, Number 78 over here figured that the law wasn't gonna help, so he'd try to stop the Clone Master himself. Obviously, he didn't succeed."

"Or maybe he did. I mean, look, the Clone Master's dead."

Milewski sighed. "He's been dead before. It never takes. C'mon, let's process this nightmare, for all the good it'll do."

THE LAST GREAT MONOLOGUE OF EVIL INTENT

James Chambers

WHY?

You ask me *why* I've chained you to a chair mounted atop a two-kiloton nuclear bomb? Is it possible after all these years, you still don't understand?

You call yourself The Bard, yet you never had any poetry in your soul nor any genuine artistic spark. No truly creative person would've come back to North Harbor City when they let you out of Spiegle Penitentiary. You would've packed your pitiful life into a suitcase, gone half away around the world, and reinvented yourself.

Did you learn anything from your time in prison?

No. I suppose you sat brooding over how to get revenge.

Well, news flash, revenge is only for those who were wronged, and I did you a favor tipping off the cops about the Perlin Street Bank job. I mean, really, what were you thinking?

Faux-Shakespearean costumes and robbing banks to the tune of "I Will Survive?"

Sure, it was the seventies and disco ruled, but cocaine and mirror balls don't give you license to discard every last pretense of artistic integrity. It was always about the money for you. About getting high and getting laid. Never about the showmanship or the crime. You missed the point completely.

There is no great crime without a great performance!

We're not simple-minded thugs snatching purses from old ladies. We're not muggers, knocking down businessmen for their wallets. We're not bandits, holding up stage coaches to steal the mail. Not sweaty-palmed suits embezzling from tech firms, or thick-necked goombas without an ounce of grace. We're not con men hiding peas under shells or transit worker unions raping the public to line their own pockets. The moment you put on a costume, you become something more.

We are not criminals—we are criminal *masterminds!*

Lords of crime, performing audacious acts of lawlessness to stun the city breathless with our *passion!*

North Harbor is our stage, and if you don't leave your heart bleeding on that stage every time you step onto it, you're not worthy of performing there. You're just another greedy mook too lazy to make an honest living.

You must take risks. Not only of being caught or killed, or of failing, or of one of your henchmen betraying you—and to this day I remain in awe that you didn't see that coming on the Perlin Street job—but real *creative* risks! Walk out on that limb. Stretch your talent, which in your case, I grant, is meager, but even the most limited of actors can push themselves.

You, though.

You picked the costume they had in your size when you robbed the Gilbert Theater and threw together some shtick from a paperback of the Sonnets you found in a car you stole. That I ever took orders from you, followed you, played into your mockery of great art wounds me to this day.

Of course, I wasn't always *The Actor.*

Long ago, I was only *an* actor, and, I admit, you took me in when no one else would.

The stage *can* be a cruel mistress. It's no excuse, but I understand your reluctance to truly consummate your romance with her.

How many countless hours I trod upon her boards in fruitless flirtation at casting calls and auditions and open mic nights, craving her approval, her consent, her open-armed embrace of my greatness. So many years I pined for her, clinging to my hope to win her heart. And when it happened—ah, such a whirlwind affair. She brought me under her wing, understudy to the great Nick Milligan, the lead in a play so daring it courted controversy before our first rehearsal. I thought myself content as her concubine when the unthinkable happened, the wondrous sort of twist only true theater in the raw provides—Nick Milligan tragically throwing himself in front of a subway train on the eve of opening night. The simple, poignant note they found in his dressing room: 'I'm so sorry, but I'm not worthy of the part.' Horror. Sadness. An outpouring of grief and mourning swept the city, and yet the show *must* go on. I stepped into that baleful spotlight before so many eyes burning with resentment because the stage chose me for her lover and tossed away her tired, old fling. In a single performance, I made the part my own and the haters forgot Nick Milligan before the curtain fell, landing me in the lexicon of North Harbor's greatest icons.

Thanks to an airtight alibi and convincing tears, no one ever suspected my hands had scripted Nick's demise.

The play ran for weeks. The reviews lauded my arrival. Offers rolled in.

Musicals, dramas, television, film, an invitation to guest lecture at the Royal Academy of Dramatic Arts—I turned it all down. My overwhelming success in a role that Nick Milligan—an actor of unquestioned brilliance—considered himself unworthy to play made it impossible to accept any lesser part. I courted only greatness, demanded to work with the best.

My agent kicked and screamed. All he saw was payday after payday lined up like ducks in a row, ready for us to pluck them all the way to easy street. I knew better.

Artistic integrity matters above all.

I held out until the right roles came.

They rewrote *Wait Until Dark* for me, and I hired a doctor to put drops in my eyes that blinded me for every performance. I played *The Elephant Man* using only secret make-up techniques passed down from Lon Chaney. I branded my arms live on stage with a red-hot iron as Neville in *The Cold Room*. I trained twelve hours a day for months to master Wing Chung Kung Fu so I could perform no-punches-pulled fights in *Gweilo's Song*. Everything I touched became a hit.

Do you know how my colleagues rewarded me?

With envy. With viciousness. With gossip, betrayal, and scorn!

They called me "difficult" to work with and too "demanding." Other actors complained I treated them like dogs and the stage crews worse. Directors bitched about how I refused to take direction and stopped casting me. My enemies spread lies about me taking certain liberties with unwilling young starlets. Crass rumors. But the offers dried up. My agent and accountant wiped me out and left me with nothing. I wound up on the street, destitute in torn blue jeans and an Elizabethan coat stolen from wardrobe, and that is when you found me.

What's that? The gag makes it hard for me to understand you. Oh, the countdown clock?

Don't worry about that. We've got plenty of time till the big finish. I never miss a cue.

There's so much that happened while you sat in that cell up at Spiegle with that insipid disco anthem playing in your head, I have no doubt. What was your fascination with that song? If you'd made even half as much effort as your henchmen to respect Shakespeare and rehearsed with us when I coached them, I would've let you be. Most likely I'd still be one of your Troupe of Terror, living in your shadow. In that sense I guess I owe you for reminding me how pointless and shallow my existence had become.

I took some time to find myself after the constabulary pinched you and the rest of the Troupe.

I henched for King Conga. Great music, but the King lacked vision. He played the same four numbers over and over. Real crowd pleasers, true, but how long can you go on resting on past laurels? Who wants to be the Tom Jones of crime?

Professor Solar hired me as one of his Sunbeams. To say my coaching and inspiration brightened all the other Sunbeams is an understatement. The professor noticed my contributions and immediately promoted me from Sunbeam #3 to Sunbeam #1. Being number one again got my creative juices flowing, but all my advice for honing our performance fell on deaf ears. The Professor ordered the other Sunbeams to teach me my place, but I was ready for them. I sent them back to him in such a wretched and ruined state that he fled North Harbor, and last I heard he'd opened a tanning salon out in Salt Lake City.

I henched for the Flying Fish after that, then the Singing Ghost, then the Vault Roach, and Hothouse, Lady Prism, and even the Dictionary—and I made them all look *brilliant*.

I coached my fellow henchfolk in the true craft and stage managed every aspect of our crimes. They learned how to mark a cue, how to emote, how to command the attention of their audience. We kindled an unparalleled crime wave. The city lived on the edge of its seat, and we raked in the rewards in riches and unspoken accolades. Though publicly they condemned us, I know in my heart they all secretly loved the awe we brought to their mundane lives.

Think about it!

You're on line at the bank to deposit the same paltry paycheck you've deposited every week for ten years, dreaming of the day you bank enough dough to take a trip to Maui, knowing it'll never happen—when the doors burst open and in walks Face Card and the Marked Deck! Sure, for the next ten minutes, you're on the floor, pissing yourself while Suicide Jack holds a shotgun to your head, but a week from then, you'll be at your rich cousin's house, upstaging him for the first time since the third grade with your story about how you almost died at the hands of one of North Harbor's most infamous villains. Hell, you're going to dine out on that one clear into the next decade. Isn't that worth a little pee in the undies and a few hundred grand in federally insured bankroll? Doesn't that make us the real heroes? We're practically role models!

That's where you went so wrong, Bard. You thought it was about *you*. What music *you* liked. What costumes *you* could throw together without half a thought. But it's about them. It always has been. We're no different from movie stars, superstar athletes, or captains of industry. If we entertain or enrich them enough, the public will look the other way when we rob, rape, and murder.

I worked the circuit a long time, you know. Every crime boss who hired me became a legend—Snow Blower, Bomb Squab, Linda Larceny, Hyper Punch, Creature Feature, the Prodigal, Madame Hatter, even Dewey Decimate, stealing rare books from libraries. Can you imagine? The entire NHPD outwitted by Dewey Decimate? They still haven't figured out it was Dewey who murdered Sean Patrick Hazlett. You'd think death by 100,000 paper cuts would be a dead giveaway. But then you'd also think a man who'd made his billions in software would know better than to drop $15 million on a Gutenberg Bible and then store it in a wall safe in his bedroom in a city where Dewey Decimate rules the stacks.

I molded them all into criminal icons to fill nightmares and wax museums for decades to come. And do you know what thanks I got? What recognition?

None.

My cut of the take, sure, but like Professor Solar, they tried to smack me down whenever I demanded fair credit or a partnership. Was it asking so much to become Creature Feature and B-Movie, or Hyper Punch and Judy, or Madame Hatter and the Red Queen? I *really* wanted to rob a bank in drag, but you can't just throw something like that into a show. It has to have an internal logic, some *gravitas.*

Well, I wised up after a while. Why was I wasting my life acting for these small-minded hacks when I possessed the talent and intelligence to change the face of crime forever? It is said those who can do, and those who cannot teach, but, no, truly great teachers have mastered their art to a level no student can contemplate when they begin their education.

I used my mastery to open The Actor's Studio for Henching and Criminal Stagecraft.

My first graduating class of twelve made waves fast. Four went to work as Lab Rats for Linus Appalling, three joined the ranks of the Pit Boss's Double-Dealers, two strapped on parachutes for the Sky Diver, and the rest became Clowns for Rodeo Rustler, all of whom went on to pull the biggest jobs of their careers.

Word spread. My classes grew with each new session. The criminal community coveted my graduates. So-called masterminds wined and dined them, and wannabees hoped some of my greatness would rub off on them. The Street Pharaoh and the Wild Huntsman were the first to ask me to train entire hench-teams exclusively for them. The tuition I charged for that—let's say it gave new meaning to the phrase "set for life." Fees, bonuses, and ten percent of their take in perpetuity. And they paid it eagerly. My school became an underworld fixture. I took on my greatest and most rewarding role yet—The Actor!

I do owe you, dear Bard, for sending me down this path.

I truly wish you hadn't come knocking on my door with your machine-gun mandolin. I hate so much to have to kill you. But what good would it do to send you back to prison? You didn't learn the first time. You are my greatest failure as a teacher. All the time I spent trying to up the ante, raise the standards, and provide my beloved North Harbor with the class of criminal it deserves all led me to this.

Now my philosophy of crime rules the streets. If your bank is robbed, your charity fund-raising gala held up, your visiting royalty kidnapped, or your most precious historical artifacts pilfered, you can damn well bet one of my alumni had a hand in it, and you're going to be well entertained while you're victimized. No criminal tries anything more daring than shoplifting a candy bar without one of my people on their crew. I won't be modest. They make me proud. I taught them well. Without me, they'd all be common thugs and gangbangers, but what they've done with my teachings—it takes my breath away sometimes.

Even some of those stalwart symbols of justice have hired me.

The criminals have been beating them so badly they want to fight fire with fire.

I accepted them as students, taught them enough to impress them, and then promptly sold that knowledge to the highest bidder. Remember when Bomb Squab put Brass Shield and The Blue Line in the hospital? They did let you read the papers in prison, didn't they?

You're nodding. Good.

So maybe you see how the pieces come together and form a picture of my hidden hand behind so much that has happened in North Harbor these last years. Brass Shield is still in a coma. No one's heard from The Blue Line for months. Rumors say he's holed up in a cabin adjusting to his prosthetic leg. Second stringers, true. Not so for The Shield Maiden, so admired and beloved by the people of North Harbor. Her steadfast dedication to "defending the weak" and "protecting the innocent" an inspiration to her fellow heroes. All heart and no brains, that one, or she wouldn't have come to me for help, allowing me to discern her true identity as WNHB nightly news anchor Janet Craig. I sold that tidbit along to Creature Feature, who attacked her during a broadcast before she could summon her mystic shield and ripped her limb from limb on live TV. Now that's showbiz! That's how you send a message.

It really got under the skin of all the powerful heroes who haven't been able to take me down. Strong Hand, Warrior Queen Kara-9, and the Solution, most of all. How do you track a master of disguise under the protection of the entire criminal community? I'm the underworld's secret weapon, a position you once aspired to after a fashion, in your pipe dreams of uniting all the crews, and ruling them as overboss. Back then it was cute how your hopes outmatched your capabilities. Now it's pathetic. Like a community theater thespian convinced their next turn as Stella in *Streetcar* for an audience of octogenarians is the one that will put them on the gilded path to a Tony or an Oscar.

Doesn't work like that. Never did.

People like you don't even know the things you lack exist.

I confess, though, it's not all bad seeing you again.

I get nostalgic for our early days. Remember when we robbed the Jewelry Exchange?

In broad daylight, we bold troubadours armed with swords and Tommy guns rushed in, and you, leaping upon a desk, crying out lines from *King Richard the Third*:

Conscience is but a word that cowards use,
Devised at first to keep the strong in awe:
Our strong arms be our conscience, swords our law.
March on, join bravely, let us to't pell-mell
If not to heaven, then hand in hand to hell.

…swords our law… hand in hand to hell…

True rallying cries.

The workers, the customers, the few guards left conscious all watched you in awe and us in fear. I believed you worthy. A belief you shattered that night in your drug-addled celebration when you conceived of "updating" your material and "getting with the times." How you failed to see what you'd accomplished in that brief, shining moment, I'll never understand.

That was a good day.

Maybe I should've been more merciful toward you. After all, as the true Bard also wrote: "Condemn the fault and not the actor of it!" When I think of all I've accomplished with the fires of outrage you fanned within me, though, I know I did the right thing.

That's what you want to do now, too, isn't it?

It's the real reason you returned to confront me. Not revenge, as you hoped I'd believe nor to return to your life of crime or to rip me away from mine. No. You want redemption. To undo the decades of lawlessness you set loose on the city when you failed me. You've come to finally do the right thing.

That's why a homing device is embedded in the flesh above your left biceps muscle.

Ah! The eyes widen! Expression! Emotion!

Sell it now! Yes! Sell your shock so the audience feels it with you!

You can't imagine how I know it's there. Neither can those watching us.

They gasp in surprise! A twist! A turn of fate! A carefully constructed plot knocked off the rails! What could possibly come next?

The clock counts down. Second by second. Minute by minute. Bringing us all closer to the heart of a white, unstoppable fire and the epicenter of the smoking crater that will replace downtown North Harbor.

The tension rises! Do you get it yet? Do you understand?

Do I have to smack your face again to wake you up or have you figured it all out yet?

Shall I give you a chance to answer? You once treated me generously. Shall I return the favor? Do you want a last chance to be heard?

Ah, you flinch from the explosions above us.

The crash of buildings collapsing. The ground shaking. The power of gods and near gods and ordinary humans armed with extraordinary weapons battling for the soul of a city.

You hear it and tremble.

I do not. I remain unflappable. I play my part no matter what comes.

The show will *go on!*

Your treachery amounts to nothing. I've known about the device in your shoulder since the day Warden Morisi let you walk through the gates of Spiegle. I've known about the deal you cut—

early release in exchange for leading the Vanquishers and their allies to me. How does it feel to fail again? To know one you plucked from the gutter will always be better than you?

I've loosened your gag. Speak your piece.

What? Speak up. You're still hoarse from where I strangled you unconscious.

What's that?

"As you from crimes would pardon'd be, Let your indulgence set me free?"

Another bit of Shakespeare. Your last words a plea for indulgence?

How misguided you are if you think I seek pardon for anything I've done. I own this city. The city should seek pardon from me. And, sadly for you, I know you're insincere. You chose that phrase as your code to trigger a final assault by the Vanquishers. Now, I've let you say it we can stick this gag back in place.

There.

And *this*—ah, it feels good to bloody your nose!

I'm not generally one to work with my fists, but I see its appeal now and then.

Did it ever occur to you that you were leading every hero in this city to their death?

Outside there now all my students fight them with everything they've got. The resources of every crimeboss united to keep me a free man. The good guys will never break through before that clock reaches zero and the bomb goes off. Envision this city without its heroes, its criminal heavyweights wiped out—and I, alone, left to seize control of every block and avenue. No one suspects. I've kept everything well hidden: "Stars, hide your fires; let not light see my black and deep desires."

If you can tell me what play that's from, I'll let you go.

No, really, I mean it.

A last chance to save yourself.

Tell me the play, and I'll untie you and let you escape with me.

Do you know the answer? I'll unbind your mouth once more. Go ahead. Guess. What can it hurt...yes, yes, a little louder, please, and—*The Tempest*?

How... disappointing.

No, no. It's *Julius Caesar*, spoken by Brutus, Act Two, Scene One.

I shouldn't have expected better—oh, that blast was close!

The battle intensifies. What a sight it must be. I'll watch it on the evening news. You'll have to rely on your paltry imagination for the last minutes of your life.

I must be going now. Not long till detonation. More than enough for my underground escape rocket to carry me clear of the blast zone. If you'd answered correctly, you'd be coming with me, but—ah, well, we say goodbye, and—

—for God's sake, no! How can it be?

The clock! It jumped ahead.

A malfunction! A programming flaw! You! You did this, hacked my system, tampered with it! Don't deny it! You've doomed us all! I'm going to perish with you and all the others!

Only seconds left! We'll be vaporized by the heat, our dust left entombed forever beneath thousands of tons of rubble.

Do you see what you set in motion all those years ago?

Three seconds!

No!

Two, one, and—

—*click!*

The clock's run down. We're still here.

One of us, however, seems to have peed himself.

Did you think I'd ever plan so poorly that I'd be caught in my own trap or that I'd ever destroy part of *my* city? Think it through, now. Eventually, the heroes will make their way down here. I'll be gone by then, hidden away in a new identity. They'll find you, chained to a genuine nuclear bomb, which absolutely would have exploded when the clock hit zero if I hadn't taken the liberty of disconnecting two simple wires. When the truth gets out about how close I brought the city to catastrophe, how no one could've stopped me, and how the city exists only because I allowed it—the people will stand and applaud me in worship.

My name will live forever, while you become a footnote in history.

The man who peed himself at the end of the world.

Well, it's been fun. I hope you've enjoyed your front-row seat.

I appreciate your part in this. A good supporting cast can do wonders, and you've helped me tremendously. You always thought it was all about money, but you see, after this I won't be playing only to North Harbor. To paraphrase:

All the world's my *stage,*
And all the men and women merely my *players,*
They have their exits and entrances;
And one man in his time rules *many parts.*

I'm playing for the world now. Everyone everywhere will watch my every performance.

What greater goal could any actor have?

BIOGRAPHIES

Greg Schauer has been a bookseller for over 33 years as the owner of Between Books in Claymont, Delaware. He has also helped produce concerts by local and national bands at the Arden Gild Hall in Arden Delaware, one of the country's oldest continuously run secular utopian art colonies, for the past 10 years. He has previously worked on *Stories in Between*, the Between Books 30th anniversary anthology with W.H. Horner and Jeanne Benzel, *Steampowered Tales of Awesomeness Vol 1* by Brian Thomas and Ray Witte, *With Great Power* with John L. French, and *The Society for the Preservation of CJ Henderson* with Danielle Ackley-McPhail.

He can be contacted at gschauer@betweenbooks.com.

James M. Ward married his high school sweetheart and she's put up with him for 44 years. He has three unusually charming sons, Breck, James, and Theon. They in turn have given him six startlingly charming grandchildren, Keely, Miriam, Sophia, Preston, Teagan, and Noah (16 months old at the time of this writing).

In that same stretch of time he managed to write the first science fiction role-playing game, *Metamorphosis Alpha*; the first apocalypse role-playing game in *Gamma World*; he worked for TSR for over 20 years and did lots of D&D and AD&D things; and designed the best-selling *Spellfire* and *Dragon Ball Z CCG*s.

Drew Bittner has been writing most of his life. In 1991, he wrote GURPS Magic Items 2 for Steve Jackson Games, following that with AD&D Circle of Darkness for TSR, Inc. Drew has written comic books and trading cards, as well as co-creating a card game for comic book publisher WildStorm (now a part of DC Comics). He lives with his wife and daughter in suburban Virginia.

Janine K. Spendlove is a KC-130 pilot in the United States Marine Corps. In the writing world she is an award-winning author primarily known for her War of the Seasons fantasy series. She has several short stories published in various speculative fiction anthologies, to include tie-in work for Star Wars. Janine is also a member of Women in Aerospace (WIA), BroadUniverse (BU), Science Fiction and Fantasy Writers of America (SFWA), and is a co-founder of GeekGirlsRun (GGR), a community for geek girls (and guys) who just want to run, share, have fun, and encourage each other. A graduate of Brigham Young University, Janine loves pugs, enjoys knitting, making costumes, playing Beatles tunes on her guitar, and spending time with her family. She resides with her husband and daughter in North Carolina. She is currently at work on her next novel. Find out more at JanineSpendlove.com.

Aaron Rosenberg is the author of the best-selling *DuckBob* series (consisting of *No Small Bills, Too Small for Tall,* and *Three Small Coinkydinks*), the *Dread Remora* space-opera series and, with David Niall Wilson, the *O.C.L.T.* occult thriller series. His tie-in work contains novels for Star Trek, Warhammer, WarCraft, and Eureka. He has written children's books (including the original series *Pete and Penny's Pizza Puzzles*, the award-winning *Bandslam: The Junior Novel*, and the #1 best-selling *42: The Jackie Robinson Story*), educational books on a variety of topics, and over seventy roleplaying games (such as the original games *Asylum, Spookshow,* and *Chosen,* work for White Wolf, Wizards of the Coast, Fantasy Flight, Pinnacle, and many others, and both the Origins Award-winning Gamemastering Secrets and the Gold ENnie-winning *Lure of the Lich Lord*). He is the co-creator of the *ReDeus* series, and one of the founders of Crazy 8 Press. Aaron lives in New York with his family.

You can follow him online at gryphonrose.com, on Facebook at facebook.com/gryphonrose, and on Twitter @gryphonrose.

Peter David is a prolific author whose career, and continued popularity, spans nearly two decades. He has worked in every conceivable media: Television, film, books (fiction, non-fiction and audio), short stories, and comic books, and acquired followings in all of them.

In the literary field, Peter has had over a hundred novels published, including numerous appearances on the New York Times Bestsellers List. His novels include *Artful, Sir Apropos of Nothing* (A "fast, fun, heroic fantasy satire"—*Publishers Weekly*), *Knight Life, Howling Mad,* and the *Psi-Man* adventure series. He is the co-creator and author of the bestselling *Star Trek: New Frontier* series for Pocket Books, and has also written such Trek novels as *Q-Squared, The Siege, Q-in-Law, Vendetta, I, Q* (with John deLancie), *A Rock and a Hard Place* and *Imzadi.* He produced the three Babylon 5 *Centauri Prime* novels, and has also had his short fiction published in such collections as *Shock Rock, Shock Rock II,* and *Otherwere,* as well as *Isaac Asimov's Science Fiction Magazine* and the *Magazine of Fantasy and Science Fiction.*

Peter's comic book resume includes an award-winning twelve-year run on *The Incredible Hulk,* and he has also worked on such varied and popular titles as *X-Factor, Friendly Neighborhood Spider-Man, Fallen Angel, Supergirl, Fallen Angel, Young Justice, Soulsearchers and Company, Aquaman, Spider-Man, Spider-Man 2099, Star Trek, Wolverine, The Phantom, Sachs & Violens,* and many others. He has also written comic book related novels, such as *The Hulk: What Savage Beast,* and co-edited *The Ultimate Hulk* short story collection. Furthermore, his opinion column *But I Digress* has been running in the industry trade newspaper *The Comic Buyers's Guide* for over a decade, and in that time has been the paper's consistently most popular feature and was also collected into a trade paperback edition.

Peter is the co-creator, with popular science fiction icon Bill Mumy (of *Lost in Space* and *Babylon 5* fame) of the Cable Ace Award-nominated science fiction series *Space Cases,* which ran for two seasons on Nickelodeon. He has written several scripts for the Hugo Award winning TV series *Babylon 5,* and the sequel series, *Crusade.* He has also written several films for Full Moon Entertainment and co-produced two of them, including two installments in the popular *Trancers* series as well as the science fiction western spoof *Oblivion,* which won the Gold Award at the 1994 Houston International Film Festival for best Theatrical Feature Film, Fantasy/Horror category.

Peter's awards and citations include: the Haxtur Award 1996 (Spain), Best Comic script; OZCon 1995 award (Australia), Favorite International Writer; *Comic Buyers Guide* 1995 Fan Awards, Favorite writer; Wizard Fan Award Winner 1993; Golden Duck Award for Young Adult Series *(Starfleet Academy)*, 1994; UK Comic Art Award, 1993; Will Eisner Comic Industry Award, 1993, and the Julie Award in 2007. He lives in New York with his wife, Kathleen, and his four children, Shana, Gwen, Ariel, and Caroline.

Keith R.A. DeCandido's other Super City Police Department stories include the novel *The Case of the Claw* and the short story "Stone Cold Whodunit" (in *With Great Power*), with more in the works. His other superhero fiction includes a *Heroes Reborn* novella (*Save the Cheerleader, Destroy the World*), the Marvel Comics-based trilogy *Tales of Asgard* (including novels starring Thor, Sif, and the Warriors Three), four Spider-Man prose stories (the novels *Venom's Wrath* and *Down These Mean Streets* and the short stories "An Evening in the Bronx with Venom" and "Arms and the Man"), and short stories in the anthologies *The Ultimate Silver Surfer, The Ultimate Hulk*, and *X-Men Legends*. His other recent and upcoming work includes the *Star Trek* coffee-table book *The Klingon Art of War*, the *Sleepy Hollow* novel *Children of the Revolution*, the *X-Files* short story "Back in El Paso My Life Will Be Worthless" in *Trust No One*, the short fiction collection *Without a License: The Fantastic Worlds of Keith R.A. DeCandido*, the short story "Streets of Fire" in *V-Wars: Night Terrors*, two *Stargate SG-1* stories (the novel *Kali's Wrath* and the short story "Time Keeps on Slippin'" in *Far Horizons*), the high fantasy police procedural *Mermaid Precinct* (latest in a series that started in 2004 with *Dragon Precinct* and includes several novels and short stories), and a whole mess of urban fantasy stories set in Key West, Florida, which have appeared in the online zines *Buzzy Mag* and *Story of the Month Club*, the anthologies *Apocalypse 13, Bad-Ass Faeries: It's Elemental, Out of Tune, Tales from the House Band* Volumes 1 and 2, and *Urban Nightmares*, and the collections *Ragnarok and Roll: Tales of Cassie Zukav, Weirdness Magnet* and the aforementioned *Without a License*. Keith is also an editor, karate practitioner, podcaster, musician, and possibly some other stuff, too, which he can't remember due to the lack of sleep. Find out less at his web site at DeCandido.net.

James Chambers writes tales of horror, crime, fantasy, and science fiction. He is the author of *The Engines of Sacrifice*, a collection of four Lovecraftian-inspired novellas published by Dark Regions Press which *Publisher's Weekly* described in a starred-review as "...chillingly evocative...." He is also the author of the short fiction collections *Resurrection House* (Dark Regions Press) and *The Midnight Hour: Saint Lawn Hill and Other Tales*, in collaboration with illustrator Jason Whitley as well as the dark, urban fantasy novella, *Three Chords of Chaos* and *The Dead Bear Witness* and *Tears of Blood*, volume one and two in his Corpse Fauna novella series.

His short stories have been published in the anthologies *The Avenger: Roaring Heart of the Crucible*, *Chiral Mad 2*, *Dark Furies*, *The Dead Walk*, *Deep Cuts*, *The Domino Lady: Sex as a Weapon*, *Dragon's Lure*, *Fantastic Futures 13*, *The Green Hornet Chronicles*, *Hardboiled Cthulhu*, *In An Iron Cage*, *No Longer Dreams*, *Shadows Over Main Street*, *The Spider: Extreme Prejudice*, *Qualia Nous*, *Reel Dark*, *Truth or Dare*, *TV Gods*, *Walrus Tales*, *Warfear*, and the *Bad-Ass Faeries* and *Defending the Future* series as well as the magazines *Bare Bone*, *Cthulhu Sex*, and *Allen K's Inhuman*.

He has also edited and written numerous comic books including *Leonard Nimoy's Primortals*, the critically acclaimed "The Revenant" in *Shadow House*, the Midnight Hour for *Negative Burn*, and the original graphic novel *Kolchak, The Night Stalker: The Poe Crimes*.

THE RANKS OF THE VILLAINOUS

Keith West, Future Potentate of the Solar System
Pamela Nery
Wes Rist
Chad A. Burdette
Silence in the Library Publishing
PLB Comics
Andromeda Pro-Tech
Mary Spila
Chris Otto
Amelia Smith
Dennis Lawson
The Dark Lord Chandra-Prime
Morten Poulsen
Chand Svare Ghei chasvag.com
Yes
Janet Craig
Lennhoff Family
Rie Sheridan Rose
Bodge Inglee
Sheryl R. Hayes
Kelli Neier
H Lynnea Johnson
Chris Cicero
Weldon Burge
Tina M Noe Good
Carol Jones
Brian Holder
Rita McClellan
Rahadyan Sastrowardoyo
zan rosin

robert early

Stephanie Fox

Anthony R. Cardno

Anonymous

Sam "Professor Voss" Conway

Alex Lyle

Dave Lewis

Dayton Ward

Roy Romasanta

dark2dawn

Kcirtap

Alex Gilmour

anonymous

Christopher S. Sanders

Tracy Syrstad

Bec

Chris Quinn

Switch

Annika Samuelsson

Nathan Seabolt

Christian Steudtner

Paul Bulmer

Kurt Brugel

Gail Z. Martin

Leshia-Aimée Doucet

J.R. Murdock

Fan of words

Stephanie Lucas

Corey W Tacker

Linda Pierce

Greg Schauer

Turn Your Allegiance

For the Other Side's Story

Turn Your Allegiance

For the Other Side's Story